THE
QUEEN
OF
CROWS

THE
QUEEN
OF
CROWS

MYKE COLE

A TOM DOHERTY ASSOCIATES BOOK

NEW YORK

THE QUEEN OF CROWS

Copyright © 2018 by Myke Cole

A Tor.com Book
Published by Tom Doherty Associates
175 Fifth Avenue
New York, NY 10010

www.tor.com

Tor® is a registered trademark of Macmillan Publishing Group, LLC.

The Library of Congress Cataloging-in-Publication Data is available
upon request.

ISBN 978-0-7653-9597-9 (hardcover)
ISBN 978-0-7653-9596-2 (ebook)

Our books may be purchased in bulk for promotional, educational, or business use.
Please contact your local bookseller or the Macmillan Corporate and Premium
Sales Department at 1-800-221-7945, extension 5442, or by email at
MacmillanSpecialMarkets@macmillan.com.

First Edition: September 2018

Printed in the United States of America

0 9 8 7 6 5 4 3 2 1

For Madeline and Kikki, Beth and Alisa.
For Daisy, Hannah, and Charlotte.
For Mom, most of all.
The women who built me, and taught me to fight.

Light a candle!
Drink wine!
Slowly the Sabbath descends
and in her hand the flower,
and in her hand
the sinking sun.

—Zelda

I

THE ARMORED GIRL

Growers—One twentieth

Builders—Render service as customary to Procurer

Drovers—Render service as customary to Procurer—No less than two teams and two carts.

Tanners—One twentieth, in custom or supply.

Herbers—Exempt. Render service to village Maior, save in time of war—then to Lord Marshal.

Menders—One twentieth in custom, save in time of war—then to Lord Marshal for service.

Tinkers—Exempt. Service to Procurer above all. Else, custom as Exchequer may see fit. Shall maintain the vault and secret Procurer's commission on pain of death. Shall teach trade only within family.

—From Imperial Edict,
"Concerning the tithes of the trades
unto the Exchequer of the Sacred Throne"

Heloise wasn't a small girl, but she'd never been a big one either. *Right in the middle,* her father had always said, *and perfect that way,* her mother was quick to add.

The war-machine made her a giant, a steel-monster puffing seethestone smoke into the gray sky. One of the machine's metal fists was hidden behind a shield heavy enough to crush an ox's skull even without the engine's brutal strength. The other fist was empty, but no less deadly for it, an unforgiving bludgeon with the implacable strength of a mountain in motion.

Her eyes were still new enough to life to widen in wonder at the world, but they looked out through a brass-trimmed slit in a helmet of burnished iron. Out and down. She towered over the tallest man in the village, Barnard Tinker, the man who'd built the machine she'd used to kill a devil and lead her village in rebellion.

Below the helmet was the heavy iron gorget, and below that, the machine's solid breastplate, covering the driver's cage and Heloise's body. Barnard had painted a red sigil across it, and again on the shield—a little girl, with a halo and wings, standing on a fallen devil's neck. The girl's hand was extended, palm outward, in the traditional pose of Palantines. Heloise felt the weight of her people's expectations every time she looked at it. She knew who she was, and it wasn't who Barnard, and the whole village, expected her to be.

The breastplate hung on a metal armature, long rods that formed a man-shaped cage around Heloise. Hung across it was more armor—pauldrons and vambraces, tassets and greaves, couters and sabbatons, and the heavy, wicked gauntlets. But where the gaps on a suit of armor would be covered with mail, the machine admitted the empty air, and Heloise shivered as the cold breeze blew through the openings and caressed her bare skin.

"They are coming, your eminence, they will be here by sunset." It was the voice of Barnard's son, Guntar, so much like his father's that Heloise had to look down to confirm. He was redfaced, breathless. He'd leapt off one of Poch Drover's cart horses, taken for his reconnaissance. Poch raced to take the animal's reins, patting its lathered flanks and glaring at Guntar. The beast was made for slow hauling, not fast riding. It looked blown, and Poch couldn't keep the anguish off his face. The old man loved his horses.

Guntar took a knee before Heloise, and the rest of the villagers joined him, as if she were a lord, or a Pilgrim.

Or a holy Palantine, a devil-slayer, a savior and protector.

She had slain a devil, but her throat still tightened at the reverence in their eyes. They had known her since she was a babe in arms. They were her home and her family. She wanted them to hold her, to tell her that everything would be all right.

But everything will not be all right, she thought, *and if it is to be even a little bit right, then it is for me to make it so.*

For all their fervor, the villagers around her were still an untrained rabble with barely three helmets between them, armed with pruning hooks and pitchforks, here and there a rusty pike or sword left over from their days as a levy in the Old War against Ludhuige and his Red Banners. They were old men, the wives and children of old men. Their names were Sald Grower, Ingomer Clothier, and Edwin Baker. None had the name "Soldier." A few, like her father and Sigir, the village Maior, were veterans of the Old War, but Heloise knew that levies attended to their trades until they were called to fight. Soldiering was not their life's work.

And the Order would be here by sunset. Heloise thought of Sigir's words after the Knitting. *The Order speaks of ministry, but it is the paint over the board. The wood beneath is killing. It is what they train to do, it is what they are equipped to do, it is all they do.*

The rebels had just one thing: the war-machine Heloise drove, the giant suit of metal and leather that made her stronger and taller than the two most powerful men in the village combined. This new war-machine was made for her, her arms and legs fitting perfectly inside its metal limbs, her movements become its own. But as powerful as the machine was, it hadn't been enough to save Heloise's best friend, the love of her life. Her gaze swept the throng, ready to follow her into war. *I couldn't save Basina,* she wanted to shout, *what makes you think I can save you?* When they'd beaten the Order before, they'd had a wizard with them. Now, there was only Heloise, her machine, and the supposed favor of the divine Emperor.

"Sigir, a word," Samson said. His eyes flicked between the Maior and Barnard, his lips working beneath his gray beard.

"Samson, there is no time," Barnard snapped. "You heard Guntar. The Order will be here soon. This"—he gestured to the massive war-machine—"is too loud. Too big and too shiny. The Order will know we're here from a league off."

"I wasn't talking to you," Samson shot back, then turned to the Maior. "Sigir, please. Now."

Heloise looked down at her father. He was so like the Maior, both men thick-necked and thick-fingered, with heavy paunches that overhung their belts and shoulders broadened from the work that attended village life. Sigir wore long mustaches, but for that and the gold chain of Sigir's office, they could have been brothers. It had only been a few nights ago that her father's approval had meant the world to her, but the fight with the devil had changed everything. A part of her recoiled from the thought of defying him, but Barnard was right, there was no time.

"Father, it's fine."

"It is *not* fine," Samson practically spat, his face reddening. "This is the other side of the sun from fine."

"Samson, please." Sigir gestured at the villagers all around them. *Everyone is watching,* the Maior's face said.

Leuba, Heloise's mother, was among the crowd. She lent truth to the old adage that a couple married long enough began to look like one another—heavy like her husband, thick-fingered and wide-cheeked. But where Samson was thunder, Leuba was the silence after its passing, and she kept her peace and let her husband speak, wringing the hem of her skirts in her hands. But Heloise remembered her mother's fierce fire when the village had thought to cast her father out after his fight with the Order. *I'll stand at your side and the town fathers will have to look me in the eye as they speak their piece,* her mother had said, eyes flashing. *Might be that will make them think kinder of what they say.*

Samson sighed, swallowed. "Barnard is right, the machine is too big, too loud, and too shiny. So we move it *back, away* from the road. We can have an ambush without risking the life of my daughter."

Heloise wanted to agree with him. Here was the chance to step down from behind that sigil, shrug off the weight of it all. She wasn't a Palantine. What business did she have leading an ambush against the Order?

"Samson," Sigir said.

"No," Samson said, "I understand that . . . much has happened in the past few days, but this is *wrong,* Sigir. You are the *Maior.* We follow *you.*"

Sigir threw an arm around Samson's shoulder, steering him away from the crowd of villagers. "By the Throne, will you be quiet? The village's will hangs by a thread as it is!" The Maior was trying to keep his voice low, but in the shocked silence Heloise could hear him as clearly as if he had shouted.

"She's my daughter!" Samson made no effort at quiet. "It is for me to say whether she fights! And I say—"

"Father!" Heloise took a step toward him, forgetting for a moment that she was in the giant war-machine. The metal leg moved with her, a lurching step that sent the villagers nearest her scattering.

Sigir's grip was tight around Samson's shoulders as he steered him farther away from the villagers. Heloise followed and Barnard and his sons came with her, Leuba trailing behind them.

"I am your father," Samson was speaking to her now, "and I am through with this . . . foolishness. A machine may make you strong, but it does *not* make you a Palantine. You are my daughter and you will come down from that thing and away."

"Samson," Sigir tightened his grip on her father's shoulders. "Enough, she is—"

Samson shook off his grip. "No! You are the Maior. It is to you to uphold the law, but she is my daughter, and she will do as I say. The village follows—"

"Samson, you Throne-cursed fool!" Sigir threw up his hands, pointed a trembling finger at Heloise. "Do you think you can go on as if the veil was not torn? As if she didn't just do what *no one* has ever done in all the days of our people? The village follows *her*, you blockhead. We are to ambush the *Order*. Do you think for a moment that we can do that without a war-machine? Do you think we can do it without the people's hearts united behind their savior? She *must* lead us, or we must flee, and I do not like our chances on the run. Not now, with the Order so close."

And there it was. Heloise's stomach tightened. *He's right. I have to do this. I must at least act the Palantine or we are all finished.*

"I don't care," Samson said, "that is my decision and it is final. She comes down now. She is my daughter."

"Basina," Barnard's voice was low and dangerous, "was my daughter. And she is dead."

The dread certainty that she must defy her father solidified. *Basina is dead. The Order is coming. Both are my fault. I have to make this right.*

"Killed by the devil!" Samson shouted back. "And the devil is dead. Avenged by my daughter. Heloise deserves life for that, if nothing else."

"Everyone deserves life," Sigir said, "and that's why everyone must fight."

"I will be fine, Father," Heloise said. "Now just stop . . ."

But Samson was striding forward, grasping the machine's metal legs and scrambling up. Heloise jerked back in surprise, the machine jerking with her. Barnard and Sigir pulled away from the sudden movement, but Samson managed to hold on. "What are you doing?"

"I am taking you out of there," Samson said, "and once I have, you are going over my knee until you learn obedience, by the Throne."

"Father, no! Stop . . ."

But Samson was not deterred, he reached the machine's metal cuisse and thrust a hand behind the breastplate, fumbling for the strap that held Heloise against the leather cushion. Heloise reached a hand over to stop him, stopped as she realized the machine's arm was matching her movement, the heavy metal shield dangerously close to her father's head. She was struggling to free her arms from the control straps to safely push him away when Barnard stepped forward, seized Samson by the collar of his shirt, and sent him tumbling in the dirt. Leuba cried out and ran to her husband's side. Samson swatted her helping hands away and rose to his elbows, cheeks bright red.

"She's a devil-slayer and a Palatine." Barnard's voice was flat. Barnard and Samson had been friends their whole lives, but now Barnard hefted his hammer as Samson got to one knee. "She's not your little girl anymore. She is the Emperor's instrument now."

"You think," Samson bit off each word, pushing Leuba behind him, "that I won't kill you, should you stand between me and my daughter?"

"No," Barnard said, "I think you won't kill me because you

cannot." The huge tinker was a head taller than her father, his gray-shot black beard trimmed short to accommodate the forge-fires that had lit his entire working life. Working beside those fires had made him as strong as he was tall, more bear than man, and still little more than a child in the shadow of the war-machine. His sons stood at his side, each nearly as big as their father, each wielding a two-handed forge hammer heavy enough to fell an ox with a single blow.

Samson stood, and Heloise knew he would try the matter even if it cost him his life. Clodio had spoken of love, of how life without it was but a shadow of life, but Heloise could see now that a father's love could drive him mad. Could even cost him his life. "I won't let you send my daughter to her death."

"My daughter is *dead,*" Barnard seethed. "Yours can fight."

Samson took a step and Heloise stepped with him, moving the machine around the Tinker men to stand it between them and her father. "Father, please!"

"You can either help us to fight," Sigir said, "or you can delay until the Order comes and we are caught unawares."

"You're mad," Samson said, looking daggers at Sigir and the Tinkers. "You're all mad!"

"She killed a devil," Guntar said, "she's a Palantine."

"Look at this!" Samson stabbed a finger at the red sigil Barnard had painted on the machine's breast. "Do you see wings on my daughter?"

"Blasphemy," said Gunnar, Barnard's other son, and stabbed a finger of his own. "You shame the Emperor, denying His chosen."

"You're lucky you're her father, Samson," Barnard said, "else I might . . ."

"What?" Samson's laugh was forced. "You'll box my ears and turn out my pockets? You'll kill me in front of my own wife and child? By the Throne, do your worst."

"You'll have to kill me, too, you animal." Leuba stepped around her husband, face white with fury. "I've known you since you was a boy, Tinker, and you'll have to kill me in front of your sons before I let you hurt my husband."

"Sacred Throne, *enough!*" Sigir shouted. "You want my word? You want the word of the Maior of Lutet? I will give it, and it is this: Heloise fights. Palantine or no, we need her and we do not have time to convene a council on the matter. This little display has sapped the village's spirits enough, I am sure. Come, Heloise, let's figure out a way to get the machine concealed."

"Damn you, Sigir!" Samson said. "I will never forgive you for this, so long as you live!"

"I suppose I can live with that." Sigir shrugged. "And this gives us all, including Heloise, the best chance to go *on* living."

Heloise turned to follow the Maior back to the knot of villagers, and Samson moved to intercept her. He stopped as the Tinkers stepped to bar his way, raising their hammers. "Don't," Barnard growled.

"Please, Heloise." Leuba sounded on the verge of tears. "I don't know what I'd do if I lost you. We only want to protect you."

"You can't protect me, not from this." She turned to her father. "Don't you understand? Basina is dead. I *have* to do this."

But she could see in his eyes that he didn't understand. It was a moment before Heloise mustered the strength to look away, ignoring the strangled choke her father made. He only wanted to protect her, but the Order was coming. And Sigir was right, they had to fight, not to win, but to *live.* *I may be a girl, Papa,* she thought fiercely at him, as if the intensity of it could make him hear and understand, *but I am the one they've chosen to follow.*

Samson and Leuba stood apart, watching as Sigir directed the villagers to gather branches and clods of earth to drape over the machine. Barnard and his sons kept a close eye on Samson, ready to move if he tried to intervene. The villagers had clearly overheard much of the conversation, and their allegiance was clear. They circled around Heloise, studiously ignoring Samson, when they weren't glaring daggers in his direction. The sole exceptions were Poch Drover and Sald Grower, who stood apart, casting worried glances over at Heloise's father, but not daring to move against the Tinkers.

Heloise could feel her father's eyes on her back. She could feel his gaze sapping her will. *What if he's right? What if I can't lead them? What if I can't fight?* She pushed the thought away. In a broken machine, she had killed a devil. Who knew what she could do in this machine, whole as it was? *Not whole,* Heloise thought as she looked down at her right arm, *the machine, maybe, but not me.* The stump of her wrist hooked the control strap, though she winced as she pulled experimentally and the leather put pressure on the bandage. Barnard hadn't bothered to affix a weapon to the war-machine's metal fist, fearing the extra weight would add to the hurt. She needed time to heal, but the Order was coming now.

Some of the villagers saw her looking at the machine's empty right hand, at the stump within. They shuffled, uneasy. *Fear's a deadly thing, Heloise,* Barnard had said. *It can drain a person of all their strength, make them weak before their enemies. That's how we were until you showed us different. But we see now, and we are not afraid anymore, so long as you are with us.*

She wrenched her gaze away from the bloody bandages and forced herself to meet the eyes of the assembled throng. "I am with you," she said, "after the devil, the Order will be nothing."

In answer, the villagers bowed their heads or tugged their forelocks and raced to cover the machine with more branches and earth.

"Now, you all listen to me," Sigir said as they worked. "Should . . . things go badly for us . . ."

"Blasphemy," Barnard said, his eyes never leaving Samson. "We have—"

"Will you shut your yob for a gnat's whisper, Tinker!" Sigir said. "The Emperor is with us, to be sure, but He will no doubt smile on a well-formed plan. Faith isn't always rushing in with your balls hanging out."

Barnard opened his mouth to reply, but Samson cut him off. "You got what you wanted, Barnard. Heloise is fighting. Let the Maior speak!"

Barnard looked up at Heloise, cheeks red, waiting for her direction. She would never get used to this man, who had known her since she was a baby, who could break her with a twist of his fingers, looking to her for orders. She swallowed the discomfort and nodded. "Let us hear the Maior out."

Sigir spoke quickly, "Should the enemy take the day, we go to the fens."

Barnard shook his head. "The frogging clans won't have us if they know we've taken arms against the Order. They're the most pious folk in the valley."

"We don't need them to shelter us, and we won't go all the way into the mire," Sigir went on. "The fens are broken ground. Close enough for us to make it on foot, but the mud will suck the shoes off the horses and the holes will snap their legs. If the Order wants to come for us, they'll have to come on foot. In all that armor, they'll be slow. We know the ground, and they don't. It's the best place to fight in skirmish order."

"What do we know of skirmishing?" Samson asked. "We're trained to the pike, formed and well commanded."

"We'll have to learn, won't we?" Sigir said. "If it comes to it, I mean."

They made little headway hiding the machine. Some tried to weave the branches into a lattice that could hold the earth, others simply piled them on, or thrust them into the frame. Some stayed put. Most didn't. After a quarter candle they'd succeeded mostly in piling a heap of brush around the machine's metal feet, and smearing dirt on Heloise's shift, face, and all over the interior of the driver's cage.

"This isn't working," Sigir finally said. "We'll need to dig a hole."

"That will take too long," Barnard gestured to the enormous machine. He stomped the frozen ground. "It's hard as stone here."

"If all of us pitch in," Sigir said, "we can get it done in time."

"Begging your pardon, Maior," Sald Grower said, "we can't. Even if we had shovels for every man, it'd take days to bury something that big."

Barnard snorted. "We don't need to bury her," he said. "She can run faster than a horse in that. By the time they know she's awaiting them, it'll be too late."

"That is madness," Samson shouted. "Barnard, Sigir, *please*. It's one thing to have her fight. It's quite another to have her rushing into battle like a . . ."

All around her, villagers were throwing in their considered opinions, shouting to be heard among the others.

"It was to be an ambush!" her father was shouting.

"She is a Palantine! She needs no ambush!" Barnard yelled.

Heloise was no soldier, but she knew this confusion wouldn't beat the Order. Everyone was giving orders, and no one was listening.

"Shut it!" Heloise's words rang through the din before she realized she had yelled them.

The silence dragged on, and Heloise realized with a start that they were waiting for her command. "I . . . I think I know what to do. Follow me."

She took a step, then another, then another, and the war-machine took them with her, the crowd parting to let her pass, then closing to follow her through the overgrown thicket and back out onto the road that led to her village. It was little more than a wide track, stretching out in a low valley bordered by two gently sloping rises. Both were well concealed, the thicket on one side, and a nearly solid wall of trees on the other.

She felt the machine's heavy tread sinking into the softer ground, still frozen, but warmed by the sparse traffic, the clods of horse dung, and the break in the canopy that laid it bare to the sun.

Samson was at her elbow in an instant, Barnard coming with him. "Leave me be, you great pill!" Samson shouted at the tinker. "I'm not going to try to take her out of the . . ."

Heloise ignored them both, dropping the machine to one knee, raising the shield high over her head.

She could hear the sharp intake of breath, feel the crowd backing away from her. She brought the machine's shield arm down with all its engine-driven strength. The point of the shield careered off a stone just under the surface of the soil, sending up a shower of sparks and making a sound like two empty pots banged together. But that only served to drive the shield point to one side, and it sank deep into the earth, digging a furrow almost two handspans deep.

The ground was hard, but it was not equal to the engine's brutal strength. Together with the heavy weight of the iron shield, the ground broke apart, clods of earth spraying as Heloise dug.

For a moment, the village watched in confusion, and then Sigir was on his knees beside her, clawing at the earth with his hands. Barnard soon joined him in the rapidly deepening pit. Gunnar and Guntar followed, swinging their great forge hammers, breaking up rocks and roots. At last, all the village pitched in, scraping and digging with shield edges, knives and swords, and here and there an actual shovel.

As the hole became shoulder deep, Barnard began waving some of them off. "We'll need to cover it. Weave a screen of branches."

"Won't hold up under a horse," Sald muttered.

"Sald, you're a Throne-cursed grower," Barnard said, "what do you know of horses?"

Heloise glanced up at the road. It was more than wide enough for a column of riders to pass without moving over the hole she would be hiding in. She forced herself to return to her digging. The sun was sinking beneath the horizon, it was too late to turn back now.

Some of the villagers went scurrying off to comply with Barnard's order. Heloise noticed that Samson was among them. *It's better this way. The less he's about, the less you'll be tempted to give in to him.*

They made good progress, but every moment Heloise thought they were moving fast enough, they hit a man-sized rock, or a root as thick around as her wrist, lost more precious time. The machine's great size had been a comfort to her before she'd started digging, and now she cursed it for needing a pit so deep to hide it.

The shadows were growing long when Guntar finally leaned on his hammer and cursed. "It can't be long now," he said, "if we don't get out of this road, we'll be ridden down."

"Then we make our stand," Barnard said, "and die on our feet."

"How many standing dead men have you seen?" Sigir asked. "An ambush is our only chance. If we cannot catch them unawares, we should run, come at them another time."

"And let them burn the village?" Gunnar's voice was heated.

"What else . . ." Sigir began, and Heloise knew that once again she would have to stop the men from arguing.

It took her a moment to find the strength. The digging had made her tired in her bones. Her stump throbbed, the bandages soaked through with fresh blood where the wound had reopened. She felt a flash of heat across her forehead, sharp enough to make her sweat, followed by a shiver. *It's fever.* She pushed the thought away. If it was, there was nothing to do for it now.

The men argued, and she glanced at the hole, still woefully shallow, but maybe . . .

She put confidence into her voice. "It's deep enough."

The men stopped fighting, raised their heads to her. They looked at each other, then at the shallow hole, then finally back to her. "Your eminence," Sigir began, "you cannot possibly . . ."

"Not to stand, no," Heloise said, walking the machine on its knees into the hole, praying she had guessed right. The metal frame groaned as she folded her legs and sat on her heels, the machine shaping itself to mimic her posture. She leaned forward at her waist, tucking the machine's head between its metal knees. The engine's bulk blocked out most of the sun, so that she could see only the dimmest reflection of light off the metal tops of the machine's knees. "You can't see me from the road, can you?"

"No." Barnard's voice, slow and deep. "Praise the Throne, we cannot."

Heloise stifled a sigh of relief. "Then cover me up. There's not much time."

"Not yet!" Her mother's voice. She winced as she heard Leuba scramble down, leaning on the machine's shoulder. The machine shuddered as she shrugged off Barnard's hand, trying to pull him back. "Leave me be!" She tried for a kiss, but there was no way to reach her, so she settled for touching her shoulder. "Oh, my dove. Be careful. I love you," she whispered. Her father's weight settled on the machine's opposite shoulder. The same touch, the same words. Heloise choked back tears and nodded. *Not now. I can't be your daughter now.*

Heloise heard the scraping of branches as the latticework was dragged toward her. A weight on the machine again, much heavier this time, accompanied by a loud clang.

Heloise sawed her head to her right, saw Barnard strapping a brass-bound, metal box to the machine's shoulder. "What are you doing?" she asked.

"The devil's head," Barnard said reverently, cinching the straps down and patting the box's huge brass lock, "will keep the Emperor's eye turned toward us. It is yours, your eminence, and you will carry it high as you lead us to victory."

The box would block her view to one side, and the thought of the devil's severed head so close to her made her stomach lurch, but as she opened her mouth to argue, they dragged the lattice over her, and all was shrouded in darkness. Tiny pinpricks of sunlight dotted the pitted surface of the machine's metal legs, but beyond that, the world vanished.

"Wait until they have all gone past, your eminence," Sigir said as they scraped earth over. "You will rise behind them and then we will strike from the sides. They will be trapped, and if Emperor is willing, we will triumph."

The scraping and thumping of earth being piled on her grew more muffled as the cover of woven branches filled in. The pinpricks of light vanished one by one, until at last Heloise could hear nothing at all, and she was alone with the darkness and the stifling chill of the pit.

Now, Sald's words seemed wrong. They had piled so much earth atop her that it would easily hold ten horses. So much that she would never see the sun again.

The tiny space stank of seethestone. She stifled a cough and shut her stinging eyes, squeezing out tears. Her skin tingled and itched as the caustic smoke, with nowhere else to go, turned on her. The only sound was her own short, gasping breaths, so loud in the tight space that the entire Imperial army could be marching over her back and she wouldn't hear them.

This was stupid, useless. She couldn't breathe, couldn't see, couldn't hear. She wanted only to stand up, throw off the oppressive weight of the earth.

She felt a tremor. No more than a ripple of the earth across her back, a pebble shaken loose to drop against the machine's metal knee. It was followed by another, and another, until the ground around her came alive with rumbling, the earth overhead vibrating under tramping feet and hooves.

The Order. They were here.

She could hear muffled voices, the creaking of leather harness, the jangling of chains. She tensed, waiting for the hoofbeats to pass, so that she could rise up behind the column, cutting off their retreat.

She felt a sharp pounding against the machine's metal back. Rhythmic, steady.

The latticework was holding. The Order rode over her. She tried to count the hoofbeats, to guess the number of animals passing, to get a count of how many enemy she would face. She tried to stifle the itching in her throat, swallow the urge to cough, and waited for . . .

A horse stumbled. Earth cascaded around her.

Shouts, hooves skittering sideways, the drumming of feet. The column had been alerted, halted. The latticework of branches, even with the thick layer of earth, had not been enough to hold a warhorse's weight with an armored rider on its back. If Heloise rose now, she would emerge at their head, giving them a clear road to retreat, and the element of surprise gone.

She heard scraping above her, men straining to pry the latticework away. In moments, they would find her. *You can either die down here on your knees, or up on your feet, breathing the air.*

It was an easy choice. Heloise dug in her heels and jerked her legs straight. The machine shuddered as it rose, metal back and shoulders exploding upward, sending the latticework spinning away. She heard men and horses screaming. Light and spraying earth blinded her, but not so much that she couldn't see two men and a horse flying through the air, sailing head over foot into a column of Pilgrims. The horses spooked, and the Pilgrims, desperate to control them, had no time to gawk at the war-machine in their midst. There was no time to count them, but their numbers seemed endless, at least a hundred riders, thick leather armor making them huge beneath their gray cloaks.

The men and horse that Heloise had thrown came down in their ranks, knocking men from their mounts and sending them sprawling in the mud, cursing. Heloise blinked, her eyes adjusting, her vision still blurry. The column was a splintered mass of plunging horses and shouting men. Most still had their flails on their shoulders, if they hadn't dropped them in the chaos.

She wouldn't get a better chance than this.

"The Throne!" Heloise shouted, and charged.

2

ROUT AND SUCCOR

Here is the brand that shall strike thee. There, the ground that shall receive thee.
Know that it is by my hand that thou art undone.
—Writ. Ala. IX. 26

Heloise had always thought killing was a heavy matter. Seeing death was one thing, but causing it was something else.

Yet here was a Pilgrim, desperately attempting to control his plunging horse, and with a jerk of her arm, his head became a red bowl, the jagged edges of his skull blooming around the corner of the war-machine's heavy shield. He flew from his horse, went tumbling into his fellows.

Now, her mind screamed at her, *attack!* But she couldn't move. It had been one thing to kill a creature out of the depths of hell, a devil scaled and horned. But Pilgrims, for all their wickedness, were people. Her throat closed, her breathing came too quickly.

One of the Pilgrims calmed his horse enough to charge her, reins in his teeth, swinging his flail double-handed. It bounced off the war-machine's metal chest, digging long scratches in the red sigil. As he wheeled his horse for another charge, Heloise saw the back of his head, knew all she had to do was punch out with the machine's empty metal fist, crack his skull like an egg. From inside the war-machine, even the Pilgrims in their boiled leather armor looked so delicate.

But she couldn't bring herself to strike, and the Pilgrim rode away and wheeled his mount, came on again, with two more of his brothers at his side.

At last, her paralysis broke and Heloise raised her shield to meet them, shouting her battle cry.

It was answered from a hundred throats. The brush trembled as the villagers came pouring out from both sides of the road, racing toward the column, which turned to meet them.

Barnard led the villagers, shouting Heloise's name as if it held divine power. Samson and Sigir were at his side, waving their short, sharp "second chances," the long knives all levy pikemen carried in case their main weapon was lost. Guntar and Gunnar came with them, dressed in fine armor that they had no doubt crafted for the Imperial Procurer. All three Tinker men fought with their heavy forge hammers, swinging them about their heads as if they weighed nothing. Behind them came Sald and Poch, Ingomer and Danad, with their sons, most of whom hadn't seen their thirteenth winter yet. Some of the braver wives, Leuba and Chunsia among them, came with their families.

The Pilgrims considered Heloise in her giant war-machine, and then the poorly armed rabble racing toward them. They turned to meet the lesser threat, snarling and digging in their spurs. The column wheeled as one man, and countercharged.

A voice was shouting orders, deep and commanding, Heloise scarcely recognized it as her father's. This must be the voice of the Serjeant of pikemen he had once been, back in the Old War against Ludhuige the Red. Samson swore and pushed, kicking rake handles and swatting shoulders with the flat of his second chance, desperately trying to get the villagers to form some semblance of a line. But while the veterans like Sigir, Poch, and Sald knew their business, the others tripped over themselves, or shouted back at him. A few threw down their weapons and fled.

Samson raced after Edwin Baker, then stopped short as he glanced back to where Barnard and his sons were charging ahead of the rest of the villagers, ignoring Samson's line and rushing to meet the Pilgrims. "Barnard! Have you forgotten everything? It's a cavalry charge! Form up, damn you!"

Barnard didn't hear him. He and his sons ran for the rushing horsemen, as if with nothing more than hammers the three of them could stem the tide. "Heloise!" they shouted. "Devil-slayer! Palantine!"

The Order thundered toward them. A couple of outriders swept past, swinging their flails in long, looping arcs. Barnard parried one blow, and Guntar the other, twisting his hammer to catch the flail's chain and pull the rider from the saddle. The other rider moved on up the rise, flanking Samson's hastily formed line, raising his flail again, heading for Heloise's father.

Heloise leapt after the Pilgrim, flying up the hill with long, clanking strides. She easily outpaced the horse, reached the outrider, and struck. Even without a weapon, the war-machine's metal right fist weighed as much as an anvil. The Pilgrim went flying over his horse's head, teeth knocked loose as the reins were yanked out of his mouth, his hands going slack, the flail tumbling. The long haft tangled in the charging horse's legs, and the beast flipped end over end, its screams abruptly cut off as its neck snapped. Its path carried it into the wavering line of villagers, sending them scattering.

Samson only had time to shoot Heloise a grateful look before he ran after the fleeing villagers, bellowing at them to stand their ground. He caught Myron Tanner by the collar of his shirt and began dragging him back into place as another Pilgrim spurred his horse over his fallen comrade and made for him, flail coming low, the spiked head whirling toward Samson's gut.

"Samson!" Sigir shouted, leaping forward. The Maior wore a pot helm and a leather coat under an old iron cuirass. He threw his shoulder into the horse's breast, madly slashing with his second chance. The animal reared, and the flail's strike went wide, the haft clanging against Sigir's helm, knocking it askew. Sigir raked the knife's edge across the Pilgrim's face, splitting his nose in two, blood sheeting down to soak his gray hood.

"Forget the line!" Sigir called to her father. "Look to your life, you fool!"

With a final furious shake, Samson let the fleeing villager go and charged the Pilgrim, hacking first at the horse's legs. The creature stumbled, sending the Pilgrim pitching forward over its neck. It only took Samson two strokes to cut the man's head from his shoulders, tumbling down to be caught in the folds of the blood-soaked gray hood.

Another three Pilgrims rode in, wheeled away as Heloise lunged to intercept them. They circled at a safe distance, calling to one another, spreading out. A fourth Pilgrim joined them, a fifth. Heloise glanced over her shoulder, saw most of the villagers in panicked flight. Maybe seven stood with her father and Sigir. It wasn't nearly enough to face scores of Pilgrims, all of them mounted, armored.

Out on the road, Barnard and his sons stood back-to-back, surrounded by a moving circle of Pilgrims, riding in to lunge with their flails before reining their horses back to avoid the great hammers. Three Pilgrims lay dead at the Tinkers' feet, blood pooling around their smashed skulls. The remaining Pilgrims were wary, but Heloise could see that even a giant like Barnard couldn't keep this up for long.

She glanced back to her father. He was safe for now. Here and there, knots of villagers were standing their ground, but the ambush was a memory. Heloise's people clung desperately to isolated spots on the road, fending off the Order as best they could. A few Pilgrims looked Heloise's way, but none rode toward her. *Easier to kill the villagers, then come for me.*

She couldn't let them.

She turned the war-machine and charged across the road toward Barnard and his sons, banging the machine's empty metal fist against the shield's edge. The Pilgrims around the Tinkers scattered, riding around behind her. A flail head scraped against the driver's cage, caught just short by the metal frame. Heloise jerked aside, threw an elbow back, sending the shield's metal point crunching into someone behind her.

The instant the attack let up, Barnard and his sons set their hammers head down in the mud, leaning on the hafts, panting. She turned, lashing out with the metal right hand, ignoring the chips of bone and runnels of blood dripping off the shield.

The metal fist met empty air.

The Pilgrims had wheeled about and were charging back across the field back toward her father. Samson had managed to get his few villagers into a kneeling line, supporting their rakes and pitchforks on their knees, bracing them with the sides of their feet. Their faces were white, cheeks trembling.

"Hold, damn you," Sigir was bellowing at them. Another three villagers stood in a tight knot around him.

A line of horsemen charged them, reined in short, striking out with their long flails. None were in danger of striking the villagers, but one flail head tangled in the tines of a pitchfork, dragging it forward. The man holding it was dragged onto his face, pulled out of the line before he finally let go.

The horsemen wheeled back around, making ready to charge the gap they'd created.

"Heloise Factor!" a voice boomed, low and haughty.

Heloise's stomach turned over at the sound of it. She knew who it belonged to before she saw him, a tall Pilgrim with burning blue eyes. Blood stained the front of his robes, some of it new, most much older. Was that Austre's blood, where it sprayed across his robes as she lay helpless in the dirt while Hammersdown burned? Was it the blood of some other friend of Heloise's from one of the other villages in the valley?

"It's good to see you, Heloise," Brother Tone said, trotting his horse toward her. "This was a very brave, very stupid thing to do. How you convinced the Tinkers to put you in the Emperor's property, I don't know, but you will all pay for it. I promise to intercede with the Throne if you leave the machine now and give yourself over to our justice. The Emperor is cruel, but there is a certain . . . fairness in that."

Heloise thought of all the people she had lost since Tone had come to the valley. Austre, Alna Shepherd, and all the folk of Hammersdown. Clodio.

Basina.

She tried to curse him, to tell him that by the time she was done with him, he would beg her for death, but all that came out was a strangled growl.

Tone smiled wider. "This is why you don't parlay with heretics. They only howl like dogs."

Heloise had seen Tone fight, knew full well his speed and skill. But he was still a man in a boiled leather shell, while she was in a tinker-made war-machine, driven by the pressure of boiling seethestone.

Heloise charged, and Brother Tone waited to receive her.

If he was frightened, he didn't show it. He moved the reins to his teeth, gently spun the flail head into motion, and dug his knees into his horse's flanks as the beast began to shy.

Heloise closed the distance, raised her shield over her head. She could feel the pressure building in her shoulders, the machine tensing to mimic her motions, enough power to cut Tone in half.

Yet when she reached the spot and brought the shield down, Tone expertly jerked the reins and was gone. The shield's point parted the dust kicked up by the horse's sudden movement, sinking into the ground deep enough to make the war-machine shudder. Her stump jerked out of the control strap, slamming against the metal frame. Bright pain blossomed up her arm, spreading across her whole body, so intense that she lost herself for a moment, and came to with a dreadful seeping feeling in her wrist. The bandages were sopping red. The wound had reopened completely, and the dizzying weakness fogging her mind told her she was already losing too much blood. *No.* She had him. She was in a war-machine and he was a just a man. Surely the Emperor would grant her justice.

"My speed is the Emperor." Tone's voice was surprisingly close, shouted over the galloping of his horse, garbled by the leather in his mouth. "His favor has made me faster than the swallow in flight. More than a match for any tinker-engine."

She saw him now, galloping past her, striking out with the flail.

He placed the blow perfectly, judging the distance from the flail to the driver's cage as if the weapon were an extension of his body. The chain rapped against the metal frame, expertly finding the gap between breastplate and gorget. The momentum of the swinging head carried it in, rising to crash into the inside of the helmet's metal visor. It shuddered, springing back off the metal.

And right into Heloise's face.

She jerked her head to the side, sending the war-machine stumbling in the same direction, but it was not fast enough. She felt the iron spikes rake across her cheek, claw their way up the side of her head.

She knew she had lost the eye before she even felt the pain. She felt the pop, the liquid dribbling down the side of her nose. The world went half-dark, and she suddenly couldn't tell what was close and what was far. The pain came next, not as bad as she would have thought, but accompanied by a deep, wrenching sickness in her belly and weakness in her limbs. She wanted to double over and vomit. She wanted to give in. *No.* She couldn't lose now. Not after all Tone had done.

She swallowed bile, felt the machine sway as her body went slack from the agony. *A moment. I just need a moment.*

But Tone would not give her a moment. He was circling back, trying to shake the offal off his flail head. "This will need cleaning," he grumbled.

Shouts from up the hill. The impromptu line of villagers had broken and now Sigir and Samson were back-to-back, fending off circling Pilgrims with their short blades. They wouldn't be able to hold out for long.

Tone slowed his horse to a canter, lined up for another pass. Heloise's stomach boiled, and now she did vomit, letting it run down her chin, the whipsawing of her neck igniting a fresh spasm of agony. She wasn't sure she could move now, hoped he would charge her. She thought she might be able to reckon the distance in spite of her lost eye if he was doing the moving instead of her, but the Pilgrim only stopped, laid his flail across his saddle. He gestured at the hole where her eye had been. "Well, there won't be any portals opening there, at least."

What little hope she'd had died. He would make her charge him. She braced herself, unsure if she could move at all, or fight when she finally reached him.

But her father shouted again, in pain this time. Samson was down, his thigh laid open. Sigir stood over him, driving back his assailant, a hound-faced Pilgrim with hanging jowls. Her father's blood still dripped from hound-face's flail head. Heloise looked back at Tone. The Pilgrim had raised his flail and transferred the reins to his teeth again. "Don't turn your back on me. Face your end."

She would be mad to turn her back on Tone, but her father's screams might as well have been ropes about her shoulders, twisting her around. The pain, the sickness, all faded behind the sound of her father's cries, the sight of his wounded leg. She heard Tone gasp as she ran from him, bounding up the hill in three agonizing strides and knocking the hound-faced Pilgrim flying. He didn't scream, only gave a strangled cough as he slammed into a tree trunk, his spine snapping with a muffled crack. Sigir helped Samson to his feet as Heloise spun, the motion nearly making her vomit a second time. "To me!" Sigir shouted to the remaining villagers. "To me!"

Tone had been chasing her, and he yanked the reins as she turned, flicking out his flail toward her face again. She got the shield up this time, squinting against sparks as the iron head struck. The act made her wounded eye sing.

Across the battlefield, what few villagers remained were racing toward Sigir, throwing down their old shields, their pruning hooks and rakes. A shout of "Cleanse! Cleanse!" rose up from the Pilgrims, and they dug in their spurs, riding them down. Tone ignored them all, cantering in a tight circle, coming around to face Heloise again.

"Heloise!" Samson panted behind her. "Are you all right?"

It broke her heart. Even wounded, leaning on Sigir for support, his first thoughts were of her. She was grateful she had turned to Tone now. She couldn't bear to have her father see her ruined eye.

Behind Tone, she could see the villagers racing off the battlefield, the Pilgrims riding hard in pursuit. None stood against them now. She could feel the sticky wetness on her cheek, tears of blood weeping from the hole where her eye had been. *No!* The rage and frustration threatened to swamp her, but that wouldn't help them. She had been a fool to think they could win this, a fool to think she could have led them to victory.

"Sigir," Heloise called over her shoulder, forcing the words out, "we . . . we lost."

"To the fens, your eminence," Sigir said.

Heloise nodded inside the war-machine, forgetting that the Maior couldn't see.

She heard Sigir dragging her father back, cursing him when he tried to stay by his daughter's side. "Father!" she called without turning. "Go! I'm right behind you!"

"She has the hand of the Emperor upon her, you fool!" Sigir added. "And she'll be a sight safer without having to look after an old man with a wounded leg."

Heloise kept her eye on Tone as the limping scrape of her father's steps told her he was finally letting Sigir take him away. Villagers streamed past her, bolting for the woods. Some were wounded, most had cast their weapons aside. Their eyes were fixed on the ground, to stumble now was to die. A few kissed their fingertips and touched them to the war-machine's frame as they passed. The three Fletcher boys hid behind the war-machine's leg, and Heloise absently swatted at them with the shield's edge. "Go!" They did.

The Order forgot Barnard and his sons, raced to ride down the fleeing villagers. The Tinkers jogged behind the rush of Pilgrims, moving as fast as their exhausted bodies would allow, giant hammers propped up on their shoulders. Barnard waved a tired hand at Heloise, mouthing, *Go.*

"No," she whispered to herself, Tone always in her peripheral vision, "not without you."

Three Pilgrims galloped toward her. They jerked the reins as they came close, and their horses reared, lashing out with sharp hooves. The sickness from her lost eye made her weak and slow, but Heloise got her shield up, the hooves striking sparks off the painted surface. She lowered the shield as the horses came back down on all fours, then jerked the shield up again, smashing the horses back and bowling the riders from their saddles. The Pilgrims tumbled backward and into the path of their comrades charging behind them, who veered aside to avoid trampling their own.

Tone alone did not join the pursuit, letting the Pilgrims stream around him. He kept his eyes locked on Heloise. "You won't escape," he called to her.

"We grew up in these woods," Heloise replied, "we slept under the trees and gleaned in the meadows for leagues around here. You ate off silver plate in a city. We'll escape." She wished she believed the words.

Tone laughed. "We eat from wooden trenchers, and I haven't slept in the same place twice in the last five winters. I've spent more time under the stars than any of you. We are called Pilgrims for a reason.

"It doesn't have to be this way, Heloise." Tone's face grew serious. "Even now, the Emperor is merciful. Climb out of your machine and surrender to me and I will call my brothers back. We will go to Lyse, and you will stand trial before the Inquisition. We will learn the truth of these rumors that you are a devil-slayer. If your testimony is pure, the Emperor will redeem you. No one else need fall."

Heloise caught her breath. *Has word spread so fast?*

"Yes." Tone pointed his flail at the scratched sigil on the war-machine's metal chest. "The story has spread beyond the valley already. They say you are a Palantine." He glanced at his flail, the remains of her eye still spattered across one bent spike. "But if that's true, I must be the mightiest saint to ever mount a horse to be able to harm you. Which means it is *not* true. Come, Heloise. You are a girl playing at war. If you would save your village, climb down from there and be a girl begging the Emperor's forgiveness."

"I killed a devil." The surge of anger made her words into an angry hiss, a sudden and welcome relief from the sickness and pain. "You will beg *me*. I swear it in the shadow of the Throne."

Tone laughed, shook his head. "You seem confused," he said, "as to the difference between the Emperor's favor and a bit of dumb luck."

He twitched the reins and dug in his spurs, and Heloise tensed for his charge. She didn't have to worry about how hard her missing eye made it to judge distance. He would come straight for her, and all she needed to do was be ready to meet him.

Except Tone didn't come for her.

His reined his horse sideways instead, plunging straight for the Tinkers.

Heloise leapt for him, but it was much too late. Gunnar was turning, raising his hammer to parry a vicious overhead swing from Tone's flail. The boy was strong, but he must have been so tired, and Heloise could see how his heavy armor dragged at his shoulders. The horizon bounced as Heloise stretched her legs, pushing the machine to go faster. But she could still see Gunnar's hammer-haft catch the flail's chain, the head slipping over to clout him hard enough to ring his helmet like a bell. Gunnar staggered, dropped to his knees.

And then Heloise reached them, striking down with the machine's empty right hand. She screamed in frustration as Tone jerked aside, and her blow landed on his horse's neck, breaking it with a loud crack, sending the animal tumbling. Tone kicked easily free of the falling beast, striking out with the flail haft, slipping the butt inside the driver's cage and sinking it into Heloise's gut hard enough to send all the air out of her. He took a few careless steps as his horse shuddered on its side, then raised a hand to his mouth and called to the Pilgrims. A few reined in and began riding back toward him.

Heloise sank to her knees and vomited again. She glanced up at Gunnar. Barnard was hoisting the boy onto his shoulder. There was a single red hole punched in the base of Gunnar's helmet, but Heloise couldn't see how bad the wound was. Barnard dropped his hammer and began to run for the trees where the rest of the villagers had fled. "Heloise! Get up!"

"Just . . . just a . . ." She couldn't breathe. The sickness and the pain of her lost eye was all.

"There's no time! Come on, your eminence!"

She lurched to her feet, the horizon swaying and her vision going gray. Guntar staggered after his father, and Heloise went with them, a slow walk for the giant machine, as close to a run as the exhausted Tinkers could manage. Gunnar flopped on his father's shoulder, blood trickling from the hole in his helm.

Twice, Heloise turned to scatter pursuing horsemen. She was too sick and exhausted to bother with the riders now, only lunged at the animals with the corner of her shield. She couldn't spook trained warhorses, but the Pilgrims had seen what the shield could do, and sawed on the reins to keep clear. It was a stuttering, maddening way to proceed, but gradually the gap between the Order and the fleeing Tinkers grew, and at last Heloise gained the rise. She set her shield behind Barnard's back and gently pressed him on.

One of the Pilgrims tried to dash up the rise after him, and Heloise was just about to turn to cover Barnard's retreat when the horse's hoof punched through the thin cover of gravel and into a rabbit hole. The horse tumbled, shrieking, and Heloise could hear the sharp crack as its leg gave way. The Pilgrim rolled almost to her feet, throwing up a useless arm to protect himself from her shield.

Heloise looked down at him. He was of an age with her father, his cheeks full and his hair gray. His pockmarked face was dusted with a few days' growth of beard. The Order was supposed to swear vows of chastity and poverty, but everyone knew that they often had lovers, and even children. Maybe this one had a daughter of his own waiting for him somewhere. *If I spare him, I will only have to fight him later.*

But the Order was always talking about the Emperor's mercy, and then never showing it. It was up to her to stand for how the Emperor should be, rather than how he was. She was no Palantine, but she could behave like one. "Tell your brothers to leave us alone," she said, and ran for the trees.

She could hear Tone calling the Pilgrims back. "To me! In the name of the Emperor, to me! You'll lame your Throne-cursed horses. Regroup on me!" Heloise could hear boots thudding on earth as a few of the Pilgrims dismounted to pursue on foot. "No, you hell-cursed fools!" Tone screamed at them. "You're not going to run them down in armor! To me, damn you!"

She could hear one Pilgrim arguing with him, "Holy Brother, we'll lose them in the woods!"

"Of course we will!" Tone roared. "We'll lose them whether we chase them in there or not! Do you know these woods? Can you find your way in them clanking about with spurs and a flail like a damned fool?"

Heloise moved too far away to hear the Pilgrim's reply, but there was no sound of pursuit, and Heloise knew the Pilgrims were following Tone's orders. For a moment, she dared to let herself hope they might escape.

The trunks were thinner along the road, but they grew denser as she forged deeper. Soon she was forced to turn the war-machine sideways, crab-stepping it between trees and stumbling as the frame caught on branches. At last, she stepped the machine sideways between two trunks, and the frame shuddered. She felt the housing of the engine on its back snag fast against something. She didn't doubt she could force the machine to drag itself free, but would that tear the engine away? She would have to get out to look.

In the broken machine, she had dangled awkwardly from the chest strap, her arms and legs barely reaching the control straps that drove the war-machine's arms and legs. In this new one, Barnard had resized the driver's cage to fit her perfectly. The metal limbs mirrored each of her motions so that she could control the machine unconsciously, simply moving as she normally did.

She raised her arms, feeling the straps tugging at her limbs, translating the motion into the machine. She braced the shield and the metal fist against opposite trunks and pushed gently outward, prying them apart.

The trunks were old, thick around as a man's torso, and they resisted at first, the wood trembling, showering the machine with dead leaves and seed pods. Heloise pushed harder, the sickness rising as she felt the straps biting into her skin, the machine's metal limbs pushing harder in response. The engine first purred, then growled, then roared as she put more effort in.

The inside of the machine was tight around her, the world reduced to what she could see through the slits in the metal head. The leather of the seat cushion behind her was slick with sweat and blood, and the tight space stank of it, mixing with the acrid stink of the seethestone.

Crack, one of the trunks splintered loudly enough to be heard over the machine's engine, and Heloise realized with a shock that the noise might be telling the Order where she was. She dropped her arms, grateful for the easing of pressure against her skin, and the engine quieted to a dull mutter.

She paused, listening. The wood was silent all around her. The birds and animals had fled the noise of battle, but she couldn't hear the other villagers. They were supposed to scatter, but had they all gone some other way? Had she gone the wrong way herself? She thought of calling out, decided against it. She'd made enough noise already. All the while, her mind chanted at her, *Fool fool fool fool fool stupid little girl fool fool fool.*

The silence and the rest slowed her heart, and she began to feel her wounds. The ragged flesh that once housed her eye pulsed and throbbed. There were lines of pain across her cheek. But the worst was her wrist. She looked over at the stump. The bandage was completely soaked, as was the leather strap snug around it. Blood had pooled in the recesses of the metal frame of the war-machine's arm.

Heloise didn't know how long she'd stared. She only knew that the quiet of the woods was like a comforting blanket. The thought of leaving the machine, of running through the woods unprotected, frightened her. Worse, it made her tired. Surely she could rest a moment before seeing to the machine. *You've lost too much blood,* she thought. *You have to get moving. Your father is out there somewhere. He needs your help. They all do.*

But her thoughts were clouded, and she began to feel strangely warm, save at her wrist, which felt as if it had been plunged into ice. She thought she saw a light in the distance, heard a distant creaking. It could mean danger, but she no longer cared. Her head was too heavy to lift. The color bled from her vision, and the world shrank to that tiny, distant light.

Basina, I'm sorry, she thought as it winked out.

3

KIPTI

The Kipti player put his lute back in his wagon, and took his gold. The Maior feared to give a heretic custom, but he was a man of his word, and the Kipti had made good on his promise to rid the shrine of the serpents. Surely, the Emperor would not judge him unkindly, for the Writ said that a word of truth was more pleasing to the Emperor than poetry, and was honoring his promise not a word of truth? But the Emperor weighed commerce with a heretic against the Maior's honesty and judged him harshly. For the Kipti returned that very night and stole away with the Maior's two sons, to be raised on the road.
  —The Lament of the Maior of Gywd

Heloise opened her eyes to a hanging toy of wood and string, tiny horses pulling tiny wagons in an endless circle. Above it, a white canvas roof stretched over wooden hoops, sloping down to become walls.

A gentle breeze was coming from somewhere, turning the toy steadily, the wagons going round and round over her head. Tiny silver bells tinkled from the horses' yokes.

"You like it?" a woman's voice asked in a vaguely familiar

accent. "My mother gave it to me back when I was with child. It was my daughter's favorite toy."

Heloise turned her head to see the speaker. A woman of an age with Leuba, only stronger, her skin dark and hardened by the sun. Her red-brown hair was streaked with gray, wrapped around a knife into a bun high on her head. She wore a red cloak, a deeper color than the Sojourners', held shut with a trefoil-shaped brass pin. Her eyes were bright blue and smiling, like Tone's might have been if he had been a kind man.

Heloise lay on a simple straw mattress. Above her, shelves were built into the wooden hoops, crammed with boxes, ribbons, and hand tools. The woman sat at a small bench before an even smaller table, cluttered with files, tiny hammers, coils of string.

The memory of the battle came back to her in a rush and Heloise sat up, her head swimming. Her skin felt . . . tight, taut leather stretched across the frame of her bones.

But there was no pain.

She tried to wink her right eye. It was still gone, but it was no longer so hard to tell what was close and what was far away. She looked down at her body.

She had been dressed in a simple cotton shift, the chest unlaced, sleeves hiked up to her shoulders. The dirty linen was gone from around her wrist. The clean, scarred surface of her stump was pink, as if it had been healing for months, not days. She reached over with one of her good fingers, pressing against it. The flesh felt hard, leathery.

Heloise flexed her leg, her arm. The phantom fingers of her right hand clenched, released. She swung her right leg off the bed and onto the floor. It held her weight.

The woman raised a hand. "Easy, now. I've purged a fever strong enough to fell a giant from your blood. I've healed the worst wounds I've ever seen on a person who still drew breath. Your mighty heart still beats, but it is trapped in the body of a girl. Go slow."

Heloise's vision grayed, rippled. She shut her good eye, gritted her teeth until the tilting world settled, then opened it, wrestling with a boiling host of questions. "Where am I? Where are my parents?"

"Your people are here with us. They are safe, and so are you. Your mother and father are just outside. I cannot mend a person with her parents flitting about my head. They tell me your name is Heloise? I am Mother Leahlabel of the Sindi band of the Traveling People. You are in my home."

The Traveling People was what they called themselves, but Heloise had been raised to call them "Kipti." The canvas, the wooden hoops, the accent, all suddenly made sense. She was in a wagon. *The Kipti steal children.* Her mother's words came rushing to her mind, she pushed them aside.

Heloise looked at her scars, pink and shining. "You . . . healed me?"

"I did, and you are well enough, by the look of it."

Unless Heloise had been asleep for a month, there was only one way Leahlabel could have healed her so thoroughly. "It's all right," Heloise said. "I won't cry out to the Order."

Leahlabel laughed, waving a hand covered with rings of different metals. "Your Order can barely find their own asses in the dark with both hands and a candle. They certainly don't find us when we don't want to be found."

Leahlabel frowned as Heloise searched her eyes. "Now, what is it that has you staring at me . . . Ah, you'd be looking for the portal. I know how you villagers think. It was my wizardry that healed you and your father both, Heloise. And the others among your village who came here wounded. Think on that before you fear me."

Heloise could feel herself blush at the rebuke. "I'm sorry. It's just that my friend was a wizard and he was going to teach me. He saved my father. But then . . . the devil . . . came out of him."

"Veilstruck. He drew too much, too fast. It is rare, but it can happen to the inexperienced. There are ways to stay hidden when reaching beyond the veil. If you are weak, or hurried, or unskilled, the devils can see your hand, and grasp it."

"The portal was in his eye, just like the stories say."

"That is not a portal, Heloise. That is the reflection of the world beyond. You are seeing a tiny sliver of what the wizard sees. Sadly, by the time you can see it, there is no saving them."

Heloise felt a stab of grief. *I didn't try to save him. I ran away.*

"But there are no portals with me, Heloise. Or with Giorgi, who you will meet. The Traveling People do not shun our 'wizards,' and we certainly don't kill them. Another reason why your Order hates us."

"The Order? Did they follow us?"

"Our outriders are . . . out riding. I have no word as yet, but it does not appear you were followed this far. Still, the Mothers are nervous and it was all I could do to convince them to give you the time you needed to heal. We are not accustomed to taking in a village's worth of refugees, and yours is the strangest village we have ever known. A young girl leading a rebellion against the Order? Bloody cloaks taken as trophies?" Leahlabel brandished a bit of gray fabric brown and stiff with blood. "There are some for turning you out lest you bring the Order upon us."

"And you're not? Why are you helping us?" This woman was a stranger, but the thought of having to run again, now, when she was too weak to walk, filled her with sick terror. She didn't have the machine. She needed time to get her bearings.

Leahlabel paused, thinking. At last she shrugged. "You are in my daughter's bed. She nearly killed me coming into this world, and didn't stay long enough to give me joy as recompense. I have lost." She sounded almost proud of the statement.

"I'm sorry," Heloise said.

Leahlabel shook her head. "Do not be. Loss is the spinning wheel, it crusheth us beneath, and raiseth us up again. There was pain, to be sure, but it made me a Mother, and I am glad of that. But I look at you, and I think of your parents standing outside my wagon just now, worried sick over you. It reminds me that loss lifts a person up, but it is a burden, too, and one I would spare others if I could. It visits enough without my help."

Leahlabel turned to her cluttered table and passed Heloise a waterskin. "Drink. Slowly. Don't make yourself sick."

As soon as the leather settled in her good hand, Heloise realized how thirsty she was. The first touch of the cool liquid against her lips sent a shock through her, the gray fog clearing from her head, and the world coming into sharper focus. "Thank you. Who are the Mothers?"

"I am just one, and all of us must agree what it is to be done with you. And so I must have your story. Your people tell me you are one of the sainted Palantines come to liberate all mankind from the yoke of the devils. If I am to advocate for you with the Mothers, I must have the truth, Heloise. I wish there was more time for you to rest, but I do not know how long they will wait. You must tell me now. How did you come to be in my wagon?"

And Heloise told her, slowly at first, carefully, watching Leahlabel's lined face for the narrowing of her eyes or the turning of her mouth that would tell her she was being judged. But Leahlabel only watched her, listening, nodding occasionally to show she had grasped some point of the story. Heloise found herself speaking faster, telling more, drawn along by the open kindness in Leahlabel's eyes.

When she was done, the Sindi Mother crossed her arms and sighed. "This is what your father says, and your Maior, and this tinker. I will admit that I didn't believe them."

"Do you believe me?"

"Yes, Heloise, I do. If there is one thing I have learned in my day it is that a lie is easy enough for one person, but nearly impossible for many. Sooner or later, one of them will get a detail wrong, and you will know. And there are no wrong details here, save one, I suppose.

"Are you a Palantine, Heloise Factor? Are you the saint your people say you are?"

Heloise wasn't sure what Leahlabel expected from her. She thought of Sigir confronting her father before the battle. *Do you think we can do it without the people's hearts united behind their savior?* Did the Kipti need the same from her?

"No," Heloise said in the end, because the Order's lies had been woven so thickly about the world that she couldn't bear to add another. "I killed a devil, but I had a machine to help me. And I couldn't save Basina, anyway."

Leahlabel's expression softened. "Who was Basina?"

"She was my friend. The devil killed her."

There was something in Heloise's voice that made Leahlabel's expression shift, and Heloise felt the tear tracking its way down her cheek from her good eye. "I'm sorry," she said quickly, wiping it away.

"She must have been a very good friend, Heloise Factor," Leahlabel said slowly. "I can see it cut you deeply to lose her."

Heloise realized with a start it was the first time she'd spoken of Basina's death since it happened. "I wish I could have . . . I tried."

Leahlabel stood. "I do not doubt you did. That is the way with loss. It spins questions that we cannot answer for the thing that has gone, but we can answer them in the things we do now. Come, Heloise. We are as ready as we will be. Let us reunite you with your people and face the Mothers."

Leahlabel took her hand and drew Heloise through the archway of light surrounded by the canvas.

The wagons were drawn in a circle around a fire pit at least as large as the Tinkers' crucible. Young saplings had been cut and leaned over it, holding up dozens of black iron hooks with pots and kettles of every shape and size. There were around forty of the Traveling People standing in a tight group so close to Leahlabel's wagon that Heloise took a half-step back. There were men and women, children still clutching at their mothers' hands, boys and girls Heloise's own age. The men wore beards, golden hoops in their ears, and short, hooked, silver-handled knives at their waists, hilts crossing over their bellies. They chattered like sparrows, speaking in a language Heloise couldn't understand, quick and light, so loud that Heloise could hear them clearly even though they were plainly trying to be quiet.

The women wore loose trousers the same color as Leahlabel's cloak, but only two wore cloaks like hers, both of them at least as old as Leahlabel. The cloaked women stood apart from the rest. They alone did not whisper as Heloise appeared.

The villagers stood off to one side, huddled close together. Heloise searched their faces, recognizing Chunsia and Guntar, Ingomer, Danad, Poch, and Sald. At last, Heloise saw her mother, with Sigir's comforting arm around her shoulders, and breathed a sigh of relief.

Samson and Barnard sat at the foot of the wagon's short stairs. Both men jumped up as soon as they heard the creaking of the boards under her feet. Barnard's eyes were red and raw, but he knelt, tugging his forelock. Samson bounded up the stairs and snatched Heloise into an embrace. With a cry, Leuba raced to join him. The speed with which Samson had stood could only mean that his leg was healed, and Heloise was silently grateful. She let herself pause a moment, accepting her father's embrace, giving in to fatigue. But the Order wouldn't care that she was tired, or that her love was dead. They wouldn't show mercy because she was young. And because of this, her father's love was poison. If she let him hold her long enough, she knew he would never let her go, that she would never want him to.

"Oh, we were so worried," Samson said. "The Kipti threw us out. Said she needed to be alone to help you."

"If you're going to be staying with 'Kipti,'" Leahlabel said, "you should know that only villagers call us that."

She saw Leahlabel's strained smile out of the corner of her eye. Like all villagers, Samson had been raised to distrust the Kipti.

"We should call them the Traveling People, Father," Heloise said, gently pushing her parents away.

Leahlabel looked at Heloise with respect, but she spoke to Samson, "'Kipti' is a word the algalifes gave us when we wandered in the desert generations ago, and your Emperor adopted it. It means 'homeless.' We are not homeless. Our homes move, and that makes us free."

"My apologies," Samson said, "and thank you for healing my daughter, and to the Traveling People for welcoming us."

"There are many bands of the people. We are the Sindi." She tapped the trefoil pin at her throat.

Leahlabel turned to Heloise. "I will speak with the Mothers and then come to you."

Barnard and her parents followed Heloise to where Sigir stood over five bodies, wrapped tightly in winding shrouds. Dead, because they had all followed her into the ambush. She wanted to weep, but she kept her voice even. "How many people died?"

Sigir's face was taut with grief. "Your eminence. We are so glad that you . . ."

"Please," Heloise said. "Is that all?"

Sigir shook his head, his eyes wet. "I cannot say for sure. At least twenty. Many may yet live and be scattered. All that we are certain remain are standing here now."

She had never thought to count how many had set out from Lutet. She hadn't known she was supposed to. *What do I know of how to lead an army?* "How . . . many . . . how many are . . . were we?"

"Ah, your eminence, it is my fault for not giving you report. We were one hundred strong, give or take."

"Do you have the names?"

Sigir shook his head. "Only of those who lie here. Myron fell, and Erik. Marta the mender's daughter. The one with the lame . . ."

"I know her, Sigir."

"It is customary, after a battle, for the victor to allow the losers to return to the field to collect their dead. The heralds take names then."

"We can't . . . we can't ask them . . ."

"No." Sigir shook his head again. "We can't. That's how it happens in a . . . regular war . . . I suppose."

"This is not a war?" Leuba asked.

"This?" Sigir said. "No. This is crime. This is rebellion. There will be no parlay and no quarter."

"It is only crime to the Order." Barnard choked out the words.

Sigir ignored him, put his hand gently on Heloise's. "It'll be all right," he said. "War or crime, it makes no difference. All ways are equally fraught now."

Heloise felt a cold spike in her gut as she surveyed the faces of the villagers one more time, noted an absence. She remembered a body bouncing on Barnard's shoulder, a red hole in the base of a helmet. "Where is Gunnar?"

Barnard's jaw tightened. He shook his head, once.

The cold spike turned to nauseating grief. Basina's brother. A fixture in Heloise's life for as long she could remember. He'd had little time for younger girls, but his strong hands had been there to pick her up when she fell down, to bring her flowers on her naming days. He looked like Basina and smelled like the Tinkers' workshop, and he had been a piece of home. The grief was followed by a surge of rage, the image of Tone's mocking smile. *I will find a way to make you pay for this.*

Barnard looked down at the freshly healed stump of her wrist. "The Kipti woman said she could heal a wound, but she couldn't bring the dead to life."

Heloise could feel every eye in the camp on her. She felt naked without the machine's protecting metal frame. She swallowed the rage with an effort. "We should say the rites for Gunnar, for everyone."

"Here?" Barnard looked over his shoulder, whispered, "Your eminence, I understand that they helped us, but these are heretics. They won't have a shrine."

"At least we can say the words. We can go outside the camp and . . ."

The tinker crossed his arms and looked at his knees, his face reddening.

"Peace, Barnard," Leuba said. "These heretics saved us."

Heloise was amazed at the kindness in her mother's voice, speaking to the man who'd thrown her husband to the ground just the day before. Her mother was slow to anger, and quick to love again.

"When Basina was little," Barnard seemed just as surprised as Heloise, "you always warned her away from the road, that she might be taken by Kipti child-thieves."

"Those are . . . things you say because everyone says them," Leuba said, "because we've always said them. I don't see any stolen children here. These people *saved* us."

A tear tracked through the grime coating Barnard's cheek until it was lost in his beard. He turned back to Heloise. "I am sorry, your eminence. I mean no blasphemy, but I . . . please do not do this here."

She touched Barnard's shoulder. "I'm sorry."

He died because I couldn't save him, she thought, *because I don't know how to lead an army, because I had the stupid idea to bury myself under the road. Because some part of me believed that maybe I was . . . something more than what I am.*

Seeing Barnard so close to tears made her want to cry, herself, but the tinker had lost his second child in less than a fortnight. If he could contain the tears, then so could she.

"I will not bury him here," Barnard said. "He will be blessed in an Imperial shrine if I have to carry him with me until he is dust. I swear it in the shadow of the Throne."

Heloise nodded. "And I swear to help you, if we have to bring Gunnar before the altar in the Imperial chapel itself." She had no idea how she would ever get access to a shrine again. The only ones she'd ever seen were in Lutet, Hammersdown, and Lyse. Lutet was on the other side of the victorious column of Pilgrims, Hammersdown was a smoking ruin, and Lyse was a town, garrisoned and surrounded by a thick stone wall.

"Oh, now that's a fine story." Poch Drover's cheeks were red.

"Hold your tongue." Barnard's voice was low, dangerous.

"You've all lost your minds," Poch said. "I love Heloise same as any of us, but she's just a girl. She's not bringing anyone to the shrine in the capital. Not now, and not ever."

"I said . . ." Barnard boomed, taking a threatening step toward the drover.

Barnard was at least twice Poch's size, solid muscle where Poch's time in the cart seat had made him run to fat, but as frightened as he looked, the drover didn't back down. "I don't care what you said! You think you're the only man of faith among us? I love the Emperor and His holy Writ same as you. Let me ask you, if His favor rests so heavily with Heloise, then why'd we just get our backsides handed to us? Why's half the village gone? Sacred Throne, man, your own son . . ."

Barnard lunged, giant hands grasping.

Then froze.

Heloise looked down at her own arm. The pink scars of her stump were nestled close against Barnard's stomach. Without thinking, she'd put out her arm and stopped him. And, as if her hand were a viper, Barnard had let her.

She could feel the heat of his anger as he bellowed, "Speak again about my son! Speak his name! Do it, you blasphemer! You traitor!"

"Traitor?" Sigir blanched. "Barnard, Poch . . ."

Spit flew from Barnard's mouth as he stabbed a finger at Poch. "You were the first to deny her after she threw down the devil and ascended to the Palantinate. The Order came to the village when she was hiding in the vault. Came right to my door. How is that possible unless they knew she was in there? And then, when she hid with Clodio in the wood, they were waiting for her when she came back. You think that was mere happenstance? The Emperor's will? Someone *told* them."

"Now, you listen . . ." Poch was red-faced.

"And then the ambush failed. They were *ready* for us." He

turned to Heloise. "This shriveled rodent told them we were coming."

"Barnard, no," Heloise whispered. Barnard's rage was a war-machine of its own. It could shield her from Poch's criticism, but that didn't make it right. "The horses felt the covering of the pit. That's what alerted them."

Barnard turned back to Poch. The cords of muscle in his neck were still visible, his breath came in panting gasps. "Doesn't mean this one isn't in the Order's pocket. Let me—"

"Barnard, don't," Heloise said, louder now, "we are hurt enough without turning on each other."

Barnard looked at her now, but she held his gaze as she repeated, "Don't, please."

Barnard's rage gave way at last. "Yes, your eminence."

Heloise could feel the weight of the Sindis' eyes on her. *How will they trust us if they see us at each other's throats?*

"Well," Poch exhaled, "thank the Emperor *someone* has some sense. Heloise did an amazing thing, but this . . . this madness that she's the Emperor's hand has to stop. We have a Maior. We should be following him. Come on, Samson." Poch gestured to Heloise's father. "She's your daughter, speak reason to her. To all of us. We need to come to terms with the Order. We need to beg forgiveness."

Heloise felt her father move closer to her. She glanced at him, saw the shame in his eyes. He *had* been her father, *had* tried to forbid her to fight in the ambush. That authority had been broken. "You said yourself that we have a Maior," Samson said quietly.

"Aye, put this on me." Sigir sounded exhausted. He was silent for a moment, then shook his head. "It doesn't matter who we follow anymore. The Order does not care."

"You can't seriously—" Poch began.

"We are in *revolt*, Poch," Sigir interrupted him. "We have consorted with a wizard, touched the body of a devil, made war on the Order. You think they'll forgive that? I am raised to Maior by your voices, but I am anointed by the Imperial observer. They've unseated me on the village rolls now, I promise you."

"We don't know what they've done or what they'll do," Poch began. "Everything's changed now. Heloise killed a devil. They might . . ."

"You're a fool if you think that," Sigir said. "They see us, they kill us. The choice before us now is to run or to fight. Who we follow down either road makes no difference."

"You're wrong!" Poch shouted. "Someone has to go talk to them. Someone has to try to—"

"You do it," Leuba's voice carried over all.

Poch's voice died, his jaw hung open. All around him the villagers looked at their feet. Even Sald Grower, his arms crossed, standing defiant at Poch's side, would not meet Heloise's mother's eyes.

"If you are so certain it is the right decision," Leuba said, "you go and speak for us."

Poch's faced reddened and he opened his mouth to reply.

Heloise took a step toward Poch, her anger at Tone leaping to this closer target. "The Order hates the Traveling People," she hissed, keeping her voice low. "If you go to them, what do you think they'll do to these kind folk who have *saved* us?"

"They didn't save—" Poch began.

"Pardon me." Leahlabel appeared at Heloise's shoulder. A knot of Sindi men stood with her, nervously fingering their knife hilts. "I see that you are . . . tired after your ordeal, and I hate to interrupt, but the Mothers are insisting on meeting Heloise, now that she is awake."

"I'm sorry." Heloise turned to her, searching Leahlabel's face for a hint of how much she'd heard.

Leahlabel's face was inscrutable. She stepped aside, making room for the two other cloaked women Heloise had seen when she left the wagon.

One of them, a woman who could have been Leahlabel's twin if not for her hard eyes, spoke first. "I am Mother Tillie, and you don't look like you killed a devil."

The words were so plain that Heloise was struck dumb.

Heloise heard Barnard gasp, spoke quickly to cut him off. "We have the head, if you need proof. It's in a tinker-vault on the war-machine."

"Ah, yes. The machine we pulled you from. It needs retrieving," Tillie said, "lest the Order's scouts find it first. We'll have a look at this head then."

"No one has ever fought a devil and lived," the other Mother said, this one old and fat, with a mole on her chin that sprouted white whiskers, "and her own father said it was a Pilgrim's flail what took her eye."

"Indeed, Mother Analetta," Leahlabel began, "but—"

"She is a Palantine," Barnard snapped. "She shouldn't be put to the question . . ."

"Please," Samson added, "she has been through hell itself . . ."

"It's true," Heloise said over them. "I don't believe it myself, but it's true. My friend was . . . Veilstruck. The devil came out of his eye."

"I believe her," Leahlabel said. "I hear truth in her voice, and I have heard some clever lies in my day. Either she is very smart, or very honest."

"Oh, come now," Analetta's jowls shook, "we are all of us Mothers. Clever children are hardly anything . . ."

"She is so clever she cut off her own hand? Took out her own eye?" Leahlabel's voice was both laughing and angry at once. "She is so clever that we found her battle-scarred and driving a war-machine, with an entire village behind her?"

"Tell us the truth of how you lost your hand," Analetta said.

Barnard seethed, took a step toward her. The Sindi, as one body, twitched toward him, the men's hands flying to the knives.

Again, Heloise touched Barnard. Again, the huge tinker froze. "It's all right," she said.

"You don't have to answer them, your eminence."

Heloise faced Mother Analetta. "I climbed into the machine . . . Not the one you found me in. A roof fell on it, crushed it, and it . . . hurt me. They couldn't save my hand."

"Are you satisfied?" Barnard snarled at the Mothers.

Analetta grunted, shook her head.

Heloise felt Leahlabel's hand on her shoulder. She turned to Analetta. "What child would craft such a tale?"

But Heloise was tired of the Mothers speaking of her as if she weren't there. "It is not a tale, and I am not a child. I killed a devil, and that makes me a woman grown."

"It surely does," Leahlabel said, "and it's not the only thing. Will you tell the Mothers about Basina?"

And suddenly Heloise was choking down tears, because she was so tired, and so hungry, and all she could see was Basina's weak smile as she bled out into the mud.

"Who is Basina?" Mother Tillie asked. Her father's arm settled across Heloise's shoulders, pulling her close.

Heloise felt a twinge of fear. Had Basina told Barnard that Heloise had tried to kiss her? If so, Barnard was keeping the secret. But secrets cast a shadow over the beauty of their friendship.

So Heloise told what truth she could. "I loved her."

"She has lost." Leahlabel raised her head to Tillie.

"She has," Tillie answered. "Not a child, obviously, but someone dear to her."

Leahlabel nodded, turning to Analetta. "She has lost. Loss is the spinning wheel, it crusheth us beneath . . ."

"And raiseth us up again," Analetta answered slowly, dragging out the words as if she didn't want to say them.

"Then you are welcome, Heloise," Leahlabel said. "The Sindi band makes room at the fire for you."

4

TO LOSE, TO LEAD

The heretics kneel before their widows and bereaved. They have a saying, "Only those that have lost can lead." They believe that wisdom and salvation are found in grief, and not in the shadow of the Throne. They see fighting as ignoble, a ritual dance reserved for their menfolk. Only their sacred "Mothers" command the bands, women touched by tragedy—those who have lost children, or husbands. To these Kipti, the world is stood upon its head. Black is white and down is up. The sooner we settle them and break them to the Writ, the sooner the valley will be at peace. The blight follows these brigands as surely as night follows day.

—Letter from Brother Witabern to Lyse Chapter House

Heloise was still eating when Mother Tillie touched her shoulder. "You are well enough to drive the machine?"

"I think so," Heloise said.

"We have left it too long," Leahlabel said. "We are good at covering our tracks, but it won't take a gifted ranger to figure out our location if they find it. We should go now, if you can."

Heloise wiped her mouth and stood. "Let's go."

"There is no need. The Order will not find it." Barnard's eyes were too wide, moving too fast. He ground his teeth. "The relic is on its shoulder. It will conceal it from their sight."

A part of Heloise feared Barnard; his new devotion to her was a kind of madness. He had thrown her father down and threatened him. What might he do to her if he ever stopped believing she was a Palantine?

But none told him that he was mad, that his words made no sense. Sigir looked frightened, and spoke slowly. "Well . . . all the more reason we should go get it now, while the Order is delayed. I don't like the idea of leaving such an important . . . relic . . . out of our hands. The Emperor cannot prefer that we leave it unprotected."

Barnard was silent for a long time, looking at his feet, giving no sign that he had heard. Guntar looked torn. He put a gentle hand on Barnard's shoulder, "Father . . ."

Barnard's head snapped up, eyes focused again. "Aye, let's go."

He turned on his heel and walked toward the edge of the camp. Guntar stared after his father, but made no move to follow. Heloise looked to Sigir. "Does he know where it—"

Sigir silenced her with a quick shake of his head. "We'd better follow," he said, and strode off. Heloise followed with Samson hurrying after. One of the Sindi, nearly a man grown, judging by the dusting of black hair on his face and the warble in his voice, called to them in heavily accented Imperial tongue. "Where are you going?"

"To get the machine," Heloise shouted over her shoulder. *I hope*, she finished in her mind. But Barnard was proceeding as confidently as if he had a map.

"He's going the wrong way," Mother Leahlabel said, motioning the boy to join them.

"I know the way," Barnard called back, not breaking stride.

Leahlabel caught up to them, hugging her red cloak around her shoulders. "He's gone mad," she said.

"I'll stop him, Mother," the boy said, breaking into a run.

"Onas, no," Leahlabel said, catching him by the collar of his shirt and hauling him back. "That one looks strong enough to break a man in half."

She cast Heloise an apologetic glance. "My son is overeager. He's only a male, after all."

Heloise stifled her surprise. She had heard that women ruled the Kipti bands, but she was still shocked to see the conspiratorial look in Leahlabel's face, as if they were sharing a private joke that the men around them couldn't understand. Onas flushed, but it looked to be from shame, not anger. Heloise's heart went out to him.

"Barnard is . . . he's grieving," she said. "He's lost two children so far."

Leahlabel nodded. "Men have ever been weak."

Heloise felt her cheeks flush. It was a cruel thing to say, especially after what Barnard had been through. "Weak?"

Leahlabel gestured at Onas's narrow back. "The same loss that makes a woman into a Mother and leader of a band will drive a man mad. They shrink from pain. Could you imagine one of them having to bear a child? This is why all mothers strive to spare their sons from grief. It takes so little to break them."

Heloise fixed her eyes on Barnard's back and focused on keeping up with his long strides. She glanced over at Onas, caught him staring. He quickly looked away, blushing. She could only imagine how she looked, her eye socket scarred over like the stump of her wrist, the long pink gashes on her cheek drawing her face into a permanent leer. He glanced up at her again, and she made sure she was looking away this time, catching him in her peripheral vision. She let him stare. The Sindi had saved her. She owed them a look, at least.

Barnard angled them through the woods, no hesitation in his stride. After a while, they turned sharply and angled deeper in. Their footfalls sounded on dead leaves, snapped branches, and Heloise thought they were loud enough to be heard for leagues.

Onas looked up at her again, no longer shy. "He's going the right way now."

"He is?" Sigir asked.

Onas nodded. "Mostly. It's wizardry, no?"

"No. None of us are wizards. You know it's death for us."

Onas considered. "For us, too, if the Order catches us, but they never do. They stop us on the road, take their taxes and tolls, call us heretics, but they cannot see the Talent unless we show it to them. I just thought . . . that it was the same for you . . . that it was talk. You know how people talk. 'I do this,' or 'I never do this,' when it isn't really true. The Order is full of lies, everything they say is a lie."

"We are not lying," Heloise said. "We are no wizards."

"But your friend was a wizard, my mother says?"

"That's different, I didn't know he was until . . ." *But you did know. You knew and you told no one.*

"Will the Order hear us?" Samson cut Onas off before the boy could ask another question.

"We must hope not," Leahlabel said, "but if they came into the woods this far, my outriders would have brought word."

Onas shook his head, standing up a little straighter. "They are a league away, at least. We could scream, light a fire. They will not hear us."

They scrambled up a steep rise, and through a brook beyond

it. The Kipti paused to dip their fingers in the water, daubing them to their lips and eyelids. "This is the *sageata de argint*," Leahlabel said when Heloise stared. "It's where we come with questions."

"It helps?" Heloise asked.

"It does," Onas said. "Once to the eyes to see the truth, once to the lips as a promise to speak it."

"Do you have a question?" Heloise asked. "Did you ask one just now?"

"Of course," Onas said.

"What is it?"

"I asked if we are really being led to your machine by the wizardry of your religion, or if your friend is just mad."

"Is he mad?" Heloise felt a chill up her spine.

"Of course." Onas smiled.

Heloise couldn't help but smile back, but she caught Samson's concerned glance from the corner of her eye. She could tell he didn't like her talking to the Sindi boy, and the thought made her impatient with him.

On the other side of the brook was a long run of dead leaves blanketing a slope that stopped at two trees. Wedged neatly between them, its head and shoulders anointed with bracken, was the war-machine.

Leahlabel stared at it, mouth open. Onas walked up to it as if he owned it, brushed some of the dust from its breast. "This is you?" He jerked his thumb at the sigil.

"It is her," Barnard said. "She is a Palantine, a devil-slayer. This is the instrument the Emperor gave her for the task."

Onas stared at Heloise until she could bear it no longer. "What?"

Onas looked away, embarrassed. "I'm sorry. It's just that . . . I've never met someone who's . . ."

"Killed a devil?" Heloise finished for him.

"No." Onas laughed. "I mean, yes, but that's not as amazing as the rest."

"What rest?"

"You warred with the Order. You laid Pilgrims low. You took their bloodied cloaks. I don't know anyone who's ever done that."

"The devil was much worse," Heloise said.

"You can . . . drive that?" Leahlabel asked Heloise.

Heloise nodded. "I'll have to if we're going to take it back to the wagons. It's much too heavy to carry."

"You could kill a devil in this, all right," Onas said, eyes wide. He turned to his mother. "We should have one. It could walk alongside the wagons, Mother. The Order'd not plague us then."

Samson was also staring, but not at the machine.

"Barnard, how?" he asked. "We've been in that camp for an entire day, and you came from the fight at a dead run, so tired you hardly knew where you were. You said you weren't with Heloise when she abandoned the machine. How did you find your way here?"

Barnard's eyes were steady, calm. "You could drop this thing into the bottom of a river and I would find it. The Emperor guides my steps."

"Come now," Samson said. "You remembered the way, or you followed some track. Something you know about the machine."

Barnard shook his head sadly, as if Samson were to be pitied. "My strength is the Emperor. It's not the machine, Samson. It's the relic." He gestured to the metal box strapped to the machine's shoulder. "A beacon to the faithful."

Then why don't I feel it? Heloise wondered.

"The devil's head," Mother Leahlabel said. "May I see it?"

Barnard stiffened, looked at Heloise. "If her eminence permits, you may. It is her prize, won by right of arms."

Leahlabel turned to her. "May we?"

Heloise wasn't eager to see what three days of rotting in a metal box had made of the head, but she nodded to Barnard and he lifted an iron key from inside his shirt. The metal chest opened silently on well-oiled hinges, and Barnard lifted the devil's head out.

It was as fresh as the moment they cut it from the devil's shoulders. The tiny nostrils, the lopsided cut of a mouth, the clusters of stalked eyes. All were pristine. Heloise half-expected it to open its eyes and shriek its ear-splitting eagle scream.

Barnard hefted it by its corkscrewing black horns. "This," he said, "is a devil."

"That doesn't look like the stories," Onas said.

Barnard shrugged and jerked his chin toward Heloise. "Then it is time to write new stories. No one has ever seen a devil and lived to tell about it, until now."

"That's right," Leahlabel said, looking at Heloise. "All of your sacred Palantines died in the fight."

Onas's gaze had turned shy again. "How did you do it?"

I don't know how I did it. It had happened so fast, Heloise thought as Barnard put the head back in the box and locked it shut. But she said nothing, climbed up the machine's leg instead, dusted the dead leaves from the seat, and pulled herself inside.

It felt good to be back behind the controls. The machine had come to feel like an extension of her body, her most comfortable set of clothes. More important, it made her feel safe. She felt the heavy solidity of the metal all around, waiting for her commands. Inside it, she had faced the Order, killed Pilgrims. It might not have saved her eye, but it had surely saved her life.

She slid her arms into the metal sleeves, her good hand reaching for the control strap.

She froze.

"What's wrong?" Leahlabel asked from the ground.

"Did you . . . did you undo the straps when you took me out?" Her stomach was fluttering, but she ignored it. Surely it was nothing. "It's just that I never undo the straps, but the buckles are undone now."

Leahlabel shrugged. "Heloise, I can't remember. It was Giorgi that took you out of the—"

Onas was looking around now, frowning. "Mother. People have been here."

"Are you sure?" Leahlabel reached up for the knife in her hair. "Perhaps it is—"

Heloise heard the rush of air before she felt the clang of boots on the machine's shoulder.

She looked up just as a slim blade slid through the gap between the machine's pauldron and the frame, missing her cheek by a hair's breadth and drawing sparks from the inside of the gorget. The man holding it had dropped from the tree trunk, and was kneeling on the reliquary box, his tight-fitting black clothes silvered by the dappled sunlight filtering in through the crowns of the trees. Loose cloth scabbards hung limp at his sides, the dagger and sword they'd held in his hands now. He was covered in sable cloth that revealed nothing, not a stray hair nor a patch of skin. It rendered him featureless, blending into the forest gloom, save the bright glint of his weapons, and the light reflecting off his eyes.

The machine shuddered as a second set of boots thumped down on the opposite shoulder. "In the name of the Throne," the man shouted, "you are taken!"

The trees to either side of the machine shivered, spewed forth more black-clad men—two, then four, then six, then more, weapons in their hands, racing toward the machine, silent save for the padding of their soft-soled boots on the cold earth.

Heloise scrambled for the salted cloth bag that kept the

seethestone. If she could somehow get the machine started . . .
The sword came sliding through the frame, piercing the bag and
forcing Heloise to slip down the seat to get out of the way. She
crouched low as the black-clad man pulled his weapon up for
another thrust.

She could hear her father and Barnard shouting. Onas drew
his hooked knives and ran for the machine. "Get out!" he called
to Heloise as he sprang onto the machine's metal knee, as nim-
ble as a cat on a tree branch, pushing off the slim surface with
his toes and leaping up the machine's arm to reach the men
above her.

She heard a clash of metal and finally slid out of the machine,
rolling down the leg and banging her shoulder painfully on the
metal foot. She scrambled to her feet in time to see Barnard, who'd
picked up a fallen sapling and was swinging it in a sweeping arc,
driving some of the enemy back. One of them charged and caught
the trunk full in his face, knocking him on his back. Another
black-clad man charged past his fallen comrade, and Samson
tackled him at his waist, slamming him into the machine's leg.
The machine shuddered from the impact, and Heloise heard a
splintering crack as one of the trunks collapsed, breaking the machine free from the tree's grip and setting it rocking.

Heloise scrambled away from it, looking up. Across the machine's shoulders, the two enemy were pinwheeling their arms,
desperately trying to keep their balance as the machine tipped
forward and back. Onas danced along the swaying surface as if it
were still. He spun, a dancer's pirouette that sent his silver-handled
knives blurring, a metal arc that swept across one man's throat,
sending him tumbling off the machine, gurgling blood.

The man's fall set the machine rocking even harder, and the
other black-clad man finally lost his footing, dropping his weapons and clinging to the reliquary box. Onas somersaulted back-

ward off the machine, turning in the air and landing on the back of the man Samson had tackled. Onas paused only to draw his hooked knife across the man's neck before throwing his shoulder against the machine's rocking leg. "Help me!"

Samson and Heloise scrambled to their feet, raced to the machine's legs, throwing their weight against them. She glanced over her shoulder to see Leahlabel, driven back-to-back with Barnard. The Sindi Mother's knife flashed in her hand, but her thrusts were nowhere near as expert as her son's, serving only to keep one of the attackers at bay. Another had reached Barnard, sinking his sword deep in his arm. Heloise screamed as the black-clad man swept his dagger up, sliding it into the tinker's side just above his broad leather belt. Sigir had been tackled to his knees, and one of the enemy had his arms pinned behind his back, knee driven into the Maior's spine.

"Heloise, come on!" Onas shouted, and she ripped her gaze away, giving the machine a final heave. Heloise felt it unbalance, the metal feet tipping up toward them. They scrambled back as it crashed down, sending most of their attackers running. Two of them were too slow, and she heard them grunt as the weight of all that metal crushed them against the ground.

Onas whirled, leapt at Barnard's attacker, the momentum carrying him into an arc that ended with his knives raking across the enemy's shoulders. The black-clad man cried out and dropped his sword, backing away, and Onas seized the tinker's thick arm. "Come on!"

Leahlabel was already running. Samson leapt to his feet and seized Heloise's arm, dragging her along. "No!" She shook free of his grip. "They have Sigir!"

Samson snaked his arm around her waist, throwing her over his shoulder. "We can't help him now! We have to go!"

He was already turning and running, Heloise bouncing like a

coil of rope against his broad back. She beat on his spine with her scarred stump, the anger boiling in her. "We can't leave him!"

"We'll come back for him!" her father panted.

She looked up and saw that her father was right. There were dozens of the men-in-black coming out of the woods now, helping their comrades up, turning to give chase. If they returned for Sigir, they would surely be killed. Heloise tried anyway, struggling against her father's grip.

In the machine, she was stronger than ten men of her father's stripe, but outside of it, there was little she could do save tighten her stomach to keep the pounding of his bouncing shoulder from knocking the wind out of her as he ran faster than she ever thought he could.

At least twenty of the black-clad enemy had recovered from the shock of the falling machine and turned to give chase, reversing their daggers to grip them by the points.

"This way!" Onas pelted back toward the *sageata de argint*, turning sharply as Heloise craned her neck to see the brook glinting in the thin sunlight. He made for a thick stand of brush that crowded the brook's edge, growing thicker as they neared, until the water slid beneath it and disappeared.

The men-in-black came behind them, fast runners, but not so sure of the ground, and not ready for a run through the woods over branches and rocks. One of them stumbled on a root, went sliding on his face. The man behind him vaulted over him, throwing his dagger as he came. It fell short, a ranging throw only, but it quivered in the earth a few paces behind Samson. It wouldn't take them long to get in range.

Leahlabel reached the brush beside her son and threw herself into it, diving low, like Heloise used to dive into the pond outside Lutet in the hot summer. She slid along the wet ground beneath the thick branches, and immediately set to crawling. Onas skidded to a stop, waving them in with one arm. "Down! Follow Mother! Down on your bellies! Go!"

Samson released Heloise and she rolled off his shoulder, slinking down onto her belly. She sighted Leahlabel's receding feet and followed them, the freezing, wet earth soaking into her dress and numbing her chest. Down here, the thick, tough bases of the bushes formed a weaving path, natural columns supporting the dense thicket of thorns and leaves above them. Heloise could feel them ripping at her back as she went. She bit her lip, ignoring the pain and focusing on moving as fast she could. She risked a glance over her shoulder, saw Barnard's massive shoulders squeeze between two bushes, get briefly stuck, then pop free as Onas pushed him from behind. The tinker reached out with thick hands and hauled himself along, his beard trailing in the mud and brook water. His face looked far too pale, and Heloise swallowed the urge to go to him, focused instead on pulling herself forward.

She heard the brush shudder as the black-clad men reached the thicket and cast their daggers into it, heard Samson grunting as he crawled in after Barnard, and finally Onas slithering along behind them all. "Go on!" the Sindi boy called to Samson. "Keep them moving! I'll hold them here!"

There were shouts as the first of the enemy reached the thicket's edge and began wading into it, slashing with their swords. Heloise risked another glance and saw Onas on his belly, slithering backward into the thicket, knives in his hands, slashing at one of the enemy who'd figured out they could make no progress standing, and had lowered himself to crawl after them. Onas drew him in with a feint, then stabbed at his unprotected face. Heloise looked away just as the man cried out.

She crawled along for what seemed an impossibly long time, her heart thudding in her chest, the fear finally seeping in now that the immediate danger was past. The ground sloped farther down, and the thicket grew denser above them, the bases closer and closer together until Samson had to shove Barnard through the gaps between the bushes.

The water grew deeper and deeper as they went, until at last Heloise was half-crawling, half-paddling, lifting her chin to keep her head above the water. At last, the soles of Leahlabel's feet disappeared, to be replaced by the backs of her heels as she stood.

"Stay low," the Sindi Mother whispered as Heloise emerged into a mire dotted with the stumps of rotted trees. Leahlabel's hand on her shoulder kept her crouched, but she could see the thicket shivering a long way off, could faintly hear the curses of the enemy and the thwacking of their blades as they tried to cut through.

She knelt to help drag Barnard out of the gap in the brush. The huge tinker merely crawled forward on his hands and knees and collapsed in the muck. He turned his head to keep his mouth clear of the brackish water at least, and Heloise felt a surge of mad hope that he would live. Samson burst through a moment later, racing to Heloise's side, running his hands over her, his eyes searching for any sign of injury as he whispered fiercely, "Are you all right? Tell me you're all right."

She was still trying to calm him as Onas emerged a moment later, his knives bloody. "Killed one in the entry," he whispered, "wedged him in good. Took them a moment to drag him out. They don't know the way if they're not following us. If we move quickly, we can lose them."

"A moment." Leahlabel knelt by Barnard's side, rolling him over onto his back. The wounds in his arm and side were puckered and gray already, the blood oozing slowly. She lay her hands across them, shut her eyes. Heloise waited in silence, felt Samson straighten beside her, crouching again at a hiss from Onas. A moment later, Barnard gasped, his eyes opening, some of the color returning to his face.

He stared at Leahlabel, his eyes terrified. The Sindi Mother was sweating, and she rolled her eyes at his revulsion. "I'll take that as thanks, you great pill. Now, get up, stay low, and follow me." She withdrew her hands, and Heloise saw Barnard's wounds had closed into shining pink scars. Leahlabel took off in a crouching jog.

Samson helped Barnard to his feet, slinging the tinker's thick arm around his shoulders. Heloise ran to this other side to give what support she could. Barnard looked even more horrified that the man he'd knocked on his back just two days ago was holding him up. ". . . Thank you," the tinker managed.

Samson spat. "I should leave you to die, you horse's ass."

Barnard managed a weak smile as he limped along. "Why don't you?"

"No heroes in a pike block," Samson grunted. "We stand and fall together."

Heloise remembered hiding outside the gathering hall what seemed like a lifetime ago, listening to Sigir speak the same words to her father. *Oh Sacred Throne, Sigir.* They had to go back for him, they just had to.

"They were waiting for us," Samson said, as Leahlabel led them splashing through the mire and behind a low ridge of gray stone, the sounds of pursuit finally cut off entirely. "They must have found the machine just after we pulled Heloise out of it. So much for your outriders."

"No scout is perfect," Leahlabel shot back. "Those were not Pilgrims."

"No," Samson said, "those were the Black-and-Grays. We had some attached to us during the Old War against Ludhuige and his Red Banners. If the Order are the Emperor's Hands, then the

Black-and-Grays are his Eyes. They're for moving quickly, and for seeing. The Order must have sent to Lyse for them as soon as we were driven off."

"They didn't move quickly enough," Onas said.

"Quickly enough to bleed me," Barnard said, "and to take the Maior. We have to get him back."

"We do," Leahlabel agreed, pausing for a moment to lean against the rock before pushing off and angling deeper into the woods, moving as fast as Barnard could hobble. "They know where we are now, or close enough as makes no difference. If they make it back to their fellows, the Order will be upon us before we can move the camp."

Heloise's mouth went dry. She'd been too focused on Sigir to think of that. "How do we stop them?"

"We move quickly, and we cut them off. They are fumbling through unfamiliar woods. We have camped here our whole lives."

"But there are so many of them," Heloise said. "Do you have enough—"

"We do not need numbers," Leahlabel said, gesturing at Onas. "You have seen the knife-dance now. All Sindi boys are raised to it. And we have Giorgi."

Heloise remembered Onas's incredible balance, the spinning arcs of his knives. Still, they would need many just like him. But she also remembered Leahlabel's words when she'd awakened in her wagon. *There are no portals with me, Heloise. Or with Giorgi.*

She opened her mouth to ask about Giorgi, but Leahlabel picked up the pace. "Tinker, you will have to find the strength to run. There's no time, and I will not have my people overrun. Come on!"

"You'll have to do your best, Barnard," Samson said, picking up the pace to match her.

"By the Throne," Barnard said, "I'll damn well drag you."

5

STANCHING THE WOUND

They curse the village ways, saying that fixing one's home makes a man a slave. They call all those who sign the village rolls "The Caged," and see them as weak. We must teach them what strength there is in settlement. A fortress is fixed, as is an army, when it is dug-in.
—Letter from Brother Witabern to Lyse Chapter House

They ran at a limping pace that made Barnard's face nearly as pale as it had been before Leahlabel healed him. Heloise stayed with the tinker, partly because he was one of her own, and partly because there was no way she could keep up with Onas and Leahlabel, who seemed nearly as fast as horses. The distance between the villagers and the Traveling People stretched, until Onas had to double back to them three times to make sure they were going the right way.

At last, panting and gasping, they broke through a treeline and into the Sindi camp, buzzing with activity as the Traveling People and villagers alike crowded around Leahlabel and Onas, all of them talking at once.

Barnard fell to his knees, Chunsia and Guntar rushing to his side. Samson stood, hands on his knees, shoulders heaving. "What happened?!" Leuba rushed to him.

"They . . . took . . . Sigir," her father managed.

"Heloise, are you all right?" Leuba asked.

"I'm fine, Mother, we need to—"

But Leahlabel was already turning. At least twenty of the Sindi men were behind her now, loosening their knives in their sheaths. At their head was a heavy man with a bushy gray beard and bright red cheeks. He alone wore no knives, and his face was open and smiling despite the grave looks all around him.

"Well, now." His voice was unworried as he called to Heloise. "You are our villager saint. I am Giorgi. They tell me you killed a devil, and Pilgrims besides."

Heloise's breath was coming easier now. The burning in her legs subsiding. The warmth in Giorgi's eyes chased the fatigue from her, made the world seem . . . brighter somehow. Clodio's eyes had done the same thing. *The world is wide and wonderful, and I am glad you are in it.*

"Some," she said, looking up.

"Some devils?" Giorgi turned to Leahlabel, a look of mock confusion on his face. "I thought it was just the one."

Leahlabel rolled her eyes. "There's no time, Giorgi."

Giorgi waved a hand, walking to Heloise's side. "There's time," he said to Leahlabel. "If they found the machine in the wash of the *argint,* then they came by way of the long meadow. They'll tend to their wounded and go back that way. We'll catch them in Wind's Teeth. It's the only way in or out of there if you don't know the ground, and they don't know the ground."

He turned back to Heloise. "Well, then, I suppose a devil-slayer could do a bit more running? We're going to need you to move that machine."

"We knocked it over," Heloise said. "It might be broken."

"We'll repair it, if need be." Giorgi waved his hand again.

"Repair . . ." Barnard managed. "It's tinker-made."

"Every one of the Traveling People is at least half-tinker." Giorgi laughed. "We'll get your Maior back, Heloise, but we have to go right now."

"No." Samson rose to his knees. "I'll come and . . ."

"You're an old man and all run out," Leahlabel said, "you can't keep up. She'll have twenty Sindi knife-dancers around her. No harm will come to her, I swear it."

"I am coming!" Samson staggered to his feet, hawked, and spat.

"There is no time!" Leahlabel was already leaving camp, the knife-dancers, with Onas and Giorgi at their head, filing out behind her.

Heloise's stomach was boiling with the strain of the run, with worry over Sigir, with fear of what it meant that the Black-and-Grays had discovered them.

"Heloise!" Samson lurched to his feet. "I'm coming with you!"

"Certainly," Leahlabel called back, "if you can keep up."

He couldn't, his cries fading in the background as the Sindi ran flat out, making straight toward the brook they'd crossed when they'd first gone out to retrieve the machine. Heloise ran with all she had, but she had had scant time to rest, and didn't have the sound of the Black-and-Grays on her heels to drive her along. She was younger than her father, but like him, she was no runner, and within moments the burning in her chest and her legs was more than she could endure. She tried to swallow air, but it seemed her throat had closed. She slowed, the line of the Sindi men racing past her.

Onas fell back to jog along at her side. "Come on, Heloise. It's not far."

"I . . . I can't . . ." Heloise couldn't get enough air to speak.

Onas put his hand in the small of her back, gently pushing her forward. "Yes, you can. You killed a devil. You can do anything."

The words didn't give her more air, or dispel the agony in her legs, but the touch of his hand on her back, the gentle pressure of his arm, propelled her along. Her stride lengthened, and the line of Sindi men grew, not closer, but at least no farther away.

Heloise stayed with them as they splashed through the brook and angled in a new direction, taking them through a thin copse of trees and down into a gully cut by an old stream bed long since run dry.

Here, Giorgi at last raised his hand, and they halted. Heloise collapsed gratefully against a rock, panting and mopping sweat from her brow. Onas patted her shoulder. "You did well."

"She did," Giorgi said, "and now the hard part is before us. Are all ready?"

The men nodded, drawing their knives, as Giorgi knelt and produced a short torch and a flint on a leather cord. He struck the flint against a rock, caught the sparks on the torch's head, and gently blew the embers until tiny peaks of flame were flickering. Heloise glanced up at the strong sun, mostly blocked the canopy of leaves above them, but still bright enough to make torchlight unneeded.

Giorgi smiled at her and stood. "Slowly now," he said.

They crept forward, keeping low and quiet, down the gully's end and out, along a low ridge of raised stones that rose high and sharp enough to stop a man from climbing over them without difficulty, until they came to a gap in the rock. The wind whipped through the crevice, sending the branches dancing to either side. Giorgi motioned them to halt, and stood, listening.

Heloise pressed herself against the rock face, straining to hear something more than the wind whipping through the gap in the rocks, but the wind stirring the leaves shut out all else save the pounding of her heart, roaring in her ears.

But Giorgi seemed to hear something; he stepped back against the rock face and signaled to the men around him. They crouched, ready.

The first man through the gap was still wreathed in the sable he'd worn when he'd attacked Heloise, but he'd lowered the cloth over his face. He was young, scarcely older than Onas, with wary eyes and thin lips. Seeing his face made him look smaller, less fearsome. A man in black, rather than a creature of spun shadow.

One of the Sindi leapt for him, sinking his knife into his chest to the hilt. The man shouted, chopping the Sindi's wrist and pushing him back. He turned, silver handle still sprouting from his chest, and turned back through the gap. His voice gurgled from the wound, but it was loud enough. "Ambush! They are upon us!"

Onas leapt past the man who'd lost his knife and cut the enemy down, throwing himself through the gap without breaking stride. The rest of the Sindi followed him, Heloise coming behind.

On the other side of the gap, Heloise could see the other Black-and-Grays freezing, drawing their weapons, stepping carefully back as they took in the numbers of the Sindi boiling out from the opening in the rock. After a moment, one of them clearly assessed that the battle was not in their favor, and the enemy bolted back the way they had come.

Onas raised the shout and the Sindi raced after them. Heloise gulped a breath and ran as fast as she could. They pelted up rising ground, Heloise searching for Sigir with every step.

At last, she saw him. His hands were unbound, but one of the enemy had him by the arm, pushing him along as they ran. Before long, Heloise spotted the fallen machine, the pinpricks of sunlight penetrating the tree cover glinting off its metal shoulder. It looked intact, and she said a silent prayer to the Emperor that it would still work. The thought of being back inside its armored frame gave her the strength to keep running.

The Black-and-Grays were slow in their soft leather boots, carrying their long blades. The Sindi gained, and before long the enemy gave up running and turned to fight. The first of the knife-dancers reached them, spinning their blades into a blur, striking and dodging in perfect accord, one slashing high while another stabbed low in silent conversation, as if the battle had been a thing they had planned.

Two of the enemy fell instantly, but the rest rallied and threw themselves into the attack. Their fighting was nowhere near so fluid and beautiful as the Sindi knife-dancers, but it was brutally effective, their long swords giving them a reach the short hooked knives could not hope to match. Heloise cried out as one of the Black-and-Grays cut through the whirling arc of blades, burying his weapon in the shoulder of the man behind them. He didn't pause, ripping the sword free and bringing it around over his head to hammer into another dancer on the backswing.

The Sindi losses gave the enemy heart, and Heloise watched them fan out in front of the machine, waving their weapons. "Heretic scum," one of them rasped, "go back to your holes and await the Throne's justice."

"Oh, no!" Giorgi laughed, waved his torch in a wide arc. "We are done waiting," and then his smile was, at long last, gone.

The fire trailed from the whipping torch, but Heloise gasped as it stuck to the air, like paint left behind by a passing brush. The flames thickened, then crackled, spit. Two orange peaks rose, like drops of oil floating on water, dripped themselves off the fire's body. They spun, thickening, the colors giving them life. Red, orange, blue, yellow, and white. They shivered, sprouted arms and legs, and set down to either side of Giorgi.

The flame-men crouched, burning arms spread.

"Wizardry!" the Black-and-Grays shouted. "Heresy!"

"More simply put," Giorgi said, "fire."

The flame-men sprang. One of the Black-and-Grays slashed at them, but his blade cut through the fire, the flames parting briefly, only to reunite as soon as the steel had passed. The burning men embraced him, and he erupted in smoking fire, his screams going higher and higher as he rolled on the ground.

The Black-and-Grays backed away at that, and the knife-dancers pressed forward. One of the flame-men stayed with the burning enemy, keeping its arms around him, ensuring that his frantic rolling on the ground did no good, while the other sprinted forward. The enemy gave it a wide berth, and the flame-man darted this way and that, trying to come to grips with an opponent. At last, one of the enemy shouted, "Water!" and went sprinting for the downed machine.

The waterskin, Heloise thought. It hung beside the seethestone, ready to squirt into the engine to start it running. She fumbled around for a weapon, settled on a good-sized chunk of sharp rock that lay tumbled in the grass, circled around the knife-dancers. She didn't know if the flame-men could be put out like a normal fire, but she doubted the enemy would be looking for a girl with a rock. She knew the Sindi would want her to stay out of the fight, but surely they would understand if she did this one thing. If she could get close enough . . .

But no sooner had she skirted the fighting and spotted the man, on his knees now, lifting the waterskin from inside the machine, than he looked up and straight at her. "It's the girl!" he shouted, dropping the waterskin and running toward her.

Heloise backpedaled, terror spiking in her gut. She had no machine now, and she was suddenly aware of how small she was, how short the reach of her rock. The Black-and-Gray raced toward her, sword raised above his head, grim and silent save for the crunching of his soft-soled boots across the dead leaves.

She fumbled backward, the ground around her suddenly far too vast, the Sindi too far away. She tightened her grip on the rock and crouched. He was too fast, and by the time she turned he would be upon her. There was no point in running, if she could dodge his first blow, then maybe she could—

She saw a flash of scarlet and he was toppling sideways, a slim knife protruding from his cheek, angling up into his skull. "Heloise!" Leahlabel paused only long enough to rip her knife from his face before running to her side. "What are you doing? Are you all right? Get behind—"

A sword pommel crashed against the side of her head and the Sindi Mother crumpled. Heloise scrambled toward her only to have a boot crunch down on her arm, pinning her to the cold ground and sending the rock tumbling from her hand.

She looked up to see the Black-and-Gray who held Sigir. His arm was across the Maior's chest now, his knife blade against his throat. He glanced down long enough to ensure his boot was firmly on Heloise's arm, then back up again.

"Stop!" he shouted. "Stop or I will cut your precious villager's throat. Throw down your weapons!"

The Sindi froze, and Heloise's heart lurched, not because she feared the Sindi would abandon their knives and let the man go, but because she feared they wouldn't. Sigir was precious to *her*, but she could see the calculation in the Sindis' eyes. They had come to stop the enemy from alerting the rest of the Order. Saving a single villager was not their first concern.

Sure enough, Giorgi's smile returned. "I have no weapons," he said, and Heloise saw the flame-man rise from the burning corpse of one of the enemy, crouch, and head for the man at a run.

The man cursed, pressing the blade harder against Sigir's neck. Heloise strained against the heavy boot pressing hard on her arm, her fingers grasping uselessly toward the rock. He hadn't pinned her feet, though, and she pushed off with them, trying to force her arm out from under him. The man rocked, stamped down harder, thrown off balance, his blade momentarily falling away from Sigir's throat. Heloise could see the flashing of silver as the knife-dancers lunged toward him.

The man shouted and raised the blade to Sigir's throat again, as Heloise's foot lost traction and skidded across the ground.

Her foot.

She threw herself as far backward as her pinned arm would allow, bringing her foot up with all her might. It skipped up the enemy's thigh to thump between his legs. Heloise winced, half-expecting him to be wearing leather armor, but she felt only the soft impact of his manhood, heard him cough and double over, dropping the knife. The pressure lifted from her arm as he stumbled back.

And then Onas and the flame-man struck him at the same time. Onas's knife pierced his throat and the flame-man's embrace set him smoldering. Sigir spun away, cursing, as the man fell across Heloise. She rolled just as he hit the ground, scrambling to Leahlabel's side.

The Sindi Mother was rising to one elbow, dabbing at the blood trickling from her temple. "I'm . . . I'm all right, Heloise. Are you . . ."

"Yes, I'm fine."

"Did we . . ."

Heloise looked up. The field was littered with dead, but she could only see Sindi standing. Sigir was blinking at the carnage, shock plain across his pale face.

"Yes," Heloise said, relief making her weak, "yes, I think we won."

Leahlabel clambered to her feet. "Giorgi! Did any get . . ."

"It's all right, Mother." Giorgi's smile was back, his calm. "We got them all."

Heloise jumped to her feet, ran to Sigir. "Are you all right? Did they hurt . . ."

Sigir blinked, distracted. He put his hands on her shoulders, but his eyes were still on the field, roving over the dead. "I can't believe . . ." he whispered, "I can't believe you killed them all."

"They didn't hurt you?"

"No, child." He finally looked down. "I'm quite all right."

Relief swamped her, and she threw her arms around his waist. "I'm so glad. I thought you were dead. I thought I'd never see you again." She felt his fingers stroke her hair.

Giorgi was helping Leahlabel to her feet, touching her face with a tenderness that Heloise had only seen among married people before. "Get off," the Sindi Mother said, "not the first knock on the head I've taken."

Giorgi frowned, glanced at Sigir. "I certainly hope you're well, villager. We lost good men here."

"Thank you," Sigir managed, still looking stricken.

"They didn't tie you," Giorgi said.

"They didn't need to," Sigir replied. "I'm one old man in the company of young, trained warriors. They wouldn't have had any trouble running me down."

"We should get back," Leahlabel said. "It won't take the Order long to start wondering why their scouts haven't returned. But first we should clean up this mess. Onas, go back to the camp and fetch more help. We must bring our own dead back to send them on up the wheel, and burn the enemy's. And the machine . . . is it broken?"

Heloise reluctantly let Sigir go and went to the machine. The metal around the engine canister was dented, but it seemed whole, and the seethestone bag was still drawn tightly shut. "It doesn't look broken . . ."

Onas began signaling to the other knife-dancers. "We'll help you stand it up."

"There's no need," Heloise said, climbing inside. "If it still works, it will move as I do. I can stand it up myself."

6

DELIBERATIONS

It was then that Shasta knew she would die, and it unbound her. She surrendered to the Great Wheel, knowing that it carried her where it would no matter what she did. Thus freed, she spent her last moment in what she loved most. While the enemy churned about her, she threw up her hands and danced. When, at last, she lowered them, she was not dead, and her foes were all around, laid open as if by the teeth of some beast.
—The First Knife-Dance, Kipti story

The sun was setting as they limped back into the camp, carrying their dead with them.

Samson sat on the steps to Leahlabel's wagon, head in his hands. He stood when he saw Heloise, but didn't go to her. "You're all right," he said.

Barnard stood beside him, arms folded. The color had returned to his face, "See, Samson?" he said. "I told you the Emperor would not let His own come to harm. I knew she would rescue Sigir."

The Maior still hadn't recovered from the shock of his rescue. He looked dazed, nodding distractedly as the villagers crowded around him, clapping him on the shoulder and shouting questions.

The Sindi had stoked the great fire in the center of the camp, taken down the hooks and pots, and laid blackened wooden wheels alongside. As Heloise watched, they tied each of the fallen knife-dancers to one. "From their families," Onas explained, "to send them up the wheel."

Other Sindi gathered around the machine, staring up at it in wonder. Many reached out to touch the metal, running their fingers along the straps and rods until Barnard cleared his throat and shooed them off.

"We lost four," Tillie said. "That was a steep price to pay."

"We got all of the Order's spies, Mother Tillie," Giorgi answered. "It will be a day at least, I would guess, before the Order realizes their people aren't coming back. We must be gone by then."

And suddenly, the villagers were underfoot. The Sindi busied themselves packing up the camp, stowing their chairs and dousing their cook fires. Women appeared with broad-shouldered cart horses and put them in their traces to pull the wagons. Heloise's people had only what they carried, and after the Sindi refused their attempts to help, they gave up, huddling miserably just outside the ring of activity as the sun sank farther and darkness enclosed them.

The Sindi shot glares over their shoulders at the villagers as they worked, but none said anything. By the central fire, the four slain knife-dancers lay strapped to their wheels like an accusation.

"What are they waiting for?" Samson asked.

Sigir shook his head. "I do not know, but they are moving on. We should speak with them. There isn't enough room in those wagons for all of us."

Heloise looked at the dead on their wheels, felt dread pricking at her stomach. "I don't know that they want us to go with them."

Sigir nodded. "I fear you are right."

"The Emperor will provide for us," Barnard said.

"We need to know." Heloise could hear her father struggling to keep panic out of his voice. "If they won't have us with them, then we need to be moving too, and now. And we need to see what supply they can spare."

The dread in Heloise's stomach rose into her throat. "Can we . . ." She turned to Sigir. "Can we outrun the Order, without horses?"

Sigir looked at his feet and said nothing.

Heloise looked across the camp. There were sixteen knife-dancers who had returned with her, and she counted at least another twenty. *You have seen the knife-dance now,* Leahlabel had said, *all Sindi boys are raised to it.*

She thought of the Black-and-Gray, his knife held to Sigir's neck. Tone, swinging his flail over Gunnar's hammer. Anger flared in her chest. "They shouldn't leave. They don't have to."

"What do you mean—" Sigir began.

"We can't just stand here, waiting," Heloise said. "If they're going to turn us out, we need to know. The Order is coming."

She strode to where the Mothers stood outside Leahlabel's wagon, talking in hushed tones with Giorgi and Onas. Sigir, Samson, and Barnard exchanged glances before hurrying behind her.

"You're all right, Heloise?" Onas looked up at her.

"Are you sure we can't help?" she asked, stalling for time, trying to suss out the kernel of an idea that was growing in her mind.

Onas looked uncomfortable. "The Mothers are . . . thinking about that just now. We will tell you when—"

"The knife-dance," Heloise cut in, desperate to keep the conversation going, to buy the time she needed to think. "Do girls do it?"

"Why would a girl want to?" Tillie asked slowly. "The knife-dance is a sop for boys. They cannot do important things like lead a band, or have children. This is their part in the Great Journey."

Onas smiled. "Nothing in the Great Journey says a girl can't do it, Mother Tillie. Shasta was a girl."

"You are no Shasta," Analetta said. "That is the difference between girls and women. We don't pine for such things."

"I am very glad I am not a woman, Mother Analetta," Onas said.

"And the wizardry?" Heloise asked Giorgi. "Can more of you work . . . fire?"

"Giorgi and I have the Talent," Leahlabel answered for him. "There are others among the Traveling People, but we leave it to each one to decide whether or not to reveal it. Some of us fear your Order more than others."

"It is not *our* Order," Barnard said. "We love the Emperor and His holy Writ, but we do not truck with the brigands in gray cloaks that claim to be his own. They serve only themselves."

"Brigands, maybe," Tillie said, "but strong brigands, and numerous, and with enough money to buy arms and good horses, and to supply themselves in the field for as long as they please."

"And they would kill you if they knew," Heloise finished for her.

"They would," Tillie said, "but since they do not, they merely rob us every chance they get, and call it a 'tariff' or a 'toll.' They take our goods, or our money, or our horses, when they can."

"When they can?" Samson asked.

"We were the Traveling People long before the Order was chartered." Leahlabel smiled. "Traveling gives certain advantages when one doesn't want to be found."

"Did you ever . . . fight them?" Heloise asked.

The Mothers were silent for a moment, exchanging glances. It was Leahlabel who finally answered. "We did. A long time ago."

"What happened?" Samson asked.

"We lost," Tillie said simply.

"And you just gave up?" Barnard asked.

"It is easier to travel carefully than to fight," Leahlabel said. "The Order can have the villages, and we can have the roads."

"Only when they're not on them," Heloise said.

"They are only on them," Tillie's voice was tight, "as long as it takes them to get to you. What are you driving at?"

"I just saw twenty knife-dancers beat a host of the Emperor's Eyes. There are at least another twenty here, and I am with you." She raised the machine's metal fist, banging it against the shield's edge. "Some of us are veterans of the Old War with Ludhuige the Red. We can fight."

"There's a *we*, now, is there?" Analetta's jowls shook. "Your people stumbled into our camp, tails between your legs. Now we are sending four of our own up the wheel, and you want us to commit more to the fire. You villagers are a plague. This is *your* fight, and we would be well advised to leave you to it."

"Mother . . ." Leahlabel began.

"No!" Analetta shouted over her. "It's good she started this talk. We must decide what to do with them and now is as good a time as any. You have been soft on these villagers from the moment they limped in here. I knew it would come to trouble, I *told* you that it would come to trouble, and now it *has* come to trouble. We should move this camp and leave them. It's *them* the Order wants, not us."

The camp began to pause in their preparations, gathering around to hear the conversation.

"We must make that decision together," said Leahlabel, but the angry murmurs of the Sindi made it plain to Heloise that the camp's heart was not with her.

"Giorgi says we slew all of the Order's spies," Analetta said to

Heloise, "so there are none left to know we helped you. If they catch us on the road alone, they might take some of our goods and let us go. If they find you in our train, they will leave none alive."

Analetta went on, but Heloise wasn't listening. She could already picture her people strung out on the road to one of the other villages—Frogfork or Mielce, begging help from terrified villagers who would surely turn them away. She could almost hear the hoofbeats of the vengeful Order behind them, catching them on the open road . . . Her people needed refuge, a place to lick their wounds and figure out what to do next. And if they couldn't take refuge with the Sindi, then there was no other place . . .

And then, suddenly, there it was. The kernel of a thought blossomed into an idea, a sudden mad plan. There was no time to think it through, but she had run on instinct since she'd first driven the war-machine out to face the devil. *All ways are equally fraught,* Sigir had said.

"You misunderstand." Heloise raised her voice. The buzzing of voices went silent. "It is not we who should come with you, but you who should come with us."

"What are you nattering on about?" Analetta asked. "Go with you where?"

"To Lyse," Heloise said.

"The Hapti band trades at Lyse," Tillie said, "and the great market isn't for another turning of the moon."

"We will not go to trade," Heloise said.

Leahlabel sounded puzzled. "Traveling People only go to towns to trade, Heloise."

"All my life the Traveling People have plied the roads," Heloise said, "coming to us only in the seasons when they could get through, even when we both needed the custom . . ."

"That is our *way,*" Analetta said, "we are the *Traveling* People."

Heloise's stomach turned over at the enormity of what she was asking. Sigir's words rang in her ears. *We have consorted with a wizard, touched the body of a devil, ambushed the Order and made war on them. You think they'll forgive that?*

"Are you traveling," Heloise asked, "or fleeing?"

"We don't have to explain anything to the Caged," Analetta practically spat. "We've taken you in and shown you every kindness. You'd be dead if it weren't—"

"We are moving," Leahlabel spoke over her. Her voice was calm, curious, "to evade the Order."

Tillie gave an exaggerated shrug. "We have always done that."

"Yes," Heloise said, "maybe it's time to do something else."

Analetta laughed. "You don't tell us . . ."

"Let her speak, Mother Analetta," Leahlabel said.

"You can't seriously be consider—"

"What do you offer, Heloise Factor?" Leahlabel asked.

"I know you would be free of the Order, given the chance. I would too. My people have beaten them once . . ."

"And been beaten by them after . . ." Tillie said.

". . . After we hurt them," Heloise shouted over her. "We have killed them, Mothers. That is more than any other villager has done, and now you have, too. Together, we can do more."

"And this is something to celebrate?" Leahlabel asked. "Men are killed easily enough."

"The Order is coming for us, and we will not be able to stop them in a forest or a village. We will not be able to outrun them without horses."

"But we will," Analetta said.

"Yes, and you will keep running," Heloise felt her chest swell as she spoke, as if some greater force were speaking through her, "as you have done for generations. You will practice your wizardry in secret. You will let the Order say when and where you come to market, and you will pay the Imperial Procurer his due before you can trade. Flight is not freedom. Running is not traveling. You are fugitives in your own valley and will forever be outside the Empire's grace until the day comes that you chock your wheels and sign the village rolls."

"We will never do that." Tillie's face was white with anger.

"If you help me, you will never have to."

"Help you how? What do you intend to do?" Leahlabel alone did not seem angry, the corner of her mouth lifting slightly with her question.

"We will take Lyse," Heloise said.

"We will what?" Sigir whirled on her. "Hel—your eminence. That isn't . . ."

Heloise raised the machine's giant empty hand and he went silent. "Help us take the town and the market is yours. You will pay no dues to the Procurer. You may say who comes to sell and who does not. Fair days when you like, come and go as you please. Sell what you like and only what you like. Put up your horses and lay down roots if you want. It will, for once, be your choice."

"And what do you want, Heloise Factor?" Leahlabel asked. "Or do you mean to march on an Imperial town simply to give us a market?"

"No. Lyse has walls, and walls stop armies. If we hold it, we can stand against the Order."

"Lyse's walls are not so thick. And as few as you are?" Analetta laughed. "Even if you can take the town, you can't garrison it."

"Maybe we can and maybe we can't." Heloise forced a smile. "But it will be easier with a band of Sindi knife-dancers at our backs."

7

TURNED OUT

*There is no place so safe as the road in company, and no
place so unforgiving, when it is taken alone.*
—**Kipti proverb**

The Mothers deliberated inside Leahlabel's wagon, sending the
villagers out of the camp to wait for their word. Heloise watched
in silence as the Sindi finished their preparations and climbed
into the drovers' chairs behind the teams of horses.

"We cannot take Lyse," Sigir said. "The Mothers are right
about that."

Barnard said nothing, but his eyes burned, and Heloise knew
he believed they could do anything, so long as she was with them.

"Then what do we do?" Heloise asked. "Do we run through
the woods until the Order finds us? Do we go to another village
and hope they take us in? Do we run all the way to the Gold
Coast and pray that Ludhuige the Red's old bannermen will protect us?"

Sigir looked stricken. "We pray to the Sacred Throne that the
Mothers do not turn us out. I wish you'd let the Order keep me."

Heloise sucked in her breath. "How can you say that?"

"It would have been bad for me, but maybe if the Kipti hadn't lost four of their own in the rescue, they'd let you stay. That would have been something."

"They didn't go out to rescue you," Samson said, "they went out to stop the Black-and-Grays from reporting back to the rest of the column."

Sigir said nothing, only stared at the rapidly dwindling traces of the Sindi camp, his face pale and drawn.

Onas finally appeared, coming so quietly it was as if he had emerged from thin air. Barnard jumped and Sigir choked on the heel of bread he was gnawing. Onas moved straight to the war-machine's empty metal fist, reaching inside the frame.

"What are you doing?" Barnard took a step toward him. "Get away from that."

Onas probed the controls where the strap connected, before standing back and nodding. "This will work." He looked up at Heloise.

Barnard drew up to his full height, towering over the boy. "You're not touching that . . ."

If Onas was cowed, he didn't show it. "It's not for the machine, it's for Heloise." He held up a small metal collar, with a broad blade emerging from the center, long enough to straddle the line between knife and sword.

"You brought me a knife?" she asked. "I can't hold it."

"You said you wanted to learn our dance," Onas said, "and you don't have to hold it. Your machine will do it for you. Let me see your hand."

The thought of letting a part of her peek outside the machine made her stomach twist, but the sight of the knife and Onas's easy smile comforted her, and she slowly loosed her hand from its grip on the control strap behind the shield.

"No," Onas said, "the wounded one."

Heloise's stomach clenched harder at that, and Barnard stiffened, only holding back at a sharp look from Heloise, but she eased her stump back and out through the metal frame. The light reflected off the shining, pink scars.

Onas slipped the metal collar over the stump, worrying at a pair of buckles until it cinched down tight.

"That won't hold no matter how tight you make it," Barnard snorted.

"The machine will hold it." Onas didn't look at Barnard, gesturing to Heloise instead. "Go on, try it."

Heloise's arm felt heavy with all that metal dangling off the end. It took some wriggling to get the long blade back inside the arm's frame, but once she did, the blade slid neatly through the fist's slot, protruding a slight distance beyond.

"There," Onas said. "Heloise, Knife-Handed."

"She can't use the strap that way," Barnard complained, but Heloise could see the curiosity in his eyes.

"She doesn't need to," Onas said. "The strap pulls the controls. She can push them with the blade now. She'll have to make the movements backward, but she can do it. And now she'll always have a weapon, in or out of the machine."

Heloise tried, pushing instead of pulling. The machine's metal fist rotated at her command, the shining metal blade refracting the light and sending rainbow patterns shimmering off the shield. "It works."

"Of course it does," Onas said. "Every 'Kipti' is at least half-tinker."

Barnard grunted, leaning in to inspect where the collar and blade slid into the fist. "This is . . . fine work, Master Kipti."

"Sindi." Onas's smile vanished. It was one thing when he said it, but another in the mouth of a villager.

"Forgive us," Heloise said. "It takes some getting used to."

Onas turned back to her. "Come on, then. Let's see you dance."

Heloise looked down at him, so tiny in the shadow of the towering machine. "I'll . . . I'll hurt you."

"You have to hit me to hurt me," Onas said, "and you can't hit me."

And in spite of everything, the mad dash through the woods, Sigir's capture and rescue, all the death and the terror, Heloise smiled. She made a half-hearted stab with the knife, and Onas sprang aside, rolling into a crouch and slashing out with one of his knives, drawing sparks from the machine's leg.

"Heloise!" Samson shouted. "Stop it!"

But Heloise ignored him, taking another swipe with the knife, forcing Onas to somersault backward, springing first onto his hands and then back onto his feet again. Samson was on his feet and shouting as Onas sprang off a rock, grasped the side of the shield, and swung his way up it, narrowly avoiding Barnard's grasping hand. He reached the reliquary box on the machine's shoulder and perched there, grinning down at the men who circled beneath him, red-faced and shouting.

Heloise laughed. "Your knife will be dull now."

"Haven't you heard?" Onas asked. "The Traveling People are a fair hand at sharpening knives."

"I do want to learn to knife-dance," she said.

"I want to teach you," Onas said.

But she looked up at him, and she knew why he had come. *It's a farewell gift.*

"Will the Mothers let us stay?"

"They will if they are wise," he answered. "I think you stumbled into our camp for a reason. I think the Great Wheel is turning, and the Sindi are on the rising spoke, the arc that will carry us to the top. It has spun you to us to lift us up."

The thought pricked at her, a strange sensation that she realized was hope.

"Will you speak for us?" she asked.

Onas shook his head. "You do not know Sindi Mothers. A young knife-dancer's word counts for about as much as a lame horse's, but what you said to the Mothers. About running. You spoke true. We . . . all the Traveling People, are tale-spinners, you know. Some of us make coin that way."

"I know." Heloise nodded. "I used to love it when you would come on market days. Though I never had the money to come into the story circle."

"We are good at telling stories. We are so good that sometimes we believe our own tales, and then it takes someone from outside the band to remind us that that is all they are."

Heloise felt her throat tighten. "I am just trying to make my people safe. We just . . . we won't last long on our own."

"I know," Onas said, "but that's the way of the Wheel, it turns whether you like it or not, and sometimes it takes you places you didn't intend to go."

"Even if . . . even if you join us, taking Lyse will be . . . it will be hard, Onas. People will die."

"Then why are you set on taking it?" Onas asked.

"Because," Sigir sighed, "she is right. Lyse has the only high walls in range of a foot march. And without walls, we are finished. There is no place in this valley or beyond where we can run from the Order, not forever. If we are to live, then we must stand."

Onas nodded to the Maior. "My people are travelers. I don't think we've ever known how to stand, but," he looked back to Heloise, "maybe it's time we learned." They were the words Heloise longed to hear, but a part of her knew they were a platitude. Onas knew what was coming.

Barnard leaned back from the arm, shaking his head and sighing. "I should have thought to do this. I was so focused on getting the tang to attach from the front."

He looked up at Onas. "Ah, the young. Your minds are so open. Age closes a man up."

Onas sketched a bow. "Does that mean I can come down now?"

"Age is coming for you too, young master," Samson said.

Onas laughed and inspected his knife's dulled edge before sheathing it. He was still smiling as he looked up.

Heloise followed his gaze to the approaching Mothers. Giorgi was behind Leahlabel, a string of Kipti men with him.

"Heloise Factor," Leahlabel said. "I see you have a weapon now."

"Onas made it for me," Heloise said, "and thanks to you too, to all of you, not just for the gift, but for having us with you. No matter what happens now my people will always be friends to the Sindi band."

Leahlabel's face twisted, and Heloise's stomach with it. "You are kind," Leahlabel said, "and my people will look forward to sharing your friendship when next we meet. But, for now, it is time to part ways, for the Sindi will move on, and where we go, your people cannot follow."

She'd known it was coming, but the words still hit Heloise hard. "Mothers . . ." the Maior began.

Leahlabel raised a hand. "Women are speaking."

"We will die out there." Sigir ignored her. "Make no mistake, you are sending us to our deaths."

"We will not leave you empty-handed." Leahlabel stepped aside, revealing two horses pulling a cart piled high with supplies, wrapped in two giant canvas tents. "There is enough food here to keep you for days, tools and clothing, too."

"At least we'll have full bellies when the Pilgrims cut them open!" Barnard snarled. "I shouldn't have expected heretics to—"

"Enough," Heloise spoke over him. She felt neither grief nor fear, just a tired numbness. "Thank you for your hospitality, and your gifts. We'll go."

"What?" Sigir spun on her. "At least—"

"They've made up their minds," Heloise said, ignoring her churning gut. "What do you want us to do? Fight them? We're lucky to have been given this much. What does the Writ say of those who grasp at joy?"

Barnard exhaled, some of the tension going out of him. "That it is as grasping the sea. Our joy is the Emperor and His will."

"And it is His will that we carry on alone," Heloise said. "He will not forsake us in it. Thank you, Mothers."

Leahlabel gave a short dip of her head. "You are wise beyond your years, Heloise Factor. With you at their head, your village can only survive and prosper."

"She isn't at our head!" Poch shouted. "We'll follow you! Those of us that want to live!"

"Villagers? On foot?" Analetta laughed. "Good luck to you. The Emperor's own Coursers on fast horses can't keep pace with Traveling People what don't want to be kept pace with."

Poch would have said more, but Barnard silenced him with a sharp cuff on his ear. "Get the Throne-damned cart," he swore, and Poch scurried to do his will. Sald joined him, grunting as they hauled it behind them, glaring up at Heloise with hate in their eyes.

"Onas, come along," Leahlabel said, gesturing to the Sindi boy, still perched on the machine's shoulder. Onas hesitated, looking down at Heloise, his mouth working silently.

"Go with your people, Onas," Heloise said, reaching up with the corner of her shield, giving him a step down toward the ground.

"This isn't right," Onas said, locking eyes with his mother.

"The Mothers are the judges of what is right," Leahlabel answered, "we who have borne children and lost them. You are just a boy, who has never known a hard day in his life. Listen to your friend. She has lost too. Come down."

Onas jumped down to the shield's edge and then down to the ground below. "I'm sorry," he said. "If I can find a way to . . ."

"I know," Heloise said, feeling more alone than she had since she had told Basina she loved her, and fled her home in disgrace. Onas returned to Leahlabel's side, paused long enough to look up at her, his eyes furious, before disappearing into the crowd of Sindi men.

"The road is—" Leahlabel began.

"We can find it well enough, thank you," Sigir cut her off with a wave, turned.

Heloise joined him, and the rest of the village came reluctantly, whispering. At last, even Poch and Sald followed, dragging the cart behind them.

They made their way through the woods in a daze, the silence broken only by Poch's and Sald's grunts as they helped the horses, muscling the cart over rocks and roots. Behind them, the sounds of the Sindi camp faded quickly, as if the forest had swallowed it.

Heloise knew she needed to plan, needed to figure out what to do next. She thought Sigir might speak, or stop. If not him, then her father, Barnard, someone. But they only kept walking, faces bleak. Samson stayed at her side, and she could feel his eyes on her, so intent it was as if he believed that if he just looked hard enough, he would see through to the girl she'd once been.

It was Poch who finally pierced the quiet, grunting his words as he wrestled the cart out of a divot. "Where to now, eh? We just going to wander the woods until we eat what's in here and starve?"

"At least this damned cart will be lighter, then," Sald added.

Poch let go of the cart edge and wiped his forehead. "We should head back to the village. It's our home, and maybe the Order won't think we'll go back."

"You're as thick as that cart," Barnard snarled. "That's the first place they'll think to look for us. We can't go back."

"Never?" Sald asked. "Then what are we to do? Ply the road forever? We're not Kipti."

"Neither are they," Heloise said. "They call themselves Sindi, or the Traveling People."

"We could try for the Gold Coast." Sald rolled his eyes, ignoring her. "Old Ludhuige's men still fly the red banners. They're no friends of the Emperor."

"Aye," Barnard said, "and we *are*, no matter what we may think of the Order. We'll not truck with the likes of them."

"It's too far," Sigir said, "we'd be caught long before we reached the border. Which leaves us with Lyse. Else, we'll have to find another village to take us in, one far enough away to give some hope that the Order will not find us there."

"What village will take us in?" Poch rolled his eyes. "We've just as much chance going home as we do—"

"No," Heloise cut him off. "We can't. We can't go to anyone."

"And why not, your *eminence?*" Heloise was almost grateful for the contempt in the drover's voice. It was better than the reverence with which Barnard spoke to her. "You said it yourself. There's no blight. We can't infect anyone else."

"No," she agreed, "we can't. But Sigir is right that the Order will chase us wherever we go. They will show us no mercy, and even less to those who shelter us. I can choose death for myself, but I will not choose it for anyone else."

"Won't you?" asked Poch. "Aren't you already choosing it for all of us? Like you did when you trucked with that wizard? Like you did when you led us out to ambush the Order?"

"That's enough!" Barnard shouted, but this time many of the

villagers shouted back, and many of them stood with Poch and Sald. Ingomer, who had bowed and tugged his forelock when Heloise had awakened after fighting the demon, stood in silence, speaking neither for nor against her.

"Why are we following her?" Danad added his voice to the chorus. "She's brought nothing but trouble, even if she did kill a devil."

"Blasphemy!" Barnard shouted, grabbing Danad and shaking him like a child's toy.

Poch grabbed his arm, trying to wrench it free, but he might as well have grabbed an iron bar. Barnard lifted his arm, and both Poch and Danad dangled in the air, kicking feebly. "Put 'em down!" Sald said, kicking Barnard in the shin. The huge tinker didn't notice, and Poch began pounding on his shoulder.

Heloise leaned the machine in, pressing the shield's corner against Barnard's forearm. The tinker's arms were nearly as big around as her father's thighs, but even he was not equal to the machine's relentless strength. He grunted as his arm was pushed down, until finally Danad's feet were on the ground and Barnard shoved him away, before spinning on Heloise. "Why do you let them . . ."

"Because they are not fools, Barnard. And because, while I love you like my own family, you are not one either. I killed a devil, yes. I want to keep us safe, yes. But I have never claimed to be a Palantine. There is no blasphemy here, only men who want to speak their piece and have it heard, and I have heard them."

Danad pulled on his shirt, smoothing the wrinkles out and nodding. Poch and Sald smiled at Heloise's words, crossing their arms.

"But," Heloise turned to them, "they will follow me anyway, and together we will take Lyse."

Poch snorted. "You're mad. It is a town, walled and garrisoned. Even if the Kipti had agreed to help us, we would still be too few to take it. Why would we follow you to certain death?"

Heloise grinned at him, feeling the scarred flesh of her cheek and eye socket stretch. It must have looked horrible, judging by the reaction on Poch's face. "Because Lyse is our only hope to survive a fortnight," Heloise said. "Because difficult is not impossible, and most of all, because I have a plan."

"Like your plan to ambush the Order? I suppose this one will work about as well as that one did."

"Poch," Leuba said.

"No." Poch had the bit in his teeth now. "I have had enough. If you are all mad enough to follow a little girl and lay siege to a town, then I will go my own way, and those of us in our right minds will come with me, I know it, and we will—"

"Poch!" Leuba's voice rang out like a peal of thunder. The drover fell silent, staring at her. All eyes snapped to Heloise's mother, and she looked suddenly shy. She glanced at her feet and swallowed hard before looking up, her eyes flashing. "Those Kipti are always going on about loss. Like hurting makes a woman a lord somehow. Well, if that's the case, then we're all of us princes here. We've lost our home and our way of life. We've lost our place in the Emperor's bosom . . . No, Barnard, let me talk. Nobody ever listens to me. You and Chunsia've lost two children now, and half the village is gone. And now you, Poch Drover, want us to lose what little we have left."

"Leuba." Poch reached for her and she pulled away to Samson's side.

"No!" she shouted. "I've known you since you were a boy, Poch Drover, and I will not sit here and let you treat me like I'm stupid." Her eyes swept the crowd. "You people are all I've ever known. You're my home, all of you. You dyed my dresses, Danad, and Barnard, you've mended every pot and sharpened every knife I've ever held. Sald, your Marta has seen me through winters where I'd have had to go hungry to feed my daughter. And now

Gunnar and Basina and Myron and all the folk we knew in Hammersdown are in the dirt. And you want to run off with half of who's left? And for what? What do you plan to do that's so much smarter than what Heloise wants? Even if you don't hold to her being a Palantine? What plan do you have?"

Poch looked at his feet, stammered.

"What plan?" Leuba asked again. "Heloise wants us safe behind walls. She's sayin' we're not fast enough to outrun Pilgrims with horses, and that makes sense to me. What do you say to that? Well?"

"Leuba, please," Poch said.

"Please, what? Sald? What's your great plan to keep us safe if what my daughter has to say is so foolish? Seems to me she's the only one talking sense here of late."

The grower joined Poch in contemplating his feet.

"You're dear to me," Leuba said, "all of you. You're dear to me, and I don't want to lose anyone else. Not to the Order, not to the road, and not because you stand on pride because it's not a man grown leading the way for once. The Kipti"—she caught Heloise's eye and corrected herself—"the *Sindi* may love loss, but I don't. I've had enough of it to last a lifetime."

The silence stretched as Poch and Sald stood shamefaced, mouths working, unable to meet Leuba's eyes. Heloise's mother's thick cheeks were flushed, her eyes glittering, and Heloise thought for a moment that, machine or no machine, she looked more the Palantine than anyone.

"Well, Poch Drover," Heloise spoke into the silence, "since you have no plan of your own, will you at least hear mine?"

·   ·   ·

But after she'd said her piece, and the village had started off, Sald Grower refused to move.

"Sald," Barnard began.

The old grower held up a hand. "We've come far enough," he said. "I'll take my chances with the Red Lords. Might be they'll turn me away . . ."

"Might be they'll string you up," Sigir said. "Don't be a damned fool."

"Who's a fool?" Sald shook an angry finger at Sigir. "Me making for the border? Or you trying to take a garrisoned town?"

"You'll never make it," Sigir said, "they'll catch you out on the road!"

"Aye," Sald said, pointing in the direction of Lyse, "much wiser to race right into their arms. They'll never catch us then. I don't care what Leuba says, or you, Barnard. I'm not going no farther, and I'll take my chances, and you shouldn't try to stop me."

"Sald, you can't—" Sigir said.

"No," Heloise cut him off. "He can do as he likes. And so can you, Poch." She turned, facing the village. "So can any of you. When we move on Lyse, there will be no more time for doubts. If any of you do not have the heart for this, you have my leave to go."

"We don't need your leave," Poch said.

"Then go," Helosie said to him. "You have heard my plan. If you feel you will be safer on the road, on your own, if you feel you can outrun the Order's outriders, or any brigands you may meet, then go on your way. I am going on to Lyse, and I am going if I have to do it myself."

"Will no one else come with me?" Sald asked the village. "Will you make me try my chances on the road alone?" None answered, but neither would they meet his eyes. The villagers looked at their feet, up into the trees, out to the horizon.

"Come on, Poch." Sald's eyes were pleading. "I don't care what Leuba said, this is madness."

Leuba only looked at her feet, and Heloise watched Poch's eyes flick to her mother, then to the Maior and back to her again.

But the old drover did not move. "If no one else is going . . ." Poch said, so low that Heloise had to strain to hear him, ". . . it's safer to stick together."

Sald muttered something under his breath and rummaged in the cart, helping himself to a small sack of bread and a waterskin. Sigir moved to stop him, but held back at a gesture from Heloise. "You're all mad," Sald said, started on his way, then turned back to the villagers.

"You're all mad! If any of you live through this . . . well, I suppose I'll be seeing you. But more likely we won't meet again until we're in the shadow of the Throne. The Emperor be with you all."

And with that, he turned on his heel, and set off into the woods.

The villagers stood in silence, watching his back until it disappeared.

There was a hollow space in Heloise's stomach, growing into an ache. "Well?" she asked the rest of them. "Are we a village or aren't we?"

None spoke, and none moved, and at last Heloise turned and walked on. The village followed, but she could feel their eyes on her back the rest of the way.

Lyse stood on the edge of a river, sprawling on a flat patch of ground cleared of trees. Samson said it had only had a palisade when he was a boy, but by the time he first took Heloise there for the fair, the stone walls were in place. They had seemed towering, impossibly thick. She couldn't imagine how many men had labored to build them, how long they had to work.

But as she looked at them through the wood's edge, she was amazed to see what a difference a few years had made. The gray walls seemed childish now, little more than oversized heaps of poorly mortared stone. The gates were close-set planks banded with iron, standing closed against the empty dirt track that wound its way along the riverbank.

Samson looked up at her. "Do you remember when we were here last?"

She nodded. "Yes . . . it looks . . . different."

Her father cocked an eyebrow. "Different, how?"

"The walls, the road. It's all . . . less . . . somehow."

"It's no less, no more than it was before." Her father sounded sad.

Heloise stared in silence for another moment before Leuba rapped her knuckles on the machine's metal thigh. "Well, I made a damn fool of myself yelling praise for your plan before, dove. Suppose I can't well talk you off it now." Sald's departure had made them all sober, but Leuba's tone was as airy as if they were just out for a summer outing.

Heloise smiled at her mother. Just a few days ago, Heloise had seen her over a bubbling pot in their hearth, stripping a chicken carcass. There had been no devil then, and the Order was nothing more than a chance and unsavory encounter on the road. "I suppose not."

"Just tell me it'll be all right, dove. Tell me you're a Palantine and that the Emperor whispers in your ear. Tell me that He says He will tear these walls down Himself if that's what it takes to keep you safe."

"Come now, dear." Samson put his arm around his wife.

Leuba leaned into her husband, but she repeated her request, her eyes earnest. "Tell me."

"I love you, Mother. You know that, don't you?"

"Aye, dove. I do."

Sigir and Barnard approached, the cart trundling along behind them. "Heloise," the huge tinker said, "the light won't hold forever. It's time."

For the second time, Heloise hunched the machine over so tightly the metal knees pressed against the breastplate. It took some work to wriggle the machine onto its side in the cart, but she managed it. They draped one of the huge canvas tents over her, lighter and less oppressive than the woven branches piled with earth had been. It was still dark beneath, but Heloise could breathe the sweet air where it wafted up through the gaps between the wooden boards of the cart's bottom. The engine's smoke puffed out through a gap between the canvas cover and the wagon's sides, a slim tendril that Lyse's sentries might notice, but she had worked out the story with Barnard if it came to that.

The cart bumped along, yoked to a single horse. Barnard rode the other, his huge body filling out the Pilgrim's gray cloak, head shadowed by the hood. Barnard was big enough that a casual look would take him for armored. Heloise prayed it would be enough.

The single horse strained with the weight of the cart, but no Pilgrim would ever be seen in a drover's chair. Sigir sat there now, handling the reins as skillfully as Poch ever could. The drover might have been more convincing, but Leuba's upbraiding and Sald's departure had left him sullen, and Sigir didn't trust him with anything so delicate. Samson had Poch and Danad both under close watch among the trees, cleared back from the walls as much as the townsfolk of Lyse could manage, but still far too close.

Heloise could feel the cart's axles strain under the machine's weight as the Lyse tipstaffs waved Barnard to a stop just beyond the treeline. "Begging the Holy Brother's pardon," Heloise heard one ask tentatively. His eyes would be downcast, keeping him from getting a good look beneath the tinker's hood. "We'd had no word that . . ."

"Nor would you." Barnard made his voice hard, but Heloise could hear the villager's lilt in his speech, the hint of the low-talk disdained by real Pilgrims. "I am on the Procurer's business, and did not think it wise to announce it and my cargo to every bandit in the valley."

If the tipstaff noticed Barnard's accent, he gave no sign. "Apologies, Holy Brother, we've never had the Order come through unannounced . . ."

"Do I look like the whole Order, you simpleton?" Barnard sneered. "There is only me. Quieter that way."

"Yes, Holy Brother. But we still must see what's in the cart. Everything through the gate is inspected, no exceptions."

"This," Barnard rapped the machine's leg through the canvas, pausing to let the dull ringing echo, "is an *Imperial* commission. Do you know the law?"

"Aye," said the tipstaff, some of the courage returning to his voice now that he was dealing with something familiar, "but there's no vault here."

"Vault or no, if you gaze on the Imperial will, which is reserved for His eyes alone, you will incur the wrath of the Order."

"Maybe," the tipstaff said, his voice frightened, but determined, "but I'll incur the wrath of the watch captain if I don't have a look. Just a quick peek. I won't tell anybody."

"It is a tinker-engine," Barnard said, gesturing to the plume of seethestone smoke wafting up from under the canvas, "as you can see. You are a tinker?"

"No, my lord," the tipstaff said.

"Then it will just look like a pile of metal to you."

"Then show me a pile of metal," the tipstaff said, "and I'll trouble you no more."

"Very well," Barnard said, "it's your own soul to damn."

She gritted her teeth, swallowing the terror as Barnard peeled back the canvas to expose the machine's bent metal leg, a handspan below Heloise's flesh one. "What's that look like to you?"

"A . . . pile of metal," the tipstaff admitted. "All right, Holy Brother. Thank you for indulging me."

"The chapter house will hear of this," Barnard said, and clucked his horse into a trot, flipping the canvas back over Heloise and motioning to Sigir, who flicked the reins of the cart horse. Heloise felt the wooden wheels bounce on the rutted track. She didn't realize she had been holding her breath until she finally exhaled.

Sigir heard the sigh and grunted. "Take another breath now, your eminence. The real test is upon us."

"He's good," the tipstaff was calling, and Heloise heard the gate guards answer, the groan of iron hinges, wood creaking as the portal bent slowly inward to admit them.

"Holy Brother," two voices said softly. Guards, bowing to Barnard's cloaked form, ushering him in.

"What in the shadow of the Throne is this?" This voice rang out clearly over the others. It was haughty, with the smooth tone Heloise had come to associate with the high-born. "Who are you? What are you doing here? From what chapter do you hail?"

Barnard's horse reared slightly, stamping its hooves as it came down. The cart jerked and halted, a corner of the canvas flap lifting on the sudden rush of air to give Heloise a glimpse of scarlet.

"My apologies, Holy Father," Barnard grunted, trying to control his horse.

Heloise could hear the jingling of a chain. "I asked you a question, Brother. Who are you? Let me see your seal."

More high-born voices, chains jingling, boots tramping in the mud.

"I am sorry I could not give you more time, your eminence," Barnard said.

"What in the shadow of the Throne do you mean?" the high-born voice demanded.

But Heloise knew that Barnard wasn't speaking to him.

She rolled onto her knees, the machine lurching to match the motion of her body, putting all of its weight on the cart's edge and tipping it over. She spilled out onto the ground, tangled in the canvas, the machine's metal knees digging furrows in the ground. She heard shouts, the pounding of boots on earth.

She stood, the engine's strength easily tossing the wooden cart aside, shredding the canvas where it tangled around the machine's legs.

Heloise blinked at the sudden light, eyes assaulted by a rush of motion.

One of the gate guards had already dropped his spear and fled, running away from the town, toward the tipstaffs farther down the track, who stood gaping at her. Barnard was struggling to control his panicking horse. The cart horse, broken free from its yoke, was a galloping dot in the corner of her eye, shrinking with each passing moment. Sigir lay on his back a few paces distant, groaning. She whirled around.

A Sojourner, flanked by two of his Pilgrims, was stumbling back from her. His face was even more pinched than that of the Sojourner Clodio had killed, pointed nose and thin lips practically converging. His squinting eyes finished the look, more hungry rat than man. He held a long staff instead of a flail, topped with the golden figure of a Palantine, wings spread, palm outward to ward off the enemy. The other two Pilgrims were spinning their flail heads, but with little confidence.

"Come on!" Barnard was shouting now, reining his horse around. He cupped his hand over his mouth and called again toward the treeline. "Come on! The Throne-cursed gate is open!"

The rat-faced Sojourner's eyes widened comically. "Close the gate!" he squeaked. "Close the gate now!"

The Pilgrims raced to the heavy wooden doors, began shoving them closed. The remaining gate guard thrust his spear at Heloise, but she parried it easily, then swept down with the shield. The guard cried out in pain, dropping the weapon and cradling his arm.

He bent to retrieve his spear, but stopped at a word from the Sojourner. "Forget it! Close the gate! Close the gate!"

Heloise risked a glance behind her and saw why.

The villagers had burst from the tree cover and were running toward the open gate, waving their weapons over their heads. A few had traded for Sindi knives, others scraps of armor. They were a ragged bunch, but they were more than the town had expected, especially with a tinker-made war-machine at their head.

The Pilgrims finally got the weight of the doors working for them, and they swung easily inward, until Heloise stretched out the machine's arms, stopping them with a bang.

The Pilgrims pushed, grunting, but Heloise scarcely felt it inside the machine's frame. Rat-face squeaked again and thrust his staff at her, succeeding only in breaking off the gold finial and sending it tumbling to the ground. "Go!" he shouted. "Sound the alarm! Bring the brothers!"

The Pilgrims seemed all too glad to get away from the towering machine, and released the doors, running deeper into the town, not even bothering to retrieve their flails.

The Sojourner tried another thrust, but Barnard swept it aside with his flail, then spurred the horse forward. The animal's broad breast knocked the Sojourner onto his back. Barnard raised the flail, but Heloise stopped him with a shout. "Leave him! Get the Pilgrims! They're raising the alarm!"

Barnard nodded and began to ride off, but the horse only took three steps before he reined back sharply. "The alarm is already raised."

Over Barnard's shoulder, Heloise could see five more Pilgrims coming at a dead run, flail heads bouncing.

She checked to ensure that the machine's arms were fully extended, bracing the gates open, and glanced back toward the treeline. The villagers were nearly to her now, the guard and tipstaffs running before them, hopelessly outnumbered and more willing to try their luck getting past the war-machine than against the shouting mob behind them.

Heloise let them through. Lyse might be a town, but what was a town but a big village? Lutet had its own tipstaffs and sentries, and they were good men all. These men scurrying past the machine's legs had never troubled her. Her business was with the Order.

But it was the sentries that charged her now, leaping down from the parapet and throwing their shoulders into the doors, heaving them back closed. She stretched the machine's arms wide. The doors shuddered against her metal fists. With so many men pushing on them, she should feel the strain now, but the machine held on, the engine bellowing, metal joints groaning.

But holding the doors open meant that she couldn't use her arms, and a few of the guards came forward, finding their courage now that the machine was pinned. The Pilgrims slowed to a jog as they saw the guards engaged. The Sojourner scrambled to his feet.

One of the sentries aimed a spear thrust at Heloise's face. She leaned out of the way, almost losing hold of one of the gate doors, which shook as the guards redoubled their efforts to push it closed. The guard grinned, and drew back for another thrust, lining his spear point up with the machine's eye slits, and then he was bowled head over heels as Barnard nearly rode him down, sweeping his flail in great arcs, driving the spearmen back. The Sojourner stumbled away, waved his Pilgrims on.

As Barnard swept past and reined around, the guards closed back in, aiming another spear thrust at Heloise, another, then another. Heloise jerked back and forth, releasing the door long enough to knock a spearhead aside, then frantically reaching out to stop the door again before the guards could slam it shut.

"Hold her!" the Sojourner shouted, no longer squeaking. "Keep her there!"

The guards reached out more slowly now, driving their spears into the machine's metal arms, pushing hard on the wooden shafts to pin them against the doors. Behind them, the Pilgrims came up, swinging their flail heads into a blur.

Heloise jerked the machine's arms free of the spearheads, knocked the shafts down, but the guards behind the doors gave a great shout and swung them closed, so that she had to reach back out to hold them open once again. The guards stepped forward, pinning her arms once more, and the Pilgrims advanced. *I can hold open the gates, or I can fight off the spearmen, or I can defend against the Pilgrims, but I cannot do all three at once.*

She kicked, driving the Pilgrims back, and the machine stumbled, the arms nearly losing contact with the doors. The Pilgrims leapt forward just as she found her feet, raising their flails to flick the heads inside the cage.

Her father exploded past her. Samson held a rock in both hands, bigger than his head. He brought it down hard on one Pilgrim, sending him stumbling back into his fellows, the flail flying from his hands. Gunnar came behind him, striking the spear from a guard's hands with his forge hammer. The villagers streamed past Heloise, and the guards gave ground, a few dropping their spears and bolting for the town's interior. The Sojourner shouted, trying to herd them back, but they brushed past him, fleeing from Danad and Chunsia, both of them red-faced and screaming, and wielding Sindi hooked knives. Leuba came with them, and Heloise blinked at the sight of her mother, her quiet, peaceful mother, laying about her with a fragment of the cart's broken rail.

Heloise watched them, all the fear and desperation of the last few days boiling up in this moment, poured out against the town's defenders. *They know these walls are our only chance*, she thought. *They know what it means if we lose.*

The Sojourner succeeded in turning the Pilgrims, who hefted their flails and shouted a war cry, advancing to meet the villagers. Harald Brewer was felled nearly as quickly as he appeared, skidding to his knees, curled up around a flail haft. Sigir leapt over him, kicking the Pilgrim square in the chest. Poch darted forward and snatched up one of the fallen flails, dragging it back behind Heloise.

Over the Pilgrim's shoulders, Heloise could see the citizens of Lyse, just like the villagers of Lutet, bakers and butchers and fencemenders. A few wore silks, and some gold, but most looked little different from the people she had grown up with, now fighting like devils around the metal legs of her machine. The Lyse townsfolk stared open-mouthed, parting here and there to admit the fleeing sentries. None moved to help the Order. None stopped the fleeing guards or called on them to get back in the fight.

The Sojourner was shouting, waving his long staff from behind his brothers, making no move to engage the swelling body of villagers inside his gates. It was just like the last man in a fancy red cloak. She'd hit him in the head with a rock. He had looked first to his men to avenge him, and only dealt with Heloise himself when they refused. *Why do people follow such cowards?*

She released the gate. The guards had fled from behind them, and the villagers were inside anyway. Closing them now would do no good.

A Pilgrim swung his flail at her, trying to do as Tone had done, catching the chain on the edge of the frame to send the spiked head inside. Heloise leaned into the blow, catching the head full on the machine's chest, the iron spikes screeching off the painted sigil. She let the momentum carry her, and the machine took a long stride into the midst of the Pilgrims, scattering them. The man who had struck her tried to leap aside, and succeeded in throwing himself sideways under the machine's metal foot, which came down with a sickening crunch. Heloise ignored the soft resistance of his body as she stepped off, reaching the Sojourner, punching down with the knife Onas had made.

The rat-faced man managed to parry the blow with his staff, turning his body away from the point, but he was powerless against the seethestone-powered strength that drove it. Heloise knocked him flat on his back, the blade sinking into the earth over his shoulder, his staff pressed against his chest. Heloise pushed, gently. The bulk of the metal fist put pressure on the staff. The Sojourner screamed, then wheezed, then struggled for breath.

"Drop your weapons!" she shouted. "Drop them and I give you back your Holy Father, and all of you can walk out of here with your skins still on."

She eased the pressure off the Sojourner's chest, letting him draw breath enough to speak, to beg for his life, to order his men to save him. Instead, he coughed out a laugh. "Do you think we who live in the Emperor's shadow hold our lives so precious? I am proud to die for Him. Holy Brothers! Kill every one of these heretics! Sell your lives dearly! Do not let . . ."

The Pilgrims were already racing to their master's defense, and Heloise pushed off with her fist, feeling the Sojourner's chest collapse beneath the pressure as she pushed the machine back to standing.

The first Pilgrim reached her, his flail tangling around her knife point even as she drove it into his head, spiking him straight down, like an apple on a stick, then flinging his limp body away with a flick of the machine's metal arm.

Another Pilgrim took advantage of the opening, driving hard for her, then suddenly crumpling as Barnard trotted past, dealing him a blow with his stolen flail that struck the Pilgrim's back hard enough to make him dance before he dropped.

The remaining Pilgrims hesitated, and the villagers washed over them. Gunnar and Chunsia and Ingomer and Sigir and her parents, blades and hammers and sticks rising and falling, rising and falling, until Heloise could no longer tell the red from the gray.

And then, it was quiet.

The townsfolk stared, the remaining sentries leaning on their spears, eyes wary, unsure if they should press the fight now that the Pilgrims were finished.

Barnard reined his horse around again and shook his bloody flail at the townsfolk. "Is that all of them?"

Silence.

"Damn you, is that all!?" Barnard asked again. "Is that all the Order has in Lyse?"

The silence stretched another moment before a woman broke it. She was well fed and wore a thick woolen shift with a gold chain around her waist. "Yes . . . that is all. The rest are but warriors."

"There's a difference?" Poch panted.

"The Order," Samson said, "gives a speech before they try to kill you."

Heloise took a step toward the remaining sentries, the blood pattering from her knife blade and down the machine's metal leg. "Do you give in?" she asked. "Must we finish this?"

The sentries said nothing, but neither did they drop their spears.

Heloise took another step, raising the machine's metal arms. "Lyse is taken! Will any of you negotiate with me?"

One of the sentries stood forward. He looked no different from the others, perhaps a bit older, gray hair straggling from beneath his helmet. "I am Wolfun. I am the Wall of Lyse."

"Not anymore," Heloise answered him, surprised at the sound of her own voice, deep and strong. "They are my walls now. They belong to my village."

"What do you want?" the woman with the gold chain asked. "What will you do?"

Barnard looked as if he might speak, so Heloise spoke first, shaking her knife in the air. "We have no quarrel with this town. Our fight is with the Order. We have taken the walls and we'll hold them, but we won't hurt you, and we won't rob you."

"What, then?" Wolfun said. "Shall we just live with you while you bar the gates and hold the town?"

"If you like," Heloise said. "We are good people. We hold to the Emperor's Writ."

"How can you say you hold to the Writ?" Wolfun gestured at the Sojourner's corpse, the crushed indentation of his chest.

"The Order are brigands," Barnard said. "We are free of them, and now we have freed you of them. It is not holy to grovel beneath their boots."

"If you would rather hold to men who quote the Writ while they spit on you"—Heloise gestured to the gate—"we will not stop you. But, if you would rather hold to the Writ itself, consider staying with us."

"You're the brigands!" someone in the crowd shouted. "How can you say you serve the Emperor if you—"

"Because she is a Palatine!" Barnard shouted. "She killed a devil, and every one of us saw her do it. She is more pleasing to the Emperor than a thousand of these cloaked bastards . . ."

"Lies!" another man shouted. "No one has ever killed a—"

But Barnard was already wheeling his horse around to the

machine's side, and Heloise was already kneeling down to offer him easier reach to the reliquary on her shoulder. "I do not know that I am a Palantine, but it is true I killed a devil, and if that will make you believe that I serve the Emperor, then you may call me whatever you wish."

8

THE WALLS

They say the Gold Coast's the richest pickings in the Empire. Ain't gold, though, Captain-General says. Sandy shore's no good for mines, it's named for how all that sand glitters in the sun. The money's in fish, he says, and in the red rocks that make the cliffs farther inland. The so-called free peoples grind these up to make a fine red dye, and they color every scrap of cloth they wear with it. "Bloody-handed, bloody-clothed," the Captain-General calls them. Hard to argue.

—From the journal of Samson Factor

Lyse was easily four times the size of Lutet, the houses tall and narrow. The roofs were slate instead of thatch, the walls built of timber and plaster instead of wattle and daub. The streets were strewn with crushed stone clearly swept clean. But it still reminded Heloise of Lutet, and the simple sight of smoke puffing from chimneys, or lanterns hung by transoms, made her heart swell. Lyse might be a town, with a market and a chapter house, but it was still an Imperial settlement, and that gave it a touch of home.

"This is foolish, your eminence," Sigir said, watching the townsfolk assemble their goods. A few had carts, or laden horses, but most simply took what they could carry on their backs. They looked frightened, but clean and healthy. Heloise surveyed the ragged ranks of her own people and knew that, on the road, cleanliness and health didn't last long.

Wolfun stood with a small knot of the townsfolk around a pile of weapons. It was the one thing Heloise had insisted the townsfolk leave behind, and the one thing she gave her own people leave to plunder. They would have need of it before long.

"If we are to hold these walls, it may be a long siege," Sigir went on, "we should make them leave their food and warm clothing behind. Gold, too, if we're to have the means to hire free-lances, or to purchase what we need, or even to bribe—"

"No," Heloise cut him off. "I gave my word. Save the weapons, we won't take anything else."

"We will regret this." Sigir shook his head.

"I know," she said, "but we have to . . . we have to be good. We can't curse the Order as plunderers and then plunder."

"Your eminence, I have been a soldier. Your father too. Sometimes . . . sometimes you must do things you don't want to do in order to win. It doesn't change who you are."

"Doesn't it?" Heloise asked. "If we're not fighting to be better than the Order, then why are we fighting at all?"

"To live," Poch grumbled, looking at his feet.

"You're alive, ain't you, Poch Drover?" Leuba asked. "You all thought that taking the walls would be impossible, and here we are holding them. All because we listened to her. If my daughter says that not acting like thieves is the best way to keep us all alive, then it's the best way. She's earned that much from you."

Poch nodded to her and stalked off, Danad at his side.

The sight of the devil's severed head had been enough for most of the townsfolk. Those standing around the weapons kept glancing up at her, and Heloise could see awe on their faces, the same fear and adoration she saw on many of the faces of her own people.

As soon as they saw her looking at them, several of them dipped their heads, tugged their forelocks. A few took a knee. "Palantine," they muttered, "savior."

My name is Heloise, she wanted to yell at them, but she held her tongue. So long as they worshipped her, they would take up arms and stand the walls when the Order came. She couldn't afford to compromise that.

But not all of the townsfolk were so awed.

"Tasha," Wolfun called to the woman with the gold chain, sitting in the drover's chair of a small cart hitched to a couple of mules. An older man, probably her husband, was loading an iron-bound chest into the back. "Don't be foolish. Where will you go?"

"To Mielce," Tasha said, "the Burgher there is a cousin."

"Don't be ridiculous, there's no place for you outside the valley."

"That's enough from you," Tasha's husband said, settling the chest into the cart and coming around to take the reins.

"Surely you can talk some sense into her, Karl," Wolfun said. "You saw the devil's head yourself. You saw her kill the Pilgrims. She is surely touched by the Sacred Throne."

"Saw the same things you did," Karl answered, "and she's surely touched by something, which is why we're going."

"You fared well against a chapter house," Tasha added, "but you will have a rougher time of it against the Pentarchy. They'll come at the head of an army once word reaches them. They won't leave any of you alive."

"And what will they do to you?" Wolfun answered. "You who let your town be taken? You who looked on the face of a devil? You who were close enough to catch the blight? They'll kill you no matter how you protest your loyalty. They'll Knit any town you rest at. You condemn every other person you meet."

"So what are we to do?" Tasha asked. "Stay here and die with you?"

"If you are to die," Heloise said, "you may as well do it on your feet with a weapon in your hand."

"Dying is dying," Tasha said. "We'll put it off as long as possible, thank you." She flicked the reins and the cart rolled off.

A group of Traveling People made their way across the town common, led by an ancient woman in a scarlet cloak. Where the Sindi Mothers clasped theirs with the trefoil symbol of their band, this woman's brooch was shaped like a cooking pot over a blazing campfire. Heloise turned to her and forced the machine into an awkward bow. "You would be a Mother of the Hapti band."

The Traveling People all froze, eyes collectively widening. The old woman's voice was dry and so soft that Heloise had to strain to hear it over the din of the townsfolk packing to leave. "I am Mother Florea of the Hapti, yes. I have never heard a villager call us by our proper name."

"The Sindi band saved us from the Order."

"From what I have seen, you do not need saving."

"Everyone needs saving, Mother Florea," Samson said. "The weak appeal to the strong, the strong to the mighty, and the mighty to the Sacred Throne."

"We appeal to our feet, and our wheels, and the road. They have not failed us for as long as I can remember."

"That does not mean they will not fail you now, Mother," Heloise said. "Will you stay with us? Help us hold the walls against the Order."

"The Traveling People are not fighters, young lady."

Heloise smiled. "I have seen the knife-dance. I know what your people can do."

"You have seen what the Sindi can do. My people care only for trade."

Heloise nodded at the gray knives belted around the Hapti men's waists. These had straight, flat blades, but looked every bit as deadly as the Sindi weapons. "Perhaps your women, yes. But your men go armed, as I can plainly see."

Florea smiled, her face sinking into a pool of wrinkles. "You know our ways very well, I see, and I like you, but my people cannot remain. The Order is no friend to Traveling People. I am afraid that . . . when they retake this town, it will go badly for us."

"It will go badly for you if you are caught outside the walls, too."

"We will not be caught."

"That is what the Sindi said. I am not so sure."

"All the same, we would go, if you will permit it."

"I am not the Order," Heloise said. "You may come and go as you please."

"That is not what your soldiers say." Florea looked at her hands.

"What are you talking about? We are villagers driven from our homes. I have no soldiers."

"When armed men accost Traveling People, they are always one of two things. With cloaks, they are Pilgrims. Without them, they are soldiers."

"What is . . ." Sigir began.

One of the Hapti men spoke up from behind Mother Florea. "Your men have stopped our wagons at the postern gate."

Heloise was moving before she knew what she was doing, the machine taking long strides across the trampled common green, between two houses that were modest for the town, but still would have dwarfed even the Imperial Shrine in Lutet, and toward the postern gate. Sure enough, the traffic there was choked by three Hapti wagons, drawn up in single file before the wooden doors.

Three sentries stood with Poch and two Hapti men, red-faced and shouting. Danad appeared from beneath the canvas canopy of one of the wagons with a double armload of thick animal hides.

He looked up as Heloise puffed and clanked her way to the wagon's side and came to a stop. "What, in the shadow of the Throne, is that?" she asked.

Danad smiled at her, hefting his load. "Winter's coming on, your eminence. Going to need these for warmth. Other one's got food, and the last . . ."

"Put them back."

"But, your eminence . . ."

"I said put them back!" she shouted. Even the Hapti stopped their arguing and stared at her. "We came to Lyse for walls, not to steal. Put it all back and let them go."

"Begging your *eminence's* pardon," Poch nearly spat out her title, "but Danad and I both fought in the Old War."

"Why should I care about . . ."

"If *you* had fought in the Old War, your *eminence*, you might know that we're about to stand to what's commonly called a siege."

"I know damn well what a siege is."

"Then no doubt you know a siege is more than walls. It's food, and clothes and wood and water and everything else you need to live day to day. You let these wagons go, you're doing the Order's work for them."

"You do the Order's work by plundering them. You make a liar of me."

"Make a liar of you?" Poch bit off every word. "You already made a liar of yourself, the moment you claimed to be a Palantine."

"I never claimed that."

Poch folded his arms across his chest. "Now, you listen to me. I have followed you this far against my better judgment. You may have amazed Barnard and your parents with your pious talk, but this is one arena where you have to trust your betters."

He jabbed an angry finger at the wagons, biting off each word.

"We. Need. These. Supplies. I'll man the walls, but I won't starve to death behind them because you want to play the saint."

The rage rose in Heloise, but not the hot fire of her anger with the Order. This was cold, quiet, and much, much worse.

"You will do whatever I tell you." Heloise's voice was barely more than a whisper.

"Or else your mother will scold me again? Because you're touched by the Emperor? You just said yourself that you're no—"

"No," she cut him off, "you will do what I tell you because if you don't, I will carve you into pieces and feed you to the ravens."

Heloise took a step toward the sentries, motioning with her knife. "Stand aside or die."

"You . . . you're just a little girl!" Poch said.

"It's not the girl you need to fear, Poch Drover," Heloise said, "it's the war-machine she's driving."

Poch's eyes ran over the machine's metal surface, taking in the point of the curving knife, the heavy shield. "I've known you since you were a babe in arms," he whispered.

"As you can see," Heloise said, "I am a babe no longer."

"They are heretics!" Danad shouted. "How can you choose them over your own kind? They don't hold to the Writ. They don't even believe in the Emperor . . ."

"*We* are heretics, or didn't you notice when you were killing those Pilgrims? Do you think we are somehow more pure in the Emperor's sight because our houses don't move? There is a devil's head on my shoulder, Danad. We didn't burn it. We didn't cry out to the Order. We cut it off and put it in a box and we carry it with us everywhere."

"It's not the same thing!" Danad shouted.

"We are not plundering them. We are freeing them from the Order. Why are we fighting if not to be free?"

Danad looked at her as if she'd sprouted a second head. "To live, Heloise. We just want to live."

.   .   .

Heloise made her quarters in the old Order chapter house. It was the closest thing the town had to a keep, with strong stone walls and only two entrances, iron-banded front and postern doors, much like the walls of the town itself. The Pilgrims lived simply, sleeping on wooden benches laid out in the nave before the shrine.

The stone walls were plastered over on the inside, painted with scenes of the Emperor's battle and martyrdom against the devils. The final painting was the scene of the Emperor seated on the Golden Throne, immortal eye bent on the shimmering veil, the devils clawing and snarling on the other side. The painting stood over a stone altar, on which stood a golden eye, flanked by small silver statues of Palantines in the standard pose, palms outward, wings outstretched.

She turned to Barnard, who stood, arms folded, jaw set. "This is a shrine." She gestured to the golden eye on the altar. "Will it serve for Gunnar?"

Barnard nodded at her. "It will, your eminence."

They brought Gunnar's shroud-twined body up from woods. It felt lighter than before, as if Gunnar had shrunk inside, but Heloise still carried it into the nave and set it before the altar.

"Will you say a word for him, your eminence?" Guntar asked, and Heloise caught her breath. What words could she say? What difference would they make? Gunnar was dead because he had followed her.

As her father's apprentice, she had transcribed the Writ at least a dozen times, and knew much of it by heart.

The last blow thou strike, strike for Me.
The last step thou takest, take it nearer My Throne.
The last breath thou sighest, be it My holy name.
Strivest thou in My service unto death, and I will keep faith,
And thou shalt be drawn to my breast, and dwelleth in My
sword arm.
Thine strength to Mine, to the confusion of the enemy,
Forever.

Chunsia wept openly, and Barnard looked up at Heloise, expectant.

She looked at Barnard, somehow managed to keep her voice even. "I'm sorry I couldn't save him, but he is where he would want to be now, Master Tinker. He is beside the Throne, at the Emperor's very hand. He's still fighting, and he will keep on fighting, for all of us, forever."

Barnard nodded, snaked an arm around Chunsia's shoulders, clapped his free hand on Guntar's shoulder, and squeezed so tightly that Heloise thought the boy must be in pain. She felt sick with guilt. She was the reason their son was in a shroud, and yet they turned to her for comfort.

She wanted to climb out of the machine, kneel at Barnard's feet and beg his forgiveness, but the thought of leaving it terrified her.

"I will make them pay." Her voice was scarcely more than a whisper. "I swear it. I will make them all pay."

Barnard's eyes widened, then narrowed. He gripped the machine's metal forearm, his huge hand looking like a child's against it. He squeezed and nodded once, firmly. "I am with you, your eminence," he whispered fiercely.

The silence stretched while the huge tinker stared into the

golden eye on the altar, as if the intensity of his gaze could some-how make sense of the loss of his children. At last, he shook his head, cuffed a tear from the corner of his eye. "Thank you, your eminence."

"Should we lay him to rest in the boneyard?" Heloise motioned toward the chapter house's postern door.

Barnard shook his head. "I'm glad of the Emperor's blessing and the final rite, but I won't lay him to rest in a false boneyard sowed by brigands. I would send him on in the old manner. That boy was a fire-forged tinker. Let him end in fire as well."

"I'll summon the village," Sigir said. "We can do it on the common."

"No," Chunsia said, her voice flat and hard, "boy's been seen enough since the fight on the road. The boneyard won't do for a burial, but it'll be enough for a burning. We'll go now, and quietly."

"Of course," Heloise said. She carried the shroud out the pos-tern door and set it in the small grid of earth, weed choked and surrounded by a tumbledown bit of iron fence. The sun was bright after the gloom of the chapter house, and Heloise blinked up at it, thinking that she was glad it was the last thing that would touch Gunnar before the fire took what remained of him. Bar-nard smiled up at her as he knelt beside his son, and Chunsia rested her head on her husband's shoulder. Heloise nodded, re-entered the chapter house, and shut the door behind her, letting the shadows rush in and claim her. She stood in silence with Sigir and her parents, who stood with hands clasped before the altar, eyes on their feet.

"Come out of that thing, Heloise," her father said at last. He leaned in to the machine, wrinkled his nose. "My dove, you are . . . you are starting to smell."

"No . . ." Heloise said, struggling for a way to make them un-derstand. "It's . . . it's not safe."

"It's a dangerous world," Samson said, "but you're safe enough with us."

"Was I safe enough when the Order came to Lutet?"

Samson flinched, and she immediately regretted the words. She wanted to apologize, but all she said was, "It is not safe. The villagers hate me now."

"Nonsense," Leuba said. "No one hates you."

"Poch does," Heloise said. "Danad too. A few others. They think I'm a heretic for letting the Hapti go."

"The . . . who?" Samson asked.

"The Kipti," Sigir said. "And she's not a child, Samson. She can reckon with the truth. Yes, Heloise. Some of the people are angry with you."

"We are fighting the Order so we can live as we choose!" Heloise said. "How can we deny that to others?"

Sigir and Samson exchanged a long look before Sigir turned back to her. "I'm sorry, your eminence, but I don't think that is so."

"Danad . . . Danad said that he just wanted to . . . live," Heloise managed.

Sigir nodded. "That is what most of the village wants, Heloise. They do not follow you to be free. They follow you to survive."

"No," Heloise said, her stomach turning over.

"Is wanting to live so bad?" Leuba asked.

"It is if you have to climb on another's back to do it," Heloise said. "That's what the Order does. The Writ says we are to lay down our lives—"

"The Writ also says we are to be obedient," Sigir interrupted. "It says we are to know our place. The Writ is a snake turning on itself. You can take a passage from the third chapter, and find one to contradict it in the tenth. It is, in the end, what men make of it."

"And what are we to make of it," Heloise asked, "now that we have the chance? Are we to throw off the Order while standing on the Traveling People?"

"Your eminence," Sigir sighed, "you have done great and incredible things, but you are still young."

"Why does that matter?"

"Because age tempers you," Samson said. "Getting old's the hardest thing I've ever had to do. But it's taught me that . . . that life is like being a mouse caught in a river current. So much of living is simply trying to keep from going under long enough to ride the water to its end."

"Think kindly of your own, your eminence," Sigir added. "They are frightened and only trying to protect their families, as you seek to protect them."

The thought of a mouse made Heloise think of Twitch, and anger surged in her, sudden and hot. "I was frightened and I drove a war-machine out against a devil."

Samson stared at her as if he'd never seen her before, and Sigir only shook his head sadly. "Not all can be so brave, and if you expect them to be, they will fail you again and again."

Heloise pictured Basina's face, blood trickling from the corner of her mouth, sight fading from her eyes. *I'm not brave like you, Heloise.*

"Try to think kindly of us." Leuba reached inside the machine's frame and touched her foot. "If you can."

Heloise felt suddenly cruel. Poch, Danad, *all* of them were here because of her, whether she had planned it or not.

"It was the same for you, Heloise," Sigir said. "When you fought the devil, were you reaching for freedom? Or were you just trying to survive?"

Heloise looked down, easier to take in her toes than the Maior's sad eyes. "Something changed . . . along the way."

"What changed, Heloise?" Samson asked. "It has only been a few days since we were safe in our homes in Lutet."

"We were never safe," Heloise said. "I didn't know what hung over us, but I was just a girl. You all knew."

"And what would you have us do?" Sigir asked. "You have seen for yourself the power of the Order."

"It doesn't matter," Heloise said. "If the Order were to ride in here now and offer to forgive us, to send us back to Lutet and put everything back the way it was, I wouldn't do it. I couldn't."

"Let us say you get your freedom, that we throw off the Order for all time, what will you do then?" Sigir asked. "Where will you go? Who will you be?"

Heloise stared at the tops of her feet and thought it over, but when she tried to cast her mind over the days ahead, she could see no further than the walls of Lyse, and how she would defend them when the Order finally came.

But something stirred deeper within her, something hotter and more urgent than Sigir's question. She looked up at last, meeting the Maior's eyes. "I don't know," she said. "I only know that I want to find out, and the Order will never let me do that."

"My dove," Samson said, "is it not better to live, and know some small measure of the world, than to die and know nothing?"

Heloise swallowed tears. Basina was gone. Clodio was gone. They had died trying to save her, to ensure that she could go on living. It dishonored them to waste that gift. But she pictured returning to Lutet, being married off to Ingomer Clothier, or some other young man from the village. To lie beneath them while they grunted and put a child in her. She remembered Clodio's hand disappearing into the shadows beside the fire in the roundhouse on the night she'd fled into the wood. She remembered what he'd said of love. *It is worth any hardship, it is worth illness. It is worth injury. It is worth isolation. It is even worth death.*

The Order would never let her live as she chose. They would never let her love as she chose.

"No," she said, "it is not better."

They were silent for a long moment, until Samson, at last, shook his head. "We're not nearly enough, even with the townsfolk who've agreed to stay and fight."

"I know," Heloise answered, "but I can't think of anything else to do."

"Might be," her father pursed his lips, eyes thoughtful, "with the veterans among them, that Wolfun fellow knows what he's about, we might be able to make a stand of it. Depends on how many the Order sends, and what they decide to do when they get here. We'll have to watch our own, Heloise. Especially Poch and Danad."

"They've had plenty of chances to run. They could have left with Sald. They're staying for a reason."

"Aye," her father said, "and that reason is they're betting that getting caught behind walls is smarter than getting caught out on the road. A man loyal to his own skin is apt to change his loyalty the moment his skin seems safer elsewhere. If the battle goes ill, there'll be more'n a few looking to open a gate in exchange for mercy."

"The Order is not known for mercy."

"Aye." Her father nodded. "For once, we can thank the Throne for that."

9

RABBIT IN THE SNARE

The Emperor is a mighty fortress, a shield that guards us. Yea, though mine enemy is vast beyond counting, 10,000 before me, and 20,000 behind. Yea, though my foe bears a glittering sword, and his countenance is terrible to behold. He shall not come nigh to me, or to my family. For a mighty fortress is my Emperor, and none shall pierce His walls.
—Writ. Ala. IX. 4

It didn't take long.

By nightfall, the first outriders were circling the walls, just beyond bowshot, their gray cloaks clinging to their shoulders, sodden by the cold rain that had begun to fall just after Wolfun set the watches. Heloise could see the sentries racing along the parapet from the front to the postern gate, long before the alarm was raised.

"What in the shadow of the Throne are you doing!" Samson called up to the tower astride the front gate.

"Keeping an eye on them," Sigir snapped back. "Or would you rather have them put up a scaling ladder right under our noses?"

"I'd rather them not see our garrison scurrying around trying to keep an eye on them, and assuring them we don't have enough beating hearts to cover our own walls!"

"When you are the Maior," Sigir shouted, "you can call the tune. For now, it's me and Wolfun up here, and you resting your fat ass below."

Samson cursed and looked up at Heloise, but she only shook her head. "Let them lead their men."

The horn sounded a moment later, and Samson followed Heloise up the ramp to the parapet walk atop the wall. The walls seemed pathetically low now that she stood on them. Wolfun's men were busy building out wooden embrasures over the battlements to add height, but Heloise still thought it would take little more than a fire ladder to mount them.

More gray cloaks were emerging from the woods, until twenty or thirty sat astride their horses just beyond the treeline, flails across their shoulders, looking up at Heloise and whispering to one another.

"The Order aren't armed for a siege," Samson said. "They'll have to send for the army."

"It won't take long," Sigir said. "Until then, they are enough to invest us here."

Wolfun leaned on his spear, grunted. "Worth a sally? While there are still so few? You made short work of the brothers here."

"The brothers here," Heloise said, "were surprised and on foot. These are mounted and ready. It's too dangerous."

"Heloise Factor!" Tone's voice drifted up to them. "How in the Emperor's holy name did you manage to get that monstrosity up on the wall?"

"She is a Palantine," Barnard shouted back. "The Emperor reached down His hand and lifted her up!"

The Pilgrims laughed at that, a soft patter that blended with the raindrops. "Well, no matter," Tone laughed, "we'll have you down soon enough. I must say, you have surprised us all. Taking an Imperial town is a bold strike, indeed. But I suppose I must thank you. You have put the rabbit into the snare, and let us bottle you up. Now, we can cleanse you at our leisure. Shall we storm the walls and have the pleasure of cutting you down? Or shall we wait out here until you eat one another? I must admit, I'm having trouble deciding."

"The Emperor will sustain us," Barnard laughed right back. "You are welcome to wait, but I am guessing you will give up come winter."

"We shall see," Tone said.

"You may as well give it a go," Barnard said. "Take us by storm. Though I think you'll have a tough time of it, a squadron of cavalry with no bows and no ladders. You could throw your flails at us, I suppose."

"We'll keep them, thank you," Tone shouted back, "but even without them, I don't think it would be too hard a task. How many of you are up there? Three? Five? Perhaps we will send our horses against your walls while we rest."

"There are more than enough to deal with you," Heloise said, her stomach sinking. Tone knew. He had seen them scurrying along the walls and he knew how few they were.

"So says the great Palantine in her tinker-engine. We are all very impressed down here, your *eminence*. How is your eye?"

"The one left to me sees clear enough. Come on up here and I will show you."

"I will be there sooner than you think." Tone reined his horse around and, shouting orders, galloped toward the front gate. A few other Pilgrims went with him, but most of them stayed where they were, their horses bending their necks to crop the grass. Even from this distance, Heloise could see the confusion on the Pilgrims' faces. They were armed only with their flails, horsemen outside a thick stone wall.

"Well, they're here," Heloise said. "Now we have to keep the walls."

"We're keeping them so far," Wolfun said. "They've not the numbers to try for an escalade. We'll put everyone over the gates, and I'll leave a lookout on the other towers just in case they try to surprise us. I think we're all right for now."

"For now," Sigir agreed. "Tone may be proud, but he's no fool. He'll have sent word. We don't have much time. Such plans as can be made must be made."

"Wolfun, will you join us?" Sigir asked the Town Wall, turning to go back to the town common before remembering to turn to Heloise. "If it pleases your eminence."

Heloise shook her head, making the machine's shoulders rock. "You have forgotten more of war than I will ever know. Lead the way."

Sigir bobbed his head and led the way back down to the green, where Wolfun had ordered the foodstuffs piled in view of all and kept under guard. "Houses got shadows," the Town Wall said. "Easier for a man to take an extra potato or a joint of meat in the dark. Having stuff out in the light is the best defense against our worse nature."

"Light is the Emperor's blood," Heloise recited, "it burneth away the dark, and the sins of man besides."

Wolfun nodded piously. "Aye, but the Emperor smiles on a well-formed plan, so I've still got Arley in the south tower looking down on it, such as there is."

There wasn't much. A few bins of ground corn and a dozen sacks of vegetables. Dried meat hung from a brace of poles pulled from their smoking houses. "How long will this last us?" Heloise asked.

Wolfun tipped his iron cap back and scratched at his thinning hair. "A fortnight at longest, your eminence. Fighting men need more vittles than most."

"And if we ration?"

"That is if we ration, but I reckon nothing makes a man more surly than an empty belly."

"We need to eat the perishables first," Sigir said, "the apples, cabbages, things that'll rot."

"Precious little of that," Wolfun said. "Most of the winter gardens are due for harvest. Would have taken it all in maybe a day or two after you arrived. Bad timing, that."

Heloise looked up at this. "Why can't we take them in now?"

Wolfun shrugged, giving a half smile. "Well, you can if you want to fight through them Pilgrims. Gardens're not far outside the postern gate."

Heloise thought of the confused looks on the riders' faces, their thin numbers. "We should go out and take the harvest in."

Wolfun's smile vanished. "You can't be serious."

"We go now, right now, before they get their bearings. Before more of them arrive. We can go out the postern, drive them back, and fill a few sacks with cabbages."

"Goat pens, too." Wolfun stroked his beard, thinking. "We could drive them in."

"It won't be long before the Order starts their own foraging. Once that happens, it'll be too late," Heloise said.

"Look at you," Samson said, shaking his head in wonder, "a soldier in your bones."

"It's too risky," Sigir said. "If we're caught outside the walls, then we lose everything."

"If we're trapped inside them without enough food, we lose everything," Heloise said. "Why should Tone risk storming the walls if he can just wait for us to starve?"

"She's right," Barnard said.

"It would help with the spirits of the Lysians," Samson said. "A raiding victory might keep a few coats from turning."

"Let's go," Heloise said, turning the machine toward the postern gate. "Wolfun, how many horses can we scare up?"

"The Order stabled their horses out by the gardens, you eminence," Wolfun said, hurrying to keep up, "It's just cart horses in here, and nobody here's good enough a rider to make use of 'em. We're better off making a run for it."

"Will five fast men be enough to take in everything?" she asked.

"Should be, depending on what we find. I don't go out to the gardens much, especially not this late in the season."

"I'm coming," Samson huffed, jogging along behind them.

"No," Heloise called back to him. "You're too slow."

"I'll keep an eye on her," Barnard said, lengthening his stride, though the big tinker wasn't much faster than Heloise's father.

Samson caught at Barnard's elbow and the tinker turned to him. "We have to go *now*. Every moment we delay puts her life in greater danger."

Samson let go at that, and stood hand outstretched, as if he could reel the machine back to him by some invisible thread.

She headed for the postern gate and picked up speed, trusting Wolfun to know his business. She heard him calling, heard men shouting in answer, the pounding of feet as they ran to join them. She permitted herself a glance out of the corner of her eye at Barnard. The man was steady off her shoulder, his huge forge hammer rocking against his own. She knew the machine was far stronger than any man, but the sight of him comforted her nonetheless.

"Open the gate!" she was shouting as soon as she rounded the corner of the chapter house and the postern came into sight. The tower lookouts, mere boys, stared at her open-mouthed and un-comprehending.

"Do it!" Wolfun shouted from behind her. "Quickly!"

There was another pause as the boys processed the command, and at last they scrambled down to obey, sliding the locking bar away and throwing their slim weight against the handles, the heavy wooden doors creaking as they swung slowly open.

"We can't give them a moment," Heloise said to the knot of men behind her. "We must strike them quickly. We will only have this one chance."

Barnard grunted, swinging his hammer experimentally. She heard swords clearing scabbards and spears rolling off shoulders behind her.

"Put arrows into 'em," Wolfun called up to the parapet, and Heloise saw men joining the boys now, stringing bows. "Make the bastards dance a moment until we get among them."

"What?" the tower sentry shouted back down. "But . . ."

Wolfun's command was clear enough, Heloise didn't under-stand why the sentry had so much trouble grasping it, but then the doors were open wide enough to admit the machine, and she charged out, raising the shield high enough to cover her, just be-low her eyes.

She shouted her battle cry, and Barnard joined her, raising his hammer up over his head as they burst out past the gate and onto the muddy track beyond.

Nothing.

There was no one there.

Heloise slowed the machine, trotting to a stop. She could hear the rest of the men following suit. Wolfun let out a low whistle. "What in the shadow of the Throne . . ."

She was certain the Order would have guarded both gates.

Tone was arrogant, but surely not so stupid as to leave Heloise a way to forage unopposed. If he wasn't here . . .

"It has to be a trap," she said.

"Trap or no," Barnard breathed, "we need to move. Either back inside, or to the work."

"One moment." Heloise could feel her muscles straining, tensing with the need to do something. She held it down with a will. She had to *think.* The risk they were taking was too great. What was Tone playing at? For what seemed like the thousandth time, she was sharply aware of how little she knew of war. She found herself wishing Sigir had come with her. He'd have known . . .

"Your eminence," Barnard growled, "we cannot stay here."

And then she heard it—shouts, coming from a long way off. The clashing of metal. She tipped her head up to the parapet, pointed in the direction of the noise. "Can you see what's happening?"

One of the sentries was leaning so far out he was in danger of falling, shading his eyes with a dirty hand. "No, your eminence. Sounds like a fight."

Wolfun appeared at her side, nodded. He heard it too. "It's a fight, for certain."

Heloise took a few steps closer to the sounds, straining to pull words out of the faint chaos. Barnard matched her steps. "Your eminence, whatever fight's on yonder, it's not *our* fight. We need to go."

But Heloise ignored him, squinting as she tried to pick out words. The curses were faint, teasing her, dancing on the edge of comprehension.

And then suddenly she had it. Not a word she understood, but one she'd heard before. Enough to recognize the language.

Before she knew it, she was off running, Barnard's shouts fading into panting as he struggled to keep up with the war-machine's great strides. The ground became a wash of frost-kissed green as the machine raced on, up a low rise and down the other side, where she saw them.

The low hill had blocked some of the sound, making the fight sound farther out than it actually was. Tone's horsemen wheeled around a line of wagons, some marked with the trefoil of the Sindi band, and others with a symbol of a pot over a campfire.

Two of the gray-cloaked riders were at the head of the wagon train, reining their horses tightly as the Traveling People tried to drive them off. Heloise could see that the damage was already done. The team of horses pulling the lead wagon were dead, flail wounds gleaming wetly, lying in their traces. Unless they were cut free and new horses brought up, the lead wagon couldn't be moved, and the rest were stuck behind it. The Traveling People were already cursing and trying to drive their teams into the broken ground to either side of the track leading to the postern gate, but Heloise could see that the heavy wagons would have rough going in that terrain.

The Pilgrims weren't risking it; their horses were already moving alongside the wagons. They swung their flails at the drovers, forcing them to drop their reins and scramble back into the wagons' canvas-covered housing.

The Sindi knife-dancers were just beginning to make themselves felt, leaping from the wagons. Heloise watched as one somersaulted over a Pilgrim, landing with a cross-slash of his knives that hamstrung the Pilgrim's horse, sending the rider crashing to the ground. Another knife-dancer took a graceful step that turned into a slide beneath a horse's belly, knife plunging upward to gut the beast from below. But there were dead Traveling People as well, facedown in the dirt, or draped across their drovers benches, all bearing the flails' ragged wounds.

Heloise looked for Onas, then for Tone, but she couldn't

distinguish one person from another in the chaos of gray cloaks and silver-handled knives. She shrieked, an animal cry, and then she was charging into the midst of them. Onas was somewhere in there. She had lost too many friends already.

The gray-cloaked riders began to turn at the sound of her cry, but she was already among them, lowering the shield and slamming into one of the Pilgrims' horses, sending beast and rider bowling sideways, the other Pilgrims scattering. But scattering did them no good, as Barnard plunged among them, swinging his great hammer at one horse's legs, already bringing the head back up and around as the screaming animal fell, until the arc brought it back down on the rider's gray hood.

A Pilgrim wheeled toward Heloise . . . and died, gurgling, Wolfun's spear in his neck. The remaining Pilgrims cantered away, still circling, but at a safe distance now, getting their bearings. It wouldn't be long before they realized that they faced just five people and not an army.

But the surprise had given the Traveling People breathing room, and five knife-dancers spun into the Pilgrims.

And now Heloise did see Onas, twirling at the head of his people, his cheeks red, his eyes lit with rage. One gray-cloaked man steered his mount with his knees, freeing his hands for an overhead swing, and Onas ducked beneath it, quick as a snake, striking out with one blade to tangle the weapon's chain, then jerking his arm down to pull the rider from the saddle.

Another Pilgrim charged him, and Heloise ran for them, banging her shield against the machine's metal fist to get their attention. The Pilgrim glanced up, reined his mount in, turned, and galloped away. Onas glanced briefly at her before racing after the Pilgrims. The other knife-dancers followed him, denying the Order a chance to catch their breath.

She itched to help the knife-dancers, to run the Pilgrims down, but she knew it was the wrong move. Her small party were too few to defeat the Order. She had bought enough time to maybe get the Traveling People free of the attack, but only if they acted fast.

She turned and ran to the lead wagon. "Get the horses clear!"

Wolfun and Barnard were already standing over the dead horses, wrestling with the traces. The Traveling People, at last given a respite from the attack, had turned their wagons back to the road and halted there, the drovers jumping down from their benches and running to help move the dead animals. Barnard fumbled with a buckle too fine for his thick fingers. "We're trying, your eminence!"

"Don't waste your time with that! Cut the leads!"

Wolfun produced a short dagger and in a few moments had parted the leather leads. Barnard and the wagon drivers grabbed the horses and began dragging the animals clear. Heloise risked a glance back toward the knife-dancers. They were surrounded, with one lying in the dirt, clutching his bloody head. She prayed it wasn't Onas. A thin, flat blade shot out from one of the campfire-marked wagons and buried itself in a Pilgrim's throat, sending him toppling from his horse.

One of the drovers ran back toward his wagon. "I'll give you one of my team, it should—"

"No!" Heloise shouted. "You need your full teams or you'll be too slow!"

The man looked at her like she was mad. He pointed at the lead wagon. "That cart is loaded, we can't pull it without horses!"

The last horse was dragged away and Heloise stepped forward, putting the war-machine between the yoking bars, her back to the wagon. "You don't have to," she said.

She reached out, curling the machine's metal arms around the bars. The wood rose, sliding into the crook of the machine's elbows. She pulled tighter, clamping them there, prayed they would hold.

"Quickly now," she shouted, and ran.

The wagon groaned, bouncing on the rutted track behind her. She could feel the weight of it, hear the clattering as whatever was inside bounced off shelves and tables. The machine's engine was bellowing with the effort of pulling the wagon, but it was more than equal to the task, and Heloise found herself going faster and faster, until the wagon seemed to be pushing her on into a dead run, faster than she'd ever driven the machine before.

She could hear the drovers behind her snapping their reins, urging their teams on, the rumbling of the wagon wheels picking up speed.

"Onas!" she shouted, praying he was alive to hear her. "Come on!"

Out of the corner of her eye she could see three of the knife-dancers detaching from the fight and racing for her, the Pilgrims turning to give chase. Another thrown knife wicked out from one of the wagons, bouncing off one of the Pilgrims' armor, but spooking his horse and turning it aside. The knife-dancers picked up speed.

"Run run run!" Heloise was shouting, her eyes fixed on the wooden ramparts of Lyse, impossibly small and distant. More riders appeared, thundering toward her, desperately trying to intercept the column before it reached the walls.

Heloise had never moved so fast, and the wagon teams were strong, but yoked horses pulling heavy burdens were no match for warhorses carrying riders. Heloise pulled with all her might, watching the Pilgrims close out of the corner of her eye. She couldn't tell if the remaining knife-dancers had reached the safety of the column, and she couldn't worry about it now.

A Pilgrim finally reached her, striking with his flail as he galloped past. She made no attempt to dodge or strike back. That would require her to stop, to drop the wagon, all of which would mean the end of them all. The flail head rapped against the machine's frame, spraying her face with sparks. *I have been a fool. All this struggle, all this work to take the walls, and now that we have them, I have doomed us all.* She heard shouts and the clashing of steel, the whisper of an arrow. The walls seemed no closer.

Three Pilgrims cut across the path directly in front of her, their horses blocking the way. "Surrender!" one of them shouted. "We have you and—"

Heloise lowered her shoulder and smashed right into him, batting his horse aside and sending him flying from the saddle. The other two Pilgrims reined aside, but kept on her, flails drawing sparks from the machine's shoulders. One of them galloped ahead of her again, charged, couching his flail like a lance. It didn't have a sharp point, but the iron ring would kill her just as surely if it slipped inside the frame and hit her at this speed.

She tried to jerk to the side, but the weight of the cart held her in place, and she was only able to move a hair's breadth. The Pilgrim compensated, adjusting his wrist and moving the flail head over, so that it grew in Heloise's vision, arrowing straight for the helmet's wide slit and her face beyond.

Her mind whirled with so many options that it froze. She should pull her arm from the metal sleeve and unbuckle her chest so she could slide down . . . she should drop the carts and move . . . she should . . . In the end she did nothing, only forged ahead, closing her eyes and praying the man would miss.

She heard a loud *thunk*, a gurgle, and a clang of metal as the flail struck the machine's shoulder, at least ten handspans wide of the mark.

Heloise opened her eyes to see the horse galloping away,

whinnying madly. The Pilgrim slumped in the saddle, an arrow protruding from his neck.

She looked up in time to see the archers on the ramparts nocking arrows and loosing them over her head. She realized with a start that she was no longer squinting against the sun, that the wall's shadow loomed over her, cloaking the wagon train in half-light.

She turned. Three knife-dancers were fanned out at the rear, the Pilgrims were wheeling away, at least one with a horse gone mad from an arrow in its rump. She could hear the thunk of the locking bar, and the slow creaking of the gates swinging open, see the relief on the faces of the drovers as they shook the reins and set their teams to running as hard as they could. She saw Barnard and Wolfun immediately, and turned back, moving again at what she'd thought had been a run, but now seemed so much slower. The sentries stood aside, staring at her in open-mouthed awe as she pulled the wagon through the gate and inside the walls of Lyse.

Sigir and her father came at a run. "Heloise!" Samson shouted, "Are you all right?"

"I'm all right," she said, "but I didn't get the forage."

"Looks like you got something," Sigir said, looking over her shoulder as the last wagon rolled in and pulled off to the side, the sentries rushing to slam the gates shut behind it. She could hear the Pilgrims making to rush the gates, and the whoosh of a fresh flight of arrows driving them back, cursing.

With the danger finally past, Barnard dropped his hammer head-down in the mud and bent over, panting, hands on his knees. Wolfun leaned his dripping spear against his shoulder and shook his head. "Sacred Throne, that was a near thing."

"No," Barnard managed, "we are beloved of the Emperor. We were never in danger."

"Tell that to the Kipti." Wolfun turned and quickly counted his men. "We got lucky, but they lost at least two of their . . ."

"Sindi knife-dancers, and a caster of my band," Mother Florea said, descending from the lead wagon with the cooking pot symbol. "The Great Wheel has borne three of us under."

"Onas . . ." Heloise moved closer to the Sindi wagons, saw Mother Leahlabel emerging from one of them.

"He is well, Heloise," Leahlabel said, as Onas appeared from behind the wagon, pale but smiling, his blades still bare and dripping gore. "Thank you for saving us."

"You are lucky we came when we did," Wolfun said. "We were only out for forage and heard the fighting . . ."

"That's not luck." Barnard stood. "It is the Emperor's divine hand. He sent us to your aid so we could bring you into Lyse."

"Aye, and gave us fifty-odd more mouths to feed," Poch Drover said, coming down from the rampart.

Leahlabel crossed her arms as the rest of the Sindi Mothers emerged. "Our wheels have turned, nothing more. For now, they turn together."

Onas ran to Heloise, embraced the machine's metal leg. "You were amazing! You threw those horses in the air!"

Heloise smiled back at him. "It was the machine. But why are you here? I thought you were moving on. Did you convince them?"

"No," Onas began, "they'd never listen to a boy, especially when . . ."

"I convinced them." Mother Florea walked over, put her hand on Onas's shoulder. "Though the lad's enthusiasm for your cause helped sway Mother Leahlabel, I'll admit."

Heloise looked from Mother Florea to the Sindi Mothers and back again. "Why?"

"Because you had us in your power," Florea said. "You had the town and could have given it over to the sack. Yet you did not.

You could have stripped us of our supplies, or pressed our men into your service defending the walls. You did not. The Traveling People desire freedom above all else, and this you gave to us willingly, when it hurt your cause to do so."

"We are most grateful for your help," Sigir said, "but that freedom will be short-lived. Those Pilgrims are an advance guard. They have sent for the army, and we will soon be invested here. If you remain, your traveling days may be brief."

Leahlabel answered Sigir, but her eyes were on Heloise. "It is easy to mistake fleeing for traveling. There are many among us who would prefer to run no longer."

"There are a few of us," Mother Analetta said, "who would prefer to keep moving."

"A very few," Mother Leahlabel added. "Too few to sway the band, and so we are here."

"I am the sole Mother of the Hapti band," Florea said. "The Order would not suffer more to be raised while we traded here, so it is my word that passes for us all. We are in accord. The Sindi and the Hapti will join you, if you will have us, Heloise Factor. Together, we will hold these walls, and either we will throw off the Empire's yoke, or else we will show the other Traveling People that there is another way to ply the roads. A braver way."

"You showed us that." Mother Leahlabel came to stand beside Onas. She reached inside the machine and touched Heloise's ankle. "And we are grateful."

Heloise swallowed a lump before she could speak. "Thank . . . thank you. Thank you for coming."

"Those knives won't do much good from a rampart," Wolfun said, "but I think we've bows enough for a few of you."

Florea shook her head. "A Hapti knife-caster can put a blade through a bird's eye at twenty paces. We will earn our keep."

"Aye." Wolfun cocked an eyebrow. "I think we can scare up a few short blades for troublesome birds."

"I hope those wagons are full of supply," Danad said, standing beside Poch. "Extra hands are good in an assault, but only when they're fed."

"That they are," Mother Florea said. "We carry our forage, and we're supplied for a fortnight, at least."

"Then we're no worse off than we were before," Wolfun said. "Still, we'd best pray that they try to take us by storm. We'll not long withstand a proper siege."

"They will," Heloise said, with a sudden certainty that surprised even her.

"How can you know that?" Poch asked.

"What was it you said to me of foolish words, Master Maior?" Heloise asked Sigir.

Sigir shook his head. "I don't remember, your eminence."

"You said that foolish words are the only things that travel faster than horses."

Samson smiled. "That does sound like something Sigir would say."

"He's right," Heloise said. "How many left when we took the town? Enough to spread word of what's happened, that mere villagers took a walled town out from under the Order's noses, and that the Traveling People have joined with them."

She thought of the stories she used to swap with Basina as they picnicked on the standing rock that overlooked the road, breathless whispers that grew grander as each saw the excitement in the other's eyes. A frog a handspan across became two-handspans. A rumble of thunder became a storm that shook the earth. "People tell tales," Heloise said.

"That's true," her father said. "They will say we are an army. Or that we breathe fire, or turn to shadows."

"They will say we are blighted," Poch groused, "and now they will say that we consort with heretic Kipti. It will not earn us allies, nor sympathy."

"You're right," Heloise said, "but it will mean they will not bother with a siege. Because every day we hold this town is a day they look like fools. We are making the Order look weak. Not only can they not stop a small village from fighting them, they cannot keep us from a town, and now they could not stop the Traveling People from joining us."

"They will fear that, if they do not crush us quickly, people might come to believe that they can be openly defied," Samson agreed. "They may come to believe we have a chance."

Leuba appeared at her husband's elbow. "Do we, Heloise?" she asked. "Do we have a chance?"

And Heloise felt her heart swell as she saw the villagers and the few townsfolk that remained clustering about her, the Sindi and Hapti, all fixing their eyes on the scratched and faded sigil on the machine's chest.

Because she realized that they did.

Heloise raised her voice. "Freedom is . . . it's like a mountain. Impossibly high, impossibly steep." She didn't know where the words were coming from, only that they were coming quickly, boiling up from inside of her almost faster than she could get them out. "And we have climbed it, step after impossible step. It was impossible that we should survive a wizard, that we should face a devil and live, that we should ambush the Order and escape, that we should travel with the Sindi, that we should take this town, that we should leave the safety of its gates and return."

She met her mother's eyes, saw the awe there. All eyes were locked on Heloise, all was silent save the sighing of the wind over the rampart. "And yes," Heloise continued, "it is impossible that we will hold this town against the might of the Empire. And before . . . before all this, that would have made me despair. But now, I know it is just one more impossible thing, and like every other impossible thing that we have done, we will do this one as well."

She turned back to Leuba. "So, yes, Mother. We do stand a chance. More than a chance. And the Order knows it, and that's why they will not wait. That's why they will storm the walls."

"And we will beat them," Barnard said.

"We will," Onas added, raising his blades, "for the Traveling People are with you now, and we are through running."

10

SIEGE

The "Free Peoples" of the Gold Coast bend the knee. All of their so-called senators are lords in their own right, rich men who claim to serve the will of their subjects, while lining their own pockets from their labor. Greatest of these is the "Red Lord" Ludhuige. He is that rarest of things: a rich man, refined and educated, with the soul of a killer. He is as wild and vicious as a starving wolf, and he will not rest until he has battered down the palace gates, and taken the Sacred Throne as his own.

—Letter from Brother Witabern to Lyse Chapter House

The first riders arrived the following day.

Not gray-cloaked Pilgrims this time, but soldiers with steel caps, breastplates, and long spears, each tipped with a black pennant, blazoned with the golden throne. A wooden frame was affixed to the back of their saddles, rising and arcing over the horse's rump. Black feathers filled it, so that it appeared as if each rider had a single outstretched wing behind them.

"The Emperor's uhlans." Samson shaded his eyes with his hand. "His light horse. They scout ahead of the main army. The rest can't be far behind."

"How much farther behind?" Heloise asked as Brother Tone

trotted out to meet the lead uhlan. They exchanged a few words, pointed at the walls. A moment later, one of uhlans reined his horse around, dug in his spurs, and galloped back the way he had come.

Samson sighed. "That'd be their rider going to tell the army that we are few in number and badly supplied, and to hurry to the attack. He's not taking supplies with him, so I'd wager not far at all."

He turned to look up at her. "They will be here soon. We should make ready."

"And part of making ready," came Mother Florea's voice as the old woman ascended the ramp and joined them on the parapet, "is seeing to your safety."

Florea gestured to two Traveling People coming behind her.

"You already know Onas," Florea was saying, but her voice was receding into a low buzz. "This is my daughter, Xilyka. She casts better than anyone in any band."

Xilyka would have been of an age with Basina, had Basina still lived. But where Basina was light, with tow-colored hair and pale eyes, Xilyka was dark, her black hair falling past her shoulders, gathered here and there into copper rings. Basina had spent her life in a tinker's workshop, and her strong arms were thick and solid. Xilyka's bare arms were long and lean, the muscle visible under her dark skin. She wore knives like Onas, but where his were silver and hooked, hers were straight and gray, without even wooden handles over the flat, metal tangs. She must have had twenty of the narrow blades thrust into her belt, a circlet of steel that wrapped her waist.

Xilyka's dark eyes locked with hers, and Heloise looked away with an effort, feeling heat rising up the back of her neck to color her cheeks. "I . . . I . . ." she stammered.

Florea smiled, misunderstanding Heloise's discomfort. "There's no need to worry, she can be trusted. The Mothers have been talking, and we've decided that you shouldn't go unguarded."

"She is never unguarded." Barnard folded his arms. "She hasn't had a moment's peace since this all started."

"That's all very well," Florea said, and Heloise risked a look back up at Xilyka. The girl was still looking at her with a mixture of curiosity and fascination. "But she is too important to trust to her friends and relations. Two bands of the Traveling People have thrown in our lot with you, and it is Heloise's . . ." She waved a hand, searching for the words.

"Legend," Xilyka finished for her, quirking a smile. Her voice was smooth and dark, just like her hair and her eyes.

Florea shrugged. ". . . Her legend that has brought us here. The Mothers agree. If she is lost, our people's will goes with her. She must be protected."

"She is safe enough with . . ." Barnard began, but Heloise stopped him with a wave, and Florea went on as if he hadn't spoken.

"Each band wants to post one guard to her, to be with her always. We offer the best dancer of the Sindi," she gestured to Onas, "and the best caster of the Hapti," she gestured to Xilyka. "Both are children of Mothers, to bind us to you. Surely," she eyed Barnard and put some ice into her voice, "you will not refuse this gift, intended as it is to ensure your safety."

"Surely not," Heloise spoke before anyone else could. "Thank you, Mother Florea. I will sleep safer knowing they are with me."

"If I speak true, Onas would probably have gutted me had we picked someone else." Onas reddened at the words, but he did not look away. "And when you come to know my Xilyka, you will see she would never have allowed any other Hapti to take the post if she could."

Xilyka rolled her eyes. "Mother . . ."

"All right." Florea threw up her hands. "Thank you, Heloise. Take good care of our children."

"It is we," Onas said, "who will care for her."

But Florea was already starting back down the ramp, waving a hand in dismissal. "Sort it out amongst yourselves."

"Mother Florea," Heloise called after her, and the Hapti woman turned. "The Talent. I know that Leahlabel and Giorgi have it in the Sindi. We may have need of it if any of your . . ."

Florea shook her head. "Then I must disappoint you, Heloise, for I am the only one among the Hapti, and I am an old woman at the end of her days."

Heloise's eyes widened. "What is it? What can you do?" She realized how excited she sounded, reeled in her ardor. "I'm sorry, Mother Florea. It's just that, if we knew, it would help us to better plan the defenses."

"The Talent is like a person's virtue," Florea said. "It is hers to bestow or to retain, as she sees fit. I do not see fit to bestow it now, and so you should plan as if it does not exist. But I promise that, should I use it, you will know it at once."

Heloise opened her mouth to protest, but Xilyka reached a hand inside the machine to touch her knee. She looked down at the Hapti girl and the shake of her head was so beautiful it nearly took Heloise's breath away. "It is not our way," Xilyka said. "Let her go."

Heloise swallowed her impatience and nodded.

It was silent for a moment, Barnard, Samson, and Sigir looking at Heloise, and Heloise doing her best not to stare at Xilyka, who clearly had no problem staring at her. Onas pointed to the box on the war-machine's shoulder. "The devil's head," he said to Xilyka, "is in there. I saw it myself. It's been there for days and hasn't rotted at all!"

Xilyka ignored him. "Do you ever come out from there?" she asked Heloise.

"That," Samson said, "is a very good question."

Heloise felt her cheeks flush again, was suddenly keenly aware of how dirty she was, of her scars, of how strange she must look wedged into a cage of metal and leather and covered with straps and buckles. "It's . . . safer this way," Heloise said, the words sounding foolish to her own ears. "You never know when the enemy might come. Best not to be caught unawares."

She expected Xilyka to laugh, or wave away the excuse, but the Hapti girl only looked at her. "That's wise," she said, "but you can come out if you ever want to. We're with you now, and we will keep you safe."

The words were so confident that Heloise, in that moment, believed them. For the first time in days, she felt as if she might safely step out of the machine, that with Onas and Xilyka at her side, nothing could harm her. "Thank you," Heloise said, her voice thick, "truly."

The feeling was followed by a flash of guilt. She pictured Basina's face, bright and smiling, as she had been before the fight with the devil. *I will never forget you. I will never stop loving you.* But the guilt and the fascination mingled in her gut, and Heloise found herself staring at the Hapti girl, unable to look away.

Xilyka said nothing, looked out over the wall. The uhlans were dismounting now, setting their horses to graze while they put up tents out of bowshot. A few sat on camp stools, sharpening their lances and their long, curving swords. More knelt in a circle, heads bowed while one of the Pilgrims read to them from the Holy Writ, hand raised in benediction.

"I've seen Onas dance," Heloise said. "Can you show us your throwing?"

Xilyka exchanged a smile with Onas before turning back to her. "Sindi boys may show off, but I am a girl and a Hapti, and when I have lost, I will be a Mother." She looked back out at the uhlans and pointed. "I promise you, you will see me throw soon enough, and you will not be disappointed."

Heloise looked out at the light horsemen, young men likely with families of their own back home. "They are not the Order," Heloise said. "They are just doing their work, same as we did. I don't want to kill them."

Sigir clapped Samson on the back. "You raised a good child."

Samson smiled. "If she were truly good, she'd come out of that machine and let me take her away."

"Do not worry," Xilyka said, looking back up at Heloise, the corner of her mouth rising. "If it is only the Pilgrims who earn your ire, then you need not kill anyone else. I will see to it for you."

·   ·   ·

The sight of the uhlans made the coming fight real somehow, a reminder of the forces that were about to be arrayed against her. The Order were warriors, to be sure, but at least they wore robes of ministry. The uhlans were soldiers. They had no function but to kill.

Xilyka and Onas took turns at watch that night, one sleeping while the other perched on the chapter house altar, receded into the shadows and all but invisible, weapons in their hands. Their presence should have helped her to sleep easier, but the knowledge that Xilyka was hovering behind her made Heloise want to change her shift and bathe, and the thought of leaving the machine then set off a wave of panic that banished all chance at slumber.

Heloise thought of trying to talk to the Hapti girl, but Sigir, Barnard, and her parents all drowsed on the altar steps, and she didn't want to risk waking them. Besides, what would she say? What did she know of the Hapti people? Xilyka wouldn't care about taking letters, or apple picking in the autumn, or how Basina was going to be marri—*Basina.* Heloise felt her stomach roll. It felt . . . like a betrayal to be thinking this way. *Don't be a fool, Basina did not love you, in the end. Not in the way you loved her. What makes you think this girl will?*

Heloise sat in the machine, straining to hear the Hapti girl breathing in the dark, and in the end she could not sleep at all. She gave up just as the sky began to lighten, the first copper rays of dawn beginning to simmer along the bottom edge of the narrow window. The machine's engine had died in the night, and she forced a fresh piece of seethestone into the chute, wincing slightly as it rattled loudly down into the canister. Her parents rolled over, moaning, but did not wake. Onas was on his feet in an instant, batting sleep from his eyes, and Xilyka jumped down from her perch, padding silently to her side. "Ready to go?"

Heloise nodded, let the rising roar of the engine drown her reply, and stepped outside. Wolfun was already up on the parapet, calling down to Poch and Danad, who were making their way toward the chapter house, but caught themselves up short at the sight of her.

"The Emperor has told you we were coming, surely," Poch said. He was careful to keep his tone neutral, but his sarcastic words were clear enough. Heloise marveled at him. She remembered him swinging her in his arms to put her up on the drover's chair when she was small. How had it come to this?

"Something like that," she said, looking past him to Wolfun on the parapet. The Town Wall was looking out beyond the walls, shading his eyes with a hand. Florea had joined him, wearing a belt of knives like Xilyka. Heloise didn't like the looks on their faces. "What's wrong?"

"We might ask you the same question," Danad said. "Where are your parents? The Maior?"

"Still rousing themselves," Heloise said. "I'm sure the machine woke them. They'll be along directly."

"I'll get them," Danad said, moving past her.

She stopped him with a jerk of the machine's metal hand. "Let them come as they are ready. If you have news, you can tell it to me."

Danad bridled. He looked back to Poch, who folded his arms. "It's not just news, your *eminence*. We can't have you unguarded."

"Perhaps the sun is in your eyes," Xilyka said, "and you have missed us standing here."

Poch ignored her. "You need proper guards, your *eminence*. Not a couple of heretic children."

Onas drew one of his knives, twirled it point first on a single finger. "Go ahead and try to harm her, and I will show you how safe she is."

Poch opened his mouth to reply, but Heloise cut him off. "Enough of this. If you have news, tell me, else, get back on the rampart where you can be of some use."

Danad shook his head, turned back to the wall. "Come and see for yourself."

Poch stood another moment, his jaw working, eyes locked on Onas.

"You have something else you'd like to say, old man?" Onas asked him, tossing the knife in the air and catching it by the handle. "I am listening."

"Onas!" Heloise said, but Poch had already turned, cords of muscle standing out on his neck, hands clenching and unclenching, following Danad back to the wall.

"That was poorly done," Heloise said.

Onas sheathed his knife. Heloise could tell from the tightness in his face how much the encounter had rattled him. "It is not our custom to stand idle when fools insult us."

"Onas, how are we going to fight them if we are watching our backs against one another? We are a handful and there is an army coming."

Onas forced a smile, but his eyes flashed with anger.

"I think," Xilyka said, "that an army is already here." She began jogging toward the ramp up to the parapet without waiting for the rest of them.

She was right.

They had come in the night, while Heloise had fretted over Xilyka's nearness, while her parents had snored, while the thick stone of the chapter house walls had screened her from the noise. They covered the grass and the newly shorn treeline, now dotted with piles of logs they had felled to build siege engines.

There were so many people that Heloise could barely see the ground, more than the market fair, more than the festival of the Fehta, which celebrated the Emperor's final victory, when he pushed the devils back into hell and drew the veil shut. It was more people than Heloise had ever seen in one place before.

The uhlans were still there, dismounted now, their horses hobbled and grazing in a clearing well back of the siege line. There were at least twice as many of them, and they'd removed the pennants from their lances, carrying them over their shoulders as spears. Here and there, behind them, were knots of Imperial knights. Their armor was the ash black of freshly forged iron, edged in shining gold. Their horses were huge, even bigger than the ones the Order rode, as encased in metal as their riders, so that together they looked like war-machines themselves, lacking only the smoking tinker-engine on their backs. Instead, they had a pair of wooden frames like the ones affixed to the uhlans' saddles, rising from their backplates and curling over their shoulders. Long black feathers ran the length of them, so that the knights looked like Palantines themselves, broad wings spreading from their backs.

"Blasphemy," Barnard muttered, joining her. "They've the look of Palantines, but not the deeds."

"And I have the deeds, but not the look," she finished for him.

"There is a devil's head on your shoulder," he said. "That is all the proof you need."

Heloise looked out over the horde of fighters beneath them, their banners fluttering the sigil of the golden throne on a field of black, the commander's tent, with the Order's chapter tent beside it. She counted at least five Sojourners and more than twice the Pilgrims than had come to Lutet. Endless ranks of foot soldiers milled about in simple black tabards, halberds or axes over their shoulders. Most numerous were the villager levies, farmers and wheelwrights and smiths come in their working clothes, homespun shirts and trousers, the tools of their trade their only weapons, hammers and rakes and pitchforks.

"It's a tide," one of the sentries said, "a tide to wash us away."

"A tide that will break against these walls," Heloise said, "and the people that hold them." But now that she had heard the words, she couldn't unhear them. The people below here were as numerous as drops of water in a river, a tide that could sweep over them in an instant. How could they hope to hold against so many? What had she been thinking?

The Sindi Mothers arrived with a small group of Traveling men, Giorgi among them. "By the Wheel," he said, "that's a lot of people."

"I don't like the look of that," Leahlabel said, pointing to a small black tent, pitched on a cleared rise some distance out from the wall. It was beside what Heloise guessed was the commander's tent, judging from its cloth of gold and fluttering banner. The black tent seemed squat and ugly by comparison, made from

coarse broadcloth and staked tightly down with thick iron. Dismounted knights stood in a ring around it, standing so close that
their armored shoulders nearly touched, their long bearded axes
at the ready.

"No," Heloise said, "I don't either. What do you suppose is in
there?"

"Nothing good," Leahlabel answered, "and nothing trifling
either, else they'd not put it under such heavy guard."

She was cut off by a horn, sounding low and loud enough that
Heloise could feel it trembling in her ears, hear it echoing in the
corners of the town behind her. Silence rolled across the land-
scape, starting with her people on the rampart, struck dumb by
the sudden noise, and gradually reaching across the army below
the wall, their ranks slowly parting for a mounted procession beneath a golden banner.

There were seven riders, all on huge black horses, save the man
in front, whose mount was white. Two Sojourners flanked him,
with a Pilgrim and three knights coming behind. The man on
the white horse wore golden armor, the breast and visor worked
to represent a radiant sun with a man's face, the countenance
stern, mouth drawn in a hard line.

As the man in the golden armor came closer, Heloise was able
to see over his shoulder. The single gray-cloaked Pilgrim behind
him was Brother Tone.

"In the name of the Emperor!" the man in the golden armor
boomed. "Where is the heretic?" His voice was high and sweet,
like a singer's, and easily as loud as the horn that had sounded
before. It did not trill as when a person shouted, was as even and
clear as if the man stood beside her.

"Wizardry," her father whispered, and Heloise felt her blood run
cold.

"It can't be," she said. "It is some tinker-work."

Giorgi laughed. "It is no tinker-work. Did you think the Order were honest men? You yourself called them brigands."

"Brigands, yes," Heloise said, "but at least I thought they cleaved to the Writ."

"They have never cleaved to the Writ," Leahlabel said, "any further than they must to excuse their excesses."

"But the people . . ." Heloise began.

"The people believe it is no wizardry, but a power given them by the Emperor Himself."

"But how can you know it isn't?"

Leahlabel looked at her like she was simple. "Because the Talent is like a . . . it is like standing in water. You can feel when the current changes, and it changes whenever someone else uses it." She looked up to Giorgi, and he nodded at Heloise in agreement.

Heloise followed Giorgi's eyes back over the rampart. "That tent," she said, jerking her chin at the squat black thing, the ring of iron-clad guards around it. "Is that wizardry too?"

Giorgi said nothing, only looked back to Leahlabel, eyes worried.

Barnard shook his head and trotted into the rampart tower.

"I am the Emperor's Song!" the man in the golden armor called. "In His name, I would address the heretic who leads you!"

Barnard came racing back out onto the rampart. He carried a broad looking glass, taken from the house of one of the rich folk who'd fled the town, and brought up to the tower so the sentries could cut their whiskers. He held it high, angled down toward the Song. "Go ahead and talk," he shouted. "You are looking at him."

The Song's horse sidestepped, and the force with which he jerked the reins to still it showed that the words had angered him. "The girl!" he shouted. "I will speak with the girl!"

"The *girl* is a Palantine," Barnard shouted, "and as such, she has adherents to speak for her."

"That is a lie." The Song raised his arms and circled his horse as he spoke, and Heloise realized that he was addressing his own troops every bit as much as Barnard. "No one has ever slain a devil and lived."

Barnard was already unfastening the lid of the reliquary on the machine's shoulder before the Song had finished speaking. He reached in and seized the head, lifting it out by the horns. Heloise shuddered at the sight of it, still perfectly preserved, as fresh as if it had been carved from stone. *I will never get used to that.*

"What do you call this, then?" Barnard held the head high, turning it so that the whole of the army could get a good view.

The Song rested his golden gauntlets on his hips and let out a laugh, loud enough to echo off the walls. Heloise could see the soldiers below grinning, clapping one another on the shoulders, pointing up at Barnard.

"I call that a clever forgery," the Song said, "a thing of tar and straw and skilled painting. I call it tinker or Kipti made. What I do not call it is a devil's head, cut from its shoulder by a little girl and somehow kept immaculate in a metal box for days on end. We are not such fools as you villagers. Save your tricks for those that might fall for them. We are the Emperor's own."

Heloise's mouth went dry. "But it's true!" she had said before she could stop herself, the words lost in the gales of laughter that swept up from the army, nearly drowning out Barnard's angry protests. Everyone in Lutet had seen her kill the thing, watched Barnard cut the head from its body. But no one else had.

She shot a glance to Onas. He was joining Barnard in shouting back at the soldiers below, but of the Mothers standing behind him, only Leahlabel had actually seen the head. The rest were looking at Heloise, making no effort to hide the doubt in their eyes.

"It's real!" Barnard was shouting. "I watched her fell the creature with my own eyes!"

"If it is real," the Song replied, "throw it down here so we can have a closer look. We promise to bend the knee and return it if you are not lying."

Barnard looked to her and shook his head. Heloise almost ordered him to do it, but she knew what would happen. The Song, or Tone, or one of the Sojourners would make a great show of examining it, declare it a fake, and all would be lost. To the villagers, the head was an icon. Perverse as it was, she couldn't afford to give it up.

No, she would not give it to the army below. But she could use it to do some good up here. She motioned to Leahlabel. "Have a look, Mothers. See for yourselves if it is a forgery."

Barnard looked even angrier at the thought of Traveling People touching the sacred relic, but Heloise matched his gaze. "Give it to them," she growled.

The giant tinker looked as if he would argue, but gritted his teeth and handed the head to Leahlabel, who turned it on its side, probing her thumbs against the meat of the severed neck. She looked back to Heloise, grunted, turned back to the Mothers, showing it to them. "If it is a forgery, it is the most clever forgery I have ever seen. This is real bone, and real flesh. There is no cloth or straw here. I can feel the wizardry in it. Can you, Giorgi?"

The Sindi man nodded. "I can, Mother."

She returned the head to Barnard as fresh gales of laughter swept up to them from troops below, dissolving into a chant of "Throw it down! Throw it down!"

Heloise turned to face her enemy, and even Barnard was quiet now, knowing it would do no good to try to be heard over them. The Song raised his arms, turning in the saddle, basking in the humor. Heloise could see Tone smiling, arms crossed, his flail tucked in the crook of his elbow.

The Song waited until the laughter died down, a good long while, until a silence had settled over besieger and defender both. He faced that wall, leaned forward in his saddle, and spoke in a low voice that still rang clearly to every ear. "You lot are prone to fantasies, like little children. I am a father, may it please the Emperor, and I have learned over the years how one deals with children.

"So, here is your lesson. We are an army, the finest fielded in my memory, ready to scale these walls and put you all to the torch. You are a rabble, a straw brigade, duped into following a fever-mad girl who aims to set herself up as a queen. If you follow her, it will be your death.

"But the Emperor is merciful! Even now His eye is turned on you, even now He sees loyal subjects turned astray by this poor girl's blight. Even now, when you have scorned Him, He stretches out His hand to redeem you.

"We only want the girl. Send her down. She is nothing, a queen of rats and crows. The mistress of stones and dirt. Send her out to us, and we will leave you in peace."

Leahlabel stepped to the edge of the rampart, cupping a hand over her mouth. "And what of us? What of the Traveling People? All heretics are alike to you, eh? How can we know the Order will keep their word if we throw down our arms and come out?"

Barnard spun on her, snarling. "How can you even ask . . ."

But the Song was already answering, not to Leahlabel, but to Heloise. "The Emperor's Song does not address animals. You do not hear us speaking with our mules, or our dogs, or any Kipti who happen to stray across our roads. Speak, instead, with the Order, for they are charged with bringing the heretic into the fold."

He gestured to Brother Tone, who spurred his horse forward. It was a calculated insult. The Sojourners were the lords of the Order, too high-ranking to sully themselves speaking to Kipti. It was a mere gray-cloaked Pilgrim who had been chosen to address them.

"Come down now, all of you," Tone called. "If I have to climb up this lump of rock I will be quite cross. Those of you from Lutet have seen me when I am cross, but it will be new to these Kipti and the Lysian turncoats with you now, so let me explain it to them.

"When I am cross, I kill things that are alive, and burn things that are not. Ah, may the Emperor not judge me for a liar. Truthfully, I burn things that are alive, too. If I have to climb up there, there will be nothing left of Lyse by the time I am done. No two stones will stand atop one another.

"But it need not come to that." Tone raised his voice louder, ensuring it would be heard inside the town as well as atop the wall. "This tinker-clad heretic of a girl has led you from the right path. You have been fools to follow her, but fools are not devils. The Song gives you this one chance to repent your actions and turn from her. Tear the girl from her machine and bring her to us, and we may yet let you live."

Barnard turned, hefting his hammer, glaring at the Lysian sentries. They looked steadily at their feet, into the distance, anywhere but at him. Heloise could see the temptation in the hang of their heads and the slump of their shoulders. *They only want to live. Tone is promising them that very thing.*

"He lies," Samson said to them. "That's a Pilgrim talking. Only thing their kind has ever done is kill. There is no mercy in them."

"I do not lie," Tone said. "Shall I swear an oath? Shall I fetch the reliquary from the chapel tent?"

Even Wolfun looked up at that, glancing quickly at Barnard before looking away. *They believe him*, Heloise thought. *They'll put me out.*

The silence dragged on, until Tone gave a satisfied nod. "Very well, then, I will fetch . . ."

Heloise tipped back her head and laughed. The sound was startling, harsh and low, like a crow's call. Even Tone let his words trail off as all eyes on the parapet snapped to her.

"Oh, you are funny," Heloise called down to the Pilgrim, "and you really must think villagers are stupid. I am, according to you, wizard-cursed, damned and blighted, contaminating everything I touch and the ground beneath my feet . . ."

"And so you are!" Tone shouted up at her, eyes blazing.

"Which means," Heloise went on, as if explaining to a child, "that you must Knit this place, that you must burn it and everyone inside. And yet here you are promising mercy if only my people will give me up. It can mean only one thing."

"That the Sacred Throne has moved my heart to pity—" Tone tried to speak over her.

"That you are afraid!" Heloise cut him off. "That your masters will be angry with you for letting us take this town. Or that you are not sure you can take it back."

Barnard's eyes lit at Heloise's words. He stepped to the edge of rampart and shook his fist. "She's right! The powerful do not bargain, they do not make promises, because they do not have to. No, you murdering brigand. You are *afraid*, frightened by villagers and our champion in her machine, and you are right to be, because we will not give her up, and when you come for her, I will kill you, and I will build another box on her other shoulder, and we will carry your head in that as a reminder of how easily fools can die."

"You . . ." Tone's cheeks burned so brightly that they looked purple even from this distance. "You will beg for your life before I am through." But his mocking surety was gone now.

"That is enough from you, Tinker," the Song said, "we will have our response from the heretic girl, or her parents. Is her father among you?"

"He is," Samson called down to them, "and he spies the Pilgrim whose eye he blackened outside Hammersdown. A mere villager beat him like a festival-day doll, and that villager will do it again, just as soon as that Pilgrim is dumb enough to mount these walls."

And now it was the defenders' turn to laugh, loud enough and long enough that Heloise knew they would remain, that they saw the Song's offer for what it was: a bid to lure them out, unarmed, to the slaughter.

Heloise looked back out over the wall, and could see Tone, visibly enraged. Perhaps the Song was, too, his red cheeks hidden by the gold sun of his helmet. But the Song's voice was just as sweet as he replied. "Foolish words from one angry man. I do not think the rest of you agree with him. I will give you one day to think it over, and return for your answer at dawn. At dawn, mind you. Anyone coming out before then will be judged a sally, and treated as an enemy. Keep to your walls, mull my words and the Sacred Throne's gracious offer."

With that he wheeled his horse, the procession following behind, the army parting to make way for them. Tone shot a glance over his shoulder up at Samson, teeth bared. Heloise could see his shoulders shaking despite the distance. Even if the Song had been genuine in his offer of mercy, she knew that Tone would not honor it for her father.

"That was well done," Samson said, and Heloise could hear the shaking sigh in his voice. He shot a glance at Wolfun and the other sentries. "They'll stick now."

Barnard took a step toward Leahlabel, and Giorgi stepped between them. Onas and Xilyka drew their weapons as well, but stayed at Heloise's side.

"What if he'd said yes?" Barnard's words were tight, clipped. "What if he'd promised mercy for all, Kipti included. Would you have sent Heloise out to die, then? Would you have given her up?"

"Don't be such a damned fool," Leahlabel said. "I just convinced every Traveling Person here that leaving these walls means certain death. Any doubting hearts have been shored up. Look beyond your own nose for an instant, you idiot ox."

Barnard's face migrated from shock to realization to understanding. He opened his mouth to reply, then closed it again. Heloise spoke quickly, in case he found words. "At least now we know when they will come, at dawn tomorrow. We must decide how we are to meet them."

"And we must go among our own," Sigir said, "and ensure that all are still with us."

He met Heloise's gaze evenly. "The Song was cunning in his speech. He knows what most of us want, a return to our old lives. He knows that dangling it for us is the best chance he has of turning you out, of ending this without a fight. Everyone in this town heard him. That is a weapon more deadly than all the flails in the Empire."

Sure enough, Poch and Danad were waiting for them as they descended the ramp from the wall, at the head of a knot of villagers. A few of the Traveling People stood by them, at a remove, but close enough to show their support.

"Maior . . ." Danad began.

"If you are thinking to turn her out," Barnard snapped, "I'll stave your skull in."

"With respect, Master Maior," Poch said, "we are talking about one life against hundreds. Why shouldn't we take them up on their offer? Everything can go back to how it was."

"How it was?" Barnard seethed. "Cowering in terror every time we heard hoofbeats? Giving up the best of our custom to strangers and turning a blind eye when they burned a village of our friends and kinfolk? That's what you want to return to?"

"She's my daughter!" Samson roared, coming to stand with Barnard, huge fists trembling. "By the Throne, if any of you send her out, I will throw your own children after her!"

A few in the crowd shouted back, and Sigir stepped between them. "There will be no fighting here."

"They may not even harm her!" Poch added. "Maybe they'll just put her in irons for a time."

"We will not send her out," Sigir said, his voice low and dangerous, "and mark my words, you two. If, for any reason, she goes out, *you* will accompany her. Then you'll see how well the Order keeps its promises."

"Their bodies will accompany her," Samson said. "I'll keep their heads."

"You just try it, you . . ." Poch took a step toward Samson, and Heloise finally moved, stepping the machine between them, bumping the drover back with its metal hip.

"I don't need my father's help," she said. "You are lucky we need everyone on the walls. If you will not fight because you want to be free, you will fight because you want to be alive. You think you will save us all by giving up one life?" She flicked her eyes from Poch to Danad. "Very well, *I* think I will save us all by giving up two."

Poch and Danad stepped back, eyes wide. "You're . . . you're no different than the Order."

Heloise kept the hurt off her face. "You're wrong," she said.

"The Order will kill you to make us slaves. I will kill you to make us free."

She pushed past them, not waiting for her entourage to follow, but hearing their footsteps behind her as they hurried to keep up.

"And who asked to be free?" Poch yelled at her back. "I didn't! None of us did!"

But Heloise ignored him, storming up the chapter house steps and pulling the doors wide with such fury that the machine's great strength slammed them against the walls.

It wasn't until they shut behind her that she sagged in her straps, letting Poch's words wash over her, reverberating in her mind. *You're no different than the Order.*

He wasn't right. He couldn't be right.

But she listened to the frightened silence of the people around her. Onas and Xilyka, her father, Sigir and Barnard. Her best friends, her kin. She could feel their eyes on her back, their minds whirling as they tried to figure what they could say.

You're no different than the Order. If the words were false, why did they feel so true?

II

FOR THE GOOD OF ALL

The mother may love her daughter, the father his son, but this is not righteousness. The lord may love his vassal, and the shepherd his flock, yet this too is not righteousness. Nor may it be said to be love, not truly. Nay, it is but the shadow of love. For only one true love exists, love of the Emperor. For all these other loves benefit but a few—a family, a herd, a kingdom. To love the Emperor is to love the world.
—Sermon given in the Imperial Shrine
on the centennial of the Fehta

Giorgi knelt on the rampart, adding another of the small casks to the stack behind the wooden embrasure painted with spent pitch. "You keep it wet," he said to Wolfun, his face serious. "If you have to choose between your men going thirsty, and keeping these casks wet, then you choose thirst."

Wolfun cocked an eyebrow. "And if they use fire-arrows?"

"Then you get the casks off the wall and under the rampart. Soak your shirts and lay them over each cask."

"That bad?" Heloise asked, striding up behind the Sindi.

Giorgi shrugged. "You've seen our fire-flowers? On festival days?"

Heloise felt a tiny fragment of the girl she'd once been. The loud bangs, the bright bursts of colors against the night sky. "Of course."

Giorgi squatted, got a good grip on one of the casks, and heaved it into position.

"That's what these are."

Wolfun's eyebrow rose even higher. "You're going to entertain them to death with colored lights?"

"The fire-flowers I saw were all long sticks," Heloise said. "Why are these so heavy?"

"The fire-flower is inside," Giorgi said, "the rest are hobnails and old spoons, broken knife points, that sort of thing. Metal scraps."

"Oh," Heloise said, picturing the bursting fire-flower, the sparks showering down, except now instead of colored light, it was shards of sharp metal, arcing and spinning.

"Are you sure it'll work?" Wolfun asked, eyeing the casks as if he expected them to go up at any moment.

"Fire-flowers are like the Talent," Giorgi said. "They always work if you know how to work them."

"And how do we work them?" Heloise asked.

"The casks are oiled," Giorgi said, "you light them, then kick them over the side. And you make damn certain the man doing the kicking doesn't take an arrow before he gets the chance."

Heloise imagined the cask going off on the rampart, the metal fragments scything through her own people. "I see."

"Your eminence," Sigir said, "are you certain this is worth the risk?"

"Don't be foolish." Giorgi stood, putting his hands on his hips. "There are ten times our number down there. There is nothing but risks from here on through tomorrow. We must take every one on offer."

Sigir looked like he might protest, but Heloise cut him off, "Giorgi is right. We cannot afford to pass up any advantage. If one of these things can cut down a squadron of the enemy, it could mean the difference between winning and losing here."

Now it was Giorgi's turn to cock an eyebrow.

"It can cut down a squadron, yes?" Heloise asked.

Giorgi shook his head. "If it lands just right, and the fire reaches the flower at the right time, maybe."

"Those are a lot of ifs," Wolfun said.

"Aye." Giorgi nodded. "Quite a lot, indeed."

Beyond the line of tents, Heloise could see the siege engines coming together. She was astonished by the speed with which they'd been assembled, stripped trees turned to beams, beams to structures in just one day. The Emperor's engineers knew their business. "Will the fire-flowers help against those?"

Giorgi shaded his eyes with a hand. "They might."

"What will they do with that tower?" Heloise asked.

"They'll roll right up to the walls," Wolfun answered. "That ram, too, see it?"

Heloise could make out what looked like the peaked roof of a small shack. "That's . . . that's a house."

Wolfun laughed. "It is, I suppose. But it don't house people. There's a tree swinging on chains under that roof, and wheels, too. They'll roll it up to our gates and knock on 'em 'til they open."

"That's not good," Giorgi said.

Wolfun shrugged. "Not bad, either. They're rushing. They took their time, they'd have twice as many. This is . . . manageable." He paused. "I hope."

Heloise looked down at the enemy soldiers, some looking up at the wall they would have to assault the following day, others gambling or napping against stacks of shields, helmets tipped over their faces. The armored knights around the squat black tent looked as if they hadn't moved since they'd been posted. If the guard had changed, Heloise hadn't seen it.

But it was the villagers that held her eyes for the longest. They looked so familiar to her, homespun shirts and woven belts that she had seen a hundred times in Lutet. Here was a gray-haired, broad-shouldered man who was the spitting image of her father, there, a boy who could have passed for Ingomer. They weren't here because they hated Heloise or the rebels holding the town.

"I do not want to kill their levy," she said.

Wolfun frowned. "They want to kill you, your eminence. And come the morrow, they will be about it."

"No," Heloise said, "they don't want to kill anyone. They want the same thing we want—to live. But they know that, if they don't try to kill us, the Order will kill them. That's not the same thing."

"Maybe not in the thinking of it." Wolfun stroked his beard. "But I don't see how that matters. In the doing of it, there is only them trying to kill us, and us trying to kill them."

"You have a good heart, Heloise." Giorgi touched the machine's metal elbow. "But I hope you can steel it for what's to come. I have seen these," he nudged the casks with his boot, "at work. They aren't pretty, and they will not distinguish between levy and Pilgrim."

"I will do what has to be done," Heloise answered Giorgi, still looking at Wolfun, "but it does matter what we want, what we think. That's the difference between us and the Order. Not wanting to do it counts for something." Poch's words still burned in her mind, making her own sound lame.

"As you say, your eminence." Wolfun bowed as he spoke, so she could not see his face.

·   ·   ·

Heloise returned to the chapter house after the casks were stacked. She had meant to see if she could close her eyes and sleep for a moment, but found herself pushing through the nave and out into the boneyard behind. The tiny, hemmed-in space felt enormous after the tight confines of the chapter house, and it took her a moment to realize why. It wasn't just the broad dome of the sky visible above her, or that the sounds of the defenders preparing for battle, carrying sheaves of arrows, fixing the rivets on pieces of armor, reached her only faintly. It was that she was, at long last, alone. Since she'd fled the village, everyone seemed to *need* her to be something. A saint, a daughter, a warrior, a leader. None of those things felt *right* to her. If she could just sit and think about it long enough, alone, she knew she could . . . not arrive at it, but get closer to making sense of it.

But the precious moment was not to last, and she kept the irritation off her face as Onas picked his way through the weed-encrusted headstones. Her gut warred with itself, sour at being disturbed and happy as always to see the Sindi youth. His smile, his confidence, his joy. Still, she would have preferred it to be Xilyka, if it had to be anyone.

"You shouldn't be alone," he said.

"I never am." The words came out more harshly than she intended, and his smile faltered, if only for a moment.

"I'm in no danger." Heloise softened her voice, tried to smile for him, though the scars on her face made it hard. "In the machine, I could take on five men by myself. And who is going to find me here?"

"Still." Onas shrugged. "You're important to all of us."

Her face fell at that, and Onas looked pained. "I realize it must be . . . hard for you. Everyone wanting a piece of you all the time. I'm sorry for that. I'm only trying to . . ."

"Do as your mother ordered. I know." She sighed. "I'm glad of you, Onas. From the beginning I have been glad of you."

Onas looked at his feet, smiling. Heloise waited for him to

speak, to leave, but he only stood there, his mouth working, and she realized that his smile was frightened. *He's working up the courage to say something.* The thought made her heart sink.

His next words set her stomach tumbling. "When all this is . . . over, I don't see how you can just go back to being . . . a villager."

"No." Heloise's mouth went dry. "I can't."

"I imagine," Onas continued to stare at the tops of his boots, "that none of your villager men will take you for a wife now . . ."

He finally looked up at her, and the shock in her face rattled him, and he stammered a hasty addition, ". . . not because of your wounds. Beauty such as yours cannot be hidden by a scar."

The forced grandeur in his words bewildered her. *Is he . . . courting me?* Heloise had never thought of herself as beautiful. Basina was always the beautiful one, for all the good it had done her in the end. Onas looked so mortified, so frightened, that Heloise felt she had to say something to fill the thick silence that cloaked them after he stuttered out the last word. "Thank . . . you." She did not feel grateful to him, only shock and anger that he had violated her one moment of privacy to talk about her marriage prospects and her beauty.

"I'm sorry . . ." he went on, and a horrible thought pierced her, a spike in her mind. *He's the son of a Sindi Mother. If I anger him, will they desert our cause?* ". . . It's just that I wonder if you hadn't thought of a different life, one I could offer you."

"You . . . can offer me a life?"

Onas mistook the disbelief in her voice for interest. His face lit as he went on. "You are a great beauty, Heloise, but most men are frightened of . . . of who you are, of what you have done, of what you can do."

Heloise was so stunned that she actually choked as she tried to draw breath. He *was* courting her. She suppressed the urge to flee, to lash out with the machine's metal fist, anything to make him stop.

"But not me," Onas went on. "We're the same, you and I. We understand one another. I know you may not . . . love me yet, but the Traveling People do not always marry for love. Sometimes, if it is a good match, something that may unite the bands, or settle a dispute we . . ."

Heloise searched for something she could say to cut him off, desperate to stop him from speaking.

"We are fighters, Heloise," he continued. "We are people who change things. Our wheels are turning together for a reason. You cannot know how much you have changed my band simply through your example. For the first time in many winters, I am hopeful for our future, and I want to be a part in making real what you imagine. I know we can do it better together, and when I think of what our children . . ."

"Our children?!" Heloise sputtered.

"Of course. So many of our people are mired in the old ways. They have lived that way for too long for them to change their minds. But we will rear children in the new way, and it will be the only way they know, and they will never accept a yoke again. We are already setting this right, can't you see? Together, we can change everything. If . . . if you will allow it, I will send my mother to your father, and ask them to promise us, one to the other, our wheels to turn together until the end of our roads."

The shock gave way to anger, and it was Heloise's turn to stammer, "You . . . you only say this because you are . . . you mistake gratitude for love."

Again, Onas misunderstood her, shook his head, smiling. "No, Heloise. I love you. I see your scars. I have seen you fight and kill. I know what you are to your village and to the Empire, and I choose you regardless. I love you, and I will have you to wife, if you will allow it."

He bowed then, a ridiculous flourish that bent his front knee and swept his arm out to his side, his free hand on the hilt of one of his silver-handled knives. *Tell him no,* her mind screamed at her, *do not let him live in hope. No good can come of it.* But when she opened her mouth to answer, she was nearly swamped by the image of his face twisting first in disappointment, then in anger, of the gates opening and the Traveling People's wagons trundling away. *Don't be stupid, the Order will never let them go.* But the image, and the terror it evoked, were overwhelming. A hundred other justifications rose to her, unbidden. Onas was good, Onas had stood by her, Onas had advocated with the Mothers to help them. None of it mattered, she could not marry him. She thought of the melting feeling when she'd kissed Basina, the breathless excitement at Xilyka's nearness. It wasn't just Onas. She could never feel that for any man.

The thought was followed by rage. Why had he waited to ask her now? Now, when they were trapped, when she could not think and could not escape. "Why now?" she managed, but the worry robbed her voice of the anger, and Onas only misunderstood her yet again.

He shrugged. "Because we may die tomorrow, and I would not go to my grave with this unsaid."

"Onas . . . I . . ." She thought of Xilyka, her dark eyes and hard voice. Why, of all the Traveling People to love her, couldn't it have been her? "I just . . . I just don't know." *Lies. You do know.* "I don't know."

Onas smiled sadly, patted the air with his palms. "No need to give me your answer now. Only promise me that we will speak of this again when the fighting is done."

No. We will never speak of this again. But Heloise felt weak with relief at the prospect of the conversation simply ending. She could put it off until after the fighting, and if living in hope made him fight more fiercely, then so much the better. He was one of her personal guard, she couldn't imagine having to fight a battle knowing he would always be at her side, angry and disappointed. "All right," she said, "after the fighting we will speak of this again."

He bowed again, even more laughably exaggerated this time. "Thank you, Heloise. I will live in hope."

And with that, he left her, standing in the weed-choked bone-yard, all the peace that solitude had brought her banished by the sick anger boiling in her belly, the hammer blow pounding of her heart.

·   ·   ·

Heloise was surprised when sleep finally took her. Xilyka was crouched in the shadows by the altar, and the enemy was still out-side the walls. Tomorrow the fight would begin in earnest. Onas's suit joined Poch's words and her father's face in the morass that had been whirling in her mind all day, and now, at last, her body had had enough of it, and refused the waking world, no matter how much worry and terror churned in her. Heloise closed her eyes, and when she opened them again, it was night and she was slumped in the machine's chest strap, and wind was sighing across the back of her neck. It was blessedly cool and sweet, smell-ing of winter's edge; she could hear it whispering in her ears, lifting the strands of her damp hair until they tickled the tip of her nose.

The machine's engine had died, and she didn't have the acrid tang of the seethestone to compete with the freshness of the air, the steady thrumming of the engine in her ears. She gave herself up to the moment, breathing deeply.

She jerked upright in the strap, panic lancing through her, set-ting her trembling fingers scrambling for a chunk of seethestone to cram into the chute. She sawed her head left and right, desperately searching the shadows.

The wind. Blowing. Inside the thick stone walls of the chapter house.

A door was open.

The sound of her fingers digging in the salted cloth pouch sounded as loud as a ringing bell, and she froze, straining her ears, squinting into the darkness, willing herself to be able to see. For a moment, the silence continued unbroken, save for the sounds she expected: her parents' soft snores, the whisper of that terrifying breeze.

And then she heard it.

A cloth-wrapped footfall, the gentle tread of someone moving behind her. The whisper of steel clearing a muffled scabbard.

She looked at the seethestone pouch again. The stone would rattle on its way down the chute to the engine, loud enough to wake the dead. It would take precious time to get the stone and get it into the chute, then more time for it to settle in the puddle of water at the bottom, to activate, to build up enough pressure for the engine to bellow to life.

Whoever had come in the night, they were trying to conceal their movements. They meant her harm, and would not wait for the engine to start. And without the engine, the war-machine was just so much dead metal around her. It might protect her from a knife thrust, but not for long.

She would have to come out.

For a moment, the threat behind her faded into the larger threat that was the whole world beyond the metal and leather frame. The tiny chapter house suddenly seemed enormous, Sigir and Barnard and her parents, her guards, all so impossibly far away that they could never reach her in time to help. In the machine, she had killed a devil, had taken a walled town, but outside it, she was only Heloise, who didn't have a weapon even if she knew how to use it.

No. Her own voice spoke up in her mind. *You have a weapon. You will always have a weapon.* In that moment, she forgave Onas's stumbling proposal. This was his gift to her.

She looked down at the machine's metal sleeve, eyes traveling the length of it to the end of her stump, where it disappeared into a slim metal collar stamped with the trefoil of the Sindi band. Beyond that, the long knife curved up, until it barely peeked out through the slot in the machine's empty metal fist. She wiggled her stump, felt the leather straps that bound the collar in place hold fast.

It would make noise to draw it out, but it would come quickly.

She reached over, undid the strap around her chest, wincing at the gentle chiming of the buckle as it fell free. She let her feet take her weight, her legs weak after so many days of not having to carry her, muscles tightening painfully at the unexpected use.

The enormous darkness around her came rushing in, and the tightness in her chest ripped her breath away. The whispering behind her came closer, darker and more terrible than any devil she could imagine.

But Heloise kept her eyes on the long, curving blade of the knife, the metal collar that held it fast to the stump of her wrist. *I have a weapon,* she said to herself, over and over and over. *I have a weapon I have a weapon I have a weapon.*

The darkness embraced her as she leapt off the machine, ripping her arms out of the sleeves, the knife sounding a rattling warning. She could hear the whispering footsteps cease as the strangers froze.

Heloise leapt down from the machine, landed on her feet, jogging until she tripped over Onas's sleeping form, curled against the altar where he was supposed to have been keeping watch.

"Xilyka!" Heloise shouted, taking a long step to keep from falling, checking her forward momentum against one of the candelabra, sending it to the floor with a crash. "Wake! Wake! Danger! Wake!"

Her eyes were already adjusting to the darkness as she turned. She could see her mother rising up on one elbow, shaking her father's shoulder. Barnard was also rising, and Xilyka had sprung already to her feet, a sheaf of blades fanning out in her hand.

Beyond them were six figures, woven from threads of shadow, living darkness in human shape, and they sprang after her, flowing around the machine, raising their weapons to strike.

Heloise recognized their slim blades, the black cloth shrouding every inch of skin.

The Black-and-Grays.

But Heloise barely glanced at them. Her gaze was fixed over their shoulders at something far more horrifying.

Sigir.

He was clothed, as if he had not slept, and he wore his armor—his iron cuirass and pot helm. In one hand, he held a sharp dagger. In the other, the handle of the chapter house's postern door, still holding it open wide to let the assassins in.

Her mind couldn't process the sight. Sigir who had loved her, who had fought for her, who had wept after the Knitting of Hammersdown, who had sheltered her father. How could he . . . Her mind spun a dozen tales to excuse him. He had been tricked, he had been forced, it wasn't really him. But there was no time to consider it. The Black-and-Grays were upon her, and Xilyka shouldered her out of the way. The Hapti girl swept her arm across her chest, letting the thin, flat knives fly.

The assassins leapt aside, rolling on their shoulders and landing on their feet, but one of the knives sank deep into one Black-and-Gray's chest and he stumbled as he tried to rise, then collapsed. Two of the assassins rushed Heloise, one from each side, knocking into the machine and sending it rocking on its long metal legs. Her mind tried to reconcile it all, the sight of Sigir holding the door wide, these strange shadow men. *This is just a dream. There's no need to fight. You will wake any moment now.*

One of the assassins' swords flicked in and Heloise raised her knife-hand to parry it. The shock against the collar tight around her wrist reminded her she was wrong, jolting all thoughts of dreams from her mind. The other assassin missed her by an inch, and then Onas shouted and Heloise could see the Sindi boy tackle the Black-and-Gray, his hooked knife rising and falling as he plunged it into the assassin's face.

The remaining three assassins tried to find a way to assist their fellows, but they were blocked by the war-machine, its huge metal bulk covering most of the floor between the postern door and the altar, and they could not strike without hitting their own. Onas dropped the man he had killed and spun his way toward them, while Xilyka drew another handful of knives.

The assassin fighting Heloise pushed his sword down, forcing Heloise's knife aside, and stabbed at her face with his dagger. She jerked aside, but still felt the slim metal pierce her cheek, bursting through her teeth in an explosion of pain that made her vision go gray. Her mouth filled with the taste of blood and she staggered back, screaming. The assassin advanced, raising his sword for the death blow.

And then his head was gone, and Barnard's forge hammer swept past. The momentum of the swing carried the huge tinker around in a circle, sent him wheeling back into the remaining assassins. Heloise looked in vain for Sigir, but the pain in her face was so great that her single eye watered, and she couldn't find him. One of the three remaining assassins dropped, gurgling, one of Xilyka's knives in his throat. Another was being driven back by the blur of Onas's flashing knives, sparks flying as he attempted to parry the Sindi boy's whirling onslaught. The Black-and-Gray did his best, but Onas's weapons weaved as if they were alive, darting over and under the assassin's sword to bury themselves in his throat.

The last assassin fell back, to where Leuba was helping Samson to his feet. He kicked Samson in the face, sending Heloise's father tumbling backward. Leuba scrambled after Samson, calling his name. *No!* Heloise thought, *You can't help him by turning your back on the enemy!* She hated her mother in that moment, weak, powerless, doing precisely the wrong thing.

The assassin kept his eyes on Barnard as he casually stabbed down with his dagger, slipping the slim blade between Leuba's shoulder blades.

Heloise and Barnard shouted in time, and the huge tinker brought his hammer down. The assassin raised his sword to parry, but the strength of the blow shattered the blade, and the hammer crunched into the man's shoulder, driving him to a knee.

She watched her mother go still, sprawled over her father. Heloise shrieked, leaping for them. An arm across her chest held her back.

She recognized the touch of the calloused palm, the pattern of hair on the back of the hand.

Sigir.

She threw an elbow behind her, was rewarded by stinging pain as it collided with Sigir's metal breastplate. She could hear the jingling of his chain of office against it, could smell his sour breath as he pulled her close. His beard was wet. *Tears*, she realized. *He's crying.*

"Forgive me, Heloise." His voice was soft, even gentle, full of the same sorrow and care she'd heard when he'd spoken to her after Hammersdown. "I must think of the whole village."

She twisted, knowing what was coming, almost feeling more than seeing the knife flash as he brought it down past her face, plunging it to its hilt into her chest.

There was no pain, only a cold, wet feeling in her lungs. Sigir released her and she whirled on him, striking out with her knife-hand, but her movements were coming to her as if from a long way off, her body responding like the war-machine did when its seethestone was nearly spent, sluggish and slow. The Maior parried the blow easily, the look of kind sorrow never leaving his face. That look made her all the more furious, and she struggled to reach him, only now she was somehow facing the cold stone of the floor. *I've fallen,* she thought dimly. *How did I get here?*

And then she heard her father give a strangled cry, and everything went black.

12

DIE TO MAKE IT SO

My hands quenched by the blood of the righteous, and still
they burn. By blood and fire are they cleansed, that they
may in turn cleanse.
The blood cleanses in the shedding, making pure, but the
fire cleanses the purest of all.
The fire is both My love and My wrath.
Even as it purifies the afflicted, it lights the way,
Even as it warms the cold, it scours,
Even as it feeds the hungry, it drives Mine enemy into the
dark.

—Writ. Ere. VIX. 7

Heloise awoke to a rhythmic smacking sound, not too different from the wet thudding of her mother's fist when she softened a cut of meat by punching it against the cutting board. She tried to sit up, couldn't. The smacking sound went on. There was a grunting to accompany each impact, and she recognized her father's voice. She craned her head to look.

"Be still," Leahlabel said. "You're going to be all right, but there's no sense in taking chances. Just give me another moment."

It was then that the pain reached her, the throbbing of her cheek and her wounded mouth, pulsing in time with the wound in her chest. She breathed weakly, the passage of air clotted and thick, as if a heavy cloth had been tied over her face. The pain pulsed and she spasmed with it, head tilting back, giving her a view of the source of the smacking sound.

Her father held Sigir by the dented collar of his breast plate, was hitting him steadily, over and over and over again. Sigir was slack in his grip, his face purple and swollen so badly that he looked more rotten turnip than man. Heloise reached out with her tongue and felt the hole in her cheek that Leahlabel had healed. The gap was scarred over and whole, but the assassin's knife had taken two of her teeth, and they would not be back.

She realized that her father was grunting words. "You. Killed. My. Wife. You. Killed. My. Wife."

Mother. She jerked upright, shrugging off Leahlabel's hands and scanning the room wildly. Her chest and face screamed at her, but she ignored them.

At last she found her mother. Leuba was gray-faced and cold. Samson had rolled her onto her back and arranged her hands across her chest, one atop the other. If not for the pallor of her skin, she would have looked like she'd fallen asleep while praying.

Heloise felt the same sense of unreality that had accompanied the assassins in the first place, the same numbness. She couldn't even bring herself to be angry with Sigir. It wasn't he who'd killed her mother. The man who did that was somewhere in that bloody pile of black-wreathed limbs at Barnard's feet.

She turned, and Leahlabel wisely backed away, eyes wide with worry. Heloise stalked toward Sigir and gave her father a shove. Surprised, Samson fell away, releasing Sigir to let the Maior's head rebound off the stone, leaving a wet smear. Heloise seized the metal collar and pulled him back up, bringing her knife's sharp point up to his throat. Her wrist throbbed where the collar had chafed against it as she parried the assassin's blow.

"Don't kill me!" the Maior burbled through his split lips. "I didn't want any of this. I didn't kill Leuba!"

"You did," Heloise said, "even if it wasn't your hand on the knife. You killed her and you would have killed me."

He tried to open his swollen eyes, but couldn't manage it. "Heloise . . . you're alive."

"Which means you failed," she said. "All of this . . . betrayal and murder. Turning your back on those who loved you. All for nothing."

"What was I supposed to do?"

"You were supposed to tell them you wouldn't take their coin, or their titles, or whatever they promised you." Heloise could feel grief building behind her cold rage. "You were supposed to keep that door closed."

She stopped speaking for fear that words would fail her, that she would weep before them all. The shock of Sigir's betrayal was fading already, leaving her with the greater shock that, even now, the sight of his battered face pulled at her heartstrings.

There were so many questions. There was so much she wanted to say, but the grief was like a swamp in her chest, and her throat struggled to force out enough air to make the words, "You said that you knew the Order was evil."

"They are," Sigir croaked, "and it doesn't matter. Good and evil are stories, Heloise. I had thought you old enough to be past them, but you've only gotten worse since you got in that blight-touched tinker-engine. You think bloodying your hands makes you a woman grown, but only time can do that."

The rage came roaring back into her. "Only a woman grown can tell that betraying your own people is evil?"

"I didn't betray us, Heloise. I tried to save us."

Heloise patted the pink scar where Leahlabel had healed the wound in her chest, wincing at the pain. "And this is how?"

"Yes!" Sigir roared, his voice finally clear. "You cannot win, Heloise! You can be as righteous as the Emperor himself and still they will kill you, and with you, all of us. Have you not stood on the walls and looked at the army below? You are a *girl*, Heloise. I have fought in a war. We cannot beat them. We can only hope they will spare us."

"They won't spare us," Heloise said, so quietly she wondered if Sigir could hear.

But Sigir did hear. "That is why I followed you," he said, "that is why I was willing to fight for you even here. Because I thought it was the only way I could keep us all alive. But now they have offered me another way."

"And their price was me."

Sigir said nothing, and it stole the last of her strength. She sagged on her feet. She felt her tongue listing into the gap created by her missing teeth. First her eye and now this. The Order was whittling her away, killing her piece by piece.

Sigir cried into the silence. "I had to make a choice! You or the village!"

"And what of the Kipti?" Heloise finally asked. "Surely the Order did not promise to spare them."

"I am the Maior of *Lutet*, Heloise. Not some heretic band."

"They are *people*, Sigir," Heloise said, grateful that he had said something that would allow her to hate him. "You're no different from the Order. You want a world for just one village, and not any others. These people can live because they pray to a throne instead of a wheel. These people can live because their homes are on the ground and not in a wagon. And someone always has to die, so everyone else can live. As if there were no other way."

It was all so . . . stupid. Basina, Clodio, Gunnar, her mother. None of them had to die.

"I want to live in a world where everyone, no matter who they are, dies from growing old, and not because someone else killed them for their own good."

"Everyone wants to live that way, Heloise," Sigir said, "but that isn't the way the world is. And you cannot make your dream real when you're dead."

"But I am not dead." Heloise leaned in close. "In spite of your treachery and your knife I am very much alive. What does that tell you, Sigir? What does that tell you about how you think the world works?"

.   .   .

Sigir tried to speak to her again, but a few short strokes from Samson relieved him of more of his remaining teeth, and he was silent. When the dawn crested, her father cradled her mother in his arms and brought her out to the town common. Barnard and Wolfun had piled wood in a bed of stones, scavenged from one of the many abandoned houses. Leuba looked tiny now, drained of color, and Heloise realized she had always seemed that way to her. The thought made the grief worse, because Leuba had done so much, and had asked for so little in return. *You are dear to me,* she had said to them all, Sigir included. She had been so worried when Heloise had folded herself into the cart to take the gates of Lyse. It had never occurred to Heloise to worry for her, as if Leuba were somehow too . . . gentle, too kind for fate to take notice of her.

The chapter house doors opened wide to admit the sun's first rays, flashing orange and yellow as they topped the town walls, falling on Sigir's swollen face and making him blink. Like her mother, he was scarcely recognizable, both eyes bulbous, purple and slitted, his gap-toothed mouth curling inward. That was good, Heloise didn't think she could bear to look on his old face, the one she had loved for so long. "Time to go, Master Maior," she said. The machine shuddered as she took a step toward him, reaching out with her knife-hand.

"Wait!" His voice whistled through his missing teeth, trying to scramble away from her. Xilyka and Onas held him fast.

"Wait! Heloise, you don't have to do this . . . you . . ."

"Oh, don't be such a baby, Sigir." Samson's voice was dead. He'd laid Leuba on her bed of wood and returned to stand in the doorway. "You've known Leuba too long to miss her funeral."

Heloise hooked the front of Sigir's shirt with the back of her knife point, and the machine's strength lifted him easily. He sagged against the filthy cloth, legs kicking. "Wait!"

But Heloise did not wait. She carried him out to the common, where the villagers and the Traveling People had gathered. They stood around the pile of stone and wood, heads bowed, as if looking at Leuba would somehow sully her. Heloise recognized it as a gesture of respect, and she appreciated it. But like her mother's death, it was useless, needless. Leuba was dead. She didn't care if anyone looked at her or not.

But needless gestures were what people needed, and what they expected of a Palantine. Heloise would at least keep them short. "My grief is too great for words," she said, "so I will use few. My mother is gone, killed by a traitor." Sigir was screaming something, a denial, a plea. Heloise raised her voice to be heard over him until her father's fist bludgeoned him into silence. "I could remind you of what happens when we die, of the purpose and joy we know at the Emperor's right hand. But instead I will ask you to tell me, what does the Writ tell of the Emperor's holy hands?"

"That they are cleansed," the few villagers who had the words of the Writ memorized responded, while the Traveling People kept a respectful silence, "that they are washed in the blood of righteousness."

"His hands are cleansed that they may, in turn, cleanse,"

Heloise recited from memory. "And how has the Emperor told us to cleanse? What manner is most clean?"

The heads came up now, eyes fixing on Sigir. "Fire," Samson's voice rang out over them all. "The flame cleans even as it lights the way. It warms as it scours. It feeds us as it drives our enemies into the dark."

Barnard produced a torch, thrust it into the wood pile. Sigir had begun to kick again, but feebly. He chafed his wrists against the twisted bit of rope that bound them. He was done shouting now, done weeping. It seemed to take forever for the wood to catch, but once it did, the flames leapt hungrily up, rolling over her mother and folding her into their embrace. Heloise straightened her knife-arm, turning Sigir so he could look. He didn't, of course, craned his neck back, lifting his chin away. For a moment, Heloise was enraged, but then she realized it wasn't her mother he was avoiding, it was the heat of the fire.

Good.

"My mother is dead." Heloise had to raise her voice to be heard over the roar of the flames. "She is dead because this man, our friend for years, our leader, killed her. He killed her because he was frightened.

"I'm frightened too," Heloise went on, "we all are. But Sigir was a man grown, and what does the Emperor say of men grown?"

"That he forgives them," the more pious in the crowd responded, "that he is merciful."

"And that," Heloise finished for them, "they must pay for the things they do. Two go into a fire as easily as one, once the flames are kindled. Cleanse and burn, Master Maior."

The machine's long, metal arm thrust him out over the fire and he danced, comically, trying to lift his legs as the flames licked at him. "Samson," he gasped, his words garbled by his broken mouth, "please! Just kill me! For the love you bear me, please end it!"

"For the love I bear you," Samson's voice was brushed steel, "I will not."

Sigir said more, but the flames were catching now, and his words ran together into a long, high wail. The fire crawled up him, making his clothes smoke and flap, his skin shrivel and bubble. He caught much more quickly than the wood had, as if his fear were a combustible thing, dried tinder laid in for this moment.

"Does it hurt?" Heloise whispered, knowing her words were drowned by Sigir's screams and past caring. "It is my mother. It is her vengeance made fire."

His hair caught with a whoosh, and Heloise was amazed at how quickly it was gone, crowning him in greasy, orange-gray gold. The machine's arm held him a good distance away, but even so, Heloise could feel the heat against her face. Even when it became painful, she didn't look away. She kept her eyes on Sigir until his shirt had burned away, and the shriveled blackness of him dropped from her blade and into fire, kicking up a cloud of embers that did their firefly dance over her head.

"Can you fish him out of the fire?" Heloise asked Wolfun. The Town Wall nodded, reaching into the coals with his spear. "And your mother, your eminence?"

"Let her be," Heloise said. "She'll need another round of cleansing after sharing a pyre with that. Bring the Maior up to the wall, and the assassins, too." She turned without looking and made her way toward the rampart, the crowd parting to admit her.

She heard the enemy before she saw them. Music was playing somewhere in their camp, and the sergeants were mustering troops into formation, no doubt expecting the gates to be flung wide at any moment as the assassin's bloody work was concluded.

She felt the smile growing on her face as she mounted the rampart. The buzz of voices was punctuated by shouts as the soldiers saw her, and then immediately settled into stunned silence as she crested the battlements and they realized it was Heloise, alive. A few more cuts on her than she'd had before, but alive.

She drank up their shock, imagined the satisfaction spiraling away from her to her mother's soul, standing beside the Emperor's golden throne. *For you, Mother. It won't make you live, but it is something.*

Heloise could feel the expectant hush below her, rippling out to silence the muttering of the sentries on the wall, of her own friends and family mounting the rampart to join her. The quiet was broken only by the squeaking axles of the handcart Barnard was pushing up to her, piled high with the assassins' corpses, Sigir atop it, twisted, black, and still smoking. Tone and the Emperor's Song were pushing their way to the front of the throng below. Tone was gaping openly, and while the Song's mask covered his mouth, Heloise thought she could see the shock in his eyes.

No, it wouldn't bring her mother back.

But it was still good to see.

"You seem busy," Heloise called down to them. "I hate to interrupt."

"We are busy," Tone gestured at the town, furious, "preparing to put this pile of kindling to the torch."

The Song settled a hand on Tone's shoulder, and the Pilgrim stiffened and went silent.

"Have you come to accept our terms?" The Song's voice was as confident, as beautiful as it had ever been, but Heloise thought she could detect an undercurrent of uncertainty.

"Thank you, no," she replied. "Rather, you seem to have left some things in my chapter house, and it wouldn't be right of me to hold them. We villagers try to be kind to our neighbors." She gestured to Barnard, and the huge tinker upended the cart with a grunt. Heloise could hear the wet smacking of the bodies as they bounced off the wall on their way to the ditch at its base.

The Song's eyes never left hers, but Tone watched the tumbling bodies come down. When he finally looked back up at her, the fury on his face took her breath away, but she forced herself to smile wider, as sweetly as if the corpses were a festival gift. "We figured you'd be hungry. Such a big army must have foraged everything there was to eat in a night or two. Did our best to carve them up for you, so you can share them out easier. Your traitor-spy," she gestured to Sigir's blackened corpse, seamed now in red where the charred skin had split during its fall, "we tried to cook for you. Apologies, I'm afraid he's overdone."

She glanced at her father out of the corner of her eye. His eyes were locked on Tone, his mouth set in a fierce grin. It lifted her heart. After all that had happened, she could at least give him this.

"You are less than animals," Tone called up to them.

"That's no way to talk to a friend who is trying to feed you. There's enough there for a night at least. More, if you're careful with sharing it out."

"We will not need it." The Song made no effort at beauty now. "We are through waiting."

He turned, rattling his sword out of his scabbard and holding it over his head. Trumpets sounded, and the silence splintered as the army sprang into action, scrambling to their siege engines, rallying to their companies, sounding the advance.

Heloise turned to her father. "They are coming."

Samson nodded. "I love you, my dove. And I wish . . . I wish it could have been different."

Heloise felt her heart swell, tears pricking at the corner of her eye. She fought it down. The enemy was coming. She stretched her ripped cheek into a smile that must have looked horrifying.

"No, Father," she said, sweeping her knife-arm out to indicate the massing enemy. "Things *are* different." And then the first shouts rose from her archers on the wall, as the enemy skirmishers advanced into range.

13

BREAKING STORM

*I can say it now, I suppose. I was at the Battle of the Bend.
I saw the Red Lords checked and driven back. I went to
the end of the march and back again, stood my post until
the disband sounded and I could go back to my Leuba. The
Captain-General gave us a rousing speech. Told us how
proud we could all be that we'd brought the Red Lords beneath the shadow of the Throne. We may be levy, but we're
no fools. The Red Lords and their "free peoples" are outside the shadow, not beneath it. They worship as they will
and do as they will, so long as they keep to the Gold Coast.
Barnard thinks they're just biding their time to make another go, but it's been winter after winter now, and I'm
betting they're just as keen to keep their border as we are.*

—From the journal of Samson Factor

The enemy's skirmishers were a mixed bunch. Some were levy,
boys and old men wielding bows and slings they normally used
to hunt rabbits or pheasants for their table. Others were professional soldiers in mail or quilted jackets and steel helmets. Their
bows were longer, their arrows scrawled with words from the Writ.
They shot singly, probing range and angle.

Wolfun raised a hand, calling to his men to wait. "We have precious few arrows. Mark your targets and do not waste a shot."

When one of the younger boys let his fear get the better of him, loosing an arrow to quiver uselessly in the dirt at the base of the wall, Wolfun admonished him with a stream of curses that would have made Samson blush.

The enemy had no such worries. Their quivers were full to bursting, and Heloise could see wagons among the tents, piled high with sacks of stones and sheaves of arrows bundled in white cloth. Their ranging shots came closer, and Heloise began to hear the twanging of the bowstrings and the pattering of arrowheads as they drew sparks from the stone wall, higher and higher as the archers adjusted their aim.

"Your eminence," Onas said, "we should get you to safety."

She did her best to ignore the nearness of him, to treat him as his role—her bodyguard—required, but the conversation between them in the boneyard still curdled in her belly. She could feel his gaze on her, did her best to avoid it.

Xilyka laughed. "Do you honestly think that she will quit the walls?"

Onas looked annoyed. "At least let us get you behind an embrasure."

Heloise tore her eyes from the arrow duel as Wolfun bellowed the order to shoot back. "All right, but make sure it's somewhere everyone can see me. And I need to be able to see the fighting."

Onas led her to a wooden embrasure a good distance from the nearest pile of the fire-flower casks. Neither the sentries on the wall nor the attackers below were great marksmen, and for at least a quarter candle Heloise saw nothing more than shouting and dodging, archers ducking behind the battlements or racing to glean arrows.

Then, suddenly, there was a meaty thunk beside her and one

of the sentries sank to his knees, an arrow protruding from his open mouth. Below him, an enemy soldier sank to his knees as an arrow clanged loudly against his helmet, and one of the levy boys kicked on his side, an arrow sinking into his groin.

"Guess we've found our range," Wolfun mused, then tapped another one of the sentries on his shoulder. "Come off the wall, Cedric, you're shot through."

The man, clean-shaven and gray haired, started as if waking from a long nap. He blinked at the arrow protruding from his arm. "By the Throne . . ." He sounded sleepy.

"Just come off the wall," Wolfun said, "and get a bandage around it. Then come right back. We can't spare you."

Wolfun was right. The defenders looked so sparse, huge gaps between them. Below them, the enemy skirmishers seemed a boiling cauldron in comparison. For every arrow one of her own loosed, the enemy loosed five. Cedric was back in a moment, arm tied in a bandage, face pale. But he drew his bow all the same, hand shaking, arrow flying wide. He grit his teeth, drew, and aimed again.

Heloise heard a creak like a forest groaning, as if the greatest cart in the world were rolling down a pitted track. She glanced up to see the wooden siege tower, as tall as the wall, rumbling forward. The levy were lined up like oxen before the tower, hauling away at ropes as thick as a man's arm. As the tower cleared the line of tents, Heloise could see the army's engineers running alongside, ladling fat onto the wheels from wooden buckets. Smoke rose from the wheels just the same. Soldiers were lined up behind the tower, pushing, their weapons strapped across their backs. They went back in rows past her vision, more behind this single tower than she had in her entire force.

She gauged where the tower would reach the rampart and moved to intercept it, but stopped at a touch from Xilyka. "Not going to try to stop you," the Hapti girl said, never taking her eyes from the rocking tower, "but you've got some time yet. No sense exposing yourself to arrows before you must."

Heloise heard a gasping cough and looked to her left, where Leahlabel had dragged the fallen sentry behind one of the watch towers. The arrow was gone from his mouth and his chest shuddered weakly, but he was alive. Leahlabel propped him up against the tower wall and turned to Giorgi, who was helping another sentry to her, an arrow sprouting from his chest. Leahlabel helped him onto his back and set her hands on him, eyes closed.

The skirmishers were falling back, and Heloise could see troops of the uhlans lining up in columns, each with a wide shield in his left hand, and the rung of a long scaling ladder in his right. Their lances were looped across their backs by loose leather thongs. Short, curved swords hung at their waists. At the head of each column was an armored knight, curved wings arcing over his shoulders, jeweled sword in one hand, wing-shaped shield in the other.

"Here they come," Wolfun said. He turned to Giorgi. "Whatever tricks you've been saving, now would be the time to spring them."

Giorgi nodded to where Tillie crouched beside Leahlabel. The Mother barked an order and a row of knife-dancers streamed past her to crouch behind the wooden embrasures. Barnard appeared at Heloise's side with Guntar, forge hammers ready. Samson had found a spear. Not the long pike of his levy days, but closer than any other weapon he'd held since the Knitting. They watched the tower trundle closer and closer, the men with the ladders keeping careful pace.

At last, Heloise heard the sergeants bellow an order, and the enemy archers withdrew, falling back to the wings of the advancing troops. Heloise could see the Song astride his horse beside the black tent. It was impossible to tell with the gold mask across his face, but she couldn't shake the feeling that he was smiling. There was no sign of Tone, but if she knew the Pilgrim at all, she didn't doubt he was in the assaulting force somewhere. That was good. If she did nothing else in this battle, she could find and kill him at least.

With each step, she waited for the sentries' arrows to fall on the uhlans, to hear the plinking of sharp metal off the armor of the knights. Surely they were in range now? She turned to Wolfun and saw the sentries ducking down behind the battlements, their quivers all but empty. She felt the muscles in her thighs clenching, her body tensing.

The tower paused and she heard a fainter creaking of great wooden wheels. She looked left and right, desperately seeking what had caused the noise. The ram! Where was the ram?!

The Town Wall glanced to Giorgi, who shook his head, mouthing, *Not yet.*

Wolfun cursed and turned to his men. "Loose what you have left. Pick your targets. Once you're dry, go to rocks." The men nodded and rose, shooting arrows at the ladder bearers. A few of them plinked off the armored knights, but others found their marks, sending levy or lighter armored soldiers screaming to their knees. It made no difference. There were too many men holding to too many rungs, and the loss of one, or two, or even three on a ladder didn't so much as slow them. As they came nearer, the knife-casters rose, sending their flat blades flicking out into the approaching mass, men packed so closely it was difficult to miss. The knife blades were heavier, wider, and one of the knights was felled now, sitting down hard with a grunt, the knife handle still quivering in his knee.

None of the casters even bothered to target the tower. The thick wooden beams would have been proof against any blade.

The tower's shadow fell across them now, a stretching column of black. Heloise strode out into it, shrugging off Onas's efforts to hold her back. She let the cool shade wash over her, banged her knife-arm against her shield edge, eyes fixed on the tower's ramp, waiting for it to drop. "Come on," she whispered. "Come on."

"Not just yet, your eminence," Wolfun said. "Might want to find some cover."

Heloise glanced at him, irritated at having her battle-focus interrupted, and noticed the Town Wall had a burning brand in one hand.

"Heloise, come on!" her father called to her, and she reluctantly let Onas and Xilyka lead her back behind the battlement as Wolfun lit the first cask and kicked it hard, sending it over the wall's edge.

Heloise crouched, wincing, waiting for the boom that she'd always heard precede the glorious flash of color of a festival fireflower. It never came. Perhaps the fire on the cask had gone out as it fell. Perhaps it had broken on the way down. Perhaps it simply did not work at all. Heloise hadn't realized how much the prospect of the explosion had frightened her until she felt the muscles in her back unknot. At the festivals, she had always thrust her fingers in her ears to shut out the thunderous crack of explosions, but if the suit didn't prevent her from doing it now, her missing hand certainly did.

At last, she began to stand, "I don't think it . . ."

There was a faint splintering of wood from the base of the wall, followed by the whooshing rush of spreading flame. By the time she'd realized the boom that followed had sounded, her ears were already ringing, her eye watering. Had it not been for the machine's weight, she might have fallen off the rampart.

The screaming from below reached her, then, howls of agony. The tower stopped rolling, mere feet from the rampart, shouts of alarm sounding from the men behind it. Heloise leaned forward to look over the rampart's edge.

Below her, a wound had opened in the field of men. Two of the ladders were broken, splintered wood fragments still smoking in the churned mud. Men were running, burning, crisping to the same slow shriveled black as Sigir, arms waving, howling out the last of their lives. Still others lay on the ground, bodies pocked with black holes smeared with red. Here and there was an arm, a leg, a jellied pool of gray that could only have been someone's guts. The base of the wall was scarred black and burning, a long smear of thick blood splashed up it as high as a man was tall.

A rain struck her then, a gentle patter against the machine's metal frame. At first, it was the high chiming of bits of metal or stone, but that was soon replaced with the softer touch of what Heloise assumed was clods of earth, until the smell confirmed it was smoking meat. She shuddered, crouched again as Wolfun sent a second burning cask over the side, and a third. The wait didn't seem so long now, and the thundering cracks barely made her wince.

When she finally stood, the ladder teams had mostly scattered, with only two farther down the wall still holding together. They stood in stunned silence, gaping open-mouthed at the carnage. One of the knights was hobbling across the field, his shield burning brightly. As Heloise watched, he bent to retrieve a severed arm, still clad in blackened armor.

Shouts from behind the tower, and Heloise saw the archers come surging to the fore again, not individual skirmishers this time, but rank upon rank of professional bowmen. They deployed in lines and fired by ranks, sending waves of arrows sheeting past the rampart. Heloise dropped along with the rest of the defenders, hearing the whooshing of the flights of arrows skimming just overhead. A moment later, she heard the creaking groan of the tower wheels again. Wolfun tried to raise his head, dropped back down as an arrow came whistling past. Another of his sentries was not so lucky, fell back to the rampart with an arrow in his eye. His comrade began dragging him toward Leahlabel, but the Sindi woman shook her head. "He's gone."

"They're making us keep our heads down long enough to get the tower in place," Wolfun said. "Going to be sword work here soon."

The arrows kept flying as the tower's shadow grew over them, the creaking of the wheels getting louder and louder. Heloise fought the urge to stand and risk herself in the storm of missiles. Surely the archers would stop shooting once the ramp lowered and the enemy spilled out? Heloise suddenly wasn't so sure. The enemy could sustain the losses far better than her force could.

At last the creaking stopped, and Heloise heard the gentle bump of the tower's side touching the wall. Two soft plunks to her left told her that scaling ladders had been placed as well.

The arrows stopped.

And then, everything happened at once.

Giorgi stood, shouting, sweeping his thick hands up toward the sky. The flames on the ground roared as if in answer, shooting upward until they topped the wall, spreading and blooming like flickering flowers. Men leapt from them, shimmering men of fire, like Heloise had seen outside the Sindi camp not so long ago. They threw themselves at the tower, their man-shapes suddenly going flat as they slipped between the cracks in the beams.

The ramp from the tower fell, heavy wood thudding against the stone, smashing the wooden embrasure flat. The enemy came pouring out, but they were screaming, burning, throwing down their shields to beat at the fires behind their armor. A few of them flailed with swords or spears against the flame-men, the metal edges passing through the burning air with no effect at all.

Into this press waded the knife-dancers, hooked blades whirling. They danced together, never speaking, but interleaving so seamlessly Heloise imagined they could read one another's thoughts. The rampart was only wide enough to permit two to stand abreast, their spinning blades flashing past one another without clashing. As one dancer began panting, their shoulders drooping with the effort of keeping the knives moving, another would whirl into position, switching places in an elegant pattern that Heloise would have sworn had been rehearsed. In the face of such precision, the enemy's superior numbers counted for nothing. The few who weren't futilely attempting to fight the flame-men, or busy ripping off their burning surcoats, were driven stumbling back by the hooked knives. Some of the attackers fled back into the siege tower, others fanned out on the rampart farthest away from the knife-dancers. The rampart ended at the edge of one of the wall's wooden watchtowers, and the soldiers began to pack up against it, driven back by the knife-dancers' onslaught. When the space there was full, Heloise watched in horror as several of the soldiers chose to jump from the wall rather than risk the burning death in the tower, or the bladed death on the rampart.

Heloise stared stupidly, the braced tension in her limbs curdling, sickening her now that she couldn't act. She had been so ready to fight, only to find that she wasn't needed. Xilyka and Onas stood between her and the combat, weapons ready, and Heloise knew they were far more concerned with preventing her from reaching the fighting than the fighting from reaching her.

She heard her father grunt, and whirled to see him thrust his spear at the first of the enemy levy, clambering onto the rampart from the scaling ladders. The climber was waving a long meat cleaver, making desperate swipes at the spearhead, cowering at the ladder's top. A butcher, then. Heloise could hear his comrades shouting at him to clear the ladder top. Her father thrust again, and the butcher batted the blow away, cringing back before his fellows shoved him forward and off the ladder. A part of Heloise wanted the poor man to survive. He was just a terrified villager shoved on into a battle, but she knew this frightened man would be just as keen to use his cleaver on her father if he thought it would spare him. For a moment, Heloise was frozen, torn between going to his aid and his destruction.

In the end, her father made the decision for her, thrusting low through the butcher's belly. Heloise saw the spear point burst through his back, and the butcher's eyes went wide, his face shocked and hurt, as if to say, How could you? And then her father twisted the spear and yanked it out, and the butcher was collapsing, the man behind him surging over the rampart, stumbling over the butcher, falling on his face. Her father speared him, too, driving the point through the top of his bare head.

Another stream of levy appeared at the top of a second ladder, rushing onto the rampart. Barnard advanced to meet them, knocking one man and then another from the wall with great sweeps of his hammer.

Heloise now did her own comic dance, swinging left and then right, trying to aid the knife-dancers, then her father, and back again. Each time, Onas and Xilyka moved to block her, forcing her to choose between standing still or crushing them underfoot. "Move, damn you!" Heloise shouted.

"They don't need your help!" Onas shouted back. "We must keep you safe!"

Heloise struggled with the rage building inside of her. There was fighting all around her, people dying for her, and her guard wouldn't let her help.

A shout rose from the postern gate. There were just two sentries in the towers there. Little boys left behind as lookouts as every available fighter scrambled to meet the attack unfolding on the western wall. The shout was followed by a booming crunch. "The ram!" Heloise could hear the voices drifting toward her.

Another boom. She could see the postern watchtowers tremble, the top of the gate shuddering between them.

The ram. They rolled it to the postern gate. That gate was shaking, and above it just two young boys, their screams coming higher and more hysterical. Beyond the gate she could see the dust plume kicked up by hundreds of marching feet, the enemy soldiers eagerly awaiting entrance into the town.

The world seemed to slow, as if some wizardry had forced time to a crawl. Heloise turned, saw Onas and Xilyka turn with her, leaning their bodies to anticipate the direction of her movement and intervene, thinking to stop her from moving farther along the rampart in the direction of the postern gate.

But Heloise wasn't moving farther along the rampart. She squatted, the machine's metal legs following suit, and when she pushed off, the tinker-engine leant its strength to a giant leap, sending her up and over her guards, her father and Barnard at the scaling ladders, Leahlabel tending to the wounded, and Giorgi with his brow furrowed in concentration, egging his flame-men on. She heard Onas shouting her name as she flew down the inside of the wall, landed on the soft grass of the common, the machine absorbing some of the impact, but not enough to keep her teeth from clicking together.

She ignored him, setting the machine to running toward where the postern gate was shuddering under the ram's assault, each stride nearly as long as her leap, the gate growing in her vision. The iron bands were bulging now, and she could see some of the black-headed rivets popping free. One of the boys was sagging limp over the edge of the tower railing, an arrow projecting from his cheek. *Hold on,* Heloise projected the thought at the straining gate, as if she could will it to hold until she could arrive. *Hold*

212 · MYKE COLE

on. The gate splintered, one of the beams sagging inward like a gapped tooth.

She could hear shouting, the light thudding of feet behind her, but she ignored it, her world shrinking to the gate and the towers above. Heloise reached the gate just as it shuddered, the locking bar groaning and cracking, and she squatted again, pushing the machine's metal legs as hard as she could, jumping straight into the air.

She knew it wasn't enough the moment the machine's feet left the ground. The tinker-engine was powerful, but the metal and leather around her was heavy, and the wall, while not enormous, was still high enough, and she would have to clear the watchtowers. The wood rushed past her, a gray-brown blur that slowed as the jump lost momentum, until at last the tower railing appeared with the boy's corpse draped across it, and she could see the cracks in the boards. She could feel the ground beneath her grasping hungrily at the heavy machine. *No.*

Heloise realized with a start that she'd shouted the word, reaching up with the corner of her shield and slamming it into the tower roof, pushing down with all her might. The thrust gave her what she needed to get over the top, and she felt the tower roof tripping her, sending the machine to its knees, skidding across its wooden shingles, tumbling off the other side.

The sky and the ground changed places and she fell down the gate's far side. She could hear the ram jingling against its chains, the shouts of the soldiers around it as they looked up and saw her hurtling toward them. She righted, getting the machine's feet under her, the world blurring again, the horizon rushing past. She glanced down to ensure that the machine's metal feet were positioned correctly, had only an instant to look at the ram's tar-soaked roof.

The impact was much less than she'd expected. Where the

ground was leagues deep, the ram's roof wasn't more than a handspan of wood shingles. Heloise barely felt it break as the machine's massive weight punched through it, spraying her face with splinters, the oddly pleasant smell of pitch and pine. She shut her eyes against the sharp fragments of wood, but she could hear the shrieking of the chains as the machine straddled the long, wooden ram, the wood thunking against the metal crotch, holding for a moment and finally ripping free to drop into the mud.

The screaming began, and Heloise opened her eyes. The ram's interior was like a comfy cottage, shadows gathering in the eaves, curling back from the light admitted by the hole she had punched in the roof. One of the supporting beams had fallen inward, crushing two of the soldiers flat. A third man, one of the uhlans, was the source of the screaming. He must have been holding the back of the ram, and he lay beneath the fallen log, arms smashed under its weight, the pale shredded skin visible around its edges, seeping crimson into the earth. There were another eight men crowded in there with her, uhlans and levy, all wide-eyed and backed against the thick walls. They wore what little armor they'd retained for the work of swinging the great log, but had left their weapons behind.

Not that weapons would have done them any good.

Because Heloise wasn't thinking of the reluctant levy, forced into the fight, and how she didn't want to hurt them. She was only thinking of her mother, her pale flesh blackening in the crackling pyre, of Sigir and his sad eyes, the look of grief as he'd plunged the knife into her chest.

She turned to one of the levy, a boy no older than Onas, so terrified that he gibbered, drooling, his palms flat against the ram's wall, as if he could somehow push himself through it.

"We fought the Order!" Heloise screamed at him, using her

shield to sweep aside one of the uhlans who found the courage to charge her.

"We're the same as you and we fought them!" She stabbed the levy boy, the knife going through his gut and the wall behind. She kept pushing, driving the point in, until it reached its end and the machine's metal fist crushed his ribs, the cracks sounding louder than the splintering wood when she'd crashed through the roof.

She leaned in, drilling her gaze into his dying eyes. "We fought them. Why couldn't you?"

The anger fled as abruptly as it came, leaving hollow, exhausted grief in its place. "Why couldn't you?" she whispered, drawing the knife out, leaving him to slump slowly down the wall, leaving a trail of fresh blood as wide as his shoulders.

One of the other levy, an older man, screamed the boy's name and rushed at her. His father, no doubt, or an uncle. It didn't matter. Kin or not, grieved or not, he would open the postern gate. He would let the Order in. There was nothing she could do for him. She met him with the corner of the shield, bringing it down so hard against his shoulder that she snapped him in half, folding him over sideways to flop like a landed fish against the ram's iron-shod head.

The rest of them fled after that, tripping over one another, jamming the ram's small doorway, meant to protect those inside from attack, but not to allow for easy exit. Heloise worked like the machine itself, cool and efficient, stabbing and smashing until they were a barricade of corpses, blocking the soldiers and Pilgrims outside, who at first tried to come to their comrades' rescue and finally stood back, watching in horror.

They tried shooting arrows and casting javelins in through the tiny opening, and then Heloise heard the crackle of flames as they finally gave up and set fire to the structure. A soldier made to force the doorway, but after Heloise gutted him and added his corpse to the pile, no one else made the attempt. And when at last the heat grew too great, Heloise squatted again, and leapt back out the hole she'd created, perched delicately on the ram's peak, then jumped again, clearing the tower easily this time, and disappearing down the far side to land beside Onas and Xilyka, panting from their long run to the gate. Two of the townsfolk had joined them, hastily nailing boards crisscross along the cracks in the gate. As Heloise watched, a third scrambled up the tower and began hurling rocks down the other side.

"Don't . . ." Onas panted, "run away like that."

"Had to be done," Heloise's spoke through the cloud of her grief, her voice coming as if from a long way off. "Had to be done," she repeated. What her father had said after the Knitting, when he excused the slaughter of Hammersdown.

Onas misunderstood her, his eyes fixed on the gate. "Someone else could have done it."

"No." Heloise looked up. "It had to be me."

More townsfolk arrived, racing up the rampart to cram into the towers, hurling stones. Children rummaged through the grass in the shade of the tower walls, finding stones big enough that it took two of them to lift, and walked them ponderously up to their parents on the wall.

"That won't hold," Onas said, watching them.

"It will, for now," Xilyka said.

"It will have to," Heloise said, looking at the wall she'd come from, where the siege tower was burning brightly now. The rampart was crammed with bodies now, so many that it looked as if it were boiling. "Are we winning?"

"We're holding," Onas said. "There's no need for you to . . ."

But she was already running, slow enough that they could keep pace with her, not because she needed their protection, but because they were two more bodies to throw into the fight, because she was not asking them to do anything she wasn't about to do herself. They did not disappoint, running fast enough that she actually lengthened the machine's stride. When she saw they had mounted the rampart, she leapt for it herself, coming down on the parapet beside Leahlabel.

The Sindi Mother knelt, her hands on the belly of a knife-dancer, brow furrowed in concentration. Giorgi slumped beside her, his face gray, a pink-scarred wound freshly healed in his thigh. His flame-men were gone, but they had done their work well, and the enemy position on the rampart was still burning brightly. The soldiers held one of the watchtowers, and had built a barricade beneath it, walling off the rampart with their own blackened corpses and timbers hacked from the burning siege tower. The knife-casters stood off at a distance, flat knives held at the ready, sending them shooting through the flames whenever one of the enemy was stupid enough to raise his head above the burning beams.

It was a stalemate, but a stalemate that favored the attackers. As Heloise watched, two more ladder teams raced forward below the wall. Behind them came a column of gray-cloaked Pilgrims. The Order joining the fight at last.

"We have to clear the rampart," Samson shouted over his shoulder, his words cracking as he saw that Heloise had returned. He grunted at her and turned back to the barricade, thrusting with his spear, trying to unseat one of the broken pieces of wood.

Barnard rested on the haft of his hammer, but Heloise could see the muscles in his shoulders bunching as he prepared to take it up again. "Don't be a damn fool, Barnard," Samson groused at him.

"That barricade has got to go, Samson. You're not going to break it with a Throne-cursed spear."

"I just need some time," Samson grunted, sending one of the

blackened corpses tumbling off the top. The enemy soldiers lurched back as it fell, then raced forward to add another beam to the top.

"We don't have time!" Barnard swept his hammer up.

"He's right," Heloise said as she pushed past them both, ignoring their shouts. The enemy cried out and she saw three archers standing to shoot her. One fell screaming, a Hapti knife buried in his chest, and the other two vanished as Heloise brought the shield in front of her, but she could hear the dull pings as their arrowheads ricocheted off the metal surface.

She lowered her shoulder, and felt the barricade break apart as the machine surged through it. Men screamed as they were knocked from the rampart. She could hear the screeching of blades, wild swings scraping the machine's metal frame. She heard a roar and the scraping stopped, punctuated by more screams as Barnard appeared on her left, swinging his hammer, each strike sending two or three of the enemy falling to their deaths below. She could see the point of her father's spear, striking beneath her arm, whisking in to hole an enemy uhlan in the gut before sliding out again, then darting in again to find some other bit of unprotected flesh. She felt the touch of something heavy on the machine's shoulder, and then Onas was leaping off her, spinning into the enemy, knives blurring out to send the enemy scrambling back. Heloise and her people surged forward.

In moments, they had passed the burning remnants of the siege tower, and the press of bodies went suddenly tight. They had reached the end of the rampart, where the base of the wall's watchtower interrupted it. The enemy could run no farther. She could feel them crushed against the surface of her shield, scrambling to reach her, Barnard and her father pressed against the machine's back. She tried to draw her knife-hand up to strike, heard Xilyka cry out as the movement pushed the Hapti girl dangerously close to the rampart's edge. They were packed much too close to move. It was all right. Heloise didn't need her knife. The weight of the machine would be enough. She leaned forward, letting the machine's weight push the shield, and heard the coughing gasp of the man on the other side as he was crushed against his fellows.

A flash of gray drew her eyes down to the rampart's edge. Hooks were glinting in the sunlight as the ladder attached to them rattled. She heard the jingling of iron chains.

"The ladders!" Heloise called to Xilyka. "Get them off!"

She heard the Hapti girl grunting as she tried to move through the press of bodies to reach the trembling ladder, as the first of the gray hoods appeared over the rampart's edge, but she could not move. She threw a knife instead, but the jostling of the fight would not allow her to aim. The blade struck the Pilgrim on the shoulder, went spinning harmlessly off into the empty air.

And then the man was up, his hood flying back, his teeth bared. He balanced easily on the rampart's edge, one boot hooked through the ladder's top rung, the other over the battlement, his flail held by the end of the haft, high over his head. He swept it down, the weapon reaching well past Heloise and her guard, and into the press of bodies behind her. Heloise did not recognize the voices that screamed and cursed, but she could tell they were Traveling People, and when the Pilgrim brought his weapon back up, the flail head was bloody.

He laughed. "Be cleansed! Be quit of heresy! Fall beneath His glory!" The flail came down again. Heloise reached for him, nearly sent Xilyka tumbling again. "Someone stop him!"

Onas turned from the enemy soldiers to the Pilgrim, and was driven back by a great sweep of the flail that would have struck him were it not for Heloise's shield corner catching the haft. At last, her father thrust his spear, the point coming in low, from between the machine's legs. It caught the Pilgrim in his groin, turning his laughter into a high-pitched shriek, sending him tumbling from the wall. Within moments, another Pilgrim had scrambled up, hooking his feet in the same way, anchoring him in place. Heloise's stomach fell. *They can do this all day.*

She felt her shield shoved, jerked her head to the side as a blade came whickering over the top edge. "The Throne!" A shout rose from the enemy pressed against the tower's edge, rallying at the sight of their Pilgrims in the fight at last. "The Throne!"

She felt a tug as Xilyka scrambled up her knife-arm, racing to find a grip as the machine was shoved backward. The sentry behind her was not so quick, and Heloise felt him lose his balance as the machine pushed him, toppling off the wall.

"Spread out!" Heloise shouted. "Make room!" But her mouth was pointed at the enemy, and even if she had been facing her own force, they wouldn't have been able to hear her over the din.

Slowly, the defenders were pushed back, until the Pilgrim was able to come off the ladder and stand on the rampart. Another swarmed up behind him, and another. *No,* Heloise thought. She had stopped the ram. She had killed that boy. They couldn't lose the wall this way, not now. But the momentum couldn't be denied. She threw her weight behind the shield and pushed with everything she had, but she only managed to slow, not stop, what was becoming an insurmountable tide. There was a drumming against her shield. A man scrambled over the top, his short hatchet drawing sparks as it clanged against the metal frame above her head. She ducked, instinctively, punched out with her knife-hand, spitting the man through his mouth and knocking him off her shield. There was another roar, and she was shoved backward again.

"Heloise!" A woman's voice, older, she recognized it. Florea. "Heloise, hold them for a moment longer!"

"I can't!" Heloise tried to yell. Flail heads drummed on her shield now. She could hear the plinking of the spikes against the surface. A Pilgrim had replaced the man she'd stabbed through the mouth. She could hear his high-born accent thundering at her from the other side of the thick metal.

And then suddenly the pressure was slackening, and Heloise heard shouts of terror from the enemy. She had been pushing so hard that the sudden lack of resistance sent her stumbling forward, the machine overbalancing. It skidded on its metal knees, sliding on the rampart to the top of the scaling ladder, suddenly empty. She looked to her left and saw Xilyka, Barnard, and her father staring open-mouthed over the wall. To her right the enemy was shrieking, cramming themselves back against the base of the watchtower, waving swords and spears as if they were trying to ward something off. Only three Pilgrims remained among them, writhing and wriggling on the rampart, their gray cloaks bound fast to them by coils of rope.

Heloise turned to look back down the ladder. The sickening height made her dizzy, but the leather straps holding her fast to the machine's seat kept the sensation from overwhelming her. At least a dozen more Pilgrims lay in the grass at the ladder's base, all bound in ropes, writhing and kicking as their comrades on the rampart. Heloise saw the same ropes twining their way up the ladder, coiling and uncoiling as they came.

Suddenly, her vision focused and she jerked back, the machine groaning as she shot upright.

Not ropes.

Snakes.

"Don't worry, Heloise." Mother Florea's voice sounded strained. "They won't hurt you."

The Hapti woman had come to stand beside Samson, her hands waving in the air over the rampart. She took a few steps closer to the enemy, until she stood beside one of the kicking Pilgrims. "You don't have to worry either," she said to the remaining enemy flattened against the tower's base. "Snakes only eat mice." She nudged the corner of the Pilgrim's gray cloak with one soft boot.

The Pilgrims shrieked and shuddered, their bodies disappearing under the growing mass of writhing serpents. A few were the big forest vipers all children learned to spot before their parents would let them go into the woods, but most of them were small garden snakes, glittering green or mottled gray, coiling and uncoiling, gripping folds in fabric, or a wrist or a finger, and biting, biting, over and over again. The rampart rippled between the ladder and the kicking bodies, and Heloise realized with a start that they were climbing. The snakes were wriggling their way up to the ladder's top and over. She looked back down to see the ground alive with them, the army scuttling back like the ripples in a pond where the stone is thrown, giving the line of snakes as much room as possible.

"You may go," Florea said to the enemy soldiers, "back down the ladder. They will let you climb. They will not harm you. Or you may stay, and they will. Make your choice."

But Heloise barely noticed the remaining enemy as they ran past her to the ladder, as the snakes writhed out of their way, coiled aside to let them begin their descent. She didn't see the soldiers' fearful glances as they passed within a handspan of her, so close that Onas and Xilyka came running to stand at her side, blades drawn.

Her eyes were fixed on the black tent, the one the armored knights had guarded so carefully.

They were gone.

The flaps were open, exposing the gray interior to the shifting light.

It was empty.

14

THE END

To the Song of the false Emperor, from Lord Ludhuige, First Sword to the Senate of the Free Peoples of the Gold Coast: Greetings. I will not waste words—you burn wizards as you traffic in wizardry. You claim to shield the people from devils as you introduce them into our midst. Your throne is heavy, and unbalanced. Soon, it shall topple upon the people of your lands, and they shall bear its full weight. In the name of these people, who have done no wrong, and warrant no hardship, I demand you quit your throne, and kneel before the people you claim to serve, and submit to their judgment.

—Letter from Ludhuige the Red
to the Emperor's Song
on the eve of the Battle of the Bend

Florea kept the snakes up until the last of the enemy had descended and the scaling ladders had been pulled up, cast down the inside of the wall to clatter on the common green. Only then did she exhale, sitting down where she was, and the snakes wriggled over the side of the wall and were gone. "That," she panted, "haven't done something like that since I was a girl."

Xilyka ran to her, kneaded her shoulders. "Are you all right?"

Florea patted her hand. "Didn't become Mother of a band by being soft, girl."

"Sacred Throne," Samson whispered, "we held."

"We did." Barnard wiped a forearm across his brow. "For the Emperor's eye is on his Palantine and her people, always."

Heloise pointed to the empty tent. "The Emperor may have a test in store for us yet."

Barnard shaded his eyes with a hand, grunted. "No matter," he said, "whatever wickedness they had in there, we will meet it as we have met—"

But the shouts had already started, from the front gate this time. "S'pose I better see what the fuss is." Wolfun was already racing down the ramp. "What is it?" he shouted up to the terrified sentries in the watchtowers overlooking the front gate. "What do you see?"

"Wizardry!" they shouted back to him. One of them had a leg over the rampart and was beginning to climb down.

"Stand your ground!" Wolfun shouted back at the man. "We've wizards of our own!" But the man ignored him, reached the ground, and ran from the gate as if it were a portal into hell. Wolfun reached for the fleeing man's shoulder, missed, then cursed and ran for the ladder, racing up it nearly as quickly as he moved running on flat ground. He froze at the tower's edge, looking out past the gate, then turned to where the defenders still stood on the wall.

"Bows!" Wolfun shouted. "Throwing knives! To me!"

Heloise's stomach twisted, and she leapt over the rampart and down to the common for the second time. The squat-leap was easier now, and Heloise reached the watchtower top, vaulting the rail. The machine thumped down beside Wolfun, startling the Town Wall.

He rallied quickly, grabbing the machine's frame and tugging

Heloise toward the railing. "It is some manner of wizardry, though I cannot say what yet."

A knot of figures was approaching the front gate. Heloise immediately recognized the Song, his golden armor gleaming so brightly she had to squint to look at him. Another Sojourner rode along beside him, as well as a knight whose chain of office marked him as a commander. Beside them was a simple Pilgrim, hood thrown back. The sight of Tone's bright blue eyes and feral smile made the anger rise hot and sour up the back of Heloise's throat.

Farther in front of them were six Pilgrims. Three of them held long iron tongs, their ends clamped around the necks of two women and a man, heads shaven, wrapped in bloody rags that had once been clothing. Their limbs were scarcely thicker than the tongs' metal arms. Their heads were down, and they stumbled, their half-starved bodies barely able to keep upright if not for the tongs around their necks. The first three Pilgrims held the tongs as far away from their bodies as they could, their faces turned away. The other three swung jeweled censers, the brass drowned by gouts of thick smoke. Heloise could smell the sweet scent of spice all the way from the watchtower.

Onas and Xilyka came clattering up the ladder, with Giorgi puffing up some moments later. He was still sweating, his face pale. He leaned hard on the railing, panting. "Had to see with my own eyes," he said.

"Can you do anything?" Heloise asked.

Giorgi shook his head. "Maybe tomorrow I can, but not now. The Talented know their limits, if they are any good. Leahlabel and Florea are blown too. Don't expect to fight Talent with Talent now."

"Is it wizardry?"

Giorgi jerked his chin in the direction of the bedraggled prisoners, the tongs driving them ever closer to the gate. "Aye," he said, "those are wizards. I can feel it."

"Do you know what they will do?" Wolfun asked.

Giorgi shook his head. "Nothing good."

More of the defenders were arriving now, clambering up the ladders to pack the towers. A few of them tried ranging shots, but the Pilgrims were careful to keep their charges out of bow range. They stopped their advance, halting their prisoners with a savage jerk of the tongs. The priests with the censers stepped as close to the prisoners as they dared, swinging the canisters at the end of their long brass chains, clouding all in spiced fog.

They chanted, and Heloise's jaw tightened as she made out their words.

"What in the name of the Great Wheel are they doing?" Onas asked.

"Cleansing," Heloise said. "They're chanting prayers to protect them from the corruption of wizardry."

"That . . . it doesn't work like that," Onas said.

"No," Heloise agreed, "it doesn't. And they know it. At least the Order must. This is for the benefit of the soldiers. For us. It is a mummer's show."

"The Talent is no show," Giorgi said, "as I expect we're about to find out."

"Liars," Samson spat, "hypocrites. 'Suffer no wizard to live.'"

"Are you so surprised?" Giorgi asked. "Did you just now learn the nature of men?"

As if on cue, the Pilgrims opened the tongs and the prisoners dropped to their knees, rubbing their necks where the iron had stripped them raw. They raised miserable faces to the wall, and Heloise wasn't certain if they saw her or not.

"Do it!" One of the Pilgrims shouted, but the prisoners only sagged, swaying drunkenly on their knees. At last, the Pilgrim set down his censer, unlooping the chain and flicking it out to rattle in the dirt. Then, as expert as a cattle drover, he sent the brass links clinking and whistling through the air, to fall like a lash across the prisoners' backs. "Do it!" he repeated.

They flinched, but did nothing. The woman's head lolled, and Heloise saw a strand of bloody drool stretching its way slowly from her mouth to the road. "Do it! Do it!" the Pilgrim repeated, sending the chain raking across them again and again, until Heloise saw it coming away bloody.

"They won't." Heloise felt hope blooming in her chest. "They won't do it."

The prisoners' reaction was sudden. One moment they were slack and empty, flinching under the strokes of the chain, and then the next moment the man shot upright, arching his back, arms spread, screaming. An instant later, the other two joined him.

Heloise saw Giorgi jerk back as the wood railing, the support beams, the floor beneath them turned suddenly slick, as if it were coated in river slime. A stink arose, the smell of rotten river mud, of places with too much water and too little light.

"Run," Giorgi's dry-mouthed whisper rose quickly to a yell. "Run! Get down!"

He vaulted over the tower's edge, catching himself on the ladder rung, the wood grown green and slippery. His grip slipped, but he managed to cling to the wood even as he slid down it, his body banging off the rungs until he sprawled on the ground, groaning. He only lay there for an instant, than was up and limping away as fast as he could. Others followed, some not as lucky as Giorgi, plummeting down the ladder to sprawl at the bottom.

Heloise heard a creak, a wet, ripping sound. The tower lurched beneath her feet. She heard the groaning of stone, saw puffs of gray dust blooming out from the wall's edge. She turned to the railing, jammed now with defenders scrambling to escape. There was no way to go over it without crushing them. "Onas! Xilyka!" But her guard were already scrambling up the machine's sides to flatten themselves across its massive shoulders. The tower slewed like a drunken man, and Heloise gathered her father to her chest, and leapt.

She cleared the people clustered by the railing, easily vaulting out over the common. Onas and Xilyka were silent, but her father groaned like he'd been punched in the stomach, and let out a yell when the machine landed with a thump.

She looked down at him, eyes squeezed shut, the corners wet. He had thrown a thick arm across his face, clinging to the machine's frame with his free hand. Heloise held her father as she knew he had held her so many times. The surge of love came so suddenly and so strong that she choked on it. *They are coming through the wall. They are coming with an army, and I have already lost Mother and now I will lose you, too.* There was no time to tell him this, no time to take his face in her hands and smooth his forehead. So Heloise instead took a moment to fix his face in her mind, to *remember* him in her arms as he was now. Whatever was coming, they couldn't touch that.

At last, his eyes opened, and she looked away before meeting them could make her cry.

"You're all right, Father," she rasped, setting him down and turning to look behind her.

The entire front wall of the town, stone and wood, its gate and towers, slumped in on itself like the mouth of an old man who'd lost all his teeth. The stone was slick and shot through with veins of ochre illness. The wood had turned gray-green, the beams flexing like spider's legs, trembling before collapsing under their own weight. The whole structure shuddered, shedding bits of itself, slime pooling at its base. As Heloise watched, the tower lurched again, the top shearing off with a loud ripping sound, as if a rotten melon had been torn in half. Heloise could see the defenders making a last desperate leap, arms and legs kicking as they plummeted through the air to bounce on the ground before they lay still. At last, the wall deflated, like one of her mother's oil-breads after the steam pocket had been burst to let out the damp, sweet-smelling air. It settled, shrinking. She made out Wolfun, limping, moving among the defenders who'd made it to the ground, trying to help them up and get them clear.

Finally, the wall spasmed, heaved, and collapsed, falling inward to splatter across the common. Some of the defenders who'd survived had managed to get clear, pushed farther into the common by Wolfun, but most of those who remained disappeared in the wall's wet shadow to be crushed or smothered. Heloise shuddered to think of either.

Barnard reached her now, with Leahlabel and the rest of the defenders, abandoning the west wall at the sight of their northern defenses ripped entirely open.

"What is to be done now?" It was Poch. Miserable, traitorous Poch, who wanted nothing more than to live, than to be left alone. Like the boy in the ram. But she could see the blood streaking his shirt and the cuts on his arms and knew he had fought. Perhaps he would keep fighting.

"We rely on the Emperor." Barnard hefted his hammer, watching the plume of greasy, heavy dust kicked up by the wall's collapse slowly drift apart, leaving a clear view of the wreckage, flat and low and no obstacle to the columns of armed men waiting just beyond.

"We rely on ourselves." Heloise raised her shield. "And make the Emperor proud."

Onas and Xilyka scrambled down from the machine's shoulders, fanned out in front of her, knives drawn and ready. Samson spat in his hands and leveled his spear.

There was nothing else to do. There was nowhere to run where the mounted enemy wouldn't catch them. There was no way to restore the fallen wall.

It was a field battle now, between the enemy in their thousands and the defenders in their dozens, wounded and exhausted, milling about in no particular order, many with empty quivers and snapped blades.

The Pilgrims advanced first, waving their censers across the wreckage, wafting the spiced smoke in great gray billows. "Theater," Giorgi panted. He hefted a great club he'd retrieved from the ground, but his hands were trembling. "Performance."

"Time." Samson shrugged. "Time to get ready."

Her father began bellowing in his sergeant's voice, pushing the spearmen into a line. Giorgi stationed knife-dancers on the wings. They both ignored Heloise and her guard, happy with their placement behind the protection of the spearwall, such as it was.

It was as much theater as the scented smoke. This tiny band of exhausted refugees would have as much effect on the enemy army as the swinging censers would on the magic that took down the wall. And yet, it had to be done, if only to give her people the grit to fight a little harder. Because if they had nothing left to live for, they might as well sell their lives dearly.

Heloise thought of her mother's pale face, Basina's confused smile as the light faded from her eyes. She thought of Clodio and Gunnar. She even thought of Sigir, as he had been before all this had started, kind-eyed and gentle. *I'm sorry*, she thought. *I would have liked to win this for you.*

But her people didn't need to hear apologies now. They needed to hear encouragement. They needed a reason to stand and fight.

"The Throne knows we are right," she shouted to them. "The

Emperor sees all. His heart can feel those who cleave to the Writ and those who break with it in His name. He will grant us victory, or He will judge us kindly.

"Either way, we have already won."

She turned from them, then, trying to ignore the exhaustion on their faces, to stop her ears to the absence of cheers. She punched her knife-hand against the edge of her shield, listening to the ringing peal that sounded like a shrine's bell, low and booming. She shouted a war cry, high and loud, sounding tiny and alone, for all its strength, in the wide open space of the common.

The enemy charged.

Heloise watched the horses pick up speed. The knights lowered their lances, fanning out into a wedge. Over their shoulders, she could see uhlans coming singly, finding their mounts and charging in as word reached them that the way was open. A dust cloud rose from farther back where the infantry were finally rounding the wall and racing to end what had been an unexpectedly hard-fought assault.

But out in front came the Order, flails raised, iron heads whipped to a blur. The Pilgrims gave no battle cry. Their eyes did their shouting for them, lit as if from within with blazing fury, with *certainty*. Heloise envied them that. It would be easier to die if she could have been sure that it meant something, but no matter how much she searched her heart, she only came up with the unshakable feeling that she was no more than a little girl in a stolen machine, having tricked this tiny, ragged band to follow her to their deaths. She had thought she had changed things, even in some small way. But she looked at the rushing tide bearing down on her, outnumbering her own troops one hundred to one, and she realized that she hadn't changed a Throne-cursed thing.

She leaned forward, bracing herself behind her shield. She

could withstand one charging horse, maybe even two. She would make their riders pay.

A trumpet sounded in the distance.

It was an unfamiliar call, a long, low blast as if from a hollowed-out horn. It sounded like a growling giant, and it was answered by a similar growl, this time from the throats of many men. She could hear the distant pounding of hooves.

A second army. The Order wished to make their victory complete. They could have crushed Heloise with half the men they had to hand, but she supposed they wanted to be sure. Or perhaps it was a garrison force, meant to hold the remains of Lyse while the other army ravaged the land as a warning to other would-be rebels. It didn't matter, the end was here, just a few hundred paces away and coming on fast.

A shout went up from the enemy infantry. Heloise took a step back, squinting past the shoulders of the charging Pilgrims. The infantry had stopped their run, turned to the side, were rushing to form a line. Some of the uhlans were wheeling off the charge, riding to their dismounted brethren.

The horn sounded again, closer and louder. The shout answered once more, and Heloise thought the accents unfamiliar. Not Traveling People, and not the Emperor's subjects either. She looked down, noticed her father had lowered his spear. She glanced at him and saw his face slack with wonder. "It can't be . . ." he was saying.

And then the second army came careering past the ruined wall, and Heloise's jaw dropped.

Many were as well armored as the Imperial knights, save they wore no wings, and their shields were simple squares, undecorated and banded with iron. Their mounts were dressed in flowing red cloth, their armor painted with what must have once been a red as brilliant as the Sojourners, but which time and service had dulled to a soft brown the color of old blood. Pennants flickered from their lances, bright banners waved aloft. All were simple red, plain and untouched.

"It's Ludhuige," Samson said. "It's the Red Lord."

Signal trumpets sounded to form the Imperial ranks and the charge splintered. The knights turned their horses, cutting across the Pilgrims' path, who reined in desperately. Within moments, all were a tangled mess, shouting and shoving. Here and there, knights and Pilgrims broke off in ones and twos to gallop back toward the infantry.

"Ludhuige's dead," Barnard said, "five winters past, at least."

Heloise scarce heard him. She realized with a start how tense her body had been, how certain she'd been of impending death. And now, suddenly, the wedge of men arrowing toward her was a confused jumble, no threat to anyone at all.

"Not his bannermen." The shock was fading from Samson's voice. "They never forgot their grudge against us."

"And praise the Throne they did not," Wolfun sighed.

The troops beneath the red banner crashed home before the Imperial infantry could form their line. There was a brief and terrible moment where the two masses surged against one another, and then the Imperial soldiers splintered apart, throwing down their weapons and making for the tents. Heloise could see the levy among them, at last having the excuse they needed to say they'd fulfilled their vows and that they could not be faulted if there was nothing more to be done. *Go,* she thought after them. *Run home. Go back and live your lives. Be free and be safe.*

The infantry were a panicked mass, but the knights and Pilgrims would be another matter. The red troops were in pursuit of the fleeing infantry now, whooping joyous war cries as they gave chase. Heloise's heart clenched at the sight of the Pilgrims and knights finding their bearings and charging toward them.

And then the red infantry came into view. There was an end-less stream of them. Not levy, but soldiers in red surcoats and pot-shaped iron helms, waving simple swords and spears, carrying plain red shields. They rushed out into the field, too quickly to form a line, but in enough numbers that the knights and Pilgrims were forced to rein in and fight them in detail.

"What in the name of the Throne are you waiting for?" It took her a moment to realize that the gruff voice belonged to her father. "The enemy gives us their backs! It would be impolite to refuse the gift!"

And then her father was racing toward the enemy, shouting, and Heloise thought he looked ten winters younger than a moment ago. It still took an instant more for the shock to subside, and then they were all running after him, shouting an array of battle cries. The names of loved ones, vows and oaths in the tongue of the Sindi and the Hapti and the Empire. Heloise alone was silent, too in awe of the sudden swing of fortune to say much of anything, unable to register the joy for fear that it might yet be snatched away. Her father was charging into danger, and that meant she had to protect him, and that was enough to guide her for now.

They were a tiny force, all exhausted, most wounded in some way or another. But the enemy had their backs to them now, were out of all semblance of order. Heloise felt her heart rising in her chest, all sense of fatigue slipping away. Her strides lengthened, the machine roaring as it matched her steps, metal legs an ex-tension of her own frantic pace. She was shrieking now, a high keening bubbling up out of her throat on its own. Her heart pounded, with rage, with excitement, with the bone-shaking re-lief that all was not lost, that there was suddenly a chance.

She reached the first of the Pilgrims, just as he was raising his flail to strike at one of the Red Lords' infantrymen. She didn't bother with the shield this time, swiping her knife-hand sideways, the point biting into the man's side and launching him from his saddle. He knocked into the Pilgrim beside him and both went tumbling to the ground. Barnard barely paused in his run to crack their skulls with his hammer, the first on the upswing, the second as the hammer came back down, sweeping back up to settle on his shoulder as he charged on.

"Leave the knights!" Heloise shouted, unsure if her people could hear her. "Break the Order!"

The enemy were turning now, wheeling their horses to face Heloise. A Pilgrim dug in his spurs and whirled his flail about his head, but no sooner had the animal moved toward her than two flat-bladed knives holed his face and he dropped his flail, slumping in the saddle. Xilyka raced past, flashing Heloise a smile that made her knees weak despite the heat of the battle.

"Keep up, your *eminence!*" Somehow Xilyka made it both a term of respect and endearment. Heloise found herself smiling back, her belly doing somersaults at the madness of it.

The Pilgrims were frozen now, heads sawing left and right, unable to decide whether they should face the armored infantry in their red tabards, or the wizard-blighted girl in the tinker-made machine and her band of Kipti and peasants.

Heloise reached a Pilgrim and he lashed out with his flail, the iron head screeching across her shield. Two of the red-coated infantrymen behind him reached out with their glaives, tangling the blades in his gray cloak and yanking him from his horse. Another Pilgrim turned to charge the footmen, his mount rearing, lashing out with its sharp front hooves. Samson reached Heloise's side and speared the creature in the rump, so deep that the animal looked as if it had sprouted a second tail. The horse's rearing turned into a shrieking backward somersault, the Pilgrim's own shout cut short as the horse's bulk fell across him, pinning his limp body to the ground.

Heloise scanned the swirling gray cloaks, desperately seeking Tone's blazing blue eyes, straining to hear his voice. But she might as well have tried to pick a single ripple out from the midst of a ranging torrent. A hundred shouting voices ran together, gray cloaks swirled like storm clouds. Any of them could have been Tone. If she were to have vengeance, then there was only one thing to be done.

"Kill them all!" she shouted. Because she would have vengeance, realized she would have done anything to have it.

She lowered herself behind her shield and charged into the midst of them, not even bothering to strike now, relying solely on the machine's weight and momentum to bring her enemy low. Most of the Pilgrims didn't even try to swing at her, and she could feel their bones breaking against the edge of her shield as she ran them down. A glance over the shield's rim told her why. The red-coated infantry had pulled back, locking their shields together in an ordered wall. Riding around their flanks came the knights of the red banners, all the more terrible for the simplicity of their armor, their plain shields and lack of wings. They slammed into the Pilgrims, thrown back once again onto Heloise and her small force.

It was the Imperial knights that gave way first. Heloise saw their false wings shaking as the battlefield shrank, slowly hemmed in by the Red Lords' infantry on the one side, and Heloise and her troops on the other. They mixed with the Pilgrims, increasing the chaos as the horses squeezed together, traces tangling, lances intertwining with flails.

At last, one of the knights turned his mount and spurred it at Wolfun. The Town Wall dodged aside, but the knight's lance still took one of the Sindi knife-dancers through the gut, pinning him to the ground. The knight made no attempt to free his weapon. Instead, he left it to quiver in the dirt and bolted for the hole he had made. The horse plunged through, and his comrades followed, turning to a steady stream of armored men, many of them throwing down their lances to get a better grip on their reins, leaning low over their animal's necks and savaging them with their spurs.

Heloise watched them, disbelieving. "Where are they going?"

"Away." Her father's voice was exultant. "Anywhere but here."

The Pilgrims were sustained by their zeal. They drew into a circle, back-to-back, baring their teeth. Heloise made to charge, but stopped at another sound of the Red Lords' horn, long and low, the growl of some foreign beast. The red banners of the knights wheeled off, the riders slowing their horses to a trot as they moved behind the line of infantry, the shield wall breaking apart to admit a cloud of skirmishers, all clad in the same red tabard worn by every warrior, high or low, in the army.

Archers. The Pilgrims could never close the distance in time. The men made a show of taking their time to knock their arrows, drawing the strings back to their ears.

The Pilgrims' eyes widened as they saw what was about to happen.

The first of them slid from the saddle, falling to his knees, his hands raised in supplication. "No! Don't shoot! Don't shoot!"

One of the Pilgrims shouted at him, cursed him for a traitor and a coward, but two more joined him on the ground. The Pilgrim cursed them again, nudged his horse forward, raising his flail to strike them, and fell from the saddle an instant later, at least a dozen arrows riddling his chest.

After that, the rest of them dismounted en masse, dropping their flails, raising their hands. Heloise could see the shame in their eyes, all of them oathbound to give their lives rather than submit to the corruption of heresy. But they were men, in the end, and the urge to live was stronger than their faith. Heloise was shocked to feel a tremor of sympathy for them. *No*, she pushed the sentiment away, *this is how we felt at Hammersdown*. Acting against everything they knew to be right, surrendering to the desire to live.

Heloise doubted that Tone was among them. She'd always seen him riding with commanders rather than the rank-and-file Pilgrims. Still, she would have to check. She started toward the kneeling men, when a flash of gold made her stop. She turned to her left and realized with a start that the battle had taken her out of the town and out into the road beyond. From here, she had an open view of the low rise where the enemy had pitched their camp. The black tent was slouching now, one of the poles knocked over. There were men running and shouting, and from her quick glance, she couldn't tell if they were friend or foe.

The golden flicker came again. She couldn't identify exactly where it came from, but only one man wore armor bright enough to catch her eye from across a battlefield.

Heloise didn't realize she had started running until she heard her father shouting her name. Xilyka and Onas came with her, and she heard her father take a few puffing steps before fatigue forced him to stop. She heard Barnard cursing at him to run faster, and then it was just the three of them, running hard for the enemy camp.

It was a shambles. The men she had seen from the distance were mostly levy, but a few Imperial soldiers as well. They were stuffing supplies into sacks: food and arrows, sheaves of paper and bolts of cloth. More than one had the treasures of the nobles in his hands, gold chains of office or silver drinking cups.

Looting their own camp. Most of them fled at the sight of

Heloise's machine. The braver ones ignored her and bent to their tasks, cutting down silk banners, or yanking pieces of armor off their stands. None moved to interfere with Heloise's progress toward the commander's tent.

What had looked small from the wall was gigantic up close. The canvas towered, striped red and white, a tiny pennant fluttering from the top bearing the sigil of the golden throne. The flaps were untied, and they rustled with the movement of someone inside. She could hear cursing from within, though she couldn't make out the voice.

"Why," Xilyka was panting, "are we here?"

"Because," Heloise said, "the bastard who took my eye is here. I hope."

"You said he was a Pilgrim," Onas said. "The Pilgrims are all back there."

"He's beloved of the leaders," she reached for the flap with her knife-hand, turning the blade to bat the flap aside, "probably because he's the vilest and cruelest of his sort."

But before she could touch the canvas, the flap was slapped aside from within and a man emerged cradling a chest, flowing over with coins.

"Come on, you damned fool," the Song was shouting over his shoulder, his voice still sweet, but so much softer without whatever wizardry he had used to amplify it. His helmet was off now, revealing the face that had been behind the golden sun, as beautiful as his voice, as arrogant. His eyes were the same blue as Tone's, but irritated rather than zealous, as if the sudden defeat of his army were a terrible inconvenience that he had to sort out so he could have his lunch in peace. Heloise marveled at that look, stunned for the moment by the thought of the kind of life he must have led to be able to wear it.

The Song dropped the chest and stumbled back, fumbling for

his sword, making a sound somewhere between a scream and squeak. Heloise lunged, sweeping him up with her shield arm, bringing the forearm of her knife-arm to his neck, pressing the metal in. The Song braced his feet against the machine's chest, first pushing, and when that failed, kicking. His boots drummed helplessly against the metal plate, his human strength useless against the might of the engine.

Another man emerged from the tent, a servant by his simpler clothing, but the softest-looking servant Heloise had ever seen, as plump-lipped and beautiful as his master. The man shook with terror, holding out his hands in front of him. "Please, no."

"Go." Heloise jerked her head, and Onas kicked the man in his ass, sending him running through the crowd of looters. She turned, still cradling the Song like a babe in arms, his back crushed against the inside of her shield, his throat slowly yielding to the pressure of the machine's metal arm.

She glanced up briefly, saw her father and Barnard now, Wolfun and Giorgi, and the rest of what remained of her people breathing hard from the long run to reach her. So few. Even if all of them, villagers and Traveling People alike, returned to Lutet together, they would not be enough to populate it. Surrounding them were the knights in red tabards, dismounted now. A few of them wore their chains of office, marking them as lords. They were simple things of gray iron, enameled in the same rusted red as their armor.

"Don't kill him," one of them said. "Do you know who that is?"

But while Heloise heard the words, she didn't understand them. The anger had boiled over once again. She knew he was not Tone, but he was *here*. She *had* him. And in a way, he was the same. He had the same arrogance, he killed good people with the same casual disregard. He claimed to own the Emperor, the same as the Pilgrims. But she knew all of this was an excuse. What mattered was that the rage was a hearthfire in her gut, and that if she didn't quench it somehow, she knew it would consume her, that she would burst into flame and all that would be left inside the tinker-engine would be ash.

No, he wasn't Tone, but he was the man with his throat beneath her arm.

"You are the Song," she whispered to him, "so sing. Sing so that the Emperor may hear."

And with that she pressed her arm home, pressed with all she had, and felt the tinker-engine take up the motion and translate it into the metal arm. The Song's gurgle softened and finally stopped, replaced by a wheeze and finally by nothing at all. At last Heloise heard a crunching, and blood bubbled from his mouth.

In the end, the Song's voice was not so beautiful after all.

EPILOGUE

DISTANT THUNDER

*The Emperor took up His hammer and mounted the stairs.
When He saw none had come with Him, He turned and
they trembled that He should name them cowards. But He
only laughed. "What is it thou fearest?" He asked. "Is it
death? It shall surely find thee here!" "How, then, shall we
live?" they asked Him, "when the enemy is all about us, so
terrible and so numerous." The Emperor laughed again, and
his voice was as the ringing of the dawn. "Wouldst thou live?
There is but one way!" "Tell it to us!" they called to Him,
hungry for His answer. "Follow me!" He said, and turned
once more, unto the fray.*
—Writ. Ere. LX. 17

Heloise wasn't sure what she'd expected to feel. The Song's broken body looked like so many others she had seen since all this had started. The dead were paler, smaller, more straw dolls than people, as if their life had inflated them the way a wind fills a sail. Even the Song's fine armor seemed . . . less, somehow. It had shrunk with him, filthy and streaked with thickening blood.

Heloise felt no sense of triumph, not even relief at having survived. She only felt a kind of numb exhaustion. She heard no cheering, no victory trumpets. The only sounds were the scrabbling of the looters in the remains of the camp, and the shouts of the Red Lords' horsemen, riding down those fleeing enemy not rich or lucky enough to have horses. At last, she tore her eyes away from the corpse, looked around her. Barnard had knelt, clasping the haft of his hammer, lips moving in a silent prayer. Her father had simply sat down where he was, letting his spear lie in the grass. He blinked, eyes wide. "Sacred Throne," he muttered over and over again, running his hand through his hair. "Emperor be praised."

Onas and Xilyka still stood, fanned out protectively before her, blades in their hands. Their posture snapped her out of her reverie and she looked around, noticing the armored men for the first time. There were three of them, all of an age with her father, yet with their faces shorn in the manner of young men. Their hair was cropped so close that the strands prickled like thorns, flashing silver and white in the afternoon sun. All wore chains of office and the same, simple red tabards of every soldier in their army. The only other indication of their rank was a strip of cloth wound around their upper arms. It was white, striped with red. Two stripes for the men on the left and right, and three for the man in the center. A standard bearer stood behind them, the plain red cloth fluttering from the top of his spear.

Beside them all stood Sald Grower, his face pale and his cheeks pinched, dressed in rags, hands bound behind his back.

"Sald?" Heloise asked. "Are you all right?"

"He is fine," the man with the three stripes said. "We caught him stealing—"

"To feed myself!" Sald said, his voice weak. "Can't be no crime to steal when you're starving—"

"—from the People's Preserve. He is our guest for now, but he told us an interesting story of a girl staring down the Empire on her own. It confirmed some of what our scouts had been saying, and we thought it worthwhile to have a look."

"And who are you?" Heloise asked.

The man with the three stripes stepped forward. He did not bow, but his posture stiffened as he inclined his head. "I am Steven, son of Roger, First Sword to the Senate of the Free Peoples of the Gold Coast."

"What is a senate?" Heloise asked. She knew she should introduce herself or thank him for his help, but the fatigue had drained her of every shred of formality.

A smile tugged at the corner of Steven's mouth. "It is a group of people who rule, together, in place of a king."

"I thought Ludhuige the Red was your king?"

The smile widened. "Ludhuige has been gone a long time, young lady. And our war against your false Emperor has taught us the importance of living free from the yoke of men."

Barnard rose slowly to his feet. His anger was plain, but he swayed on his feet, and Heloise could see that he lacked the strength to summon more than hard words. "Our Emperor is not false, and he is no man."

Steven ignored him, addressing Heloise. "You would be Heloise Factor, yes? I have heard many titles for you. Some call you 'the Queen of Crows,' others 'the Armored Saint.' I have even heard you called 'the Knife-Handed Devil.' They say you lead here."

"I am neither queen, nor saint, nor devil," Heloise said, "but it is true that I am knife-handed, and I do lead here."

She realized that it was true. With Sigir gone, there was no one else for the village to turn to. She supposed they could choose a new Maior, but who would certify him? Would they send to the capital for an Imperial Legate? And even then, the Traveling People were here for her.

"That man," Heloise pointed to Sald, "is one of mine."

Steven's smile was thin. "That is not what he said, when we caught him in our gardens. He said that he had quit your company, as his people had gone mad, and followed a girl they had set up as a saint. He said that he was willing to do penance for his crime and put his plea before the Senate to take up residence among the Free Peoples. His first service was to accompany us here, to prove that his story was true."

Steven turned back to Sald, and smiled wider. "I'd say that part of his bargain is fulfilled."

Sald met Heloise's eyes briefly before looking away. "Can't believe it," he muttered. "Didn't think you'd . . . it's impossible."

Steven turned back to her. "He is our man now. But the Free Peoples are truly free. Once he has completed his contrition, he can make his own choice to rejoin you or no, as he will."

"He walked away from us when we were at our lowest," Barnard seethed. "We don't want him."

Steven ignored the huge tinker, gesturing at the Song's broken body. "That was poorly done, Heloise Factor. Do you know who that was?"

"That man had my mother killed. Did you think to ransom him?"

"Certainly not," Steven said, "but a prisoner is useful in negotiat—"

"There will be no negotiation," Heloise said with sudden heat. "I will put an end to the Order and their tyranny. When the people of the Empire can live as they like, go where they like, pray how they like, do what they like, then I will negotiate. Until then, I will visit upon the Order what they visit on others. Again and again and again, until they learn." She nudged the Song with one of the machine's huge metal feet. "This man lived his entire life never fearing anything, never wanting for anything. It is too late for him, but perhaps the lesson will not be lost on those who come after."

Steven shook his head. "I have heard of your zealotry."

Heloise laughed. "I'm just a woman who has been hard done, who has lost those who she loved. I am angry, and I am tired, and I am through making deals."

One of the men with the two stripes touched Steven's shoulder. "Come, sir. It is as Sald said. She is a mad brigand."

"Bite your tongue." Barnard had found some of his heat. "She is a Palantine, and she—"

Heloise stopped him with a wave. "Enough, Barnard. They do not hold to the Emperor, and you cannot expect them to hold to Palantines."

"We do not need your gratitude," Steven said, "and we will not tell you how to lead your . . ." He paused, gesturing at the few survivors. "Company. We will camp here to see to our wounded and regroup, and then we march on the capital. There is a place in our auxiliary if you wish to join us. If not, then we will not hinder you."

Steven swallowed, stiffened. "But I will express my gratitude to you, Heloise Factor, and my admiration. Ever since we raised our banners against the false throne, we have waited for a moment to finish the fight. We never thought it would come from . . . such an unlikely quarter. I know you did not seek to aid us, Heloise, but you have helped my people to realize a dream we have held closest to our hearts since I was a younger man. And whether you will avail yourself of it or no, you have our thanks, and yes, our debt. Therefore, you may see my quartermaster to reprovision. My surgeons will tend to your wounded, if you will permit it. We will clothe you and arm you, and if you will not march with us, you may march beside us, and my pickets will watch over you, and permit no harm to come to you should you be overtaken by the enemy. This much we can do, and we will do it, and gladly."

"The capital," Barnard snarled, "is not yours to take. It is our Empire, and it should be ruled by its own people."

"I have told you," Steven's voice was cold, "what I can do. And if there is something I have not said I can do, then you must assume that I cannot do it. You are welcome to our supply and our protection. However, should you hinder us in our aims, or give succor to the foe, then you will be just as welcome to our wrath." He swept his arm across the battlefield, the kneeling prisoners, the heaps of dead. "You can see it is a warm welcome, indeed."

Barnard opened his mouth to say more, but Heloise cut him off. "We will take the night to think on it. We are the villagers of Lutet, the townsfolk of Lyse, and the Sindi and Hapti bands of the Traveling People. I lead, but we take our decisions jointly."

Steven smiled, made a formal bow. "I understand. That is wise. My people also take our decisions jointly, and it is their will that I serve here." He pointed at a clearing off the main road some distance from the looted camp. "If I may prevail upon you to make your camp there, I will send my sutlers and surgeons straight away. Whether we will be friends or not, I cannot say, but at least let us do this one small thing for you. Your man," Steven inclined his head toward Sald, "will be well cared for. You have my word."

Heloise nodded. "You are . . . kind, sir. Thank you."

"It is my honor," Steven said, and turned on his heel, making his way toward a larger knot of officers clustered around the kneeling Pilgrims.

"Sir Steven," Heloise called after him, and he stopped, turned, eyebrow cocked.

"There is one of them, the Pilgrims. His name is Brother Tone. He has wronged me. I would have him delivered to me, if he is among them."

Steven bowed. "Of course, Heloise. You may have whatever prisoners you wish, after we have questioned them. We ask only to hold the Sojourners and greater lords, if there are any left alive."

"I only want the one."

"Then you shall have him, if he is here to be had.".

"And there were three . . . prisoners," she said, unsure if she should admit to their wizardry, in case these red men hated them as much as the Order. "Their heads are shaved and they are ragged. I would see them, if they are still about."

Steven frowned, turned to one of the men with two stripes on his armband. They held a brief, whispered conference before he turned back to her. "We found three bundles of rags, jumbled amidst some . . . priestly vestments."

"Yes," Heloise said, "do you have them?"

"No," Steven said, "we only found the rags. I doubt the prisoners you seek survived."

"Why?"

"Because they were burned." One of the two-striped men waved to one of his valets, who came forward bearing one of the jeweled censers Heloise had seen the Pilgrims waving around the prisoners. It was blackened and melted, the brass hardened into solid runnels after it had cooled. "It did this to the vestments," Steven said. "Of the rags, there was little more left than ash."

· · ·

Steven was as good as his word, and no sooner had Heloise's band sprawled exhausted in the grass than she heard the creaking of a cart. It was a camp kitchen built into a single wagon, complete with a cook fire in an iron basin, and a tub for washing the carving knives. Leahlabel and Florea circled it, unable to keep the frank admiration from their faces. Five servants rode on the wagon, two surgeons and three others who scrambled to lay out blankets, which they covered with bowls and trenchers, heels of bread. They set up a field table and chair, covered it with a fine cloth, and set it with silver plate before motioning to Heloise. "My lady," one of them motioned her, "come down so we tend to your wounds and see you fed."

At the thought of leaving the machine, the now familiar fear rose in her. "Shall I eat fine food at a table while my companions sit on the ground and eat from wood trenchers?"

The servant bowed deeply. "You are a good leader to your people, but the First Sword was specific that—"

"The First Sword does not rule here. Whatever finery you'd set out for me can still be set out, and let all have run of it."

"As you wish," the servant bowed lower, "but at least come down so we may tend to your wounds."

Heloise swallowed the fear, forced it down into her belly. "After all others have been tended to, I will consider it." Her body itched, rubbed raw where she'd wrenched against the leather covering of the seat. Her muscles ached, as did the wounds Leahlabel had healed over. But even now, with the danger truly passed, the world outside the machine's frame still felt too big, too close. She knew that by the time the surgeons had seen to everyone, they would have forgotten her, and she knew that she would let them.

"Did you find Brother Tone?" she asked.

The servant bowed again, so deeply his face was level with the flat ground. "Begging the lady's pardon, but we did not. But our pickets are still searching the boundaries, and our heralds still name the dead."

Her people ate in silence, their faces masks of fatigue and shock. None spoke of Sald, just over the rise in the Red Lords' camp. Even her father did little more than pass by her, reaching out to touch her foot, before snatching a few bites of bread and a swig from a wine flask then curling on his side in the grass. Onas and

Xilyka ate from the fine table, laid out with fruit, cheese, and a whole roast fish, but only because it kept them close to her.

Onas brought her a handful of grapes and a heel of bread smothered in oil, and Heloise ate these, as well as accepting a swig from a waterskin before hanging in her straps. Heloise could see the question in his eyes, met them with as hard a stare as she could muster. Now was no time for him to press his idiot suit. He held her gaze for a moment, then turned away, anger flashing in his eyes. Heloise was simply glad to have him gone.

She knew she should call a counsel, should discuss what was to be done. But she saw Leahlabel drowsing on Giorgi's shoulder, Wolfun slumped against the stump of a tree that had been felled to build the tower that still smoked against Lyse's battered walls. *No,* she thought. *Later. For now, let them rest.*

She wasn't sure when she had fallen asleep, only that she came awake suddenly in the night, roused by the tramping of feet, of shouts and the cracking of branches, the creaking of wheels. She fumbled a piece of seethestone from the bag, slamming it into the chute, squirting water after and waiting for what seemed an eternity before the engine roared into life. It was then she realized that she heard no clashing of metal, and that the shouts of alarm were not the screams of the wounded or dying. There was no fighting yet.

She blinked into the darkness, lit now by lanterns and flickering torches. Down the road to the ruins of Lyse the looting was still going on, the lanterns bobbing like fireflies, and the Red Lords' camp beyond, lit by so many campfires it was as if a pocket of day had been preserved.

All around her, people were converging on her tiny camp.

A column of villagers, almost all of them men grown, carried improvised weapons over their shoulders, farming implements or smithing tools. They looked sleepless, hollow-eyed, and hungry.

A few warriors marched with them, men in boiled leather, with thin blades, wearing packs on their backs and riding calm horses, their hides crisscrossed with scars.

Beside them was a wagon train of the Traveling People, the canvas showing the sigil of a thicket of thorn bushes. The Mothers walked out front, and behind them came a cloud of their men, short and strong, girded with the pair of silver-hooked knives that Heloise had come to know so well.

Both columns halted as Heloise moved the machine forward. Leahlabel and Florea ran to the Mothers of the newly arrived band, chattering in their own language and pointing at the ruined town.

The newly arrived Mothers looked at Heloise with dawning smiles, but the men at the head of the villager column knelt. "Palantine," the one in front said, "deliverance from hell. Bless us, your servants."

Heloise's stomach sank, and she could hear her father's sharp intake of breath, but the truth was that she was grateful. A man who knelt and called her Palantine wouldn't be likely to try to kill her or those she loved.

"I am Heloise Factor," she said, deliberately omitting the saintly title.

"You are Heloise the Armored Saint," the man said, "who turns back the tide, who delivers the wretched from misfortune, who will save us all."

Heloise opened her mouth to refuse, but Barnard interrupted her. "She is, and I assume the Emperor has called you to her banner."

"He has," the man said. "I am Ernst, of the Vold. The men grown of all the villages of the coast have come with me. Seal's Rock and the Shipbreakers, the Iron Bay and Fire Point and

Smayd, and a dozen other settlements. We have heard the Order has been thrown off and the true faith proclaimed, that you march to free the Emperor from the fetters of His false servants. We have come to add our arms to your holy cause."

Heloise caught her breath. She had never thought of herself on a mission to free the Emperor from the Order's influence. To punish them, surely, and to free the world from their yoke. But the Order had always been part of the Emperor, and He of them. He was divine and they were mortal, and that distinction had been the difference between the holiness of the Throne and the evil of its servants. But the story had changed as it traveled. She remembered how rumors spread through the village, a secret whispered in one girl's ear had become a totally different story by the time it was revealed by another. It was the same thing here. Her immediate thought was to correct Ernst, but she looked out over the column of villagers, at the fire in their eyes and the weapons on their shoulders.

The Traveling Mother stepped forward now, and while she did not bow, her face was lit as she addressed Heloise. "The Great Wheel has turned us unto you, Heloise Factor, and it would have us travel the road together for a time. Word has reached us of one who has gathered travelers to her bosom, who would see them travel where and how they will, who will keep the Order's hands from our purses, who will restore the free and open road. I am Mother Andrasaia of the Brock band of the Traveling People. We are careful of when we fight, but we will fight for this."

The first of the Red Lords' pickets arrived then, Steven at their head, galloping on unarmored horses. The men hadn't even had the time to don their armor, wearing only their red tabards for protection, swords naked in their hands. "Heloise!" Steven called to her. "What is going on?"

And suddenly, Heloise knew. The truth was that she hadn't believed she would survive Lyse, and so had made no plans for what to do beyond holding the walls.

But now, she felt the weight of expectation from her own villagers gathered behind her, Samson and Barnard at her side. Heloise met Ernst's eyes, then Andrasaia's. No, she hadn't thought of what to do next, but they clearly had.

She nodded before turning to the First Sword. "I have been thinking of your offer, that we might march alongside you when you progress to the capital. After some consideration, I have decided to accept."

ACKNOWLEDGMENTS

I set out to write *The Armored Saint* as a test of my ability to push beyond the limits of my subgenre, and to prove to myself, and all of you, that I was a Writer with a capital W. The book sold out its print run and went into its second printing within its first week of publication. No book is ever perfectly reviewed, but *The Armored Saint* has come as close to a uniformly positive reception as any book I've ever written.

Jews have a Hebrew word we use to express boundless gratitude, דַּיֵּנוּ or, *dayenu*. It means "it would have been enough," and we sing it with joy every Passover. I sing it now to everyone involved in this project—if Tor had agreed to take the book on, but it hadn't met with such a great reception, it would have been enough. If you had loved it, but it hadn't sold out its print run in the first week, *dayenu*.

This is all a very fancy way to say thank you. If you're holding this book in your hand, that means you're back for the next round, and that *The Armored Saint*, such an important book to me, meant something to you, too. I have said before that I am no Emily Dickinson. I write to communicate. Without readers, I cannot be a writer. It is to you, most of all, that I give thanks.

While I can't thank every reader by name, there are some

who I can. Thanks to Irene Gallo for backing my play and taking a risk on a writer stepping outside his comfort zone. Thanks to my editor, Lee Harris, who helped whip the book into its current shape. Thanks also to my agent, Joshua Bilmes, for detailed and probing editorial work. To Justin Landon, who, while no longer my editor, provided a critical sanity check at the eleventh hour. To my incredible cover artist, Tommy Arnold, for bringing Heloise to life and readers, stunned by his gorgeous work, into my fold. To Katharine Duckett and Mordicai Knode, who are largely responsible for whipping up the enthusiasm that has surrounded this series. And to fantasy illustrator Greg Manchess, who has been a constant friend in a sometimes unfriendly city, a calm voice, a gentle hand on my shoulder. Greg is, as anyone who has met him knows, one of the kindest men alive.

Heloise has a tough journey ahead of her, and trials and triumphs yet to unfold. She's a brave young woman, and if you're reading this, then odds are that you love her as much as I do. We owe it to her to bear witness.

EXPERIMENTING WITH ELECTRICITY AND MAGNETISM

BY OVID K. WONG

A VENTURE BOOK
FRANKLIN WATTS
NEW YORK   CHICAGO   LONDON   TORONTO   SYDNEY

On the cover: A Van de Graaf generator (courtesy of the Museum of Science, Boston).

Photographs copyright © : Archive Photos, NYC: pp. 13 (Lambert), 36 top (Dean); Patsy Kelley: p. 17; Photo Researchers, Inc.: pp. 18 (Will & Deni McIntyre), 36 bottom (SPL), 70 (Andrew McClenaghan), 85 (SPL); The Bettmann Archive: p. 27; American Museum of Natural History, Library Services/Lee Boltin (neg# 322264): p. 27 inset; Randy Matusow: p. 53; Con Edison: p. 101.

Library of Congress Cataloging-in-Publication Data

Wong, Ovid K.
    Experimenting with electricity and magnetism / by Ovid K. Wong.
       p.   cm.—(A Venture book)
    Includes bibliographical references and index.
    Summary: Provides instructions for a variety of simple experiments demonstrating the principles and properties of electricity and magnetism.
    ISBN 0-531-12547-5
    1. Electricity—Juvenile literature.   2. Magnetism—Juvenile literature.   3. Electricity—Experiments—Juvenile literature.
4. Magnetism—Experiments—Juvenile literature. [1. Electricity—Experiments. 2. Magnetism—Experiments. 3. Experiments.]
    I. Title.
QC527.2.W65 1993
537'.078—dc20   92-37672   CIP   AC

This book is dedicated
to the thirty-five
Honors Science Teachers
of Illinois (1989–91)
for their inspiration,
collegiality, and friendship.

CONTENTS

FOREWORD

Electricity is an amazing physical concept! This idea has intrigued mankind for at least twenty-six hundred years. An ancient Greek philosopher, Thales, observed that amber would attract small objects after being rubbed. The charged amber exerted force over a distance like magnetism. In fact, the Greek word for amber is *electron*. People have been studying electricity ever since.

Dr. Ovid K. Wong in his eighth science book addresses this amazing commodity, electricity. There are ample opportunities for young scientists to test ideas, gather data, draw conclusions, and apply principles in new and diverse situations. This book presents the historical flow of electricity and magnetism over time, but it goes well beyond mere description. You will be stimulated by experiments, the hands-on approach to investigations, which are both challenging and exciting.

The main idea to remember is this: We do not know "all about" this topic yet. There are wondrous discoveries yet to be made with new and undiscovered applications awaiting the curious and questioning mind.

This book presents a springboard to new thinking. Trade new lamps for old ones as you go beyond the known and into the unknown realm. Remember these sage words of the American chemist Albert Szent-Györgyi (1893–1986):

Discovery consists in seeing what everybody has seen and thinking what nobody has thought.

Happy Discovering!

Thomas C. Fitch, Ph.D.,
the Distinguished Professor
of Science Education,
Illinois State University,
Normal, Illinois

INTRODUCTION: ELECTRICITY AND MAGNETISM

Although seemingly different, electricity and magnetism are actually two forms of the same force. It's important to remember that statement as you experience the many experiments in this book. The relationship between electricity and magnetism can be stated simplistically: whenever electricity moves, magnetism is produced; whenever a magnetic force field changes, electricity is produced.

We are not usually aware of electrical effects when we use magnets in our daily lives; nor are we aware of magnetic fields when we use electricity. Unfortunately, like other forces, electric and magnetic forces are invisible. If only we could see or feel electric and magnetic forces, and know they were there without needing to use special detecting instruments, their close relationship would become obvious to us because we would find them always acting together.

Experiments in this book are clustered under specific topics of interest. Beginning experiments are typically simple, while projects and invention activities are more challenging. Welcome to the wonderful world of experimenting with electricity and magnetism!

A Note About Safety

Please remember the following important safety rules:

1. Do not experiment with electricity from wall outlets. Household electricity is dangerous and can kill you.

2. Never work with lights or appliances that are plugged into a wall outlet.

3. Avoid downed power lines and electric company substations. They are extremely dangerous.

4. Wear safety glasses when cutting metal and when working with hot or corrosive liquids (including soldering).

1

ELECTRICITY
AT REST

You have probably experienced electrical effects like these: You scuffed your shoes across a nylon carpet and then created a spark by touching a doorknob. You unfolded nylon clothing taken from a clothes dryer and noticed a crackling noise and sparks. These and many other examples indicate the presence of electricity transferred by the frictional contact between objects. Electricity produced by friction can be stored on the surface of nonconducting substances such as rubber, glass, and cloth materials. This type of electrical charge buildup is known as static electricity. *Static* means non-moving. If static electricity remained static we might never notice it, but it doesn't. When you saw a spark when touching a doorknob or heard a snap when unfolding clothing you were actually seeing or hearing static electricity in motion. Static electricity makes sparks when it jumps. The branch of physics that studies electricity at rest is known as electrostatics.

The spectacular display of lightning in thunderstorms is a good example of powerful electrical movement in the atmosphere caused by the buildup and discharge of electric charges. On hot, humid days, heavy clouds become charged with static electricity. Typically, positive charges tend to build up at the top of the cloud and negative charges move to the bottom. Eventually, a heavy charge builds up and the negative electrons discharge, or jump, in an attempt to balance themselves. The air gets very hot. This causes the flash of lightning, accompanied by the shock wave of pressure that we hear as thunder.

HISTORY

Benjamin Franklin ● Most Americans know Benjamin Franklin (1706–1790) as a hero of the Revolution, a prominent statesman, and a Founding Father. However, Franklin, a self-made man who achieved wealth and fame through determination and intelligence, was also a scientist who made important contributions to the understanding of static electricity.

Franklin's best-known discovery is that lightning is caused by discharges of static electricity in the atmo-

12

Buildup of electric charge in the atmosphere, especially on hot, humid days, causes lightning.

sphere. To test his hypothesis, he conducted his famous kite experiment. He flew the kite during a thunderstorm using conducting silk thread as the string. Attached to the silk kite string was a metal key. Franklin found that electric charges from the atmosphere traveled through the silk thread to the metal key. In this dangerous experiment, Franklin diverted some of the deadly electricity through the key into the earth. The immediate practical result of Franklin's work was his invention of the first lightning conductor, a device that safely diverts intense electric charges from buildings, thereby preventing the loss of life and property. The lightning conductor is still widely used today.

Henry Cavendish • The British scientist Henry Cavendish (1731–1810) is known for his outstanding work in electricity. His earlier research established basic concepts for understanding the nature of electricity. In his experiments he defined the nature of electric force as the attraction and repulsion existing between two charged bodies. These forces play a key role in explaining electrostatic phenomena.

Charles Coulomb • The French physicist Charles Coulomb (1736–1806) formulated the law that describes the forces that exist between electric charges. The law states that like charges repel and opposite charges attract, and that a force exists between any two charged objects. That force is proportional to the product of the two charges divided by the square of the distance between them. Thus Coulomb's law is expressed as

$$F = k(Q_1 \times Q_2) / d^2$$

where F is the force, Q_1 and Q_2 are the charges, d is the distance between them, and k is a constant.

BACKGROUND INFORMATION

Electricity is closely related to the atomic structure of matter. Everything in the universe is made of very small particles called atoms. You are made of atoms; so are the chairs and tables in your home, the food that you eat, and the air that you breathe. Each atom is so small that it takes millions of them to form the head of a straight pin, for example. An atom has a positively charged nucleus in the center surrounded by negatively charged electrons in orbits. The sum total charge of an atom is always neutral because the positive and negative charges equal and cancel each other. The movement of "loose" electrons in orbits causes atoms to gain or lose one or more electrons. Consequently, atoms gaining one or more electrons will become negatively charged while atoms losing one or more electrons will become positively charged. Keep in mind that electricity is the result of moving electrons. Can you mathematically visualize how the movement of the negatively charged electrons affects the total charge of a neutrally charged atom?

Static electricity is produced in various materials by rubbing them with other substances. These materials build up either negative or positive charges, depending on whether they gain or lose electrons. As we know from Coulomb's law, substances of opposite charge attract each other. Conversely, substances of the same charge repel each other. When wool and plastic are rubbed together, electrons can be made to move from

15

one to the other. The atoms in the plastic pick up some loose electrons from the atoms in the wool. There are now extra electrons on the plastic, so it is no longer balanced but negatively charged. The wool has lost electrons so it too is no longer balanced; the larger number of protons than electrons makes it positively charged. The wool and the plastic will attract each other because unlike charges attract.

EXPERIMENT 1: What Are the Effects of Electrostatic Charges?

Materials ● Ne2 neon light bulb (from an electronic hobby store), zip-lock plastic sandwich bag, newspaper strips

Procedure ● (see Figure 1)

1.   Spread the leads of the neon light bulb so that they point in opposite directions.
2.   Place the bulb inside the plastic bag and seal (zip-lock) the opening.
3.   Rub one side of the plastic bag with a silk cloth in a dark place (for example a closet).
4.   What do you see? Can you explain what happened?

(*Hint:* Rubbing will cause one side of the bag to become positively charged, the other side negatively charged.) Here is another simple experiment to determine the effects of electrostatic charges:

Materials ● Old newspaper, television set, wool blanket, miscellaneous objects found in your home

16

Two spherical terminals mounted on insulating columns are the basis of this high-voltage electrostatic generator, called a Van de Graaf generator, at the Museum of Science in Boston.

Young girl with a static electricity generator

Procedure ●

1. Cut a strip of newspaper about 3 cm wide and 20 cm long.
2. Hold the paper strip and bring its free end to the screen of a turned-on television. What happens to the paper? Can you explain why it behaves as it does?
3. Move around your home with the paper strip.

18

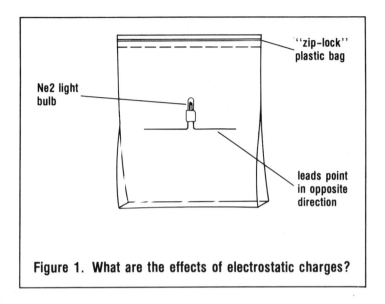

Figure 1. What are the effects of electrostatic charges?

Bring it close to a windowpane, a wool blanket, or other items that you think of. Can you explain how the paper strip may be used to detect static electricity?

Time to Think ●

- If you charge a balloon by rubbing it with wool, the balloon will stick to a wall but not to a metal door. Can you offer an explanation?
- Two charged balls, A and B, are separated by a distance of 2 cm. The charge of ball A is 2 coulombs; B's charge is 8 coulombs. What is the force exerted between the two balls? Apply Coulomb's law of static electricity.
- Static electricity is most easily created on a cool, dry day. Can you figure out why?

EXPERIMENT 2: How Can a Homemade Electroscope Be Used to Detect Charges?

An electroscope is built in this activity. The instrument is later used to detect static electric charges.

Materials ● Old audio tape, two aluminum soda cans, metal cutter, masking tape, sandpaper, sharp knife, plastic pen with a smooth barrel, work gloves

Procedure ● (see Figure 2: Making an Electroscope)

1. For safety be sure an adult is helping or supervising while you do this step. Put on work gloves and use the metal cutter (heavy-duty scissors) to cut away the top and bottom of an aluminum soda can. The work gloves will protect your hands against sharp metal edges.

2. Flatten the can into a rectangle. Nip the corners as shown.

3. Fold it in half again the other way. Nip the corners with the metal cutter as shown.

4. Open the can and fold it into a four-sided frame. When it is viewed from the open ends it should look like a box with the two side walls missing.

5. Cut an X on top of the frame with the knife. (Be careful to avoid cutting yourself.) Push in the tabs and fold them to make a smooth square hole.

6. From the old audio tape, cut off a length of about 25 cm.

7. Cut a strip of aluminum from the can about the width of the audio tape and about 15 cm long. Use a piece of sandpaper to remove the coating from one side

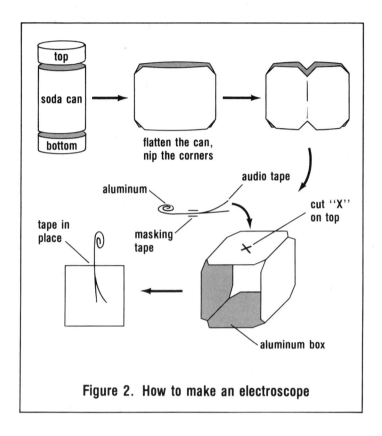

Figure 2. How to make an electroscope

of the aluminum strip. Roll one end of the strip until about 4 cm is unrolled.

8. Cut a short strip of the audio tape and fasten that to the unrolled end of the aluminum strip with a piece of masking tape. Make sure that the dull side of the tape faces the sanded side of the aluminum.

9. Hang the piece in the center of the hole with the help of tapes. The rolled end should be outside, and the end with the audio tape should be inside. Now you have successfully constructed a simple model of an electro-

scope. This instrument is used in the following steps to detect static electric charges.

10. Obtain a plastic pen with a smooth barrel and end. Rub the pen with a piece of fibrous cloth (*note*: a sweater sleeve will do). Immediately bring the smooth end (not the writing tip) of the pen near the rolled part of the electroscope.

11. Observe the audio tape and the aluminum strip inside the electroscope. What happens? Can you use the electric charge theory of attraction and repulsion to explain what you saw?

Time to Think ●

Before anything happens the electroscope is neutral. That means that the number of positive and negative charges are equal. When the plastic pen is rubbed with a piece of fibrous cloth, the pen is loaded with extra movable negative charges. What will happen to the distribution of charges on the aluminum strip and the audio tape when the pen is brought near the electroscope? Can you use a simple diagram to illustrate your explanation?

EXPERIMENT 3: What Is Electric Induction?

Materials ● Grains of puffed rice or wheat (from a cereal box), thread, large glass test tube, piece of silk cloth

Procedure ●

1. Hang a grain of puffed wheat or puffed rice by a thread.
2. Bring the large glass test tube close to, but not

close enough to touch, the grain. Can you describe what happens?

3. Rub the test tube with the silk cloth. Again bring the test tube near the grain. Can you describe what happens?

Time to Think ● Can you hypothesize the electric charge (positive or negative) of the grain? Can you hypothesize the electric charge of the test tube before and after rubbing it with silk? How do the answers help you to understand electrical induction?

EXPERIMENT 4: How Does a Charged Object Affect Other Objects?

Materials ● Plastic wrap, sheet of paper towel, ruler, paper clip, salt, pepper, small pieces of aluminum foil, Styrofoam pieces

Procedure ●

1. Place the paper clip, salt, pepper, aluminum foil, and Styrofoam on one side of a table, leaving as much space as possible between them.
2. Place a piece of plastic wrap flat on the other side of the table. Rub it with the paper towel to create static electric charges.
3. Predict what will happen when the wrap is brought to about 3 cm of the small objects you placed on the table. Record your predictions on the chart that follows.
4. Hold and stretch the plastic wrap flat above each of the objects in turn. Record your observations on the chart.

Objects	Predictions	Observations
Paper clip	_____	_____
Salt	_____	_____
Pepper	_____	_____
Aluminum foil pieces	_____	_____
Styrofoam pieces	_____	_____

Time to Think ●

● Why did the plastic wrap pick up some objects but not others?

● What are the differences between your predictions and observations? What did you learn?

● How does a statically charged object affect other objects?

2

NATURE'S
ELECTRICITY

Because we are so familiar with man-
made sources of electricity such as batteries, power generators, and the like,
we often are surprised to learn that
Mother Nature also generates electricity.
Have you seen or used a gas grill pilot
igniter? How does the igniter spark a
flame? When you click the button of the
lighter, the sparks that result are produced not by the rubbing of a flint but by
the deformation of a crystal. The igniter
and other sophisticated devices such as
microphones, phonograph pickups, mu-
sical toys, smoke detector buzzers, tone

generators in watches, ultrasonic cleaning devices, and ultrasonic submarine detectors are all examples of the use of piezoelectricity in our everyday lives. Piezoelectricity is produced by piezoelectric substances such as naturally occurring crystals.

HISTORY

In 1880, the French chemists Pierre and Jacques Curie discovered that electricity could be produced by various naturally occurring substances, such as crystals of quartz and tourmaline. They found that when these piezoelectric crystals change form under pressure, electricity is produced. Interestingly, the physical change in shape is not permanent because the same effect can be produced repeatedly. And conversely when electricity is applied to a piezoelectric crystal, that crystal will vibrate and change size. Another way of looking at this interesting phenomenon is in terms of converting energy from one form to another and back again. That is, in piezoelectric substances, mechanical energy will change to electrical energy, and in turn electrical energy will be converted back to mechanical energy.

Just what causes piezoelectricity in some naturally occurring crystals is not fully understood.

EXPERIMENT 5: How Can Piezoelectricity Be Generated?

Materials ● Safety glasses, piezoelectric disk, Ne2 neon light bulb, speaker wire, solder, soldering iron, alligator clips, hammer

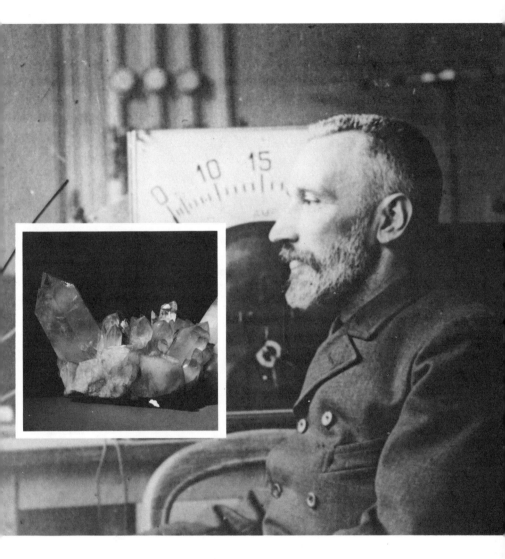

Pierre Curie (1859–1906), French scientist. He and his brother Jacques did extensive research on piezoelectricity. One of their discoveries was that quartz crystals (inset) could produce electricity.

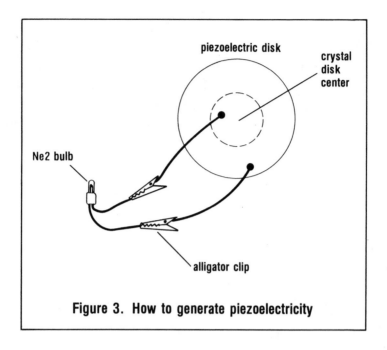

piezoelectric disk

**crystal
disk
center**

Ne2 bulb

alligator clip

Figure 3. How to generate piezoelectricity

Procedure ● (see Figure 3)

1. Obtain a flat piezoelectric disk either from a science supply store or from an old radio or other electric device that is ready to be thrown out. The metal disk has a crystal disk center. Treat the disk with great care; do not twist it. A damaged disk will not work in the experiment. An Ne2 neon light bulb can be obtained from a science supply or electrical store. The bulb is used because of its low voltage.

2. **Put on safety glasses.** Solder the leads from a 30-cm-long speaker wire to the disk. Be careful not to inhale the harmful fumes from the soldering, and re-

member that a soldering iron gets very hot. One end of the wire should be soldered to the center of the disk. The other end should be soldered to the rim of the disk. (See Figure 3 for soldering locations.)

3. Connect the leads from the neon bulb to the two ends of the speaker wire not attached to the piezoelectric disk. Check all the wire connections.

4. Place the disk on a smooth, hard surface.

5. Hammer the center of the disk with a sharp, steady blow.

6. What happens to the neon light bulb? Can you explain?

Time to Think ● Can you explain what you saw based on the piezoelectric theory?

EXPERIMENT 6: How Do You Light a Barbecue Gas Lighter?

Materials ● Barbecue gas lighter (e.g., a Scripto Aim Flame), Ne2 neon bulb

Procedure ●

1. Depress the trigger of a barbecue gas lighter several times to get a flame. Do you hear a rather distinct *click*? Do you hear the sound before seeing the flame or vice versa?

2. Carefully insert one lead of the Ne2 neon light bulb into the butane orifice. Let the other end of the lead hang over the side to touch the metallic outer frame of the lighter.

3. Remove the butane cartridge. Depress the trigger.

What happens to the neon bulb? Do you recognize any similarities between this activity and the previous one?

Time to Think ●

Did you hear a rather loud *click* when you depressed the trigger of the gas lighter? Is a flint and striker wheel used to light the butane gas? Are batteries needed for this lighter?

EXPERIMENT 7: How Does the Patio Gas Grill Igniter Work?

Materials ● A replacement gas grill igniter (from a hardware store)

Procedure ●

1. Identify the different parts of a gas grill igniter. These parts are the red button, the black housing which is the body of the device, the red wire, and the insulated metal lead from the housing.
2. Hold the insulated end of the red wire and the black housing in each hand. Bring the end of the red wire close to the insulated metal lead, but not close enough to touch.
3. Depress the red button. What do you see?

Time to Think ●

What could be inside the housing of the igniter? Can you make a connection between this device and the piezoelectric disk used in the previous activities?

EXPERIMENT 8: How Can Sound Be Generated From Piezoelectricity?

Materials ● Piezoelectric disk, stereo speaker plug, electric wire cutter, soldering iron, solder, tape recorder or stereo receiver

Procedure ●

1. Prepare a piezoelectric disk with soldered wire leads (see Experiment 5). If you used the same disk you constructed in the earlier activity you need to remove the Ne2 neon bulb.
2. Take an ordinary stereo speaker plug and carefully strip off about 2.5 cm of insulation. You will find two types of wires beneath the outer insulation. One type is a thin insulated wire and the other is several strands of thin, bare wire.
3. Solder the leads from the piezoelectric disk to the leads of the stereo plug.
4. Plug the stereo plug into the tape recorder or stereo receiver. Turn on the recorder or receiver. What happens to the disk? Can you see or hear any vibration?
5. Put the disk flat against the desktop or window. How does this affect what you saw or heard earlier?

Time to think ●

How do you explain what you saw/heard by applying the "reverse piezoelectric theory"? What happened when electricity from the tape recorder was applied to the piezoelectric disk?

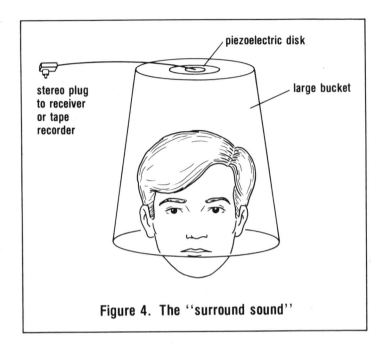

Figure 4. The "surround sound"

EXPERIMENT 9: How Can an Inexpensive "Surround Sound" Be Made?

Materials ● All the materials used in Experiment 8 plus adhesive tape, cardboard bucket like those used in fast-food restaurants for fried chicken (large enough to fit your head)

Procedure ● (see Figure 4)

1. Prepare the piezoelectric disk, the stereo plug, and the tape recorder or stereo receiver as you did in Experiment 8. Follow steps 1 through 4 of that experiment.

2.   Tape the piezoelectric disk flat to the bottom of the bucket.

3.   Place your head inside the bucket and turn on the tape recorder or stereo receiver. Can you describe what happens?

Time to Think ●

- How was the quality of "surround sound" different from the sound production of Experiment 8?
- How did the bucket act as a chamber of resonance?
- Based on what you learned from this activity, can you hypothesize how microchips are similarly used in buzzers and watch tones?

3

ELECTRICITY
IN MOTION

When you turn on an electric appliance, the electricity that makes it go is not magically produced at the wall socket. Electricity has to be generated from an energy source such as a power station generator or a battery (which basically is a portable power station). The electricity is then delivered to the consumer through cables. The cable is like a water main between the reservoir and your home.

In order for our homes to receive electric power, there has to be a power station to generate the power and a cable to deliver it. In other words, both the source and the pathway are needed to convey the moving electricity. If either the station generators stop working or the cable is broken, electricity stops running.

Put simply, electricity is a form of energy that makes things go and glow, a form of energy that can be changed into mechanical, light, or heat energy. A great deal of the moving electricity used in the home is changed into heat energy. The flowing electrons are used to heat the elements in an electric range, a toaster, or a heating system.

Electrical energy also may be converted to light energy in a light bulb, or to sound energy in a radio or a television speaker. Electric current can also produce mechanical energy, which can be used to turn motors in a dishwasher, washing machine, or electric blender.

HISTORY

Alessandro Volta ● The Italian physicist Alessandro Volta (1745–1827) invented a device called the electrophorus, which used metal plates to store electric charge. The stored electricity could be drained and used. This could be considered the primitive model of today's electric battery and condenser. Count Volta, a nobleman, established an important theory of current electricity, which deals with the movement of electrons. The theory states that electrons move from a location of high energy to a location of low energy by virtue of their relative position in the electric field. The term *electric potential* is used to describe the energy level of electrons. The unit of electric potential is the volt, named after Volta.

Volta invented his "voltaic piles," a forerunner of the modern battery, in 1799. It consists of alternating disks of copper and zinc, with salt-water-saturated pads layered between them. Volta is credited with the discovery of constant-current electricity.

Georg Simon Ohm (1787–1854) demonstrated that flow of current is directly proportional to difference in electric potential and inversely proportional to the resistance of the conductor. This became known as Ohm's law.

Georg Simon Ohm ● Georg Simon Ohm (1787–1854), a German scientist devoted to the study of electricity, discovered that the flow of electricity is not only related to the electric potential as stated by Volta, but also to the resistance of the conducting pathway. Ohm tested the hypothesis by passing current through conductors of different length and thickness. He discovered that for a given type of metal, the flow of electricity increased as the metal's length and thickness decreased. In other words, electricity tends to seek a pathway with the least resistance.

BACKGROUND INFORMATION

Earlier we said that the electricity we use every day requires both an electric source and an electric pathway. What we were talking about, in effect, was the electric circuit—the source and pathway put together. The electric circuit is a continuous path through which electric charges flow, and the flow is called an electric current. Electricity must travel in a complete circuit in order to be used.

Conventionally, we use electron flow to describe the movement of current. The amount of current is measured in terms of a unit called the ampere, or amp. The ampere unit measures the quantity of charges that passes by a point in a given time. For example, a typical household light bulb (100 watt) uses 1 ampere of electricity.

Every circuit must of course have a source of energy supply, which can be a battery or a generator. In a battery, current is generated by stored chemical energy. Because the current always flows in one direction, it is called direct current (DC). Current flow from a generator, on the other hand, changes, or alternates, in direction and is therefore called alternating current (AC).

EXPERIMENT 10: How Much Electricity Do You Use?

Materials ● None needed

Procedure ● (see Figure 5)

1.   Locate the electric meter in your house or apartment, which measures kilowatt-hours. Look at it carefully. It will be either the new-style digital display or the old-style dial meter. Both types of meters will change their number as electricity is being used in your home.
2.   If you have the dial meter, note that the dials are organized to be read in multiples of 10. The dial farthest to the right indicates kilowatt-hours in 1's, the next dial in 10's, the next dial in 100's, then 1,000's, then 10,000's.
3.   Read the dial of your dial meter from left to right, just as you would numbers. It can be tricky because some of the dials read clockwise, others read counter-clockwise. The main thing to remember when reading a dial-type electric meter is that when the pointer is between two numbers, it is always read as the smaller number. If the pointer is exactly on the number, read it as the number. If it is only half a millimeter in front of a number, read it as the smaller number. Note that if the pointer is between 9 and 0, consider 9 to be smaller than

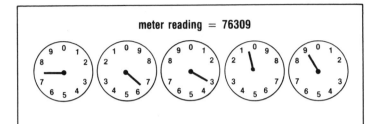

Figure 5. How much electricity do you use?

0. The 0 is really a 10 in this case. If the pointer is between 0 and 1, read the number as 1.

4. For either type of meter, look to find the wheel that turns when electricity is being used in the house. Ask an adult to turn on some electric appliances and watch the turning wheel of the meter.

5. Look at the meter about the same time every day. Record the reading for several days. Find out how much electricity your house uses on average each day.

Time to Think ●

● Did your home use roughly the same amount of electricity every day? Were some days more expensive than others? If so, can you think of several reasons why?

● The turning meter wheel indicates that electricity is being used. Which appliances use the most electricity? Is it the microwave oven, the blender, the radio, the television, or the vacuum cleaner?

EXPERIMENT 11: How Many Ways Can You Light a Bulb?

Materials • Aluminum foil, scissors, flashlight bulb, 1.5-volt dry cell (D cell) (*Note:* technically, a single dry cell should not be called a battery because a battery is two or more electric cells connected together.)

Procedure •

1. Cut a strip of aluminum foil about ½ cm wide.
2. Construct a complete circuit using the dry cell as the energy source, the foil strip as the pathway, and the flashlight bulb as the energy user. Does the bulb light up?
3. Record all your attempts with simple diagrams. You may use the foil strip to connect the different parts of the light bulb to the different parts of the cell. How many different ways can you light a bulb?

Time to Think • Examine all the circuit diagrams that you have recorded. Divide them into two groups, the successful circuits (those that light the bulb) and the unsuccessful circuits. What is one major difference between the two groups?

EXPERIMENT 12: How Do You Build a Copper-Zinc Plate Battery?

Note: In 1880, Alessandro Volta (see "History," above) invented a primitive device for producing electricity by chemical reaction. Today, simple chemical cells are called voltaic cells in his honor.

Materials ● Copper strip, zinc strip, two insulated wires, crystals of ammonium chloride (sal ammoniac), thin strip of felt, hammer, scissors, rubber band, sandpaper, ruler, sheet cutter, nail, safety glasses, lab apron

Procedure ●

I. Use the sandpaper to thoroughly clean both sides of the zinc and copper strips.

2. Use the sheet cutter to cut the zinc strip into six 2-cm squares (**caution!**). Cut the copper strip likewise to obtain six 2-cm squares. Flatten the squares by hammering them on a hard surface.

3. Use scissors to cut six squares of felt smaller than the 2-cm squares.

4. Put on safety glasses and lab apron. Dissolve the ammonium chloride in a few teaspoons of warm water in a bowl. The ammonium chloride solution is the liquid conductor of the battery. **Handle the chemical solution with care**.

5. Thoroughly soak the felt squares in the ammonium chloride solution. Press the soaked felt slightly to get rid of the excess solution.

6. Place a zinc square flat on a table and cover it with a wet felt square. Then put a copper square on top of the felt square. In other words, the piece of felt is sandwiched between the zinc and copper squares. Repeat the arrangement to form a single multilayered "sandwich" as follows.

Z/F/C/Z/F/C/Z/F/C/Z/F/C/Z/F/C/Z/F/C
Zinc = Z Felt = F Copper = C

7. Use a nail and hammer to make a small hole on the first zinc square and the last copper square.

8. Tie the stack together with a rubber band. Now you have made a zinc-copper plate battery. Now complete steps 9 and 10 to find out if it will work.

9. Strip the end of an insulated wire to expose the metal. Connect the wire to the zinc square that has the hole. Similarly attach another wire to the copper square with a hole. Wash your hands clean of the chemical solution.

10. Touch your tongue with the two wires. How does it feel? Can you feel the mild electric current?

Time to Think ●

● How does the battery generate electricity?
● What would happen if just zinc or just copper squares were used?
● Is the electricity generated by your homemade battery strong enough to light a flashlight bulb? How do you find out?

EXPERIMENT 13: What Is Inside a Dry Cell?

Materials ● D cell, hacksaw, insulated wire with exposed ends, flashlight bulb, work gloves, safety glasses

Procedure ●

1. Examine the outside of the D cell. Hypothesize what the inside of the cell would look like if it were cut in half lengthwise. Illustrate your hypothesis with a simple diagram.

42

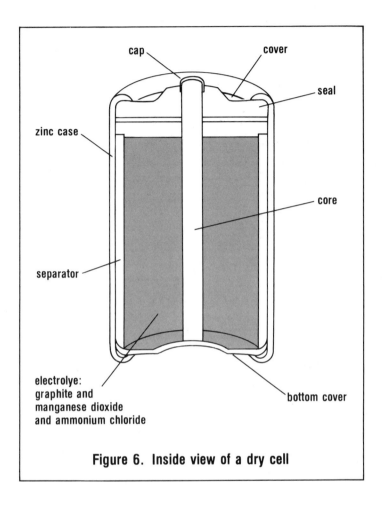

cap

cover

seal

zinc case

core

separator

electrolye:
graphite and
manganese dioxide
and ammonium chloride

bottom cover

Figure 6. Inside view of a dry cell

2.   Put on work gloves, safety glasses, and a lab apron. Cut open the cell the long way with a hacksaw. Position the saw so that it is off the center contact point. Can you identify the following parts: carbon rod, black carbon electrolyte paste made of manganese dioxide and graphite powder, and the zinc can (see Figure 6)? How does the real interior compare with your hypothesis?

(*Note:* Hold on to your cut-open cell. You can use it again for Experiment 14.)

3. Test the cell with the flashlight bulb and wire, much as you did with the bulb and foil in Experiment 11. Does the cell still produce electricity? How can you tell?

Time to Think ●

● The function of the zinc container is to produce electrons and the black electrolyte receives them. Draw a complete circuit diagram to show the flow of electrons when you connect a bulb and a wire to a cell. How does that flow of electrons explain why the bulb lights up?

● Was the inside of the cell you cut open moist or dry? Do you know why?

● Dry cells have a limited shelf life. Expired cells usually develop leaks through the cell container. Do you know why?

EXPERIMENT 14: How Do You Recycle Dry-Cell Parts to Make a Wet Cell?

Materials ● D cell, insulated wires with exposed ends, flashlight bulb, hacksaw, salt, glass jar, nail and hammer

Procedure ● (see Figure 7)

1. If you saved the cell you cut open in Experiment 13, go right on to step 2. Otherwise, put on work gloves

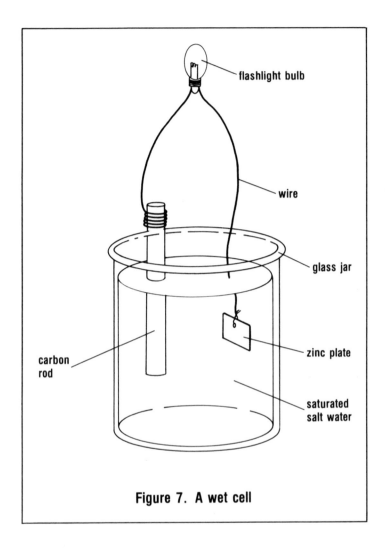

Figure 7. A wet cell

and safety glasses and cut open the D cell lengthwise
with a hacksaw.

2. Remove the carbon rod in the center and clean it.

3. Cut a strip of the zinc can (this is the shell or

container of the cell) about the length and width of the carbon rod. Clean the strip well.

4. Using a nail, hammer a small hole on one end of the zinc strip. Attach a wire to the zinc through the hole. Loop another wire around the rod to attach it. Make sure that the ends of the wires are stripped to expose the metal.

5. Lower the carbon rod and the piece of zinc into a glass jar of saturated salt water (water with a lot of dissolved salt). Make sure that the wires hang outside the jar. Now you have completed the construction of a wet cell. Why is it called a wet cell?

6. Connect the wires to a flashlight bulb. Did you build a complete circuit to produce electricity? How can you tell?

7. Draw a diagram of your hookup to show the direction of electron flow through the wet-cell system.

Time to Think ●

● What is the major structural difference between a dry cell and a wet cell? Which parts are comparable and which are not?

● Are the contact points on the wet cell similar to the contact points on the dry cell? Can you explain?

● Can you explain the flow of electrons in the wet cell with reference to the electric potential of the zinc and the carbon? Which one has a higher electric potential? The electrons always flow from a point of higher electric potential to one of lower potential.

● Insert a carbon rod and a piece of zinc from a used

46

dry cell into a fresh lemon. Using insulated wires, connect the rod and the zinc to a flashlight bulb to make a complete circuit. The bulb lights up. How do you explain what you saw?

EXPERIMENT 15: What Is Inside a Light Bulb?

Materials ● Frosted household light bulb, hacksaw, work gloves, cloth rag, hammer, safety glasses, pliers

Procedure ●

1. Examine the frosted household light bulb to identify the glass and the metal base. What do you think the inside of the bulb would be like if you were able to see through the frosted glass and the metal base? Draw a diagram of your hypothesis.

2. Wear your safety glasses to protect your eyes. Wrap the bulb completely with a cloth rag and hammer lightly enough to break only the glass and not the parts inside the bulb.

Now, what do you see? Can you find the coiled filament and the glass support? Why are the two ends of the filament separated by glass?

3. Cut open the metal base of the bulb carefully with the hacksaw. Remove the metal covering with pliers. Wear your work gloves to protect your hands from sharp edges. What is inside? Can you trace the ends of the filament through the metal base? Where are the wire contacts inside the metal base?

4. Draw a diagram showing the inside of the entire light bulb. How is this diagram different from the one

you hypothesized earlier? In your notebook, write how you think a light bulb works.

Time to Think ●

- Why are the metal base and the wire contact points of a light bulb separated by ceramic material?
- In order to light up a bulb, a complete electric circuit has to be established. Based on what you see inside the bulb, which two specific contact points should the wire touch to light up the bulb?

EXPERIMENT 16: How Do You Build a Cell Holder, a Bulb Holder and a Switch?

Materials ● D cell, masking tape, two large paper clips, two wood boards (5 × 6 × 1 cm), clothespin, thumbtacks, noninsulated copper wire, ruler with a shallow channel in the middle, flashlight bulb

Procedure ● (see Figure 8)

Dry-Cell Holder ○

1. Place the two large clips against the two ends of the D cell. Make sure that the clip touches the end contact of the cell. The loop end of the clip should extend beyond the diameter of the cell. With the clips in position, secure them by wrapping masking tape around the cell lengthwise. Place the cell on the shallow channel of the ruler; the channel will hold the cell in place and prevent it from rolling. Now you have assembled a dry

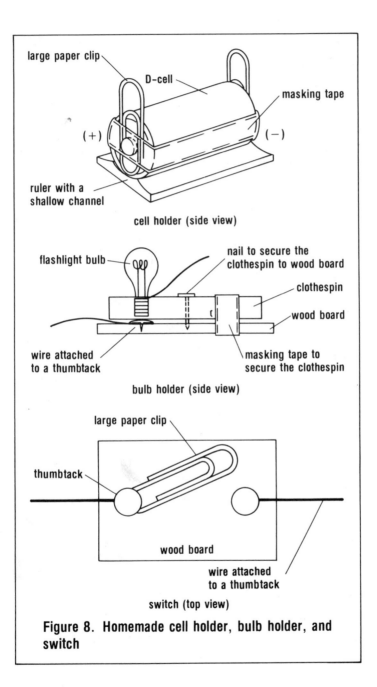

large paper clip

D-cell

masking tape

(+)

(−)

ruler with a
shallow channel

cell holder (side view)

flashlight bulb

nail to secure the
clothespin to wood board

clothespin

wood board

wire attached
to a thumbtack

masking tape to
secure the clothespin

bulb holder (side view)

large paper clip

thumbtack

wood board

wire attached
to a thumbtack

switch (top view)

**Figure 8. Homemade cell holder, bulb holder, and
switch**

cell with two terminal attachments resting on a holder (Figure 8).

Bulb Holder ○

2. Push a thumbtack gently into one end of one of the wood boards. Wrap a wire under the tack and allow a length of the wire to hang from it. Carefully hammer the tack into the board after the wire is in place.

3. Use a clothespin to hold a flashlight bulb. Place the metal base of the bulb right above the tack. Secure the clothespin and bulb by putting the clothespin flat on the board. Drive a small nail through the hole in the middle of the clothespin and use masking tape to attach the clothespin to the wood block.

4. Wrap another wire around the metal base of the bulb and extend a length of the wire from the bulb. Now you have made yourself a bulb holder with a flashlight bulb in place.

Switch ○

5. Push two thumbtacks into the opposite sides of a wood board. Wrap a wire under one tack. Place a large paper clip and the end of another length of wire under the second tack. You should make sure that when the paper clip is turned it touches the other tack. The paper clip is the bridge between the two tacks that acts to turn the circuit on or off.

6. Hammer the tacks carefully into the board after the wires and paper clip are in place. Now you have made yourself a switch. A switch can be used to open a circuit

(make it an incomplete circuit) or to close it (make it complete).

Time to Think ● What is the key factor to consider in putting the bulb, the dry cell, and the switch together to make a complete circuit?

EXPERIMENT 17: How Can You Make a Circuit Using a Switch, a Bulb and a Cell?

Materials ● D cell with holder, flashlight bulb with holder, and switch—all from Experiment 16

Procedure ●

1.   Connect the D cell with its holder, the flashlight bulb with its holder, and the switch to make a circuit. (*Hint:* connect the paper clip of the D cell to one end of the wire of the bulb holder. Connect the second end of the wire from the bulb holder to one wire of the switch. Connect the second wire from the switch to the other clip of the D cell.) Do you now have a complete circuit? Can you explain?
2.   Turn the paper clip to bridge the two thumbtacks. Do you have an open or closed circuit? How can you tell? How can you turn the light on and off by using only the switch?

Time to Think ● In a simple circuit the cell is the energy source and the bulb is the energy user. Will an open switch make the circuit complete or incomplete? What then is the function of the switch?

EXPERIMENT 18: How Do You Test Conductors and Insulators?

Materials ● Flashlight bulb, D cell, wire, paper clip, eraser, chalk, pencil lead, paper, glass

Procedure ● (see Figure 9)

1.   Construct a complete electric circuit using the cell, the wire, and the light bulb. If you have completed Experiment 17 this should not be a new experience.
2.   Place different objects between the contact points of the circuit (for example, between the bulb and the cell or between the wire and the cell). Test some other substances that you have in mind. Record the results in the following chart.

Objects	Lights the Bulb	Does Not Light the Bulb	Conductor/ Insulator
Clip	_____	_____	_____
Eraser	_____	_____	_____
Chalk	_____	_____	_____
Lead	_____	_____	_____
Paper	_____	_____	_____
Glass	_____	_____	_____
Other	_____	_____	_____

Time to Think ●

●   Conductors permit electric current to flow through them while insulators do not. Can you classify the

What are the conductive properties of these materials?
You can find out by doing Experiment 18.

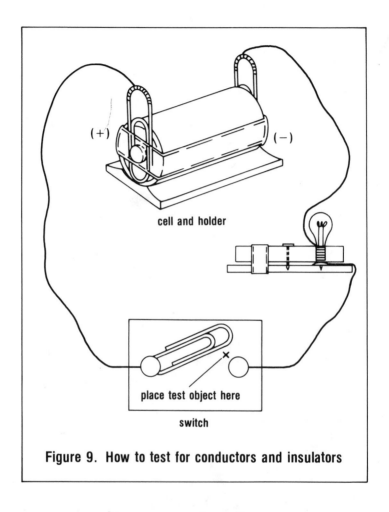

Figure 9. How to test for conductors and insulators

objects in this experiment into two groups: conductors and insulators?
● Can you identify the different parts of a dry cell
and a light bulb as either conductors or insulators?
Why are both conductors and insulators used in
making a dry cell and a light bulb?

EXPERIMENT 19: What Is an Electrolyte?

Materials ● D cell, three insulated wires, small glass jar, flashlight bulb, bulb socket, sugar, vinegar, salt, starch, cooking oil, water, masking tape, six small paper cups, teaspoon

Procedure ● (see Figure 10)

1. Strip the ends of all three insulated wires.
2. Connect one wire between one terminal attachment of the cell and the bulb socket.
3. Connect one end of the second wire to the socket, leaving the other end free.
4. Connect one end of the third wire to the other terminal of the cell.
5. Place the wire from the socket and the cell into a jar as shown in the diagram.
6. Fill one of the small paper cups with cooking oil and another with water. Use the masking tape to label the two cups "water" and "cooking oil" and set them aside. Now fill the other four cups with water. Prepare these test solutions by stirring each of the other substances—the sugar, vinegar, salt, and starch—into a separate cup until the water can dissolve no more of the substance. In any case put no more than two teaspoons of the substance into its cup. Be sure to identify what you have placed in each cup with a masking tape label right after adding the substance.
7. Separately pour each of the six test liquids into the jar. Before adding another liquid, be sure to empty the jar and thoroughly rinse it with plain water. Whenever

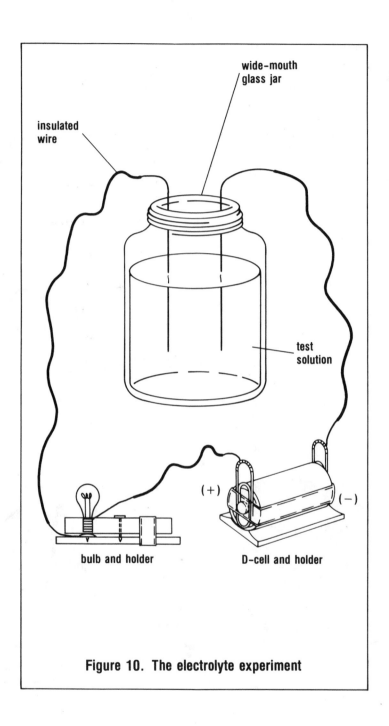

Figure 10. The electrolyte experiment

you pour a liquid into the jar, make sure the free ends of the wires are submerged. Use the following chart to record your observations.

Test Solutions	Does the Bulb Light Up? (Yes/No)
Water	
Oil	
Sugar water	
Vinegar water	
Salt water	
Starch water	

8. Look at the completed chart. Which liquid permits electricity to flow through? Liquids that permit the passage of electricity are nonmetallic conductors in which current is carried by the movement of ions. Liquid conductors are called electrolytes.

EXPERIMENT 20: What Is Electroplating?

Materials • 6-volt cell, old door key, copper strip, nail, hammer, salt and vinegar, small glass jar, insulated wire, masking tape

Procedure • (see Figure 11)

1. Fill the small glass jar about half full with vinegar. Stir in salt (about one tablespoon) until the vinegar can dissolve it no more. You will notice a small deposit of salt at the bottom of the jar when the salt-vinegar solution is ready.

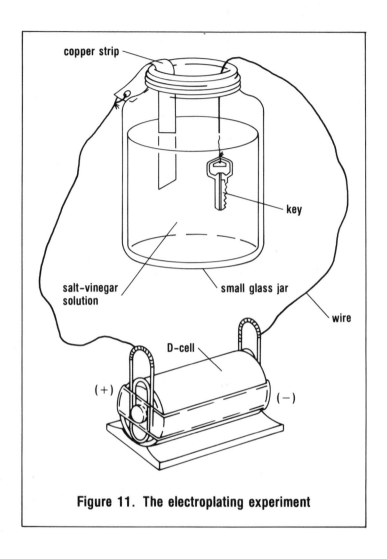

Figure 11. The electroplating experiment

2.   Hammer a small hole into one end of the copper strip with a nail. Bend the copper strip so that the long end is submerged in the solution while the short end with the hole hangs outside the jar.

3. Strip the ends of the insulated wire to expose the metal. Connect the wire between one terminal of the cell and the nail hole of the copper strip. Use the masking tape to secure the wire to the dry cell terminal.

4. Strip the ends of another wire to expose the metal. Connect the wire between the free terminal of the cell and the key.

5. Submerge the key in the salt-vinegar solution. Make sure that the key and the copper strip are not touching each other.

6. Wait for a few minutes and record your observations. What happened to the color of the solution? What happened to the key?

Time to Think ●

● Can you trace the path of electricity in the electroplating system by identifying all the components? (*Hint:* the source of electricity is the dry cell. Begin with the dry cell and trace the path through the wire and back to the dry cell.)

● Predict what will happen if plain water is used instead of the salt-vinegar solution.

● How does the copper deposit on the key?

● How is electroplating used in industry? Can you give examples?

EXPERIMENT 21: How Can Two Light Bulbs (in Series) Be Lit at the Same Time?

Materials ● D cell with holder, two flashlight bulbs with holders, switch, four lengths of noninsulated copper wire

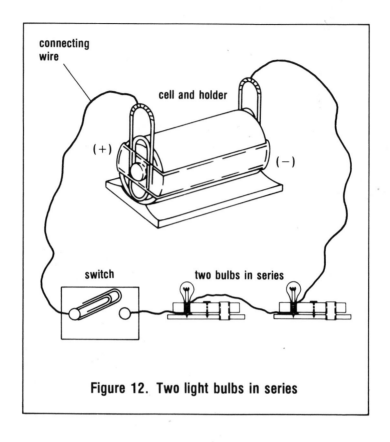

Figure 12. Two light bulbs in series

Procedure ● (see Figure 12)

1. If you skipped Experiment 16, then you will have to go back and make the D cell holder, bulb holder, and switch described in that experiment. You will need to build an extra bulb holder, however. If you have already completed Experiment 16, then of course all you have to build is the second bulb holder.

2. Connect one wire to the terminal (that is, the paper

clip) of the cell and to one end of the switch. You may twist the wires together to secure the connections.

3. Connect a second wire from the other terminal (paper clip) of the cell to one terminal of the bulb holder.

4. Connect a third wire between the remaining terminal of the first bulb holder and one terminal of the second bulb holder.

5. Connect a fourth wire between the remaining terminal of the second bulb holder and the last terminal of the switch.

6. Now you have connected all the parts of a circuit with two light bulbs in series.

7. Close the switch. What happens?

8. Remove one light bulb from the holder with the switch closed. What happens?

Time to Think ● ·

● Draw a diagram showing the flow of electrons through the complete circuit from the energy source to the energy user. Use arrows to indicate the direction of flow.

● Compare the brightness of the light bulbs in this experiment and Experiment 17. Can you explain the difference?

EXPERIMENT 22: What Are the Effects of Connecting Two Cells (in Series) in a Circuit?

Materials ● flashlight bulb with holder, switch, two D cells with holders (you will have to build one more D cell holder), noninsulated copper wire

61

Procedure ● (see Figure 13)

1. Connect a wire between the terminals of cell 1 and cell 2. The remainder of the connections are similar to those in Experiment 17. Remember when two cells are connected in series, the positive terminal of one cell must be connected to the negative terminal of the other cell. The experiment will not work if the terminals of the cells are not connected right.

2. Connect one wire between the other terminal of the cell holder and one terminal of the bulb holder.

3. Connect another wire from the other bulb holder terminal to one terminal of the switch.

4. Connect the last wire from the other terminal of the switch back to the terminal of the bulb holder. Now you have built a circuit with two cells in series.

5. Close the switch and observe. What happens?

Time to Think ●

● Compare the brightness of the bulb in this experiment with the one in Experiment 17, where only one cell is used. Can you explain the difference?

● When you connect two cells together what is the total voltage?

EXPERIMENT 23: How Can Two Light Bulbs (in Parallel) Be Lit at the Same Time?

Materials ● From Experiment 21: two flashlight bulbs with holders, switch, D cell with holder, noninsulated copper wires

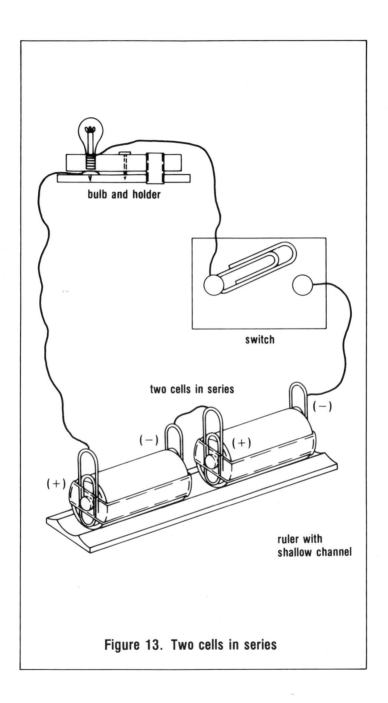

bulb and holder

switch

two cells in series

(−)

(−) (+)

(+)

ruler with
shallow channel

Figure 13. Two cells in series

Procedure ● (see Figure 14)

1. Connect one bulb and its holder, the switch, and the D cell and its holder in a complete circuit. Please see the preceding experiment for the setup.

2. Now bring in the second bulb and its holder. Connect another wire between other terminals of bulb holders 1 and 2. Notice there are two wires coming out of each terminal of bulb holder 1. Now you have completed all the parts in a circuit with two light bulbs in a parallel configuration.

3. Close the switch. What do you see?

4. Remove one light bulb from the holder with the switch closed. What happens?

Time to Think ●

- Draw a diagram showing the flow of electrons through the complete circuit from the energy source to the energy user. Use arrows to indicate the direction of flow.
- Compare the brightness of the light bulbs in this experiment and Experiment 17. Can you explain?
- If you could use either a series circuit or a parallel circuit, which one would you choose and why?
- Look around your house. Can you find examples of series circuits and parallel circuits?

EXPERIMENT 24: What Are the Effects of Connecting Two Cells (in Parallel) in a Circuit?

Materials ● From Experiment 16: two D cells with holders (unless you have done Experiment 22, you will

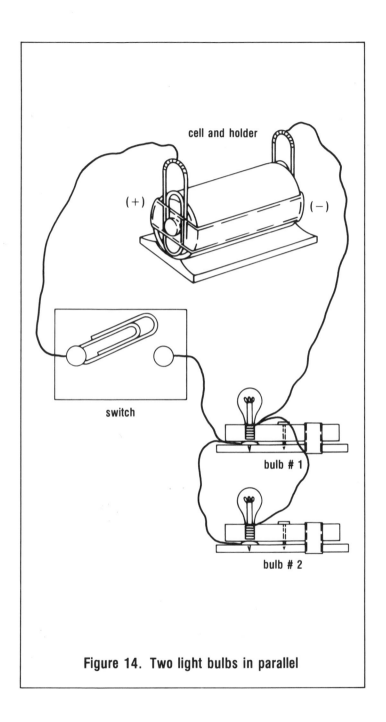

cell and holder

(+)   (−)

switch

bulb # 1

bulb # 2

Figure 14. Two light bulbs in parallel

have to build a second cell holder), flashlight bulb with holder, switch, noninsulated copper wire

Procedure ● (see Figure 15)

1. Place the two D cells in parallel and connect the terminals with wires. Remember to place the cells so that their positive/negative terminals face the same side.
2. Connect one wire from one terminal of cell holder 1 to the bulb holder.
3. Connect the other terminal of the bulb holder to the switch with another wire.
4. Make the last connection between the switch and the cell holder. Now you have completed a circuit with two cells in a parallel configuration.
5. Close the switch and observe. What happens?

Time to Think ●

- Compare the brightness of the light bulbs in this experiment and Experiment 22, when two cells were used in series. Can you explain the difference?
- Now that you have seen a circuit with cells in series and another with cells in parallel, which one do you think is more useful or functional? Can you support your choice?

EXPERIMENT 25: How Can Electricity Be Regulated by a Rheostat?

Materials ● Flashlight bulb with holder and D cell with holder (both from Experiment 16), soft lead pencil, two iron nails, sharp knife, insulated wire, ruler

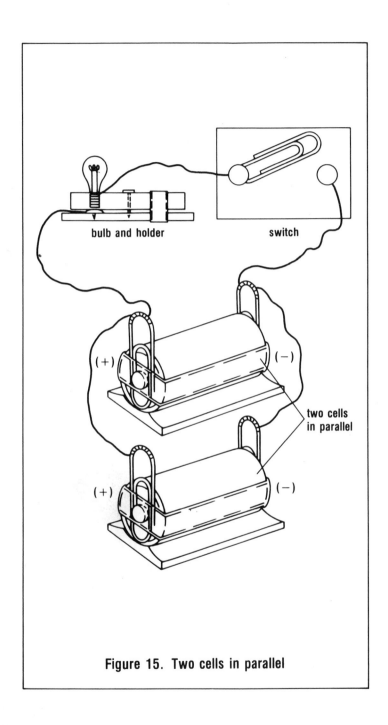

bulb and holder

switch

(+)   (−)

two cells
in parallel

(+)   (−)

Figure 15. Two cells in parallel

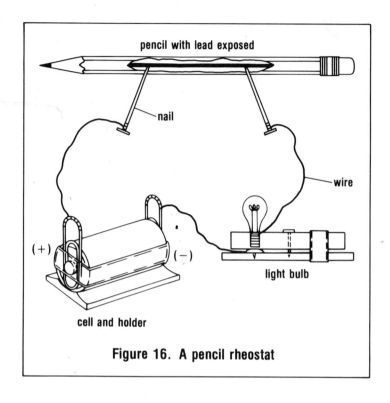

Figure 16. A pencil rheostat

Procedure ● (see Figure 16)

1.   Construct a simple electric circuit using the cell
holder, the bulb holder, and wires as in Experiment 17.
2.   Modify the circuit by wrapping the wire ends from
the bulb holder and the cell holder tightly around the
heads of the iron nails. The nails will be used as probes.
3.   Have an adult help you to carefully cut open the
soft lead pencil lengthwise with the sharp knife to expose the lead. Be careful not to break the lead. You will
need its entire length for this experiment.

4. With all the circuit components in place, press the two probes (that is, nails) gently against the pencil lead. If you press too hard you will break the lead. Note that the probes should not be touching each other. What happened to the light bulb?

5. Vary the distance between the two probes along the lead and record your observations using the following table.

Distance Between the Probes (in millimeters)	Brightness of Bulb
1	
2	
3	
4	
5	
6	
7	
8	
9	
10	

Time to Think ●

● The "lead" of a pencil is mostly graphite. Is graphite a good conductor of electricity? How can you find out?

● According to the experiment data collected, how does the length of the lead affect the amount of electric current that flows through a circuit?

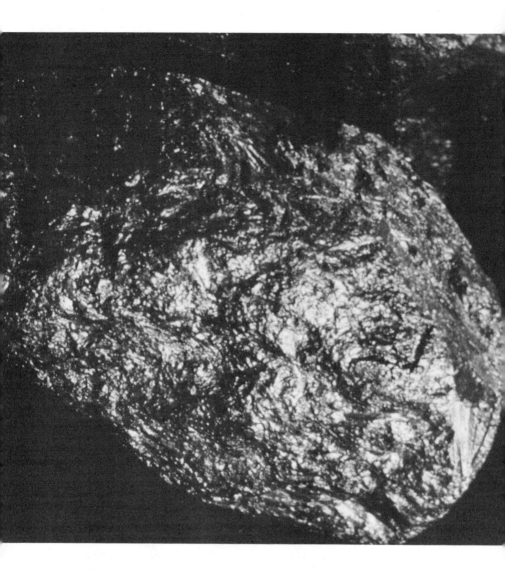

Graphite is a form of carbon. A pencil
"lead" is actually mostly graphite. What
do you learn about graphite's ability to
regulate electric flow by making
the rheostat in Experiment 25?

- A rheostat is a device for controlling the flow of electricity. For example, ordinary room lights can be dimmed by a rheostat. The volume of a radio can also be controlled by a rheostat, although nowadays electronic circuitry is used instead. How was the pencil lead used to control electrical flow? What is the major variable used in a rheostat to control the flow of electricity? Is it the length of the substance? Its weight? Its volume? What did you learn from the experiment?

EXPERIMENT 26: How Does a Two-Way Switch Work in a Circuit?

Materials ● Bulb with holder and D cell with holder (from Experiment 16), two two-way switches, noninsulated copper wires

Procedure ● (see Figure 17)

1. Use the diagram to prepare two two-way switches. Please note that a regular switch has only one contact, which is represented by the metal tack. The two-way switch has two contacts, or two tacks.
2. Use Figure 17 to build an incomplete circuit. In this circuit, the battery holder is connected to the bulb holder and one two-way switch. The other terminal of the bulb holder is connected to the second two-way switch.
3. How do you connect both two-way switches to make a complete circuit? (*Hint:* two wires are needed for the connection.)

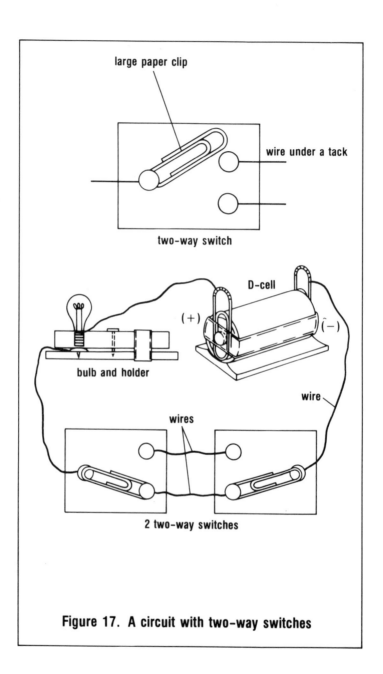

large paper clip

wire under a tack

two-way switch

D-cell

(+)

(-)

bulb and holder

wire

wires

2 two-way switches

Figure 17. A circuit with two-way switches

4. Close the two switches. Does the bulb light up? Open either of the switches. What happens? Can you explain with a simple circuit diagram?

Time to Think •

- Why would anyone want to have two switches to turn the same light on or off? What is one major advantage of having two switches?
- Why is the special switch called a two-way?

EXPERIMENT 27: How Does a Fuse Work in a Circuit?

Materials •

6-volt cell, wooden board (5 × 6 × 1 cm), aluminum foil, scissors, noninsulated copper wires, masking tape, iron nail

Procedure •

1. Cut a strip of aluminum foil so that the center is as thin as a wire. The thickness of the wire is critical to the success of the experiment. This prepared strip is called a fuse.
2. Place the fuse flat on the wood board and connect each end with a wire. The connections between the wire and the fuse can be secured by masking tape.
3. Connect the wire to the two terminals of the 6-volt cell.
4. Observe what happens and record your observations.

Time to Think ●

● Can you locate a fuse box (circuit breaker box) in
  your house? How is the fuse box similar to the fuse
  in the experiment?
● Can you explain how a fuse protects an overloaded
  electric circuit? Please keep in mind that most
  wiring systems today use circuit breakers instead
  of fuses.

EXPERIMENT 28: What is a Circuit Resistance?

Materials ● Thin insulated wires, thick insulated wires,
thumbtacks, two wooden boards (5 × 15 cm), flashlight
bulb with holder, D cell with holder, switch

Procedure ● (see Figure 18)

1. Use the flashlight bulb and holder, the D cell and
holder, and the switch to build a simple electric circuit
like the one in Experiment 17. Use thin wires for all
connections.
2. Use an extra-long piece of wire between the bulb
holder and the cell holder. Wrap the wire around a piece
of board, and secure it with two thumbtacks hammered
into the board.
3. Close the switch, and record what you observe.
4. Disconnect the wires and replace them with thick
wires. Again, use an extra-long piece of thick wire
(about the same length as the extra-long thin wire)
between the bulb holder and the cell holder. As before,

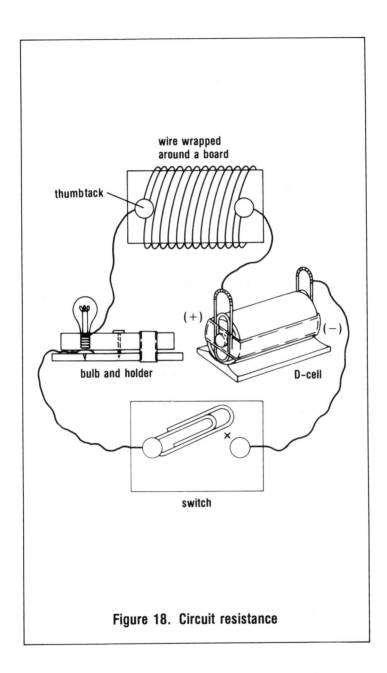

wire wrapped
around a board

thumbtack

(+)

(−)

bulb and holder

D-cell

switch

Figure 18. Circuit resistance

wrap this wire around a piece of board and secure it with two thumbtacks.

5. Close the switch and record your observations.

Time to Think ●

● How does length affect the electrical resistance in a wire?
● How does thickness affect the electrical resistance in a wire?
● Does electrical resistance affect the brightness of a light bulb?
● Which component—the light bulb, the D cell, or the switch—offers the most resistance to the flow of electrons? Can you support your answer?

EXPERIMENT 29: How Is Electricity Changed to Heat?

Materials ● D cell with holder, switch, nichrome heating wire (from a science supply store or an electronic store), connecting wire, thermometer, graph paper

Procedure ● (See Figure 19)

1. Use the D cell with holder, and the switch, to build a simple electric circuit like the one in Experiment 17. Note that instead of a flashlight bulb and holder, you will be connecting a special nichrome heating wire between a terminal of the switch and a terminal of the cell holder.
2. Coil the nichrome wire tightly about ten turns around the bulb of the thermometer (Caution! the nichrome wire will get hot!)

76

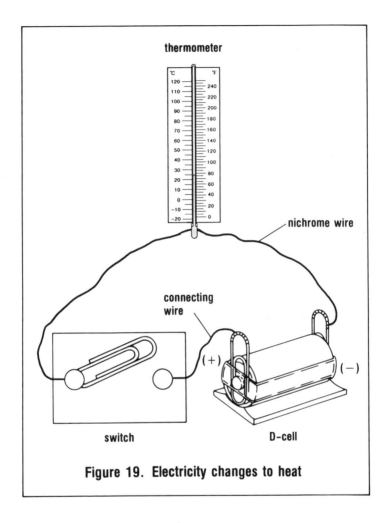

thermometer

nichrome wire

connecting
wire

(+)

(−)

switch

D−cell

Figure 19. Electricity changes to heat

3. Record the beginning temperature of the thermometer. To avoid affecting the accuracy of the temperature reading, be careful not to touch the glass stem or the thermometer bulb.

4. Close the switch and read the thermometer at 15-

second intervals. Use the following table to record your observations.

Time (seconds)	Temperature (degrees Celsius)
Start	
15	
30	
45	
60	
75	
90	
105	
120	
135	
150	
165	
180	
195	

5. Use the data you collected to construct a line graph. Place the time variable (seconds) on the X axis and the temperature variable (degrees Celsius) on the Y axis.

Time to Think ●

- The nichrome heating wire has very high resistance to the flow of electricity. How is this property related to changing electricity to heat?
- Can you name a few household examples where electricity is turned into heat?
- A heating element is an object made of a high-

resistance substance like nichrome which is tightly coiled to concentrate the heat produced. If you were an electrical technician, how would you design the heating element for an electric coffeepot?

● Examine the contour of the line graph from the experiment. What is the maximum temperature? What is the difference between the maximum temperature and the beginning temperature?

EXPERIMENT 30: How Is Electricity Changed to Light?

Materials ● Two D cells with holders, three wires, switch, nichrome wire, ruler

Procedure ●

1. Connect the two cell holders and cells with a length of wire. Add the switch to the circuit you are building.
2. Wrap the length of nichrome wire around the ends of the two wires coming from the incomplete circuit.
3. Close the switch. What happens? (*Caution:* the nichrome wire gets very hot!)
4. Vary the length of the nichrome wire connection and complete the following table.

Length of the Nichrome Wire	Brightness of the Wire
5 mm	
10 mm	
15 mm	
20 mm	

5.   How does the length of the nichrome wire connection affect the brightness of the wire?

Time to Think ● Based on your experience of the experiment, can you explain how electricity is changed to light energy?

EXPERIMENT 31: How Does a Diode Work?

A diode is a semiconductor device that permits electric current to flow in one direction. A diode is like a one-way street for electricity. It is one of many devices used by engineers to make televisions, radios, and other electronic appliances.

Materials ● D cell with holder, flashlight bulb with holder, long piece of wire, switch, simple diode (from an electronics store)

Procedure ● (see Figure 20)

1.   Connect the D-cell, the light bulb, and the switch to make a complete circuit similar to the one in Experiment 17.
2.   Now connect the diode to the circuit as shown in Figure 20. What happens to the light?
3.   Now turn the diode around 180 degrees so that the connecting wires are attached to the opposite ends of the diode wires. What happens to the light now?

Time to Think ● How would you define *diode*? Write your definition in your notebook.

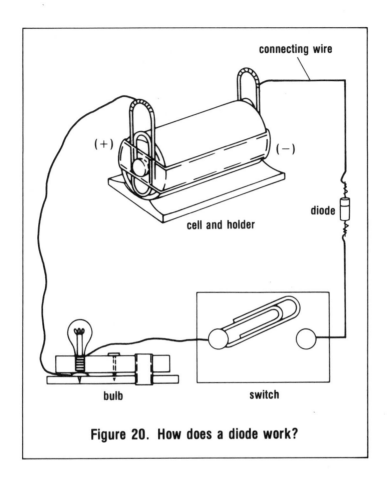

connecting wire

(+)

(−)

diode

cell and holder

bulb

switch

Figure 20. How does a diode work?

EXPERIMENT 32: How Do You Wire a "House"?

Now that you have worked with different circuits in this chapter, you can try to wire a shoe box in the same way that an electrician wires a house.

Materials ● Shoe box, cardboard, scissors, pencil, ruler,

wires, four flashlight bulbs, switch, D cell with holder, masking tape

Procedure ●

1. Cut up the cardboard and use the pieces as dividers to make four rooms in the shoe box "house."
2. Draw a plan for placing a light in each of the four rooms. Consider the following questions: Where will the light be placed? Where will the switch be placed? Where will the electrical source be placed? How will you connect everything to make a complete circuit?
3. Go ahead with the wiring after you have completed the wiring plan in your notebook. Turn on the switch. Does your wiring plan work? If it doesn't, try a different plan.

Time to Think ● How should the switch, bulbs, and cells be connected so that the lights in the house are the brightest possible?

4

ELECTROMAGNETISM

What do doorbells, television sets, vacuum cleaners, hair dryers, fans, electric razors, electric can openers, washing machines, telegraphs, telephones, electric motors, and generators have in common? They all use electromagnets activated by the flow of electricity. Electromagnetism works wonders in our daily lives, as you can see from the roll call of household gadgets and appliances that use electromagnetism to do their jobs. In the following experiments you will experience firsthand the close relationship between magnetism and electricity.

HISTORY

Hans Christian Oersted ● In 1820 the Danish physicist Hans Christian Oersted (1777–1851) discovered the close relationship between electricity and magnetism. The story of the discovery is an interesting one. While giving a college physics lecture, he noticed that a nearby compass needle twitched when he flipped a switch to start an electric current. Further experiments convinced him that a magnetic field is present whenever electric current flows through a wire.

André-Marie Ampère ● The French physicist and mathematician André-Marie Ampère (1775–1836) repeated Oersted's experiment many times to define a rule. The rule relates the direction of current electricity along a wire to the deflection of the compass needle. Ampere then proposed a theory of magnetism that explained it in terms of the flow of an electric current. The theory reflected his conviction that electric current causes the phenomenon of electro/magnetism.

In recognition of Ampere's contribution to the understanding of electromagnetism, the unit of electric current was named after him. An ampere of electricity is defined as the amount of current in a wire that will exert a certain force on another nearby current-carrying wire.

Background information ● Electricity and magnetism are inseparable aspects of the same phenomenon: you cannot have one without the other. Simply stated, wherever there is a moving electric field, a magnetic force may

Danish physicist Hans Christian Oersted (1777–1851) demonstrated the effect of an electric current on a magnetic compass needle. His discovery became the foundation of the study of electromagnetism.

be induced in a nearby conductor. On the other hand, wherever there is a moving electric current, there is a magnetic field.

One common application of electromagnetism is the electromagnet, a device used in such machines as the telegraph, the buzzer, and the motor, among other gadgets and appliances. A simple electromagnet is a loop of wire coiled around an iron core and connected to the two terminals of a battery. Due to the connection between magnetism and electricity, the current produces a magnetic field; therefore the loop of wire acts as a magnet. The strength of the electromagnet can be augmented by increasing the number of coil turns or by boosting the electrical input from the source. Unlike the permanent magnets that you use to hold things on your refrigerator, the electromagnet can be turned on and off by opening and closing the switch that controls the current.

The other side of the electromagnetic coin relates to the ability of the magnetic field to produce electricity. If the magnetic field in the region of a loop of wire is changed by moving a bar magnet near the wire, electrons will flow in the wire. Why? Because the magnetic field pushes the electrons, and moving electrons produce electricity. This phenomenon is called electromagnetic induction.

EXPERIMENT 33: How Do You Make a Galvanometer (Electric Current Detector)?

Materials ● 6-volt dry cell, various lengths of insulated wire, magnetic compass, cover of a small cardboard box, four thumbtacks, switch (from Experiment 16), wooden board, two paper clips

Procedure ● (see Figure 21)

1. Coil an insulated wire about fifteen turns around the cover of a small cardboard box.

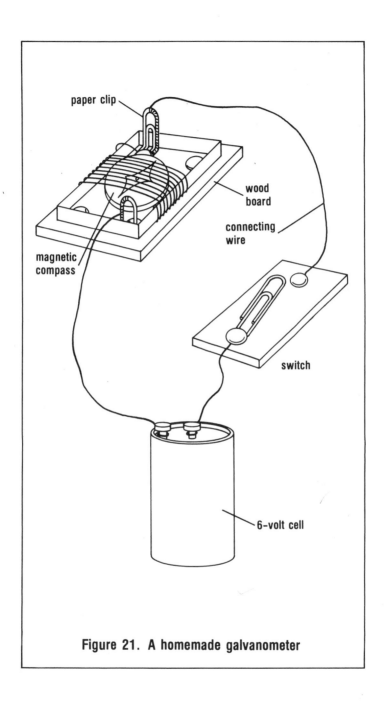

paper clip

wood
board

connecting
wire

magnetic
compass

switch

6-volt cell

Figure 21. A homemade galvanometer

2. Place the box cover on the board. Secure it in place at the corners with four thumbtacks.

3. Bend two paper clips in half as shown. The paper clips are the leads.

4. Slip the paper clips under the tacks. Wrap the ends of the wire around the thumbtacks. Press the tacks into the wood.

5. Put the magnetic compass inside the box, that is, inside the wire coil.

6. Connect a wire between the cell terminal and the switch terminal.

7. Connect two other wires from the cell and switch to the paper clip leads.

8. Close the switch. What happens? Open and close the switch several times and record your observations.

9. Reconnect the terminals of the cell to reverse the poles. In other words, the wire used to connect the positive end now connects the negative end and vice versa. Close the switch. What happens? Open and close the switch several times and record your observations.

Time to Think ●

● Based on the results of the experiment, can you formulate a simple rule to describe the relationship between the direction of the current and the movement of the compass needle?

● Consider the close link between electricity and magnetism—that is, when electricity moves through a coil, magnetism is produced. Explain how a galvanometer is used to detect electric current.

EXPERIMENT 34: How Do You Make a Simple Electromagnet?

Materials ● 6-volt cell, insulated bell wire, large iron nail, switch (from Experiment 16), straight pins

Procedure ●

1. Coil an insulated wire twenty turns around a large iron nail.
2. Connect one end of the wire to the switch and the other end to the terminal of the 6-volt cell.
3. Connect a wire between the switch and the cell to make a circuit.
4. Close the switch to make a complete circuit. How many straight pins can the electromagnet you have just made pick up? Record your observation in the chart.
5. Increase the number of turns around the nail to forty, sixty, eighty, etc., according to the chart. Each time test the electromagnet on the straight pins. Record your observations in the chart.

Number of Coils	Number of Pins Picked Up
20	
40	
60	
80	
100	
120	
140	
160	
180	

Time to Think •

• What happened to the strength of your electromagnet whenever you opened the switch? Does
this suggest any advantages of using an electromagnet?
• Use the data from the chart to plot a line graph. Use
the axis for the number of coils and the X axis for
the number of pins picked up. What does the graph
look like? What does it mean? What can you gener-
alize about the number of coils versus the strength
of the electromagnet?
• Can you imagine how a junkyard operator would
use a powerful electromagnet to move metal
scraps?

**EXPERIMENT 35: How Can You Make a Stronger Electro-
magnet?**

Materials • Two 6-volt cells, insulated bell wire, large
iron nail, switch (from Experiment 16), straight pins

Procedure •

1.   Construct a twenty-turn electromagnet as you first
did in Experiment 34.
2.   Place two 6-volt cells in series.
3.   Secure all wire connections to make a complete
circuit.
4.   Close the switch. What happens? Open and close
the switch several times and record your observations.
5.   Increase the number of coils around the nail to

forty, sixty, eighty, etc., according to the chart. How many pins can each electromagnet pick up? Record your observations in the chart.

Number of Coils	Number of Pins Picked Up
20	
40	
60	
80	
100	
120	
160	
180	

Time to Think ●

● Use the data from the chart to plot a line graph. Use the Y axis for the number of coils and the X axis for the number of pins picked up. What does the graph look like? What does it mean?
● Compare the graph to the graph in Experiment 34. What generalization can you make about how to strengthen an electromagnet?
● How would you design an electromagnetic device to detect counterfeit coins?

EXPERIMENT 36: How Do You Build a Telegraph Set?

Materials ● 6-volt cell, wood block, two large iron nails, switch, pieces of unpainted ferrous metal such as iron, nickel, steel, noninsulated bell wire, screw, hammer

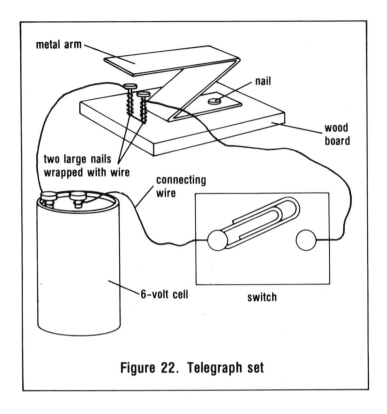

Figure 22. Telegraph set

Procedure ● (see Figure 22)

1.   Bend a piece of metal into a Z-shape and nail it on the block of wood as shown. This piece of metal is the receiver of the telegraph set.

2.   Hammer the two iron nails under the free end of the metal.

3.   Connect a long piece of wire to one terminal of the 6-volt cell.

4.   Wrap the wire many times around the nail until the

nail is covered with layers of coil. Start at the top of the nail and work downward.

5. Bring the wire across to the other nail. Coil it around as many times as before, but this time work upward.

6. Connect the other end of this wire to one terminal of the switch.

7. Connect a second wire between the free terminal of the dry cell and the switch. Now you have completed the circuit.

8. Close the switch. What happens to the telegraph receiver? If nothing happens, you need to adjust the space between the arm of the metal Z and the nails. You might bring the metal arm a little closer to the nails. Open and close the switch a few times. Record your observations.

Time to Think ●

●   How does the telegraph set use electromagnetism? Can you use a circuit diagram for your explanation?

●   In 1844, the great American inventor and painter Samuel F. B. Morse (1791–1872) invented the telegraph, a device that made it possible to communicate with people in distant places much faster than ever before.

    The telegraph sends signals in the form of a code called the Morse code over electric wires. Obtain a copy of the Morse code. Find out how you can send a simple message on your telegraph by using the Morse code.

EXPERIMENT 37: How Do You Build a Buzzer?

Materials ● 6-volt cell, wood block, two large iron nails, switch, piece of metal (unpainted), noninsulated bell wire, screw, hammer

Procedure ● (see Figure 23)
Note: Instead of building another telegraph set, you can use the one you built for Experiment 36. However, you will have to modify the sounder, or telegraph receiver, to make it a buzzer.

1.   Prepare the telegraph receiver as in steps 1 and 2 of Experiment 36. See the note above if you have already completed that experiment.
2.   Hammer a tiny hole into the free end of the metal with a nail.
3.   Connect a wire between one terminal of the cell and the hole of the metal arm.
4.   Coil a long wire around one nail many times, working downward. Begin at the top of the nail and make sure that the free end of the wire sticks out from the top as shown. It is critical that the free end of this wire should lightly touch the free end of the metal as shown in the inset of Figure 23.
5.   Bring the wire across to the other nail. Coil it around as many times as before, working upward.
6.   Connect the other end of this wire to one terminal of the switch. Connect a second wire between the free terminal of the cell and the switch. Now you have made a complete circuit.
7.   Close the switch. What happens? Continue to open and close the switch, and record your observations.

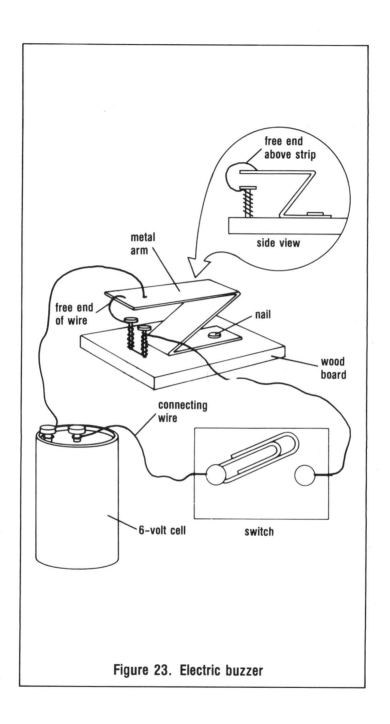

Figure 23. Electric buzzer

Time to Think ●

● How does the buzzer system work on electromagnetism? Can you use a circuit diagram to support
your explanation?

● Predict what will happen if the free end of the wire
from the nail is permanently connected to the free
end of the metal arm. Can you support your pre-
diction by what you know about an electric circuit
and an electromagnetic circuit?

EXPERIMENT 38: How Do You Build a Simple Motor?

Materials ● Styrofoam cup, two paper clips, D cell,
masking tape, two square magnets, thin enamel-covered
wire (magnet wire), sandpaper

Procedure ● (see Figure 24)

1. Coil the thin enamel-covered wire around your
index finger four times. Pull the wire from your finger
and you will get a wire loop. The two ends of the wire
should extend from the loop at right angles as shown.
Use a small piece of sandpaper to completely remove
any coating on the ends of the wire. Set the loop aside.
2. Bend two paper clips as shown to form a hook for
supporting the wire loop horizontally.
3. Tape the paper clips on each terminal of the cell in
a vertical position. Check to see that the clips are equal
in vertical length.
4. Place the cell with the clips on the bottom of an
inverted Styrofoam cup. Tape it down with masking tape.

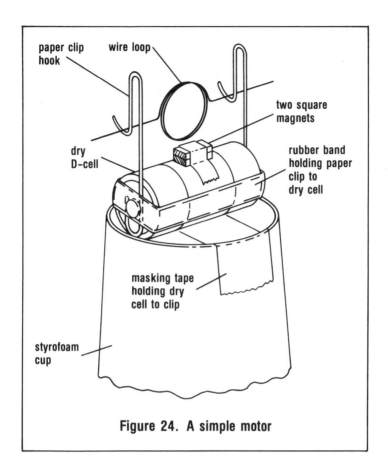

paper clip
hook

wire loop

two square
magnets

dry
D–cell

rubber band
holding paper
clip to
dry cell

masking tape
holding dry
cell to clip

styrofoam
cup

Figure 24. A simple motor

5.   Tape two square magnets on the cell between the two clips.

6.   Place the wire loop gently on the paper clip hooks directly above, but not touching, the magnet. Make sure that everything is in a perfect horizontal position. Trial and error will tell you the best position. Record what happens.

● Examine the following components of the motor and its function. (1) The wire loop with the current flowing through it is the electromagnet. (2) The paper clips (hooks) deliver electricity to the wire loop. The hooks permit the wire loop to move or rotate. (3) The permanent square magnets interact with the electromagnet through repulsion and attraction.

After putting together the information from (1), (2), and (3), can you explain how the motor works on electromagnetism?

● Steam and running water are used to move an electric generator. There is a big motor inside the generator. Find out how a generator transforms mechanical energy to electric energy.

5

PROJECTS IN ELECTRICITY AND MAGNETISM

INTRODUCTION

Scientists have unique ways of solving problems—the scientific method of investigation. When scientists are confronted by a problem, they carefully set goals. Next, they collect background information on the subject by tedious research before actually pursuing the investigation. It is true that scientists sometimes make important discoveries by chance, but even these would be impossible without the scientists' special training and their ability to make sense of the accidental discovery.

HISTORY

Thomas A. Edison ● Thomas A. Edison (1847–1931) epitomizes the spirit of American ingenuity. Edison is without a doubt America's most celebrated inventor and technologist. He owed his success in giving the world the incandescent carbon electric lamp and so many other important inventions not only to his genius but also to his remarkable persistence. Although his first attempts with various inventions often failed again and again, Edison always kept trying and learning from his failures until he eventually succeeded. He was issued a total of 1,093 patents.

Now that you have gained knowledge as well as skills in the basics of electricity and magnetism from the previous experiments, you are ready to go on to the next level of experiments and to more fun and challenging projects. You will have an opportunity to experience some exciting moments of Edison's actual work when you do Experiments 39 and 40, which replicate two of his investigations in electricity and magnetism.

EXPERIMENT 39: How Do You Make an Electric Light?

In Experiment 15 you investigated the inside of a light bulb. In this experiment you will actually make a light bulb yourself and thereby get an idea of how Thomas Edison must have felt when he invented the incandescent lamp in 1879.

Materials ● 6-volt cell, insulated wires, copper-strand lamp wire, switch, small birthday candle, wide-mouth jar with lid, masking tape, soda bottle cap, match, hammer, nail

You can replicate two of the discoveries of the
great American inventor Thomas Alva Edison—the
electric light bulb and the relay telegraph—by doing
Experiments 39 and 40.

Procedure ●

1. Use the hammer and nail to make two small holes 4 to 5 cm apart in the lid of the wide-mouth jar. The best way to do this is to lay the lid (not the rim) flat on a board. Strip the ends of two wires and insert them into the jar. Bend the wires and tape them down on the lid with masking tape.

2. Remove one copper strand from the lamp wire. Coil it around a nail several times. Remove the coil. Connect the coil between the two wires from the lid.

3. Connect one wire from the lid to the terminal of the cell. Connect the other wire from the lid to the terminal of the switch. Connect another wire between the free terminal of the cell and the switch. You have now completed a circuit.

4. Place a lighted candle inside the jar using the soda bottle cap as the candle base. Screw in the lid tightly while the candle is still burning.

5. Close the switch to complete the circuit as soon as the flame goes out. Wait a few minutes. What happens? Record your observations. *Note:* this experiment is more dramatic if the last step is performed in a dark room.

Time to Think ●

● The experiment will also work without burning the candle. You can try that for comparison. What is the purpose of burning a candle inside the jar? (*Hint:* when the candle is out, what does it tell you about the air in the jar?)

- When you break a light bulb, it pops. What does that tell you about the inside of the bulb?
- What is inside a neon bulb? Why does it light up differently from an incandescent bulb?

EXPERIMENT 40: How Do You Build a Relay Telegraph System?

In Experiment 36 you had the opportunity to build a simple telegraph set. In Edison's time (around 1870) he found that the electric current flowing from a distant station was too weak to operate the electromagnet of the telegraph set. He therefore made an improvement of the old model and invented a relay system to boost the weak force and make it much stronger.

Materials ● Strip of metal, small wood block, Popsicle stick, thumbtack, masking tape, iron screws, insulated wire, 6-volt cell, flashlight bulb and holder, 1.5-volt D cell, switch, sandpaper, solder and soldering iron (optional), hammer, nails

Procedure ● (see Figure 25)
There are three major components to the relay telegraph system: the relay unit with the electromagnet, the low-voltage circuit, and the high-voltage circuit.

Relay Unit ○

1. Bend a metal strip in the form of a Z. Note that one end of the Z is longer. Secure the short end of the Z strip into the wooden block with a metal screw.

103

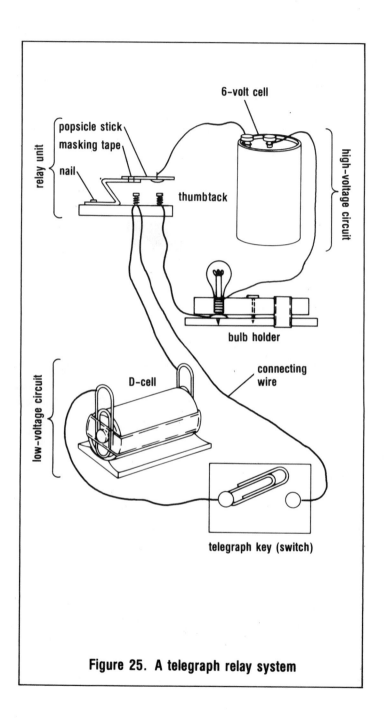

Figure 25. A telegraph relay system

2. Extend free arm of Z with a Popsicle stick and tape it down with masking tape. End of the Popsicle stick should not extend beyond the wooden block.

3. Press in a thumbtack near the end of the stick. Sand the head of the tack to ensure good conduction. You have just finished making the contact arm of the relay unit.

4. Hammer two nails onto the block. One nail should be located under the metal strip, the other directly under the thumbtack.

5. Coil about 100 turns of long insulated wire around the nail beneath the metal, leaving enough wire to make other wire connections. Twist the free ends together so the coil will not come apart. You have now made an electromagnet.

Low-Voltage Circuit ○

6. Connect one wire from the electromagnet of the relay unit to a 1.5-volt D cell.

7. Connect the D cell to one terminal of the telegraph key. The telegraph key is actually a modified switch.

8. Connect the second wire from the electromagnet to the other terminal of the telegraph key. Now you have made the low-voltage (1.5-volt) circuit and connected it to the relay unit.

High-Voltage Circuit ○

9. Connect a wire between the one terminal of the 6-volt cell and the thumbtack. You may choose to solder this connection since this is the moving part of the system. If you do, have an adult help you, and be careful not to inhale the harmful fumes from the soldering.

10. Connect the other terminal of the 6-volt cell to a 6-volt bulb. (*Note:* a flashlight bulb will burn out immediately with a 6-volt cell.)

11. Connect the third wire between the bulb holder and the nail beneath the thumbtack. Now you have completed the high-voltage circuit.

12. Depress the telegraph key. The closing of the key makes the low-voltage circuit complete. As you may recall, this represents a message coming in from a distant station. Open and close the key several times as if you were sending a telegraph message. Record what happens by completing the following chart.

Telegraph Components	What Happened?
Electromagnet	_____
Contact arm	_____
Light bulb	_____

Time to Think •

- Draw a simple diagram to illustrate the flow of current in the low-voltage circuit and the high-voltage circuit.
- How was the low-voltage circuit used to control the high-voltage circuit by going through the relay unit? Can you explain?
- Which way is it easier for a telegraph operator to receive an incoming message: through the clicking of the contact arm or through the blinking of the light bulb?

EXPERIMENT 41: How Do You Build a Watchdog That Doesn't Eat or Sleep?

Anyone opening a door equipped with this "watch-dog," which is actually an alarm, will be in for quite a surprise! You may want to take it anywhere you go; it is truly portable.

Materials ● 6-volt cell, two wood blocks, tape, electric doorbell, insulated wire, wooden clothespin, rubber bands, masking tape, eye screw, thumbtacks, hammer and nails, solder and soldering iron, string, sandpaper

Procedure ● (see Figure 26)
Like the circuits you have built earlier, the alarm basically consists of a power source (the cell) and power user (the bell) connected in a complete circuit with a set-off device (the switch).

1. Nail two wooden blocks together at a right angle. Place the 6-volt cell next to the upright block and secure it with rubber bands.
2. Place the doorbell flat on the horizontal board, next to the battery. You may want to nail it in place.
3. Place a wooden clothespin next to the doorbell. Tape it down in place. Push one thumbtack into each jaw of the pin. Make sure that the tacks are sanded to permit good conduction.
4. Place a piece of cardboard between the jaws of the clothespin. The cardboard is the insulator between the two thumbtacks. Attach a trip string to the cardboard. The other end of the trip string should be attached to the door.

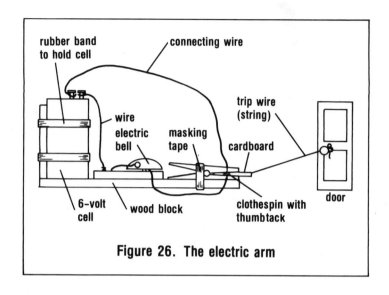

Figure 26. The electric arm

5. Make the following wire connections:

- From one terminal of the cell to one terminal of the bell
- From the second terminal of the cell to one thumbtack
- From the other thumbtack to the second terminal of the doorbell.

6. Put the alarm in place. The system is now ready to work for you.

7. Have someone open the door. The door will pull on the trip string, which in turn will pull out the cardboard to permit direct contact between the two thumbtacks. Now you have a complete electric circuit. What happens?

Time to Think ●

● Make two simple diagrams to show the flow of electricity (1) when the cardboard was in place and (2) when the cardboard was pulled. Which of the two is the incomplete circuit? Which is the complete circuit?

● How would you make additional wire connections to include a flashlight bulb so that the light turns on at the same time the alarm bell rings?

UNITED STATES USE OF ELECTRICITY IS INCREASING

In recent years, 37 percent of the nation's energy has been used to produce electricity. Scientists predict that the figure will increase to 40 percent by the year 2000. The United States is becoming more and more dependent on electricity to meet its energy needs. In the past sixteen years the U.S. demand for electricity has grown by 45 percent, even though the population has grown by only 16 percent and our total demand for energy by only 8 percent.

To meet this increasing demand for electric power, a variety of energy sources are tapped. Some of those sources contribute a substantial amount of the electricity needed, while others contribute less than $\frac{1}{2}$ of 1 percent.

Do you know the major sources of this country's electricity? Can you rank them in order of their contribution to the U.S. demand for electricity?

The following nine sources were identified by a survey from the Energy Information Administration.

- *Biomass* energy results from the burning of wood and solid waste. This provides less than 0.1 percent of the nation's electricity.
- *Coal*. Eighty percent of the nation's coal output is used by electric utility companies to produce electricity. The burning of coal provides 57 percent of the nation's electricity.
- *Geothermal*. The use of geothermal energy, which is tapped from underground sources, is limited to the western United States. Geothermal energy produces 0.33 percent of the nation's electricity.
- *Hydropower*. Almost 10 percent of the nation's electricity is generated by running water. It is the leading renewable source used to provide electricity.
- *Natural Gas*. About half of the natural gas output was used by gas turbines to produce electricity during peak hours of demand. Natural gas produces 10 percent of the nation's electricity.
- *Uranium*. About 109 nuclear power stations presently provide the United States with almost 20 percent of its electrical needs.
- *Petroleum*. Six percent of the nation's electricity is provided by the use of petroleum.
- *Solar*. *Solar* energy provides about 0.0001 percent of the nation's electricity. The use of solar power is largely limited to certain geographic areas in the United States.
- *Wind* energy provides less than 0.0001 percent of the nation's electricity, and 95 percent of our wind-generated electricity is in the state of California.

U.S. ELECTRIC POWER GENERATION SOURCES

Sources	Rank
Coal	1
Uranium	2
Hydropower	3
Natural Gas	4
Petroleum	5
Geothermal	6
Biomass	7
Solar	8
Wind	9

More than half the electricity consumed in this country is generated by burning coal. Unfortunately, coal burning is also our main source of carbon dioxide gas pollution, which causes environmental problems such as global warming and a higher incidence of respiratory disease. As a result, more people are switching to using alternate sources of clean and renewable energy. Energy from the sun and wind seems to be the promising solution.

Scientists estimate that sunlight shining on the United States on a typical bright summer day can provide more energy than this country can use in two years! The problem is how to collect the energy and turn it into a usable form. Although solar energy has the potential of providing us with clean, renewable energy, it is unfortunately quite expensive to generate at present.

EXPERIMENT 42: How Do We Harness Electricity From the Sun?

Materials ● Block of wood, silicon solar cell (from electronic hobby store), magnet wire (no. 18), soldering iron and solder, tape, compass, two small alligator clips

Procedure ● (see Figure 27)

1.   Purchase a silicon solar cell from an electronic store. It is not expensive. You are all set if the solar cell comes with connecting wires. If it does, skip step 2, which deals with attaching those wires.

2.   Lay the solar cell faceup flat on a surface. Scrape the ends of two connecting wires. Put on safety glasses and gloves and, with adult supervision, solder a length of wire to the silver edge on the face of the cell. Turn the solar cell facedown and solder another length of wire to the silver surface anywhere on the back.

3.   Tape the solar cell and its connecting wires onto a block of wood as shown.

4.   Now place the solar cell aside and, unless you have already done so, build a simple galvanometer according to the directions in Experiment 33. A galvanometer is a sensitive instrument used to detect the presence of electricity.

5.   Connect the two wires from the solar cell to the wires of the galvanometer.

6.   Expose the solar light system to the following conditions and record your observations. Use the following chart to record your data.

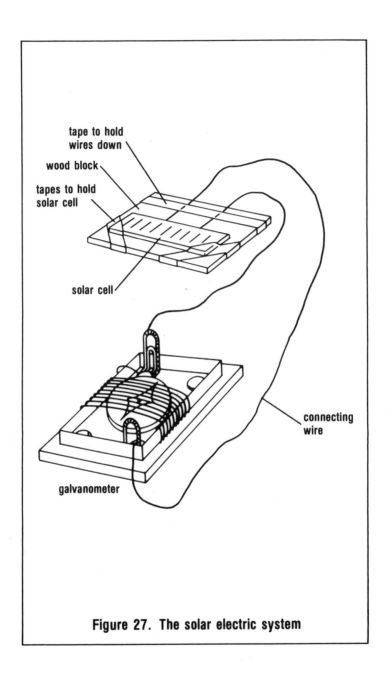

tape to hold
wires down

wood block

tapes to hold
solar cell

solar cell

connecting
wire

galvanometer

Figure 27. The solar electric system

Light Condition	Needle Deflection of the Galvanometer
Flashlight	_____
Direct sunlight	_____
Indirect sunlight (overcast)	_____
Incandescent light	_____
Fluorescent light	_____
Sunlamp light	_____

Time to Think ●

- Look at your experiment data. Can you rank the movements of the galvanometer needle? What can you conclude about one disadvantage of using solar energy?
- Many space satellites use solar collectors to power their equipment. Find out (from the library) how solar collectors transform light into electricity.
- Have you ever used a solar calculator? Can you compare a solar calculator to a conventional dry-cell-operated calculator?

EXPERIMENT 43: How Do You Harness Electricity From the Wind?

Wind is related to the heat of the sun because air movement is caused by differences in air temperature, which result from solar heat. The concept of harnessing wind energy has been used since ancient times. Centuries ago

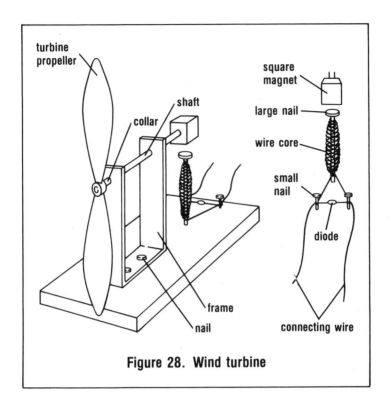

Figure 28. Wind turbine

wind was being used to propel sailing ships, to grind grain, and to pump water. Many scientists feel that in most locations the cost of converting wind energy to electricity would be too high at present to justify its use.

Materials ● Wood block, 6-inch (15.2-cm) model air-plane propeller, large iron nails, smaller nails, small square magnet, metal strip, hammer, drill, magnet wire (no. 18), diode (1N34A) from an electronic hobby store, tape, solder and soldering iron, super-glue, electric tape

115

Procedure ● (see Figure 28) The wind electric generator has two major components: the turbine and the wire core. The turbine moves a magnet to push electrons in the wire core and thereby generate electricity.

Turbine ○

1. Glue the square magnet flat on the head of a large iron nail. Set it aside because it takes time for the glue to set. The nail is going to be the shaft of the turbine.

2. Prepare a tin can frame support as shown. Nail one end of the frame to the wood block.

3. Mark on the uprights of the frame where you will later drill holes for the shaft to go through. It is better to drill the holes later because you might need to change their position.

4. Attach the propeller to the other end of the nail when other parts of the system are ready to go.

Wire Core ○

5. Coil a long magnet wire around a large iron nail about 1,000 turns. The coil should be about 5 cm long. Leave two lengths of wire uncoiled for connections. Twist the ends of the wires together so they will not come apart.

6. Drive the nail into the wood block next to the upright of the turbine frame. The wire core standing up should be shorter than the frame upright. Hammer two smaller nails as shown in the wood with wires from the coil.

7. Put on safety glasses and work gloves. Solder a diode between the two small nails as shown. The pur-

116

pose of the diode is to convert the alternating current (AC) from the core to direct current (DC). DC is what you will use in the experiment.

8. Insert the shaft of the turbine through the frame. The bar magnet of the turbine must be directly above but not touching the head of the wire core when it moves. Wrap a collar of tape on the shaft as shown. This will prevent the shaft from sliding.

9. Carefully drill a small hole on the propeller and fit it snugly on the nail.

10. Expose the wind turbine to the wind or put it right in front of a fan. You may want to turn the blade of the propeller just to help it start.

11. The ultimate test of the system is to connect a light bulb or other test items to the two small nails. Use the following chart to record your data.

Test Items	What Happened to It?
Light bulb (1.5-volt)	_____
Light bulb (6-volt)	_____
Galvanometer (from Experiment 33)	_____
Heating wire	_____

Time to Think ●

● Based on your experiment data, what can you tell about the strength of the electric current generated by the wind turbine?

117

- Use your knowledge of electromagnetism to explain how electricity can be generated from the wind. (*Hint:* when the propeller spins, it also turns the magnet on the shaft. What will that turning magnet do to the wire core?)
- What other sources of energy can drive a turbine to generate electricity?

GLOSSARY

Alternating current. Electric current in which the flow of electrons reverses direction in regular cycles.

Amber. A hard, translucent fossil resin from pine trees. Amber, usually yellow or brown in color, is commonly used for carvings, jewelry, and electrical insulation.

Ammonium chloride. A white or colorless crystalline compound of ammonia that is commonly used in dry cells. The chemical formula for ammonium chloride is NH_4Cl.

Ampere. The standard unit of strength of an electric current. It is equal to the amount of current produced by 1 volt acting through a resistance of 1 ohm. The unit is named after the French physicist André Marie Ampère, 1775–1836.

Atom. The smallest particle of an element that has the chemical properties of that element. The atom has a positively charged nucleus in the center surrounded by one or more negatively charged electrons.

Attraction. A force exerted by bodies on one another. The force tends to pull the bodies together.

Battery. Two or more electric cells connected together.

Biomass. That part of an environment consisting of living matter. Biomass is expressed either as the weight of organisms per unit area or as the volume of organisms per unit volume of the environment.

Circuit. A complete path through which an electric current passes.

Circuit breaker. An automatic switch which breaks the circuit when too much electricity is flowing. It is similar to a fuse, but, unlike a fuse, it can be reused.

Condenser. An electrical device that controls the supply of electricity by means of two plates that hold the electric charges.

Conductor. A substance that allows energy such as heat or electricity to pass through.

Crystal. A rock that is bounded by plane surfaces. Crystals are arranged in an orderly and repeated pattern. Sodium chloride, or table salt, is an example of a crystal.

Current. The flow of electricity in one direction.

Direct current. Electric current in which the flow of electrons goes in only one direction.

Dry cell. A combination of two metals in a chemical solution that produces electricity. Dry cells are used in flashlights and other devices.

Electric charge. A fundamental property of matter. An

electron carries a negative electric charge; a proton a positive electric charge.

Electric field. An area in which an electric charge experiences a force, as happens at the two anodes in the cathode ray tube of a television set.

Electricity. Energy carried by electrons, protons, and other subatomic particles. Electricity is capable of producing heat, light, and other effects.

Electric potential. The difference in electric pressures. The flow of electricity goes from a point of high electric potential to a point of low electric potential.

Electric resistance. The opposition to a flow of electricity. A substance that does not allow electricity to easily pass through has a high electric resistance.

Electrolyte. A solution which permits electric current to pass through.

Electromagnet. An iron core with insulated wire wound around it. The iron core becomes a magnet when electric current is supplied to the electric coil.

Electron. A subatomic particle that carries the smallest negative electric charge.

Electrophorus. A device for generating charges of static electricity by means of induction.

Electroplating. To apply a metal coating to the surface of an object by means of electrolysis.

Electroscope. An instrument used to detect and measure electric charges.

Electrostatics. A branch of physics that studies static electricity, or electricity at rest.

Flint. A hard, fine-grained stone that produces sparks when struck against steel. Flint is commonly used in cigarette lighters.

Friction. A force that resists motion between two surfaces that are in contact with one another.

Fuse. A safety device consisting of a strip of metal inserted in an electric circuit. The strip will melt and break the circuit if the electric current becomes excessive.

Galvanometer. An instrument for detecting and measuring the flow of electricity.

Generator. A machine that converts mechanical energy into electrical energy.

Geothermal. Related to the heat generated from the earth's interior.

Graphite. A soft, black crystalline carbon commonly used as a lubricant when mixed with oil and as "lead" for pencils. Graphite is a conductor of electricity.

Hypothesis. An educational guess or assumption based on known facts. A hypothesis can be used as a basis for further investigation and experimentation.

Igniter. A device that triggers burning, commonly used in cigarette lighters and gas grills.

Incandescent. Glowing with heat. An incandescent lamp is a light bulb in which light is produced by passing electric current through a thin high-resistance wire, causing it to glow.

Induction. The process of giving an electric charge to an object by bringing it close to a charged body.

Insulator. A material that prevents the flow of an electric current. Many nonmetals are insulators.

Ion. An atom whose outer electron shell has gained or lost one or more electrons. Positive ions are formed by the loss of electrons, negative ions by the gain of electrons.

Kilowatt-hour. A unit of electric energy indicating the amount of energy used at the rate of 1 kilowatt for 1 hour. Example: an electric heater takes electricity at the rate of 4 kilowatts.

Neon. A nonmetallic element that makes up a small percentage of the gases in air. Gaseous neon is used in electric lights. The chemical symbol for neon is Ne.

Neutral. In electricity, neither positively nor negatively charged.

Neutron. An elementary particle in the atom that has no electric charge.

Nichrome. A metallic substance with very high electrical resistance. Because of that unique property, nichrome wire is used as heating elements in such appliances as toasters and heaters.

Nucleus. The positively charged center of the atom. The nucleus consists of protons and neutrons.

Parallel circuit. An electric circuit in which two or more components (for example, the electric source and the electric user) are arranged in the same direction in parallel positions relative to each other.

Piezoelectricity. Electricity generated by the action of certain crystals showing negative and positive electric charges under mechanical pressure.

Polarization. The state of having two opposing forces or positions.

Quartz. A very hard form of silica that occurs in crystalline form. Quartz is the most common of all minerals and is the principal component of sand.

Repulsion. The force exerted by two bodies pushing away from each other.

Rheostat. An electrical device for changing the resistance of a circuit. Rheostats are commonly used for dimming lights.

Semiconductor. A solid whose conductivity is less than a conductor's and more than an insulator's.

Series circuit. An electric circuit in which the components (for example, the electric source and the electric user) are arranged in a linear fashion, positioned one after another.

Silicon. A nonmetallic element that exists in its pure state as either brown powder or dark-gray crystals. Silicon is the second most abundant element in the earth's crust. The chemical symbol for silicon is Si.

Solar. Relating to the sun.

Tourmaline. A glassy crystal of complex composition. It is often used as a semiprecious stone.

Ultrasonic. Relating to sound waves having a frequency beyond the range audible to human beings. Ultrasonic sound is usually above 20,000 cycles per second.

Uranium. A heavy silvery element with many forms, some of which are used in the production of nuclear fuel.

Volt. A unit for measuring electric pressure or force. One volt consists of the amount of electric pressure needed to produce 1 ampere of electric current where the resistance of the material carrying the current is 1 ohm.

Watt. A unit for measuring electric power. One watt is equal to 1 joule of work per second.

FOR FURTHER READING

Ardley, Neil. *Discovering Electricity.* New York: Franklin Watts, 1984.

————. *The Science Book of Electricity.* San Diego: Harcourt Brace Jovanovich, 1991.

Asimov, Isaac. *How Did We Find Out About Electricity?* New York: Walker, 1973.

Berger, Melvin. *Switch On, Switch Off.* New York: Crowell, 1989.

Graf, Rudolph. *Safe and Simple Electrical Experiments.* New York: Dover Publications, 1984.

Gutnik, Martin J. *Electricity: From Faraday to Solar Generators.* New York: Franklin Watts, 1986.

Taylor, Barbara. *Electricity and Magnets.* New York: Franklin Watts, 1990.

Wood, Robert. *Physics for Kids: 49 Easy Experiments with Electricity and Magnetism.* Blue Ridge Summit, Pa.: Tab Books, 1990.

INDEX